"*The*
suspe
good
that
and
librar

"*The*
whic
comp
Both
that
it!"

"Mo
New
her l
elem
most
of pr
enga

DATE DUE

e,
of
re
ts
y

or

y
a
g.
y
el

er

te
h
e
d
er
n

st

"A suspenseful read that you won't want to put down. Darkness and light collide in this compelling tale. Spiritual battles come to life in this mysterious cauldron of events."

Cheryl Peterson — Children's Book Writer

THE
DIVIDING
Stone

*To all
who get
carried away
by stories*

THE DIVIDING Stone

ANITA ESTES

TATE PUBLISHING
AND ENTERPRISES, LLC

Published by Tate Publishing & Enterprises, LLC
127 E. Trade Center Terrace | Mustang, Oklahoma 73064 USA
1.888.361.9473 | www.tatepublishing.com

Tate Publishing is committed to excellence in the publishing industry. The company reflects the philosophy established by the founders, based on Psalm 68:11,
"The Lord gave the word and great was the company of those who published it."

Book design copyright © 2016 by Tate Publishing, LLC. All rights reserved.
Cover design by Maria Louella Mancao
Interior design by Richell Balansag

Published in the United States of America

ISBN: 978-1-68187-200-1
1. Fiction / Religious
2. Fiction / Christian / General
15.10.23

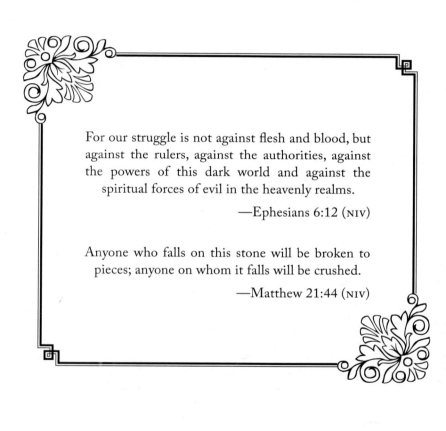

For our struggle is not against flesh and blood, but against the rulers, against the authorities, against the powers of this dark world and against the spiritual forces of evil in the heavenly realms.

—Ephesians 6:12 (NIV)

Anyone who falls on this stone will be broken to pieces; anyone on whom it falls will be crushed.

—Matthew 21:44 (NIV)

Dedicated to those who have wrestled in prayer,
my writer's group and my husband

PROLOGUE

New Covenant

Early 1800s

A cold autumn wind swept down from the rock cliffs, wailing like a woman in travail. The gusts battered a set of newly painted shutters against a large stone-hewn house. They knocked relentlessly like the spirits of the dead desiring their release.

Margaret tossed and turned feverishly as she watched dark forces hunting in the night, gathering en masse like a thousand evil creatures smothering life, bent on destruction and bloodthirsty for revenge. The rapid beating of their wings stirred the tree branches, threatening to break them. A thousand pairs of glowing yellow eyes peered through the darkness, waiting.

She screamed.

A large, grotesque, dragon-like creature, known since ancient times, threw back his head and laughed with hysteria. "The hour is now ours. We have awaited this for decades."

He paced back and forth in front of his troops with his wings folded and his long tail arched in midair. "The Light is flickering and soon will extinguish. They have been fools who played into our hands."

Cackling erupted throughout the camp.

"Their houses of prayer are stone cold or divided. Our most detestable rival will soon lose His most passionate ally in this town, and we shall rule!"

A roar of assent and beating of wings spread like wildfire through the gathering crowd. Margaret bolted upright in bed. Her nightmare was upon her in the flesh.

A forceful hand covered her mouth and silenced her scream. She kicked and writhed trying to break free, only to be bound by another.

Rough hands gagged her with rags, and a strong man tossed her over his shoulder. They pushed her though the open window into the waiting arms of a gnarly creature, who lowered her down a ladder to the cool grass below.

Outside, the moon hung full in the sky, casting a silvery light.

From the corner of her eye, Margaret spied the shadows of several cloaked figures. They crept along the stone-walled house, concealed by the darkness. Her long golden tresses spilled over a black robe as she shook her head in defiance. Thick rope bound her arms and legs.

As they approached the cemetery, the moonbeams cast eerie shadows across the gravestones. A group of hooded figures encircled a stone, like specters presiding over their dead. Though gagged, Margaret cried for help, but no sound escaped her lips. She moaned. *Holy Father, I beseech Thee. Please send assistance!*

A heavy hand thrust her head to the side, scraping her cheek against the cold millstone. Her eyes teared. Through blurred vision, she stared at the shadow of a face—somehow familiar.

A rough hand tightened the gag while her eyes countered the other's cold stare. He backed away, returning to his position in the circle.

A bloodcurdling sound pierced the night like the high-pitched howl of a frightened woman. Margaret choked on her own suppressed scream then recognized the cry of the screech owl. She held her breath and prayed for mercy and courage.

Suddenly Margaret caught a glimpse of a ghastly yellow-green ribbon of light streak though the night sky, like an apparition. It twisted and writhed, breathing a putrid odor, like rotten eggs, down on them. Then it disappeared into the branches as quickly as it had come. She wondered if anyone else saw what she had seen, or was it all just a nightmare?

The high priest's voice startled her, making her painfully aware this was indeed no dream.

He commanded his falcon to search out the owl. "Go, my little Beelzebub, and make quick work."

The bird fluttered into the darkness, though Margaret thought she heard something else besides the falcon. It soon became unmistakable—the whirring of a thousand wings, screeching, sputtering obscenities, over and over until she felt they were driving her mad.

Through the horror of it all, Margaret heard the muffled voice of the master of ceremonies. Her mind registered recognition. She heard someone proclaim him as the Worshipful Master. It chilled her to the core. *Lord, only You are to be worshipped.* Tears stung her eyes. *What darkness is upon me?*

The men chanted, their voices hypnotic. As they intensified, her fear heightened. Terror flooded her being and washed through her body as she understood her fate. She closed her eyes tightly and prayed.

The chanting stopped.

A dagger glistened.

Margaret cried out to her Maker for one last time. *Father, forgive them for they know not...*

The horror gave way to the sound of angels' wings accompanied by golden shafts of shimmering light. Though brilliant, they did not blind her, and she basked in the glow of their radiance. Tenderness bubbled from their touch as the angels gently lifted her spirit upward and soothed her aching heart. She passed from the cold, wretched darkness of the night, through layer upon layer of increasing light, until a liquid-gold atmosphere enveloped her. The warmth filled her heart with an overwhelming joy—one she had never experienced on earth.

Celestial music blended with the sounds of rushing waters, and they harmonized to produce a heavenly experience. The music wrapped around her and dwelt within. She and the music of the ages were one, enveloped in rivers of love. Only one thought disturbed her:

Now who would uncover the truth she discovered?

1

New Coven
The Present

Margo stared at the tattered piece of brittle paper in disbelief. A gust of wind almost tore it from her hands, but the cold blast quickly died. Her eyes raced across the faded, amber-colored letter as she struggled to absorb its meaning. She stood transfixed and read the vehement warning written with a fountain pen in red ink.

There is a diabolical evil that stalks this town.

The next sentences were barely legible, but she could make out a phrase: "a true-blood Dubier." The name sounded familiar from her research. Margo thought it might be one of the founding town fathers. She backtracked and deciphered a few preceding words. "They are closer than you think. Beware!"

Though several undecipherable sentences followed, the whole thing read like a line from a bad horror movie in the 1900s when melodrama ran high. And her hands shook as she squinted to reread another fragment. *I believe one of our ancestors was one of them. One of our ancestors?* Margo, a nickname for Margaret, knit her eyebrows. *Who wrote this? A Dubier?* She had to find out.

With the letter in hand and handbag flapping at her waist, Margo raced across the backyard to the studio and flung open the door. Mumbling to herself, she almost forgot her mission to inform Chris. *Maybe this was the secret Grandma had referred to for years.* It didn't seem plausible, but what if it was true?

Her husband stepped out of the office. "Talking to yourself again?" he teased as he walked toward her, passing stacks of pots waiting to be fired.

Margo jumped—her usual response when jostled from her inner world. If only she didn't plunge so deep in thought she'd be more aware…and not carry on a one-sided conversation.

"What's true?" Chris raised his eyebrows. His playful smile irritated her.

Margo waved the ripped note in her hand. "I don't know…but all those years my grandma alluded to a mysterious ancestor in our family line and—"

Crash! Margo jumped and absentmindedly let go of the paper, which fluttered to the worktable. The sound of shattered pottery echoed in the studio. She dashed to the scene of the crime and saw one of her stoneware mugs smashed on the floor. The culprit sat on the top shelf of the rack licking his paws.

"Shadow, how did you get up there?" She reached but couldn't quite retrieve him. "You bad boy. Get down immediately."

The smoky-gray cat's tail wrapped around the neck of a vase. He didn't want to be coaxed down. She turned around. "Chris, help me. I can't get Shadow, and I need to go. I was coming in to tell you when the pot—"

Shadow jumped off the shelf with a thud. Margo picked him up with one hand and marched him straight toward the door. Retrieving the torn letter, she folded it with trembling hands and placed it in her bag that doubled for a purse and portfolio of sketches.

"Leaving already?" Chris bent down and cleaned up the shards. "With all this pottery to glaze?"

"Sorry, but I have to. I'll be back in an hour or so." She knew time would be of the essence.

Chris smirked. "And what's this about your long lost ancestor?"

She tried to think of a quick answer to satisfy him. "I found something important in Mom's old stuff…a letter. I'll explain all about it when I get home."

Margo rushed out the door, leaving Chris holding the dustpan. This discovery couldn't have come at a worse time. But if the letter was true, there wasn't much time to waste. It might be a matter of life and death.

The autumn leaves blazed a trail down the mountainside, spilling into a pool of cornfields outside of town. Mesmerized by nature's beauty and mulling over the letter's contents, Margo missed the stop sign. A car went speeding through and nearly crashed into her. She jumped and slammed on the brakes. Her car skidded to a stop.

The driver shook an angry fist. "Watch where you're going, you idiot," he yelled out the window.

Margo's leg shook as she slowly pressed her foot on the gas. Could this be a warning? Perhaps she should just forget about the letter and go back to the studio. Yet an unseen force compelled her. *Dear God, protect me and show me the meaning of this letter.*

With no time to waste, she raced up the steps of the old stone library, determined to find the truth—or at least one more clue. She reached to open the heavy wooden door and slipped on some pebbles on the landing.

Her foot skidded across the stone and her hair whipped in front of her face. She couldn't see and nearly lost her balance.

Another close call.

She brushed aside her long honey-brown tresses and took a deep breath. *I need to slow down and pay attention. First the stop sign, now this. Margo, get a grip!* She tugged at the oversized door, but it didn't open, so she knocked.

Still no answer.

Just my luck. She peered into the window. A lone librarian sat at her desk, filing cards. Margo tapped on the aged glass that made the figure inside appear somewhat distorted, almost dreamlike. Surprised, the old woman looked up from her work, squinted, then hobbled forward.

Hurry up. I don't have all day. Margo twisted her hair. Her multilevel strands of thought turned to her previous computer research concerning her missing relative, part of the family secret. It had proven somewhat successful, but not complete. After that, nothing but dead links—frustrating. So she'd abandoned the search for a while, until now.

She just happened to be looking for a picture in the attic and rummaging through a box of her mother's overlooked belongings when she discovered the letter—tucked in a box of old photographs. It certainly shined new light on the subject, but not enough. What she needed lay behind those four walls.

If only she could get in.

The door creaked open and a blast of musty air assaulted Margo's nostrils. It brought back memories of her grandfather's collection of old books. For a moment, Margo stood mesmerized and envisioned a nineteenth-century woman with her hair tied up in a bun, velvet hat and muff, long trailing coat with petticoats and bustles—similar to the portraits she knew hung in the foyer. *Could one of them possibly be…?* She fingered the paper in her purse.

Margo crossed over the threshold. She had hoped to avoid the librarian, but it didn't look good.

The old woman smiled, and her wrinkles deepened. "Good morning, dear. Haven't seen you in a while. Looks like you've been working at the studio." The librarian looked down at Margo.

"Oh, that…" She brushed off the dried clay on her work jeans.

The gray-haired woman stared at her. "So what will it be today, my dearie—the world of the River Valley artists or a Victorian mystery in the drawing room perhaps?"

Margo let out a long breath. She knew no matter what she would tell her she'd prattle on about this book and that, pouring out her wealth of wisdom and knowledge in a ten-course diatribe that left Margo's head spinning. She decided to take a chance.

"Truthfully…I've been researching my family tree."

"Oh, how exciting." The elderly woman clasped her hands together.

Her pause gave Margo just enough time to slide past the rolltop desk and into the hallway.

The librarian called after her, "Just let me know if you need any help. My father was the local historian and he knew…"

Her voice faded as Margo disappeared. Maybe she should ask the librarian, but then again, she might suspect something.

No. Better do the research herself…then maybe her recurring nightmare would make some sense.

She entered into a network of small rooms crammed with leather-bound books but bypassed these for the moment. The next room narrowed, and on the walls hung the aging oil paintings. Though she knew the paintings here, she'd never studied the names before. They were darkly rendered portraits of the founding fathers and their families, stark and rigid. She read their nameplates—Hasbrocks, DuBois, and Eltin—but none with the name in the letter.

On the opposite side hung one woman's portrait that looked unlike the others. She'd never seen it before. Her hair was not pinned up in a bun, and the corners of her lips turned up just a little. Margo read the engraved brass plate, "Sarah E. Dubier, wife of Colonel Louis Dubier." The letters flashed recognition. *Dub*——just like the note.

Margo's legs wobbled as she came one step closer to the truth.

———⟫◆⟪———

Light radiated in golden shafts through the clouds, mirroring the brilliance of angels' wings clapping in the heavens. One very tall, imposing, warrior angel named Zuriel sheathed his sword. "Excellent work, Veritas, disclosing the letter. With her thirst for the truth, she will discover the clue in no time."

"Yes, but she will need a little more help and protection, so I must get busy revealing the truth and dispatching others. Then it will be time for you to take over with your troops."

The leader of the prayer warriors folded his wings, which from tip to tip were almost forty cubits—or, in modern-day measurements, approximately seventy feet long. "This is indeed true, but I must wait until the saints pray. She has begun, but much more is needed."

The two took flight and descended through the clouds until they landed on a stone church steeple in the small town of New Coven.

"It is true there weren't enough people praying for Margaret back then. The believers didn't even realize the danger she was in at the time, but I think there is a house of true prayer in a town nearby, which has the potential to be activated. Margo may be the key."

The powerful being looked down to his companion, Veritas, the guardian of truth. "Indeed back then, they didn't recognize the danger among them, not until it was too late, and so the evil one had his way…for a time. Some of our ranks did not understand."

"Yes, it was difficult for many of us to appreciate the Sovereign's plans at that time. It looked as if the enemy had ruined a wonderful Christian family, but now, Margaret is rejoicing together with both her earthly and Heavenly Father."

Both angels bowed their magnificent gleaming heads, recalling the time of prayer and the changes that took place after Margaret's incident. Her death had caused repentance in her father and in others in the town. Perhaps change was on the horizon again.

Zuriel, the archangel of prayer, lifted his radiant face. "It will come again soon."

"Yes, it will. I can feel the saints are gathering. Now it is time for the Master to complete His mighty plan, whatever it may be."

Veritas looked up at the shining soldier. "Margo has a gift, although she is not yet aware of it. I am certain the Master will reveal it to her soon."

"She probably won't understand it at first, but that is one reason many prayer warriors will be needed."

"Indeed we must work closely together on this assignment. It has been long in the making. Many before her have failed."

"Yes, but the Master knows the perfect timing."

"I pray it is now."

As the two departed, the sky shone with a magnificent brilliance.

Margo sank down into her favorite overstuffed chair with a book that might help with her investigation. Rummaging through her bag for the envelope, she found it and carefully removed the aging paper. As she unfolded it, her hands began to shake again, but she managed to stop them and read some more.

> I believe one of our ancestors, a true-blood Dubier, was once one of them and others before him.

Yes, there was the name—Dubier. But what did "one of them" mean? She continued to read.

> But you must not speak of it...or they will discover who has revealed their...

Their what? She squinted her eyes to see better. Of all words, why did this one have to be missing? She reread the warning.

> They are closer than you think. Beware!

She hoped the following sentences would provide a clue, but they were not legible. Instead she skipped to what she could see.

You will suffer a frightful…along with your daughters.

A frightful what? Injury? Scare? Death? It seemed so menacing and urgent. Whose daughters did the writer mean? Most importantly, who was it written to? Her grandmother? Mother? It appeared older than that. Perhaps her great-grandmother, but why hadn't her mom shown it to her? Maybe she considered it a prank or passé. Margo shook her head. Too many questions and not enough answers.

The small room seemed to close in on her as she picked up the old book on her lap. Maybe it was just the mustiness of the place that brought to mind her grandparents' small attic where she liked to play as a little girl. Margo, born Margaret Bernadette Bevier, examined the book's spine. A faded Dewey Decimal sticker showed its age along with the book's title, *The Founding Fathers of New Covenant*, by Michael W. Dubier. That was the name that interested her. Intrigued, Margo scanned the chapters until she saw number 12, "The Miller's Daughter: The Mystery of Margaret L. Dubier." She wondered, *Who's Margaret?*

Margo skimmed the chapter and took out a notepad then scribbled a few dates and facts about the Dubier family: the father was a member of a ruling body of a dozen men and a French Huguenot, the mother Dutch; they had five sons and two daughters. They lived in one of the largest homes and owned a mill. She hoped this information would prove helpful later.

She read on. "Although Margaret was descended from two prominent families in the community, the Eltins and Dubiers, she did not meet with fortune." The paragraph described the young woman's relationship with the dashing Colonel Abram Hasbrock, although the engagement terminated. Margo wondered what caused the breakup. Was he, as her mother used to say, a cad?

She mused about her own life. Although Chris possessed a great personality, their first two years of marriage were stormy. She'd expected romance and roses but discovered a few prickly thorns hidden in the bush. After five years, Margo faced the truth—marriage wasn't all about romantic love but a different kind that forged bonds through tough times. Maybe Colonel What's-his-name was all looks and no substance. But she didn't have time for this hypothesizing.

She quickly turned the browning paper, and a fragile page fell out onto her hand. She slipped it back in place as best as she could, although it stuck out just enough to annoy her. Small things out of place distracted her, but today she ignored it and kept on reading.

At that moment, the librarian entered. She looked at the book and sighed. "Are you reading about the tragic death of Margaret, my dear?"

Margo jumped. "What are you talking about?"

"I saw the well-worn page sticking out, the one that recounts the tragedy." The librarian pointed to the previous fallen sheet.

Margo turned to it and read about the incident. It spoke of tragedy, broken engagements, and the early death of—

"Every local town historian wants to know about Margaret." The librarian interrupted Margo's reading. "We had her portrait hanging in the foyer with the others, but it disappeared—stolen one weekend. Strange incident—the door locks never seemed tampered with, nor the windows. Anyway, it's never been recovered, but you can see her picture on the next page."

Margo turned to it and examined a faded black-and-white photograph of the large Dubier family—father, mother, sister, and brothers—all strikingly handsome, except for the father. She thought he looked imposing with his bushy eyebrows and large protruding nose. But looks could be deceiving. Maybe he was a good guy after all.

The librarian peered over Margo's shoulder and pointed to the opposite page.

Margo looked then gasped.

"What's wrong, my dear?" the librarian inquired. "You look like you just saw a ghost."

Margo gaped at the portrait. Staring back at her was the image of the woman in her nightmare!

The Dragon Master of the Dark Abyss breathed fire and summoned all his minions. He roared with a fearsome anger like rolling thunder. "You fools! What bumbling idiot allowed that book to fall into her hands?" His red beady eyes swept across the assembly.

Bickering and confusion followed as each foul creature pointed a bony finger at the next. A cacophony of "Not me!" resounded.

"There will be hell to pay for this!" The dragon who was once an angel of light, Lucifer, arched his spiked tail in the air and swooped down upon them. It knocked out the first several rows of his prized princes and overlords. Pride, Division, and Deception as well as Lust and Witchcraft sailed into the air and banged against a cave wall.

"That is only a taste of what will come if any more of these slip-ups occur," the beast hissed. "You will pay dearly if this problem gets any worse. Now, go leave my presence and blind those souls."

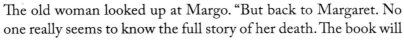

The old woman looked up at Margo. "But back to Margaret. No one really seems to know the full story of her death. The book will tell you a gruesome tale that Margaret took her own life!"

"Suicide?" Margo dropped the book in disbelief. She hadn't been prepared for such a tragic incident. *Dear God, I hope this isn't true. The letter mentioned nothing of this.*

The librarian continued. "I don't believe that rubbish for a moment! The Dubiers were not like that at all." As she bent down and retrieved the book, the loose page slid under her desk. She tried to grasp it but couldn't. When she stood up, her body erupted into a series of jerking motions.

Margo jumped up. "Are you okay?" She'd never seen someone acting so strange. Maybe she was having a seizure. The woman's face appeared different, her mouth contorted, and Margo couldn't believe the sudden transformation. "Should I call 911?"

"No, no, I'm fine...but I'm sorry I, I...lied to you." Her voice cracked.

"Lied?"

The old lady stiffened. "I'm sorry, I was trying to protect you, but we can't throw away history just because we don't like it. I was being a foolish old woman. She did indeed commit suicide." She sounded huskier than before.

This was too weird. *What does that page really say?* She bent down to retrieve it, but the old lady swooped it up.

Margo met her gaze. An odd, faraway look appeared in the librarian's eyes.

"I was just trying to help." Margo shrunk back as the woman clutched the paper. "I'm sorry I dropped the book, but the thought of suicide shocked me." How could this be happening? Was God trying to warn her once again not to get involved?

"Yes, it's very disturbing, but true."

"But," Margo interrupted, "you just said you thought it was a bunch of rubbish."

"I told you I wanted to protect you," she said in a sharp tone.

Margo thought she saw a shadow pass over her face and the room grew chillier.

She shook it off. This was ridiculous. "I'm leaving."

But what about Margaret?

2

Margo, a nickname she earned as a young, feisty child, woke early the next day eager to start working in their studio. As she stretched, she was surprised to find an empty space next to her in bed and no sign of Chris.

Early bird catches the worm, she repeated the childhood saying. *Uggh! Chris could have it.* She yawned and stretched. *He's probably mixing clay, I better get down there.* She jumped up and nearly stubbed her toe on the bedpost.

Reminding herself today was exactly two weeks before the most important craft fair of the year, she quickly dressed in faded work jeans and hurried into her pottery shop, a small converted barn on the edge of their property. She pushed away thoughts of Margaret and the message in the letter.

Not today.

In the studio, Margo settled into working at the wheel, throwing pots, while Chris mixed clay and glazes in the back room. Powdery dust wafted in the air and settled on the worktable. Margo hunched over the whirring machine and focused intently on centering the clay, an art she had mastered. The clay easily complied. Margo wished she could be as easygoing and moldable. Not an easy task for a stubborn artist. She wanted her life to be more centered on what truly mattered, though she wasn't quite sure what that involved. Was chasing after some nebulous evil and dead ancestor really necessary at this busy time? She doubted it, and she tried to dismiss the message the letter contained.

Margo deftly sliced the bottom of the finished cup, and a chill ran down her arm. She'd done this a thousand times before, so what was wrong? She lifted the mug and set it on the table. The words of the correspondence jumped out at her: "There is a diabolical evil that stalks this town. Beware!" What *diabolical* evil could it mean in this beautiful, quaint village?

The loud chugging of the clay mixer in the other room brought Margo back to reality. The clay was finished. After a few minutes, Chris appeared with the vat of new clay. "How's the throwing going?" He plopped the slime onto the kneading table.

Margo looked up from the wheel. "Good. You mixed some great clay. Thanks for kneading out all the lumps."

"Makes for great muscles." Chris laughed as he made a fist and flexed.

Margo twittered. "You're my hero." She then changed her voice. "Now please get to work."

Chris smiled and approached with clay-covered hands. "And what do you think I did while you investigated?" He held up his hands and walked like a zombie. "I'm coming to take you away, Margo Pierson."

He brushed his fingers against her face, smudging it with clay.

"And I'm going to bury you!" She stuck out her hand and a big blob of clay landed in his shirt pocket.

"Truce," Chris called. "Break time."

The angry demon warrior, the Prince of Deception, paced back and forth, his talons clacking along the stone floor, his wings bristling close to his side, exaggerating the tremendous hulk of his shoulders. Two Division captains, Lies and Gossip, quivered in the wings, awaiting their commander's wrath.

The Prince of Division was not present; he had been sent on a special assignment with his eminence, Pride. Deception seethed with anger. "So Lord Division has teamed with Pride," he hissed under his breath. "They think they can do better than me," he murmured as he paced across the rock cliff.

Every click of his claws against the floor sent shivers down the backs of the writhing creatures, until the ugly beast stopped dead in his tracks and faced his troops, avoiding his stupid captains off to the side. He would deal with them in private and teach them an unforgettable lesson.

"No one is craftier than me!" he bellowed.

Everyone stood at attention.

His eyes gleamed yellow in the darkness as his shattering voice pierced all within earshot.

"As you know," his voice mocked, "there has been a breach of trust. Some fool has not properly covered his territory." His beady, red eyes scanned the audience, and they quaked at his penetrating gaze.

Throughout the day, Margo continued throwing clay pots, vases, bowls, and cups. She held up a vase and smiled at its shapely form. *Not bad at all. I'm on a roll.* After dinner, she continued working until evening, but the batches of stoneware got stiffer and stiffer and more difficult to center on the wheel. Margo pushed back a strand of wayward hair and battled with a hardened lump of clay. She squeezed a little more water from the sponge, but it didn't help. Her strong hands firmly clasped the spinning clump, but it would not comply.

It shifted first to the left and then to the right, wobbling as she tried bringing it up higher into a cone and back to center. Patience for such annoyances was not one of her virtues, but another lesson glared at her. She could be demanding. But was she as difficult as this clay? She hoped not. *Lord, have patience with me and soften my heart.*

Throwing her hands up in exasperation, the clay slip trickled down her arm. She wiped it on her apron.

"Okay, what's going on around here?" Margo objected.

She wondered if Chris had botched up the formula.

"Chrriiiis," her voice sailed across the open space. "Did you mix this with stone?" No one answered. She mumbled, "Just what I don't need before a big show—stiff-necked mud!"

In frustration she stopped the electric wheel, wiped her hands on her apron and looked up. Her artistic eye caught the brilliant sunset from the big picture window. She sat mesmerized as the sun shot its last rays of golden light across the indigo sky. It disappeared behind the Overlook Tower, swallowed by the silhouetted mountains.

She had grown to love the natural beauty of her surroundings, but today, the cliffs looked dark and foreboding. Shivering, she turned away from the window. The October chill had already set in, and her thoughts turned to the letter. A diabolical evil stalks this town. *What evil?* She shuddered and reflected on another portion she deciphered last night. "Men who scheme against anyone who loves the Lord God." What men would do such a thing? Was it true or just the imagination of a hysterical old woman?

Margo watched as the last ray of sunlight disappeared.

She looked back down at the lifeless clay before her and spoke to the silent mass that would not budge. "You stubborn lump. I'll get even with you!"

Chris never appeared. She assumed he must have taken a break or was in the office. Margo decided to leave him alone if he had surmounted the task of paying the bills, one she hated. She sat down and started the electric motor again. The whirring noise was a familiar, comforting one, and she plopped down another chuck of clay from the same batch. Determined to make this lump obey her, she bore down harder and squeezed the clay tighter.

What in the world got mixed up in this—cement? The piece continued to wiggle and thump, thump, thump off center.

Great, just like my life lately—off center. Time to soften you up, baby. She reached over to the pail and attempted to dunk her sponge in the liquid. While stretching, she pulled her bad shoulder out of whack. Her arm dropped like a dead log into the wet clay, and her hand overturned the bucket. Water spilled everywhere.

"Blasted!" The angry words flew out of her mouth.

"Chrissssss," she cried. A sharp twinge shot across her shoulder. What in the world? Margo grimaced and looked down at her arm covered in clay. *How did I ever get myself in this mess?*

Margo caught her breath and screamed again. "Chris, come here!" But her words fell on deaf ears.

An eerie feeling engulfed her, like the ominous presence of the orcs from *Lord of the Rings*. It inched its way up her spine, like a slimy creature. Margo tried to breathe, but an awful stench filled the room. It suffocated her. She wondered if the fumes from the kiln were not properly vented. Heaviness embraced her, so she couldn't move—trapped by fear.

Then a faint, piercing cry split the air in two.

"What's that?" Margo yelled.

Her eyes darted back and forth, desperately searching the room. The sound grew in intensity to an ear-splitting screech like a banshee shrieking, but Margo couldn't distinguish whether it was human or animal. Before she could determine its origin, the room filled with the fluttering of wings she could only feel. One brushed against her face.

"What's happening?" she screamed. A sharp pain dug into her arm, like the claws of an animal. Tears sprung to her eyes as she struggled to lift her lifeless appendage off the soaking wet table. It would not budge. *God help me.*

"Chris...pleeeease, come here," she yelled and slumped down on the wheel. Thoughts of her recent discovery washed over her. *Was this the evil?* She wanted to dismiss the thought as ridiculous, but somehow she sensed this incident was connected. Though she grasped to understand, she didn't know how or why.

She wondered if God was warning her, but she struggled to understand how a letter written years ago could be a warning for her in the twenty-first century. *I really better stop reading all these mysteries and start focusing on my pottery.* A rustling noise outside in the bushes startled her.

"Who's that?" She picked up her head, tears streaming down her face. Before long the latch on the studio door began to jiggle. Margo stopped short of screaming when Chris burst through the barn door, his face white as a ghost.

"Margo, what's wrong?"

Her voice trembled. "I can't move my..."

He rushed to her side. "How can I help?"

"My arm...it's cramped up something awful and my shoulder too." She winced in pain and tried to move.

"Should I massage it?"

"Yes, but be careful."

Chris carefully kneaded the cramped area, and Margo sat back in the metal chair. Slowly, the muscle responded to his touch and relaxed. He brushed aside a few wisps of her light-brown hair.

"Whew, scary." She patted Chris on the shoulder and left a trail of clay. "Thanks a lot. It feels better now." She looked up at him and squinted her eyes. "Where were you?"

"I went into the house to get an after-dinner snack. What happened?"

Margo smiled sheepishly. "I'm not sure. I was working on a piece of clay when..." Margo recounted the whole incident, minus a few details, while he continued massaging her arm. The tension drained.

"I know this sounds crazy, but I felt like I was battling some dark force trying to…hurt me."

Chris raised an eyebrow. "Well, we'll definitely have to pray about it, but don't tell—"

Margo's dark eyes widened and she gasped, "Look, something moved." She pointed toward the picture window. "Out there. I think there's a prowler!"

Chris gazed toward the dark glass and calmly replied, "I don't see anyone. Do you?"

"No, not now, he's gone, but could you please look outside and check around the bushes?" Margo lifted her arm and massaged it a little. The remaining knot loosened. "I'll watch from the window. Signal me if you see someone." The urgency in her voice propelled Chris into action.

———◆———

Outside, night had fallen and the mountains were etched in black against the darkening sky. Chris looked up at their form and shuddered; he too felt an ominous presence. Although he believed in the existence of demonic forces, he didn't think they could attack people, at least not physically. Anyway, he didn't think it happened these days. He'd need to discuss this with a few of the other Christian brothers and see what they thought.

As he swept the flashlight back and forth through the bushes and around the house near the studio, he hoped to find a clue, but there was no sign of anyone. Then he walked toward the sloping hill behind the barn and cast the light in an arc across the trees and then down their massive trunks. Chris loved his wife and wanted to help her, but he thought she might be too tired. Maybe if he could divert her thinking, she would feel better.

He tramped back to the studio and observed Margo at a distance from the doorway. He loved the slender curve of her neck and the determined stance of her body as she stood waiting for him. She looked so beautiful with her long hair cascading over her shoulders. As he approached, he puzzled over her ability to be tough as nails and soft as a kitten, all at the same time. He walked into the studio.

Her bright eyes questioned. "Find anything?"

"Nope, nothing." He thrust his arm out and threw something in her lap. "Nothing, but this big fat spider."

She stepped back and screamed, brushing off her jeans. "You big…" She looked down at a leaf and glared at him, then took it and ripped it to pieces. She gave him one of her scolding looks he knew so well. Then he met her gaze and smiled broadly. He knew she couldn't stay mad for long, even though she hated spiders.

"I think you better stop reading those murder mystery novels. They're making you jumpy."

Margo grabbed a wooden clay tool and poked him. "Take that." She playfully jabbed him in the waist. "And that." She got him in the arm. "You little fiend."

"Who, me?" He loved to tease her, but he never thought of himself as a *fiend*.

"Not really."

Chris wrestled the tool from her and threw his arms around her in a big bear hug. Tousling her honey-colored hair, he smothered her cheek with kisses. He loved this crazy artist, no matter what she imagined.

Across town, two friends of Chris and Margo, Mark and Jessica Dart, plopped down on the living room couch after finishing a quick dinner. Jessica wondered if Margo remembered her favorite classic episode of *I Love Lucy* was on tonight, but she felt too lazy to call and remind her. Anyway, she wanted to get the remote before Mark did and claimed all rights to the TV.

Jessica completed her assignment successfully and turned the set on. The familiar music filled the room. Mark walked in and scrambled for the remote, but Jessica held it triumphantly.

"Give me that!" he demanded in a tone much sterner than normal. "You've been home all day and can watch *Lucy* whenever you want. It's my turn to sit and relax." A dark cloud passed over his face.

Jessica, hurt by his harshness, turned toward him and glared. "So you think I've been sitting around all day doing nothing? Well, there's a lot to do to keep food on the table and run a house." She wondered why she snapped at him so ferociously, but she didn't care.

"So you think I've been doing nothing all day at work?"

Jessica knew Mark worked hard, but she couldn't control what came out of her mouth. "No, but I deserve the TV tonight."

"Well, I think the man of the house should get first preference."

That statement, along with the others he'd been making lately, started a small crack in their relationship, like a tenacious weed slicing through macadam.

Jessica screamed, getting angrier by the minute. "Okay, man of the house, but first you have to do your job and clear the table."

Mark stomped over to the dining room table. "Okay, but you have to wash them."

Jessica fumed and watched the show as Mark cleared the table. Her anger bubbled within. *He knows how I hate to do dishes right after cooking dinner*, and she thought of a plan. "Fill the sink with water and I'll get to them, dear." She didn't like to trick Mark, but it was an easy way out. She heard the water running, and sat back in glee. *Serves him right, treating me this way.*

Mark returned to the living room and saw her watching *I Love Lucy*. He exploded, "Get in the kitchen!"

Jessica whimpered then fled to the dining room. "I hate you." Her anger seethed as she turned around to confront him. She saw the downcast look on Mark's face. She knew she'd wounded him, but at that point, she didn't care. *He deserved it.*

She ran into the kitchen and began to wash the dishes. Mark came in to apologize. Standing at the entranceway he watched

Jessica and then approached a little closer. "I'm sorry. I don't know what came over me."

Jessica wondered the same thing. They didn't usually get so riled up about trifles, but then again, they were having more disagreements lately. Mark was being selfish and getting more difficult to live with.

The two of them stood there in the kitchen—Jessica on one side, Mark on the other—and stared at each other for a few moments.

Mark asked, "What was that all about?"

Jessica shrugged her shoulders and replied, "I don't know."

Zuriel looked concerned with his wings folded and head bent down. "The enemy dispatched his forces in number," he announced as he rose from his seat. "They have gained territory, and those who were once for us are now against us, but a few faithful saints have lifted their voices in prayer. We have sent guards and are mobilizing troops according to His command."

His gaze fixed on his fellow workers. "But this is all I can do until His Majesty orders them to intervene. Perhaps He awaits the people's prayers, though I fear many will suffer and fall prey."

Veritas nodded. "Yes, what you say is valid, but I'm sure the All-Knowing has a perfect plan. Margo already has a hunger for truth, though she fears what it will entail."

"The problem remains that few are as aware as she, and even fewer have kept their swords sharpened with prayer."

"Yes, Zuriel, that is true, but if we look further, we will find who we need. For now, we both face a tremendous challenge with these humans."

3

Margo finished glazing the last batch of pottery and set it on the shelf. Throughout the day, she couldn't erase last night's encounter from her mind. Was it connected to the letter and what she had learned about Margaret? It seemed improbable. But what had actually happened? Suicide, as they said, or something far worse? She walked into the office and opened the clay box where she'd hidden her mother's letter. She picked it up gingerly. The faded words taunted her. Was this the evil spoken of in the note? She needed to know.

Looking up, she spotted the copy machine. She walked over and carefully placed the fragile letter on the glass surface and changed the settings to darken the copy. The light flashed across its surface. Excited, she picked up the warm copy. Yes! Several sentences and words too faded to decipher were now legible when copied in black:

> There is a diabolical evil that stalks this town. They are closer than you think. Beware! Though few are aware, they are hateful, evil men who scheme against anyone who loves the Lord God. They worship their own gods of ancient civilizations and of power. I believe one of our ancestors, a true-blood Dubier, was once one of them and others before him. But you must not speak of it or they *will* discover who has revealed their S—— Society. And you will suffer a frightful d—— along with your daughters. I know this because one day he renounced this abominable society but

lived only a few months more! Though he left a d——, we discovered it was burned; only one page survived. It told of this society of S——, their lust for power and the meaning of their Divi—— Stone.

What! She could hardly believe her eyes and read it over again. It was easy to decipher a few more missing words, like *secret society* and *diary*. Yet was it true one of her relatives was involved? But who? The letter indicated he died just months after leaving the society! Would she need to find out about another ancestor to solve the mystery? It was useless to think about it now with so much to do. How could she possibly have the time to investigate something that had happened centuries ago?

Unless it related to the show.

Margo wheeled the bone-dry pottery into the kiln room where Chris was preparing it for firing. "How are we doing?" She didn't wait for him to answer as she thought of a way to accomplish two things in one trip. "What if I go into town for an hour and take some pictures of the historical buildings. It would make a great backdrop for our booth, don't you think?"

Chris turned from setting up the kiln shelves and looked at the rack of pottery. "Well, we seem to have made up for our losses last night."

"Great, I just finished my work and need a break. How about I call Ashley and see if she'd like to do a photo shoot in town?"

Chris tapped his finger on the door. "I think that would be a nice idea to invite Mark's sister along. She needs some good influences, but you have to do one more thing before you go."

"What now?"

He stepped closer. "Give me a big hug...and be back in an hour."

"I don't know, that's a pretty tall order, but for you—"

Chris hugged her before she finished her sentence, and Margo felt his warm embrace. She laid her head on his chest for a moment and listened to his heartbeat. It made her feel loved and secure. She hated to release him, but she needed to investigate Margaret Dubier just a little more.

He let go. "Remember, one hour or you'll turn into a pumpkin."

Margo and Ashley ambled down the cobblestone street with camera, lenses, and tripod in tow. As they rounded the corner of the three-hundred-year-old street lined with stone houses, Margo tingled with excitement. "Look at that beautiful old house." She pointed.

Ashley looked up. "Which one?"

"The Dubier house." Margo studied the stone work that formed the walls of the building and the tiny windows that probably let in little light. It looked different now that she was searching for a clue to Margaret's untimely death and maybe her own past.

"This would make a great picture with the mountains in the background. I'll set up here." Ashley planted her tripod.

While she arranged everything, Margo snapped pictures of the stone foundations, the heavy wooden doors, the small wavy glass windows, and the herb gardens. She hoped the camera's eye would reveal some significant detail.

She set her hopes on investigating the cemetery, and she sauntered over to the area near the stone church next to the graveyard. After Ashley took a number of pictures from several angles, Margo returned. "Hey, look over there. I bet that place has some really old gravestones. Let's go check it out."

"Oh yeah, perfect place for an afternoon stroll." Ashley objected with a playful tone, "If I didn't know better, Margo Pierson, I'd say you're one morbid artist."

Margo smiled and walked up the stone path. She hadn't told Ashley about her plans for rubbing the gravestones. Her new friend might have a hard time understanding her real purpose for her investigation. Today she had one goal: to find Margaret's gravestone and do an imprint.

Ashley tagged along then stopped at the iron gate when she saw Margo take out her paper and weird-looking pencils. "What in the world are you doing?"

"Oh, just some research about my family."

"Don't tell me you've gotten into this whole genealogy craze?"

"Not intensive, just some possibilities I wanted to track down. Reminds me of my Nancy Drew days."

A gust of wind howled through the trees. Margo thought she heard whining voices, but she was not deterred. She walked through the iron gate, and her friend soon trailed behind.

"You've got to learn to look beyond what you see with your eyes," she said and waved Ashley over. "Take for example the gravestone over there," she said, pointing to one of the oldest ones. "That's the grave of one of the ten men who formed the original ruling body in this town in 1657." Margo marched over and pointed to the dates of the man's birth and death. "That's the grave of Mr. Hasbrock, one of the—"

"So what?" Ashley interrupted.

"I was about to say one of the wealthiest and most powerful families in town."

Ashley frowned.

Since Ashley was Mark's younger sibling, Margo overlooked her brashness and continued. "I bet you didn't know that King George granted him a large tract of land from New Covenant to the Upper Estates, a total of six thousand acres."

"Whew, he'd be one wealthy dude today. How'd you find that out?"

"I read about it. Those musty old books aren't as boring as you think. A lot of things happened in this town because of his decisions and those of eleven other powerful men who formed the ruling body."

"Hmm, unchecked power?"

Margo marched over to another grave she knew from past exploration. "Mr. Dubier, among other French Huguenots, would not cooperate with the Dutch settlers who moved into the territory and caused a huge argument over which church to attend. The Dutch built their own church over there." Margo pointed to a boxlike brick structure with a white wooden steeple, and they strolled over.

A blue historical marker confirmed her research. Ashley read the embossed yellow-and-blue sign. "First stone church built in 1707. Services in French to 1753. New stone church built 1773. Dutch language used until 1800."

She turned to Margo. "So you're saying the town was divided soon after it began, just like today. Those townies don't exactly like us college students."

"Yeah, exactly." Margo raised her voice in excitement. "Did you know the town disagreed over whether or not to allow the college here? They thought it might bring in the wrong element."

Ashley laughed. "Well, they might have been right about that if they looked at some of the students today." She hesitated for a moment. "But these divisions seem to go way back."

Margo looked directly at her. "Now you're getting the picture." She meandered through the graveyard, weaving in and out of the well-worn paths, reading the faded names and inscriptions, looking for the graves of the Dubier family in hopes of finding Margaret's.

Leaves swept around the gravestones, and a gust lifted them up. Swirling into a funnel, they rose higher and higher in the air. Suddenly, the gust stopped, and the leaves tumbled to the ground.

Margo reflected about the spiritual lesson played out before her. *The wind is a perfect illustration of God's Holy Spirit. You can't see Him with your eyes or touch Him, but when He's moving, you can certainly see His effects. But what did this have to do with the letter and Margaret?*

She felt an unexpected poke on her shoulder and jumped. Ready to scream at any moment, she turned around and realized it was only Ashley. "Hey, don't do that. Remember how I used to jump when Professor Eagleton interrupted me while I was painting."

Ashley laughed. "Oh yeah, I forgot. You certainly go into another world when you concentrate."

"Oh well, that's me." She stared past her new friend, and an unusual gravestone came into focus. "Wow, look over *yonder*." Margo emphasized the last word in a playful tone and pointed straight ahead.

Ashley turned around. "Looks like an obelisk. Strange. I wonder if it's a grave marker?"

Margo walked over and deciphered the worn engraving. Her heart pounded as the letters formed the name: M-a-g-a-e D-u-b-e. She easily filled in the blanks: Margaret Dubier. Born 1786. Died 1807.

Margo covered her mouth and suppressed a scream of excitement. "Oh my goodness. This is it!"

"What?"

"The gravestone I've been looking for."

"You mean your relative?"

"Maybe." Her photocopying of the letter made several lines clearer, but it didn't help her locate anything more about her relatives. "A true-blood Dubier." Was this her family? She assumed so since the letter said, "Your loving mother," and it was found in her mother's possessions. However, her mother was a DuBois and her father a Bevier. People said she was a perfect blend of both. They were well-known families in New Coven, though neither talked much about their ancestors. She'd have to investigate further. But when?

For now, Margo nodded and scanned the next line on the stone. "Died from a heart broken in two." *Wait a second, the book never said that, or maybe I didn't read far enough.* She thought about her encounter in the library. Why had the librarian waffled between belief and disbelief over Margaret's suicide?

Ashley walked over and read the gravestone carving. "Hmmm, that's a strange inscription. Why would anyone put that on a grave?"

"I read she committed suicide because her father wouldn't let her marry the love of her life, but some disagree." Margo reiterated what she'd just learned.

"That would explain it."

"Maybe so." Margo looked around and realized the stone was set off from the others and asked Ashley to look for more Dubier family markers—William, Mary, Louis, and Sarah.

Margo hoped, as she rubbed her carbon pencil stick over the engraving, some hidden code would appear, but nothing looked apparent. The letters of the gravestone appeared as written with no mysterious underlying words. *Maybe I've read too many mystery novels.* Her mind trailed off to the latest one as she worked.

When she finished, Margo rolled the newsprint into a small cylinder and put it in her backpack for further inspection. The air current picked up again and moaned through the trees, as though signaling the girls it was time to leave.

Margo couldn't wait to get home.

⟫◆⟪

The following afternoon, the wind died down, and Margo returned to the old grave site alone to gather more information. During the day, it was a tranquil site, situated next to the stone church. She climbed up the grassy hill and located the area of the other Dubier grave sites. The sun shone through the trees and created shadowy patterns on the gravestones.

The night before, her examination of the rubbing proved futile. No hidden markings or coded messages jumped off the page. Yet the lettering proved interesting. The letter *M* stood out against a faded background in what appeared to be another sentence, but the rest looked like it had worn off. For now the best thing to do was to take rubbings of the remaining Dubier family gravestones on this side of the cemetery. She thought a clue might be embedded in the stones.

Even if there weren't an answer in the rubbings, she'd hang them up to study their engraving style. *If God wants to show me something else, He'll just have to make it clear.* She was doing her part and giving Him the opportunity to speak to her through the pictures. Then again, He could talk to her through any means he wanted.

Margo took out the soft pencil from her leather satchel and placed the large manila paper over the gravestone. She held it in place with one hand and with the other she rubbed the side of the pencil over the surface of the cold stone. Little by little the letters appeared like magic on the paper. After she finished the last one, she packed up her materials and hurried toward one of the older houses in the community to inspect its historical marker.

It read, "Colonel Hasbrock House built 1677 by one of the original…" Margo gasped. That was Margaret's fiancé's name. *Wouldn't it be awful if he had something to do with the murder? Maybe it's why her death was covered up as a suicide. No, that's not possible…but then again…*

Margo looked up and examined the structure. The windows were small and the house short. Situated next to the Dubiers', it was dwarfed by its neighbor. Off to the side was a small well with a large round stone covering the opening.

Curious, she sauntered over and wondered if the Dubier family shared this well with the Hasbrocks. Her hand explored the bumpy surface of the carved lid and gave it a push. It wouldn't budge.

Feeling tired, she leaned against the well. She recalled seeing stones like this before when she visited one of her favorite romantic spots with Chris: an old mill near a waterfall. She thought for a moment. That's it—a millstone. She remembered *it* was used for grinding wheat into fine flour for baking bread. The placement of it over a well struck her as strange.

Mr. Dubier was a miller. Margo knew from reading the book yesterday. *I wonder if this was one of his grinding stones. But why would someone place it over a well?*

After a few moments of examining the stone, Margo decided the Historical Society probably made that decision in order to prevent accidents. She dismissed the thought and returned to her present concern: the miller and his daughter, Margaret.

The sun hid behind gathering clouds, and a cold wind swept down the street. Margo shivered as she walked briskly down the stone path, wrapping her sweater around her.

Shutters banged on the stone house and gave her an eerie feeling. *Lord, protect me*, she prayed. Then she scolded herself for being spooked so easily. Margo peeked through one of the wavy glass windows. It was very dark inside, and she could barely see a thing. Walking back down to the well, she decided to do a rubbing of the millstone, but she would have to hurry. Her pots from yesterday would probably be dry soon to load for a bisque fire, though it was never wise to rush the drying process and cause breakage. *Another fifteen minutes won't matter.*

She took out her largest piece of heavier paper and began marking with a cake of rubbing wax. As she worked, a pattern appeared, different from what the millstone looked like on the surface. There were places where the stone must have been scraped away, just enough to leave a break in the rubbing, a blank space.

Margo's eyes scanned the street. *Good, no one in sight.* She didn't need some nosey body prying into her business. As she worked, she could hardly believe her eyes. Letters appeared, formed by the empty spaces. She examined them; so far they spelled out N-b-s-h. Makes no sense. Maybe someone's initials. No, they would be in capital letters.

Just then an old lady emerged from the Historical Society's building. Margo felt panic rise in her throat. Her nimble fingers worked swiftly as the woman slowly approached. As she came closer, Margo rolled the paper up and stepped away from the well.

The woman turned into a side parking lot, and Margo breathed a sigh of relief. *That was a close call.*

Margo resumed. Her fingers flew across the paper. When finished, she held it up. There, in broken letters, interspersed with blank spaces in a circular design an embedded message appeared: C-ic Pr-ki- N-b-s-h-b-su.

Margo stared at it, bewildered. *Maybe it's a sentence or a code, but what does it say?* Margo assumed the spaces in between were for more letters, but she wasn't sure.

What could this mean?

It seemed like the first few words were etched using the regular alphabet, but the last word seemed to be a jumble. Since it began with a capital letter, perhaps it was a name? She rolled the paper and stuffed it in her knapsack.

Maybe it was just a prank...some college student's idea of fun. If so, it was distasteful and disrespectful of the Historical Society's property. But why hasn't anyone else found this before? Perhaps I should report it, though what good would that do? Margo's head spun with questions, but uppermost in her mind was who did it and why?

That night, dark forces gathered in the cemetery as they did hundreds of years ago, when all that existed in that very spot was a churchyard. The gravestones came later, as the settlers began to pass on to another life, watched over by an increasingly dark force seeking to entangle and divide the faithful.

At present, the spirits swept through the yard, howling. Their bulging eyes glowed a fluorescent green in the darkness. Several large and dark creatures loomed in the shadows outside the heavy wooden door of the old church. Hundreds of sniveling, writhing, and cackling underlings crept behind each other.

A loud voice boomed. "All legions of New Coven's division are to come to the forefront immediately!"

A great mass of writhing creatures mounted the air with a loud whirring caused by the flapping of a thousand wings. Several bumped into each other, eager to be first and please the master. With one piercing look from the most prominent one, they settled down.

The meeting was called to order. "We are gathered together tonight," the commander's voice echoed, "to put a stop to what has been set in motion." The ancient dragon's nostrils flared, and his eyes pierced the legion. "We have another breach. Someone was not watching the cemetery carefully and now..." His voice trailed off, punctuated by heavy breathing, as he pointed a bony finger in the air and seethed. "But I have a plan, so you are fortunate." He breathed fire and singed a few underlings. They yelped.

"Come forth, Deception."

A tremendous creature with a radiant face on one side and a hideous one on the other stepped forward. He bowed and streams of light followed. "Yes, my lord."

"It is because of you that the detestable Veritas is now lurking around the corner." He lifted a powerful wing, and the wind almost knocked Deception off his feet. Light from his radiant face went dark for a moment, but Deception quickly recovered.

"It was not my fault, sir, you see." His voice hissed like a snake. "Those sniveling idiots over there were sleeping." He pointed toward a pack of lies and their lower-ranking captains: Falsehood, Dishonesty, and Deceit. "But I will double my efforts, sssirr. Set posts at every church and—"

"You imbecile," the commander shouted. "It's too late for posts. You must infiltrate the church. Forget about the others, they are ours already. To do this, I have chosen others to assist you." He pointed to Pride and Lust.

As the Prince of Division stood up, his tail sliced a number of Deception's cronies in half, and a fight broke out between several of their troops.

The dragon flew at them and breathed down fire, incinerating them.

Pride stepped out from the shadows, and the crowd shivered. They all recognized him, as all of them were under his command also.

Lord Division sat down, and His Eminence Pride strutted to the podium, puffing out his feathery chest. The crowd screeched in approval.

He spoke with confidence. "All of you have a great tool to wield against this puny representative of truth. I dwell within each of you as well as in those you ensnare."

Loud war whoops erupted from the crowd as Pride swept his magnificent wing over the troops. "I have already laid the foundation, the remainder is easy." His height and breadth appeared to grow to twice its original size. "Now go do your work. I, The Great and Mighty Pride, will assist you. Rally your troops and take charge!" He grinned broadly. Division pouted.

The Prince of Deception lurked in the corner, whispering to a snakelike figure as old as time.

4

Margo's heart pounded wildly as she raced through the dark network of streets and alleyways pursued by two large hooded figures. Without warning, she found herself lifted up and transported inside a strange building. She began running down a hallway of doors. At the end of the corridor, one door was open. She sprinted to reach it. As she leapt inside, her body cried out in pain.

Frightened, she slammed the door shut and collapsed. Her chest heaved up and down as she breathed heavily, gasping for air. Blood rushed through her ears, seemingly exploding within her. Tears stung her eyes and trailed down her face. She crumpled to the floor and fought to understand what had happened. Where was she? Nothing made sense; nothing was familiar. Had the two men lost her trail?

Barely able to stand up, she wobbled on her legs, trying to summon enough strength to move. She heard the thudding of footsteps and froze. In an instant she sensed the men's x-ray vision expose her hiding place and see right through the door. Suddenly, a celestial creature penetrated the walls and whisked her away from the darkness.

Outside, Margo touched down on a mountain road that looked vaguely familiar. She breathed a sigh of relief. Now she understood. The dark forces were after her discovery, but it was safely hidden. As she stood there thinking about her next move, a monstrous bird swooped down and seized her by its talons. It hovered over a steep cliff, threatening to release her when—

A clap of thunder jolted Margo awake. Torrential rain followed, matching the terror she felt coursing through her veins. Buckets of rain drove themselves like spikes onto the roof. Margo bolted upright in bed and looked around the dark room. Grabbing for Chris, she encountered dead air. Where was he? Her hands felt cold and clammy just like the the night before.

An ominous presence crept into the room. Dread poured over Margo. Throwing off her covers, she heard something flutter away with the rustling of the sheets. A bat? She suppressed a scream... then all was quiet. It was gone. She had to find Chris. He must be working in the studio office.

Margo groped in the dark, moving quietly along the edge of the bed then to the dresser and finally, to the hallway. The night-light glowed, but it flickered off and on again several times. It made for an eerie atmosphere like lightning flashes. She quickened her pace to the living room as she looked over her shoulder, scanning the lengthened shadows made by the light. Shivering suddenly, she half-stumbled, half-ran the rest of the way down the hall.

"Chris, where are you?" she called, but no one answered.

Reaching the living room, she forced cold, shaking fingers to find the round knob on the lamp. In her anxiousness, Margo sent the lamp wobbling on its base and nearly knocked it over. With her other hand, she grabbed the light and rescued it from falling. Finally, her finger located the knob and she turned it on. Light flooded the room, and Margo saw a note lying on the table.

> *If you wake up, don't worry. I'm just catching up on some work in the studio. I'll be back when I'm finished. Love ya, Chris.*

Margo sunk into her favorite chair and wrapped a blanket around her. She didn't want to venture outside in the dark to find Chris.

What should she do?

If she stayed here, the ominous presence and her fears might take over. If she went outside to find Chris, someone might sneak up on her. She felt torn, divided—not only over this but about so many things. Should she pursue the path of uncovering the truth about Margaret or spend more time developing her career?

What was God's will in all this? And how could she know it?

She searched the coffee table and glanced over an odd assortment of reading material—a local history book, several mystery novels, a museum brochure on ancient pottery and stoneware, and finally, her devotional. Ignoring the other items, she picked up her cloth-covered Bible and opened it in her lap. As she leafed through the pages, it fell open to a Psalm.

Margo read aloud, "Yea, though I walk through the valley of the shadow death—" She abruptly stopped. *Great, just the verse I didn't need.* She continued to read. "I will fear no evil, for thou art with me." The words leapt off the printed page. Wasn't there a T-shirt with a similar saying? Fear nothing.

But how was that possible? The next phrase provided the clue: "For thou art with me."

I know that's true, God, but where, Lord…where? Where are you?

She had pleaded with God many times before to show up in her duress, and He often did, but not in a way she expected. Tonight, though, she sensed Him in a different way. Something inside her began to move.

A warm glow coursed through her body and spread throughout the room. Then it actually began to light up. Wondering where the light came from, she got up to check on the outside lights and was surprised to see a full moon shining after the storm. Dark clouds passed through the orb, causing it to appear very dramatic, but Margo no longer felt frightened.

The chilling presence began to ebb. Even though it had palpably left the bedroom earlier, the manifestation had left an imprint upon her spirit. Now Margo felt warmth and peace. She opened her eyes and read on, "Thy rod and Thy staff comfort me."

Her tense shoulders relaxed as she clutched her Bible. She loved the truths of His Word. They were her consolation, but even more so, it breathed life into her. She wished she spent more time reading it and applied its truth more readily. *Oh, Lord, forgive me.* She reflected on the day's strange occurrence. *Help soften this heart of mine. I don't want to be like that hard lump of clay. I want to do Your will, but I'm not sure what it is. Please show me.*

Outside the house, the moon grew dimmer and more rain clouds moved in from the north, but fear no longer gripped her. Feeling reassured, sleep began to take over. Her head drooped as she hesitated a moment in that place between slumber and wakefulness, hazily recalling a disturbing saying an old college professor often quoted: *If religion is the opiate of the people,* she argued with herself, *then why do I go so long without it? I guess I'm just human, Lord, and You know that. I forget so easily, just like Your servant David. Thank You for the reminder.* Margo drifted off to a blessed sleep, embraced by a peace-giving faith.

A black Jaguar sped along the escarpment overlooking New Coven while a host of wildlife awoke to their nocturnal cycle. Raccoons sniffed their way down to the bottom of garbage cans, and mice scampered along trails, searching for scraps and tidbits left by hikers. But tonight, there was more than just the normal activity of the wood's creatures. An unusually large hawk circled high above, his sharp eyes surveying the scene as the speeding car snaked up the mountain. His spirit communicated with the master.

Though born Bill Guiles Eville, he choose to use Guiles as his surname as not to draw attention to his last. Even though he couldn't see the bird, he felt the presence of the falcon spirit guide as the car screeched around the hairpin turn faster then he'd ever gone before. He loved the speed and thrill of living dangerously on the edge. His vehicle sped past the famous climbing cliffs, The

Trappings, where many a young man and woman tested their skill. Behind that rock wall lay a series of over fifty challenging rope climbs: the Gargoyles, Devil's Kitchen, and the Headless Horseman. Other than climbers, few ventured farther, except Bill. He had business to take care of, and he didn't care where he had to go—he would get there.

In a seemingly deserted area of the woods, a strange light emanated, flickering and dancing like a candle, drawing the car like a moth to a flame—though Bill never thought of himself that way. He pictured himself at the apex, high above his accomplice who was presently sitting next to him. Yet even Bill followed the Grand Master's orders, though he believed he stood on a much-higher plane and would one day supersede them in power. He had learned his craft from his father and climbed upward in the society.

But Bill wanted to get to his destination as soon as possible, so he spun into the gravel parking lot. He enjoyed his role as master of ceremonies, as he had attained that position. Turning to his helper, he barked, "Grab the backpack and my suitcase. We're late."

They slid out from the bucket seats of the sporty vehicle. Bill slammed the door shut and grabbed the expensive leather case from his companion.

"Let's get going."

His shadow obeyed and immediately fell behind. "Okay, boss."

Bill led the way, pushing aside branches and small bushes partly covering the trail. He watched the moonbeams spill along the wooded pathway, and he navigated with confidence. His body moved swiftly, and his mind was occupied with thoughts about the ceremony to come, the payoff, and the girl.

Halfway up the mountain, Bill looked down at his watch then stopped and slid open his cell phone. He scrolled to the desired contact, called, and left a message. There was always business to take care of, but Bill didn't mind. It meant more of everything for him—more money, more women, more danger, but most of all, more power.

He felt in complete control of every situation. His companion, Paul, said nothing but surged ahead. Bill slipped the phone in his jacket and, in several large steps, was behind Paul. Illuminated by the moon, Bill watched Paul's strong muscular figure ascend the mountain path without skipping a beat. He observed how the heavy backpack didn't affect him. Bill congratulated himself. Paul was the best man for the job. He executed all Bill's commands as intended. It was a great relationship.

Bill and his companion confidently picked their way through the brush-covered trail, which took several twists and turns. The higher they climbed, the more the vegetation thinned. When they reached the timberline, the trees looked more stunted and squat from the lack of rich, pure oxygen, but Bill felt refreshed from the exercise. He wasn't out of breath or panting. A surge of adrenaline filled Bill's body in anticipation of the night.

As they approached, he spotted a small flicker of light and heard an unusual monotonous sound. A faint *ha-umm* filled the night. The closer they drew to the light, the more discernible the sounds became until there was no question as to what it was or where it came from. Bill recognized the mantra immediately. He clicked his suitcase open, checked its contents, and motioned to his partner. "Look...over there, to the left. The cave is around the corner. Stay outside until I signal for you to come in."

"No problem," Paul obediently replied.

Bill shut the suitcase and sauntered over to the cave. He smoothed back his hair, brushed off his black leather jacket, and ducked into the entrance, crossing over the earthen floor. A blast of cold air assaulted him.

Once inside, Bill listened as the chanting reverberated and bounced off the projections on the rock wall. To some, it may have sounded spooky; but to Bill, it was peaceful, rhythmic, like floating on a cloud. Its cadence lent a dreamlike quality to the scene. He approached the group. In the middle of the cave's chamber he spotted a rectangular wooden table with a black fringed tablecloth. Bill carefully observed its border woven with white rectangular designs interspersed with dots. Of course he recognized the cipher and knew their significance: Great Architect of the Universe. As he anticipated, six candles were arranged in sets of three on either side. A merger of forces.

Bill joined the circle of priests from the ancient cult. The druid-looking figure acknowledged him with a nod of his hooded head. A woman with long blond hair in a sheer white gown approached Bill and handed him a folded garment. He locked eyes with her for a minute and then traced the outline of her supple body with his eyes. A shock of electricity passed though him as he took the robe from her long, slender fingers and slipped it over his head. When he finished, she handed him another robe. Time for his lackey to join them.

He grinned and watched longingly as the young woman turned around and returned to her place in the circle. The arch of her back and her thighs swished the flimsy material back and forth. Bill's eyes followed her every move. After a hooded figure signaled, he went out of the cave and returned moments later with his accomplice, Paul.

No one spoke. Chanting filled the room. Bill watched carefully as the other four men acknowledged their presence with a bow of their heads. The leader raised his hands, and the chanting stopped. A robed figure handed Bill a long black scarf with embossed red symbols and tassels at the end. He draped it over his shoulders. The clothing made a striking statement of black against red.

The transaction complete, everyone except Bill and Paul began chanting again. The blood coursed though Bill's veins as his eyes fixed on his prize. As the cadence became hypnotic, a small animal emerged from the shadows of the darkened chamber. Its hooves tethered and mouth wrapped shut to prevent it from bleating.

The creature was led to a small wooden sawhorse placed behind the ceremonial table.

Immediately, Bill motioned to Paul, and the two became the center of attention. Paul reached for his tools from the backpack and produced a strong piece of rope. He tied the feeble creature to the post while Bill lifted the long sharp knife from the case. As he inspected the ceremonial blade, the priest began to recite a rhythmic incantation.

Bill Guiles breathed deeply, immersing himself in the reverberating sounds, letting his spirit ride their undulating rhythms. He emptied his mind of all thought but one and handed the implement to his accomplice.

Steadying the animal as the priest approached with a large wooden bowl, Paul placed the vessel under the goat's head. He positioned himself and raised the blade to enact the deed. Its razor-sharp edge glittered in the candlelight, suspended as if frozen in time. With a powerful swoop, he slit the goat's throat, stripping life from its flesh. Blood poured into the bowl.

The priest announced, "It is finished."

Bill grinned.

It had only just begun for him.

A huge, handsome creature puffed out his chest feathers as his voice echoed in the small chamber of the cave. He addressed three others in the upper echelons of his majesty's court. "I am indeed the right one for this job. I've already spun a plan and set it in motion quicker than any of you can think."

"Don't be so overconfident," a thin black-hooded creature spurned. "My magic is ancient and very powerful, going back to the dark ages when we ruled over men's fate. Our priests realize this. Look what we are able to do in New Coven. Bill thinks he knows the deeper magic, but he is my pawn."

His Eminence Pride laughed mockingly. "So you think. Let's just say Mr. Eville and I are intimately entwined as one. We go back ages."

The Prince of Deception lifted his cloak and spread his arm across the table like a bird in flight.

"We do not doubt your powers, especially since they learned the power of blood sacrifice from you, but you have grown weaker in these later years. Your numbers are few throughout the world. The people of New Coven are an exception. If you want to reach the masses, you can only succeed with *my* help."

Sorcery sneered and moved into the light from the shadows. "I needed you in the last century, but now, a new day is dawning. I grow stronger every day in the covens. They dot the land and soon will be under every tree and bush. No longer do I sneak around undercover. I have my own brand of *enlightened* magic epitomized in New Coven and beyond. It is now seeping into the culture at large. The best thing is—they don't even know they are falling under my spell."

Pride guffawed. "But all of your minions dance to my fiddle… all of your precious coven's leaders are *mine!*"

5

Chris stumbled across the dew-soaked grass as he headed toward the house. A mist covered the landscape, and he could barely make out the edge of the doorway. *Wow, it must have rained like the devil last night! I sure hope this fog lifts soon.*

He furrowed his brow as he thought about driving up the mountain to attend the Saturday-morning prayer meeting. He knew the winding mountain road with the sharp hairpin turn was difficult to negotiate in good weather. What a nightmare this mist will be!

As he crossed the threshold into the living room, he felt a chill in the air. He wondered if the electric had gone off in the middle of the night. Not an unusual occurrence. It made him feel even guiltier about falling asleep after firing the kiln. Chris hoped Margo hadn't missed him. As he wandered into the living room, he was surprised to see her sleeping on the recliner with the Bible closed next to her. He wondered if the storm had awoken her. Grabbing one of the fringed blankets, he draped it over her slumped body.

"Guess I'll have to make my own breakfast today. Serves me right. " Although he wasn't the world's best chef, he cooked a batch of scrambled eggs. Just as he was about to sit down to eat, a bleary-eyed Margo shuffled to the stove to boil water for tea. Chris greeted her with a gentle "Good morning."

Margo spun around and snapped, "How in the world did you get there?"

Chris teased. "I flew."

"Don't say that, not after last night."

"What do you mean?"

She dropped a teabag in a cup. "I had a terrible dream…about some kind of huge eagle or hawk that grabbed me by its claws and held me in its grip." Margo buried her face in her hands. "I can still feel the terror as he screeched and swept me up the mountainside. He nearly dropped me when…thank God the thunder woke me up."

"That's odd," Chris mused. "I didn't hear a thing last night."

"I noticed. Where in the world were you?"

Chris grinned sheepishly. "I fell asleep in the studio."

"This is the second time you weren't around when I needed you. I saw your note, but I wasn't going to tramp out there"—she pointed to the studio—"in that rain."

Chris shrugged his shoulders. "Sorry."

"Anyway, after I woke up I got up and read the Bible. I must have fallen asleep. It sure was weird though…that strange feeling, like the night—"

"When I couldn't find the prowler?"

"Yeah, it was the same spooky feeling. You guys need to pray about this."

"Sure, I'll ask the guys to pray my wife doesn't get carried off by some huge bird. They'll really think I'm going off the deep end with this spiritual warfare stuff."

"Oh, come on. You know what I mean." Margo slumped into the chair.

"Okay, I'll mention it to them in a slightly different vein, but first I need to get out of here and up that mountain in one piece." Chris pointed out the window in the direction of Lookout Mountain. He noticed the mist lifting from the valley, but it clung to the mountains like a mother bear to her cubs. He hoped he could find his way.

Chris's car skidded around the hairpin, brushing the shoulder. Fog covered the roadway, but the car seemed to know its way, as if some unseen hand was guiding it up the mountain. He crested the top of the cliff, which usually offered a panoramic view of New Coven, but today it was shrouded in mist. Pulling into the parking lot, Chris saw only a few vehicles. Although he was late, he had a single purpose in mind.

He walked quickly along the narrow path and came within view of the small prayer group. As he approached, he heard the men discussing various issues. Their voices climbed higher with each retort. Mark, their campus minister, was arguing with the senior elder.

As Chris approached, everyone looked up and stopped talking.

"Hi, guys, sorry I'm late," Chris greeted them. "Thought you'd already be in prayer."

"Yes, that's a good idea. Why don't we put our differences aside and pray?" one of the senior elders, Lance, suggested.

Everyone bowed his head. "We come against the dark forces at work in town," the youth leader, Mark, prayed. "Father God, I see the enemy prowling around the church. Keep us on guard from him and the forces he sends to divert our attention." Silence followed. Only Lance and Chris said "Amen" in agreement.

Chris didn't understand the unusual coldness of the others in response to this prayer. Maybe they didn't think the church needed prayers of protection. He thought about the church's successful ministries: a coffeehouse, soup kitchen, street evangelism, missionary work to the underprivileged in the city, a college ministry, and a newly formed crisis pregnancy center. God was blessing the church, and that's all some of them saw.

As time progressed, Mark turned his prayers to the college students. Chris felt a little leery over some of the relationships Mark had formed with these coed girls, but a few came to know the Lord. He tried to keep his thoughts solely on the prayers, but he couldn't help it when his mind wandered to Margo and her strange dream.

Finally, Mark stopped praying and Lance began. "Lord, there are so many wounded people out there trying to heal themselves. They fill their lives with things—cars, money, alcohol, drugs, and sex. Open their eyes to see it's worthless without You." Chris always enjoyed Lance's honesty and cut-to-the-chase insight. Several others added a few short prayers, but to Chris, it felt like something was keeping a lid on the meeting. It ended abruptly, and the group soon disbanded. Chris approached Lance to discuss the prayer ministry in general, but he had an appointment in town. Lance promised to talk to Chris later.

Contemplating the prayer meeting, Chris stood for a moment and hesitated before he walked toward his car. He watched as the others climbed into theirs. He noticed the fog had lifted.

Darn, he admonished. *I forgot to ask them to pray for Margo.* It was still early, so Chris decided to venture off for a short hike. *Lord, if there's anything to what Margo has been feeling lately, show me the way to understanding her.* He followed the small path leading west toward the rock-climbing cliffs and passed by the well-known escarpment. He was surprised at how few people were climbing today. He decided the fog must have kept them away.

Usually, on the weekends, a trail of cars a mile long snaked their way up and around the infamous hairpin turn. Chris recalled seeing license plates from as far away as Colorado. A friend of his was an avid climber, and one day he explained to Chris all about carbines, chocks, pitons, and of course, the different ways to handle the ropes.

He convinced Margo and him to try rappelling down the rock face. His friend said it was a great place for beginning climbers because the wall sported enough crevices to get a foothold. But it was a mistake. Margo was handier with clay than rocks. Chris dismissed the thought of what could have happened as he passed by the place where Margo almost fell, but he said a prayer. *Thank*

You, Lord, for Your protection over Margo. Please continue to watch over her. Show me if she's under too much stress or if what she's feeling lately is real.

He walked farther down where the path became overgrown with branches and bushes, but Chris decided to press on anyway. He was not in the mood to be with other people, and hikers might arrive soon since the fog lifted. His feet moved swiftly along the path while his arms and hands pushed aside overgrown branches. The growth grew thicker, and he felt like giving up. *This is too much work*, he complained. *Time to turn back.*

Then something up ahead caught his eye. Stuck on the end of a branch, a small red piece of cloth waved in the breeze. Chris moved ahead to inspect it. He thought it odd since few hikers came this way. Curiosity got the best of him, and he wondered if a bushwhacker tied it there to warn of danger. Carefully choosing his steps, Chris proceeded along the barely visible path. It seemed mysterious until he walked about thirty paces farther. The trail ended at the edge of a steep drop-off. So that was it, Chris thought, the red flag was indeed a warning sign that the trail was about to end at a cliff.

He turned around, relieved. Margo's dream had left him somewhat unsettled. Snooping around the woods, even in broad daylight, made him a little tense. Chris retraced his steps and approached the red waving flag again. When he arrived at it, he stopped for a moment and inspected the area. To his surprise, a small path, not visible from the other side led off to the right. A thick clump of bushes were slightly pushed aside, and Chris thought he saw another trail. "What in the world…" He ventured ahead to investigate.

Sure enough, behind the thick brush and undergrowth he found another small but negotiable path. Chris thought about recent events. *Life sure brings us on some strange paths.* His feet led him onward and up a small rise then around a bend to an outcropping of rock. He climbed steadily to the top. It got hotter, and he removed his jacket. By the time he got to the end of the path, he was panting.

Chris leaned against a rock wall. It felt cool and refreshing. He took a deep breath and felt his heart pounding in his chest. Overhead, several turkey hawks circled. One of them let out a screech, sending a chill up and down his spine. Chris felt his heart beat faster as his imagination ran wild. Visions of Alfred Hitchcock's *The Birds* flashed across the screen of his mind. His palms grew sweaty, and he struggled to gain control of his rising fear. "Oh great," he addressed the winged creatures. "I've been led down this mysterious path to be attacked by an army of turkey vultures." He figured it was time to pray aloud. "Lord, I don't know what's going on or why I ended up here, but would You please give me a clue if I'm supposed to stay or get out of this strange place."

———————◆———————

Margo counted the same clay pots over again. She kept losing track. The potter wanted to know how many more items she needed to meet her quota for the show. *Where in the world is that husband of mine. I'm lousy at doing this.* She put down the pencil. *No use working now.* She walked over to the glazes and tried to evaluate what colors she needed to buy, but once again, she couldn't concentrate. *Okay, that's it—time for prayer.*

She bowed her head. *Lord, please keep Chris safe, and help me to—*

A pot fell off the shelf.

Margo yelled. "Shadow, is that you?"

He plunged off the shelf, his tail held high, and landed a few paces from her. "You've been a naughty boy lately." She picked him up and rubbed his neck. Walking over to the tray of pottery, she inspected the floor.

"Now let's see what you've broken." She picked up a glazed mug that shattered into pieces.

"Well, thank God you didn't break a vase or something more expensive." She swept up the remains and walked to the oversized garbage can. On the way, she brushed up against the stone rubbings and loosened the tack that held it and the accompanying photo. They fluttered to the floor, and she picked them up.

Margo stared at the letters and tried once again to unlock the code. Frustrated, she brought both over to the table and examined them more closely. She scrutinized the second word, comparing it to an enlarged photograph she had developed from the day before. The k-i stood out, and Margo noticed something she hadn't before. Two faint vertical scrapings nearly jumped out at her. They were more worn than the others, so the pencil rubbing did not pick them up as well, but the camera did. Staring at her as plain as day were two *l*'s forming the missing word: *killed!*

A gust of cold air hit Chris on the face. Where did that just come from? He regained his breath, but his heart pounded like a hammering woodpecker. Turning a corner of a big boulder, he looked around. Just a few feet away from the path, a black hole met his gaze. Chris slowly climbed down from the rock and stood in front of a cave's mouth. Cold air swept up, chilling him through the bone. He put his jean jacket back on and then peered inside to see if he could see any signs of life. Since there appeared to be none, he cautiously stepped inside.

The interior of the cave was both cool and damp. Chris rubbed his arms to keep warm. It took a few moments for his eyes to adjust to the darkness. Once he could see, he surveyed the surrounding area. There weren't any signs of a wild animal inhabiting the cave. Nothing unusual or out of place, he thought, nothing at all.

Feeling somewhat safe, Chris cautiously stepped to the middle of the cave. It wasn't very big. He estimated it could comfortably fit about twelve people inside, but he wondered who would ever want to hang around there. Continuing his exploration, he found the back of the cave was entirely walled in; it didn't lead to any other mysterious caverns. So he sized up the place as a somewhat ordinary, average cave. Yet his gut feelings told him something else.

Thanks, Detective Margo, now I think everything is eerie, even this run-of-the-mill cave. He tried to convince himself nothing was out of the ordinary.

Standing in the middle of the darkness, Chris wondered about the use of the cave and what it would be like to live in it. He squatted down, and his hands explored the cool rock floor. His eyes had totally adjusted to the darkness, and he could see more than he did before. He searched the walls up and down. What he was looking for he didn't know. Just as he was about to get up, something on the floor caught his eye. He stretched his arm, but he couldn't reach it. Chris inched closer. His fingers confirmed what his eyes revealed: dried red droplets spattered all over the ground.

Immediately, Chris stood up and looked around the room for a clue, but there was no trail of blood. A wounded animal could not just appear in the middle of the cave without some other telltale signs. He bent over again to see if there was any blood leading to or away from the spot. There was none. *That's strange.*

His mind raced. Where did those drops come from? At that moment, a turkey hawk's cry reverberated off the outer cave walls. Chris jumped to his feet. He thought of Margo again. Then he looked at his watch. Time to go.

When Chris stepped out of the darkness, the bright light blinded him. He squinted and put his arms over his eyes to block the sun. After he got his bearings, he looked up in the sky and saw a couple of falcons riding high overhead. Normally, they inspired him, and he liked to watch their outstretched wings soaring on the wind currents. But today, they frightened him.

As if they wanted to scare him away.

6

Bill surveyed the valley below as he descended the mountain into the town of New Coven. He recalled the events of the previous evening and how he enjoyed the ritualistic ceremony. Unlike groups who combined Eastern mysticism and occultism, last night went beyond dabbling in the arts. The small gathering held themselves above those who spoke of a "New Age." Their power descended from the ancient arts and not for mere fun or a few harmless spells. They took advantage of any means available and employed the best, like him and Paul. Though Bill believed his society held greater power, he saw the advantage of joining forces. The blood spilled last night had a specific purpose and target. The thought of it made him heady with power.

Driving his black Jaguar into town, Bill laughed at the people who thought they didn't exist anymore. Their ignorance gave them more freedom to participate in the order's rituals. The vast resources of the corporate office, which sent him here, attested to their power and influence. Though his position differed from the priests, they paid a handsome bounty for his work, which he hardly considered work at all.

Bill pulled his car into a parking space a block away from his destination and picked up his expensive leather briefcase. As he crossed the street in broad daylight, he looked up to the rooftops and grinned. He felt the presence of his comrades. *Perfect for our task.* He felt a sense of agreement.

When he arrived at the old bar in town, he looked the outside over. The place was exactly what he wanted. A faded sign hung on the door: "Come on in, ya dang fool." Fools indeed. He walked up to the entrance. The siding on the building needed repair. All the better. He'd take the shabby little place and convert it into an upscale café. The business would serve as a perfect front and make money to boot. He'd already called the corporate office.

Bill peered through the darkened window, and it reminded him of the ceremony last night when the priests mixed their incantations with the power of visions. As their chants grew deeper and they emptied their minds and souls, the priests invited the Dragon Master, Satan, to take full residence within them. Bill was already well versed in this practice, now part of his makeup. He would soon attain the coveted position his father had wanted.

He knew he performed the society's tasks well, and they handsomely rewarded him. The female they provided gave him everything he wanted, and the two created an unholy alliance. Their bonding would be almost impossible to break since the ceremony was sealed with blood and targeted a specific population.

Bill put his hand on the doorknob and twisted it open. He threw open the door and peered into the darkness. His pupils dilated quickly, and his eyes adjusted to the lack of light. The figure at the bar, framed in darkness, looked familiar—one of the boss's cronies. Bill sat down next to him and ordered a double scotch on the rocks.

Bill broke the ice. "So how do you like the place?"

The man leaned into him. "It'll do. As long as you do what you're supposed to."

He slapped a bill on the bar table. "Get me another one," he growled.

As the bartender poured his drink, the man in the shadow slipped a folded paper into Bill's open hand. He opened it and read the name and address. A wide grin spread across Bill's lips as the nameless man threw back his head and downed a shot of Black Velvet. It was an assignment Bill would fully enjoy.

The inner circle of darkness gathered together before their supreme master and bowed. Pride unfurled his wings with a loud *swoosh* and nearly knocked Division down.

"Silence, my principalities and captains!" the Dragon Master commanded from his dais. Division stood rigid. "You have done well, but we have only just begun." He pointed a clawed finger upward. We must continue to send more troops to the appropriate places."

"Your Majesty, I have sent out many forces against the New Way," Pride boasted.

"Yes, I know, very good. But there is one in particular you haven't been able to captivate."

A dark hooded figure stepped forward. "I have already set in motion a plan from the old ways of witchcraft."

Satan stepped down and stared at his companion. "Good work, Captain. Indeed, we are gathered here to ensure its success. Today, I'm also giving you greater power and promoting you." He turned around and strutted back to his position on the platform. Pounding his claw like a gavel, he announced, "We must all work together to ensure that relative of Margaret's falls under our spell."

Margo prayed earnestly for Chris's safe return as she paced the kitchen floor, but her mind was filled with confusing thoughts and fear. She tried to get the picture of the terrifying creature out of her mind but couldn't. *How can I pray in faith, Lord, when I'm a bundle of nerves?* When Chris finally came walking through the door, she ran over and threw her arms around him. She tried to mask her anxiety and teased him with a line from a favorite song of theirs. "So where have you been, my darling young one?"

He shrugged his shoulders. "How about fixing me a roast beef sandwich? I'm dying of hunger."

"Okay, so what happened?"

"Nothing much. I just went for a short hike."

"I bet," she remarked and then made his sandwich, piling on the meat with mayo. She thought of the tried and true saying, "The way to a man's heart is through his stomach." Better to have him fed first and then ask questions later. He gobbled the food and drank two glasses of soda, but Margo sensed a cloud hanging over him.

When he finished his last bite, she asked cautiously, "Did something happen at the prayer time that made you three hours late?"

Chris didn't respond.

"Hello, are you there?"

Chris looked up at her.

"Was it the fog?"

"What do you mean?"

"Was it the fog that made you late?"

"No, everything is fine. I'm just a little tired. I think I'll take a nap and finish loading the kiln later on."

"That would be great. I tried to do some work while you were gone, but some of the pieces are awkward to handle and you do a better job than me." Margo knew a little rest could change his disposition in five minutes flat. She figured tonight would be a better time to discuss what was really on his mind.

A pair of bulging eyes peered from behind a tree watching the mist shroud the woods in deep fog as an old mangy bear lumbered along a nearby path. He scrutinized the pitiful creature, soaking wet from a torrential downpour.

Just what I wanted.

Weighing in at a mere four hundred pounds, the brown bear would be easy prey for a gang of his underlings. As the unsuspecting creature ambled through the forest, he slapped branches of trees and bushes aside. The bear's hunger would make the infestation easy.

The Overlord of Witchcraft called into the night, and a dozen fiends burst from behind trees and bushes. Just then a horde of whirring wings attacked from all sides. They sunk their claws deep into the creature's back and sides. He roared and bit his neck and shoulder to no avail. The demons tore at flesh and entered in though the blood. The animal threw himself against a tree, but the unearthly bats took control. With an angry slap of his front paw, he reared up two feet taller than normal and sharpened his claws on a tree trunk. The demons enjoyed their new senses and plotted their next step.

In the late afternoon, Margo received an unexpected phone call from Melanie Eltin-Carson, Richard's wife. She called to invite them for dinner, which she had never done before in the two years they knew each other. Margo was surprised at the invitation especially since Chris and Rich didn't always see eye to eye on important issues. She wondered if the two of them clicked today and that's why Chris was so late.

In Margo's estimation, Rich was outspoken and had a tendency to be a bit too sure of himself. In contrast, Melanie was quiet and almost sullen, as though she were brooding about something. Perhaps she was being a bit too critical, but something bothered her when she was around either one of them. Maybe tonight, they could get to know the couple better and dispel some of her misgivings.

Margo looked out the window as Chris drove the car up the long driveway to the Carsons' house. Their old reliable Chevy, which was suitable for Margo, looked somewhat out of place at the back of Rich's new BMW. She eyed the surroundings for a few minutes before getting out of their car.

"Now I know why they didn't invite us over to their house before now," Margo commented.

"We definitely don't fit in with this crowd."

"Yeah, I wonder why they asked us over?" Margo furrowed her eyebrows and added, "I thought maybe the reason you were late today was because the two of you spent some time together."

"Where did you get that idea?"

"I don't know. I was just trying to figure out if there was a connection between you being late this afternoon and this invitation."

Chris nodded his head and mumbled. "You're always trying to figure things out."

"Come on, you know that's just the way I am."

"Okay, okay."

"So why were you late?" Margo couldn't keep from asking.

Chris coughed. "Like I told you, I decided to go for a hike up in the mountains. I found an interesting cave and explored for a while. I'll fill you in on the details later if you really want to know."

She looked at him and raised her eyebrow. "Of course I do."

They walked up the brick pathway hand in hand. Margo felt a little uneasy as Melanie ushered them into the house. She couldn't help but think of the contrast between their humble and pieced-together home. The artist in her noticed everything matched and was color coordinated. She could see Rich was successful in the eyes of the world, but Margo wondered where he actually stood in spiritual matters.

The Carsons were friendly enough and very hospitable, although Melanie was quiet and reserved. Her dark eyes seemed to hold some secrets Margo carefully probed to uncover, but Melanie dodged Margo's questions. Bored, Margo opened their wedding album on the living room table. The first page displayed their invitation, "Mr. and Mrs. Eltin cordially invite you…" *What? Eltin? That was Margaret's maiden name. I wonder if Melanie knows anything about the suicide. Probably not, but maybe.*

"Supper's ready." Melanie requested their presence.

At dinner, Rich engaged Chris. "So what did you think of today's meeting?"

Chris hesitated. "I'm not sure what to think."

They continued to talk while Margo tried to get Melanie to communicate. She complimented her hostess on the delicious meal complete with appetizer, soup, salad, and entrée, but Melanie just smiled and continued eating. Margo thought she would burst if she ate another bite.

After dinner Chris and Rich cleared the table, and Margo helped Melanie clean up in the kitchen. Margo hated this role assignment, but she thought it would be a good opportunity to get to know Melanie, though it only got as far as chitchat. The college grad hated small talk that led nowhere. She felt the main purpose for speaking was to communicate ideas about truth and beauty, with some exceptions like the bantering she enjoyed with Chris. This idle talk was nearly killing her, so her mind began to wander to Margaret's odd death.

Margo couldn't wait to get out of the kitchen. She hated cleaning up after dinner and felt trapped, caged like a bear. She carefully handled the crystal glasses then loaded the dinner plates into the dishwasher slots and noted how much easier it was than stacking a kiln. She decided to plunge into a deeper subject.

"Melanie." She waited to get her attention. "I've been doing a little bit of genealogy research about the town and found out one of the Dubier woman may have committed suicide. Have you ever known anyone to do such a thing, especially back then?"

"Umm..." Melanie stammered. "I've done a little research about the furnishings and architecture, but not much about the people, except for reading the portrait captions in the library and what's in the Historical Society building."

"Have you ever seen the picture of Margaret Dubier?" Margo hoped to lead Melanie into a revealing conversation.

"I don't recall, except some of those portraits in those old houses remind me of my own family, with their sad eyes and no smiles." Melanie's hands began to tremble.

Margo thought she may have hit on something and continued to probe. "I'm sorry to ask you such a personal question, but do you know anyone who has committed suicide in your family?"

Melanie buried her face in her hands and didn't answer.

Margo realized she'd gone too far out on a limb. "I'm sorry; I just know so little about the subject and thought you could help me. I also noticed you're an Eltin, and I read something about one of them committing suicide. But you don't have to answer."

Time seemed to stand still.

"I'm sorry. It was many years ago, but I was young and impressionable. They think my grandfather killed himself, but the family covers it up."

Margo was startled by her response. "I see. Well, if you ever want to talk to someone about it, just let me know."

She had been probing about Margaret's supposed suicide, and this new information may be related. But how? When they finished cleaning, she strained to hear the men's conversation. "So, Chris, how do you think things are coming along in our church?"

Margo heard her husband's muffled voice reply. "It depends upon what 'things' you're talking about."

"Oh, I just meant in general: the meetings, prayer on the mountain, the finances, worship—things like that."

A plate rattled to find its position on the rack. Margo missed Chris's answer, but as they finished up and walked into the living room, she caught the last part of Rich's sentence. "Some shady dealings going on."

As they entered the room, Margo darted over to Chris and wrapped her arm around him. "So what important things are you men discussing?"

Melanie perked up a little for the first time all evening and waited for Chris's reply. He answered Margo.

"We're discussing church business." Then he turned back to Rich. "Now what were we talking about? Oh yeah…what do you mean by dealings?"

"I'm not talking about money here, Chris. You know just because I'm successful, that's not all I think about. Anyway, you know, our elders have their own jobs and don't get paid for their church work. Even though I think they should get something, it's their own business, not mine."

"So then what's the problem?" Chris asked.

Margo wondered the same thing. She didn't completely trust Rich's answers and thought he had other motives for discussing church business.

Rich answered right away. "I don't think they make decisions properly. Shouldn't the congregation have more say in church matters? The elders think they've got a hotline to God."

Margo wondered what Chris thought about this just as he answered. "It seems to me they choose the deacons based on how they minister to others and the way they live out their Christianity."

Melanie objected. "Well, maybe that's true for some people, but Rich has been working at the coffeehouse for over a year, and he isn't a deacon, but Mark is. And I've been working at the soup kitchen for six months, and no one even notices me."

Rich added, "I know you and I have been faithful in attending those Saturday-morning meetings, and no one even mentions it in church."

"Truthfully," Melanie hesitated, "I think it's wrong. People should be recognized for their efforts."

Margo shifted in her chair. She didn't like the direction of this conversation, and she prayed it would end soon. Rich had appeared somewhat ambitious when he first came to the church, but Margo thought she was being judgmental and tried to be less so. Tonight confirmed her initial impression. Was there anything she could do to help them realize being a Christian wasn't always about being recognized?

7

Late Saturday night, Margo and Chris finished loading the
kiln. Chris handed her a vase, and she stared at it, trying
to decide where to place it. She tried several different
locations, but none seemed right.

"What's the holdup?" Chris asked.

"I can't seem to figure out the best place for this one. It's so
delicate. I don't want it to fall over." She let out a sigh. "I don't
seem to be able to think right. I can't make the smallest decisions
without deliberating over it."

"Let's take five. You seemed distracted. Something on
your mind?"

Margo sat on a bench. "What isn't on my mind? The pottery
show, the whole ordeal about Margaret and the alleged suicide,
the note I found in my mom's belongings, problems at church—"

"Okay. I get the idea. I think we need to pray."

Chris bowed his head and Margo followed. "Dear Lord, we
need You. Margo has a lot of things on her mind, and she needs
Your help to sort it out."

"Yes, Lord, help me focus on what's important and what I
should do. Show me the way." She opened her eyes and saw one
of her older pieces. "Hand me that big pot over there," Margo
said. She pointed to an urn on the floor. "That one."

"When did you make this?"

"A couple of years ago."

"So where's it been?"

"Hiding in a corner." Chris handed it to her.

"I think I'll add some high-fire glazes, gold or silver. Spruce it up." Margo walked over and studied the piece. "I'll reglaze it when we do a higher firing." She smiled. God gave second chances; she would too.

"And where are you going to get the money?"

"Don't worry. I've been saving."

Chris shook his head. "Have you seen that stack of bills in there?" He pointed to the office.

Margo nodded. "Yeah, but this show is going to wipe them out."

The golden-yellow flames of a campfire leapt against the black backdrop of the night as three demonic lords surveyed their territory. Their penetrating stares zeroed in on two large shadows looming in the fire's circle of light. The smell of fish permeated the camp.

Surrounded by a forest of darkness, the Chief Captain of Fear cast a dreadful glare. "I can unravel these two with the slightest effort." He arched his wings, and the other two demons trembled as if mocking him. He took flight, screeching an ear-piercing scream.

The two men dressed in bulky jackets and hats looked up from the shadows. One wore an old cowboy hat and the other a baseball cap, which he took off and slapped on his leg. "Whew," he declared. "Sounds like some mean old screech owls have taken up residence nearby."

A cross pin on the younger man's jacket glistened, caught in the firelight, as the other fisherman, Bob, shook his head back and forth. "Yeah, their bark is worse than their bite, if you get my drift."

The overlord, Witchcraft, snickered at Fear's paltry efforts to scare them. Filled with pride, he recalled his more successful efforts in capturing men's minds and filling them with stories of ghosts, goblins, and dwarflike men. As he watched the big old, ornery bear stumble through the woods, he concocted his own plan.

Later that evening, the leftovers of the fishermen's dinner wafted through the air and tempted the possessed creature. He followed his nose. Famished and fearless, the bear stepped out of the woods into the clearing. He rose with grizzly strength and walked straight ahead. A slick material blocked his way, and his sharp claws sliced through it like a sharp knife through soft skin.

A ripping noise pierced the darkness.

One of the fishermen in the tent awoke with a start. "What the heck's out there?" His question was riddled with fear, and the demon smiled.

Enraged by the hunger of the dark forces, the bear fished for human flesh.

A light flashed on, illuminating the inside as a figure sprung into motion, gripping his large-framed companion. The light switched off and Witchcraft mumbled to his companions, "Watch my work."

The creature growled, and the sides of the tent billowed like sheets in the wind. The wiry figure escaped. Though he tried to help his buddy, the stockier man didn't make it out in time as the tent collapsed and engulfed him in nylon. "I can't breeeeathe," he yowled.

A gaggle of high-pitched whines filled the air. Fear dispersed his troops and blanked the area.

The enraged animal bore down with a crushing weight. The three demonic powers watched as the tent undulated and the fiends attacked from all sides. Witchcraft lurked in the corner while his underlings penetrated the bear. Animal flesh ripped in his minions' claws. A loud growl filled the night. "Grrrrrrrrrrrrrrrr."

In the cover of darkness, the other human, Mike, sprang to his feet, screeching like the owl he had heard earlier. He frightened the hordes. The bear stopped, sniffed the air, and slowly turned from his prey and lumbered toward the noise. The tough fisherman moaned but worked his way out from under the tent as the bear leapt at Mike, and confusion broke out.

He prodded the bear with a shiny metal object, and blood oozed from the creature. A flurry of bat wings was overhead rushing in, disguising the flutter of yet another being. The Prince of Division arrived and immediately dispatched his minions. They seized the man, Mike, as he pummeled the creature. The bear gained more fury.

The two winged creatures stood in the shadows, hoping not to be seen. Still, Pride boasted, "We will soon eliminate yet another of these stupid humans who have joined the enemy's army. And he thought he could overcome me. Ha! I have proven stronger!"

Fear snickered. "The Dragon Master will be pleased, but not with you...you fool. Prince Division has gained the victory for himself."

Kingsland, North of New Coven

Dave Light tossed and turned in his bed as hundreds of dark-winged creatures invaded his sleep. They were about to pounce on someone when he yelled, "Mike, watch out. They're above!"

A hand touched his shoulder, and terror seized his being. *They must be after me.* In the dark recesses of his mind, he heard a gentle voice calling.

"Wake up, honey." He thought it a dream, but the voice sounded familiar.

"Wake up, dear." Fingers caressed his forehead. "You're having a nightmare."

His eyes flew open as he clutched the blankets. In the dim shadow of the moonlight, he saw his wife's silhouette. "I must've been having a dozy. What'd I say?"

"You called out to someone to watch out."

"Who?"

"I think the name you said was Mike, but I'm not sure."

Dave sat up in bed. "Isn't that strange? I just met a new guy in church, Mike. He was the cowboy who sat in the back last week."

"Oh yes, you told me about him."

"He had a real interesting story about an angel saving him from drowning."

"Really? You never told me that."

"You know I don't like to tell you everything people tell me, especially new attendees."

She smoothed the covers. "I know, I'm just the pastor's wife."

Dave leaned toward her and stroked her hair. "Beth, you know it's not that." He slumped back on the pillow. "Must've had him on my mind. Hope he's okay. Even though it was just a nightmare. Maybe the Lord wanted me to pray for him."

"Then let's do it."

Her husband fluffed the pillow and sat back on it. "Good idea."

Margo peeked out of the bedroom window and yawned. In the south, near the pottery barn, the sky darkened and threatened rain. The sky cast its dark oppressive spell, and Margo flopped back into bed. She fumbled with the clock and turned off the alarm.

In what seemed like a few minutes, the sound of banging pots and pans rose loud enough to raise the dead. The noise in the kitchen startled Margo awake. Her eyes popped open and she glanced over at the clock.

"Eight thirty already," she moaned.

She thought she had set the snooze alarm but in fact she had turned it off. It hadn't been a terrible night, but she remembered something about a bear. It made no sense.

Ignoring her dream, Margo recalled the small spat with Chris after they returned from the Carsons' house. She didn't totally agree with Rich, but on the other hand, she did side with his evaluation. In her estimation, Chris should be made a deacon because of his spiritual insight and understanding. He had a gift for praying for people and listening to their problems. *Oh well, no use staying annoyed about it.* She hopped out of bed and dressed for church.

Services at the Kingsland Free Church started later than unusual. Joy Hopelyn noted more than half of the two hundred seats were unfilled. She hoped the recent split hadn't discouraged the other members. The pastor, David Light, had tried to keep the congregation together, but some members had deserted. He spent a lot of time in prayer over it, and he looked like he hadn't gotten a good-night's sleep again. Neither did she. Someone had disturbed her dreams last night, someone in trouble.

But was it just a dream? She didn't think so. Joy had experienced dreams and visions like this before, but this was different. Had God allowed her to hear a man's call for help? As strange as it seemed, she also felt he might be here. She looked around searching for him, though she didn't know what he looked like.

Joy struggled to put this person out of her mind and concentrate on worship. She began to sing and think about the Lord when thoughts about an angry bear invaded her mind. Then a man in a flannel shirt flashed across her brain. Perhaps a clue?

She filed the image and put it out of her mind for now. Listening to the music, she focused on worship while her husband, Ray, looked down at his watch for the umpteenth time. Joy knew he felt uncomfortable and wanted to get out of there, but she didn't know why. Perhaps he felt the same heaviness in the worship as she did. She wondered if they were experiencing the aftereffects of the church split.

Ray turned to his wife and whispered, "Hon, I've got to step outside for a few minutes and get a breath of fresh air. I feel like I'm going to fall asleep right in the middle of worship."

Joy turned toward him. "All right, dear, if you must." Unlike her husband, Joy had the ability to override the oppressive spirit. Though she enjoyed the upbeat music, it hadn't lifted the congregation. As a whole, today they experienced difficulty worshiping. All around her, church people yawned or spoke to their neighbor, hands fidgeted, and feet shuffled back and forth. Joy felt relieved when Pastor Dave approached the pulpit.

She flipped open her Bible to the reference and listened. His words stirred her. Punctuated with force and clarity, they opposed the feeling permeating the church. He paced back and forth and spoke about the cleansing power of the blood.

"The blood washes away our sins. Isn't that wonderful news?" Dave turned directly to the audience and spoke with compassion. "Brothers and sisters"—he stopped at the lectern—"we can no longer allow sin to crouch at our door. If we ignore it, it will overtake us in the night. We must be vigilant and cleanse ourselves under the blood."

Joy looked around. People began to pick their heads up and listen attentively. The pastor's eyes swept over them. She felt the Spirit stirring, bringing conviction. She followed his gaze to the back of the room. Her eyes fell on the same spot as his…to a man wearing a red-checkered shirt!

8

Margo watched the clouds rip apart as she tore down the highway toward the church. High winds brought a welcome change in temperature from the oppressive summer heat, which easily broke the clouds apart like pieces of cotton candy. In the distance, several hawks circled the tower of gray rock wall. Even though they looked like mere dots to Margo, their presence was imposing. The whole scene gave Margo the willies as she recalled similar feelings from the night before.

While in church, Margo's mind flashed back to the dramatic scene. How easily the clouds dispersed and disappeared. The picture made her shudder as she recalled the dream from a few nights ago. A birdlike creature had carried her far away up into the mountains. He intended to destroy her, to eliminate her, rip her apart as easy as the wind blew the clouds away.

Was it a warning about the church, something to do with her vision? Or did it have anything to do with her stumbling upon Margaret's tragedy? Did she really commit suicide, or was her young life ripped away like these clouds? The thought plagued her, but she had no answers. She needed to reel her thoughts back in and focus on the service.

Worship appeared lively—people clapped their hands, lifted their arms in praise, and danced. Margo and Chris joined in, but something troubled her spirit. She whispered to Chris, "We need to talk…later." He nodded in agreement.

Mark Dart, one of the elders, delivered the message with power. Margo laughed to herself, Mark was barely twenty-five, and he had the title of an elder. New Way Fellowship believed in a plurality of leadership, a hierarchy of elders and deacons who ruled over the church. According to them, they were following the doctrinal mandates laid out in the Bible. It had its advantages, but it also caused some division between them and the local churches. But they were alive, on the cutting edge of what they thought God Himself was doing with His church.

She reflected that all in all, the church seemed successful. She looked around at the numbers of people in church today. Attendance was good. The professional-sounding music team— composed of guitars, keyboards, drums, and trumpet players— inspired people to worship. Off to the side, a few brave women even danced. Like a smorgasbord, it had variety.

Today, something different hung in the air. Could it be what the letter referred to? Sure wickedness reigned in the big cities, but this was a small town. What evil could the letter be referring to in New Coven?

Closer than you think.

Margo fidgeted in her seat, restless. She couldn't wait until Mark finished his message. She felt he was too young and inexperienced to be an elder. Although, she had to admit what he lacked in wisdom and experience, he made up for in enthusiasm. Usually she enjoyed his animated sermons, but today, it seemed out of tune.

She glanced toward the door several times. The last time she looked, her eyes fell on a tall, handsome stranger who was sitting next to Rich. Margo watched the newcomer as he listened for a while; then his eyes swept the congregation. He caught a glimpse of Margo before she could turn away, and she felt his stare go right through her. Another reason she couldn't wait to get out of there. The minute the sermon finished, half of the church filed quickly out the front door. Normally, this bothered Margo; but today, she wanted to leave with them. As they walked down the aisle, Chris greeted Lance and started a conversation. Margo sighed and waited. She tapped her shoe, and her eyes roved the church. Her gaze fell again on the guy who accompanied Rich. His back was turned to her, and he appeared to be speaking with Rich and Mark. For some odd reason, she got goose bumps up and down her arms, and she rubbed them to warm herself. She nudged Chris and pleaded, "Come on, let's go. I'm starving."

He grinned. "What's for lunch?"

Margo enticed him. "Pepperoni pizza."

"Okay." He smiled and turned to Lance. "Gotta go. The wife says so. I'll call you later." Chris left quickly with Margo.

"What's your big hurry? Big date tonight?"

"*No.*" She emphasized the one word. "Let's just go."

Driving down the road, Margo finally spoke. "All during worship, I kept flashing back to the clouds. I don't know if my imagination was running wild, but it seemed as though an unseen force ripped those clouds apart and devoured them."

Chris laughed. "Maybe they were hungry."

Margo glared. "Don't play dumb. Anyway, Rich brought some new guy to church today. I felt like he was…I don't know…like he was boring a hole through the back of my head." Margo rubbed the nape of her neck. "I just had to get out of there!"

"C'mon, Margo, I think you're exaggerating. All these nightmares and visions are getting to you.

Over at the Kingsland Free Church, people formed a line in front, seeking prayer. Several members, including Ray Hopelyn, joined the pastor in a tight circle. Ray's wife, Joy, watched as tears flowed, but the atmosphere wasn't filled with sorrow and oppression like in the past.

Joy wanted to meet the guy in the flannel shirt, but she didn't dare run up to him and spout off her dream. She had more decorum than that. The pastor would finish praying soon enough, and maybe he could introduce them. Dave seemed to have something to say to him.

In the meantime, Joy spoke with the pastor's wife, Bethany, who was also sensitive to the spirit world. "The service was wonderful today. Did you feel the difference?"

She agreed. "Yes, much more warmth. I'm so happy to see Ray praying with people again."

Joy looked around the church and watched others with bowed heads. "Yes, there appears to be a cleansing going on."

"And both you and Ray are also partly responsible for it." The woman gave her a hug. Joy hugged her back. She felt a little uncomfortable with the comment, but agreed. It had taken a lot of prayer, but the spirit of heaviness was replaced with a lighter feeling.

"Your husband's sermon hit the nail on the head, and it's great to see people responding."

"Yes, we're beginning to get new people in the church, like that cowboy type over there. Have you met him yet?"

"No, I don't think so. Well, come on over and I'll introduce you. He's in the back."

As the woman ushered her to the back of the church, a tall lean man in jeans and a checkered shirt stood up and approached them. Joy recognized him immediately.

<hr />

After lunch, Chris joined Mark and Jessica on an excursion to the mountains. Earlier, Chris had made the mistake of telling Mark about the cave, and of course he wanted to investigate. Margo stayed home to work on the pottery, and she told Chris she needed some time alone in the afternoon to sort things out. Chris promised to be home for dinner.

On the way up the mountain, Mark raced up the winding roads in his sporty red car. Chris knew Mark loved excitement and danger, but he wondered if Mark wasn't showing off a little. Jessica didn't appreciate his tires squealing around the turns, and she protested.

Mark chided, "Oh, come on, Jess, don't be an old lady. I'm just having some fun. Besides, I'm not driving too fast."

Jessica answered with a trace of malice in her voice. "I won't make it to old age if you keep insisting on driving this way." Chris wondered if Jessica was angry at Mark for something else, but he didn't seem to notice, and he continued on a lighter vein.

"Well then, you'll get to see the Lord earlier than you expected, and then everything will be just perfect. The way you like it. So no need to worry. Right, Chris?"

Chris didn't want to be put in the middle, but he couldn't prevent it. "I don't think she's worrying, just being sensible."

"Well, thanks for the backup, buddy."

Mark pressed on the gas pedal as the car climbed higher. As they approached the hairpin turn, he yelled. "I'm slowing down. I am. I am. Didn't you notice it was me who was preaching today? Now that takes maturity!"

Jessica conceded, "In the spiritual realm, you have some insights, but I wish you'd apply them to everyday life."

"Oh, Jess, give me a break. I'm only twenty-five years—"

"Yeah, that's obvious," Chris interjected.

Mark kept the car's speed in check while they negotiated the tricky curve. From a bird's-eye view, the car probably looked like an ant crawling up the side of a mountain. The backdrop of the green valley and the bright-blue summerlike sky made it look like a child's painting. Chris knew Margo would like the scene, and he hoped she was okay.

The three walked up to the area where the elders and deacons prayed on Saturday mornings. The sun lit up the scene, so different than the other day when fog covered the landscape. Today the fields spread out before them like a patchwork quilt.

Mark walked to the ledge, but Jessica stood back with Chris. "I'm glad you're here with us. Mark would make me go to the edge if you hadn't come."

It was warm and sunny, so they sat down on the rock, away from the edge. Mark joined them. Chris walked over to the ledge to give them some alone time. Out of the corner of his eye, he saw Mark try to kiss her, but she pulled back from his advances.

Chris overheard snatches of their conversation.

"Not here," she protested. "In front of—"

"It doesn't matter. We're married." Mark's voice carried.

"Yes, but I don't like to kiss in public. It makes me—"

"Fine, then let's go." Mark stood up and called over to Chris. "Hey, let's take a walk to the cave."

He grabbed Jessica's hand and led her down an overgrown trail he had hiked down previously. They wound around it as they scraped against bushes and reached a small footpath. Jessica complained her legs hurt, but Mark pushed on anyway. Chris sensed the tension in the air.

Finally, they came to a clearing and sat down on a rock. The gray cliffs looked dramatic, etched against the deep-blue sky. Chris and Mark watched several turkey vultures circle above, climbing higher on the warm air currents while Jessica massaged her aching calves. A slight breeze, tinged with the first chill of autumn, blew across their faces. Chris liked the cooler weather.

Jessica shivered and wrinkled up her nose. "Did you smell that?"

"What?"

"That stench. It's terrible."

Mark took a deep breath. "Probably a dead rabbit." Pointing to the encircling vultures, he added, "It's probably what they're interested in." The breeze brought in another wave of the nauseating smell.

"Maybe there's a hidden lair over there. Let's investigate." Chris motioned to a small path leading to the cave.

"No way. I'm staying right here where it's safe. I don't want to look at…some mutilated animal carcass."

"Okay. Suit yourself, but I want to see if there's any prey."

Chris and Mark left Jessica and walked in the direction of the pungent odor. It grew stronger as they approached the cave. They followed it around to the other side. The stench smelled putrid to Chris.

Just around the bend, they saw a trail of blood. Chris wondered if an animal dragged a carcass along the path, and the two followed the droplets until it ended. When Chris looked up, he stood in front of the cave.

"This is the cave I found," Chris informed Mark. He peeked inside but saw nothing out of the ordinary. His eyes swept across the cave floor and searched for a clue. Nothing. He walked around the outside of the cave, and there he found it.

Just beyond the trail of blood was a mound of dirt. Chris hadn't noticed it before, but now it stood out. He stepped on it, and his foot sank down. A putrid odor rose to meet his nostrils. "Let's go."

"No," Mark protested. "I want to dig it up." He searched the area for a tool and spotted a long stick. He bent it back and created an L-shaped shovel. Chris stood back as Mark dug. The putrefying odor almost gagged him, but Mark continued.

"Hey, I found something." Mark brushed the dirt away and gagged from the smell. The stick uncovered a swarm of maggots. Chris came closer and covered his nose. Within a matter of moments, Mark exposed a grotesque sight—the mutilated body of an animal. Mark dropped the stick.

Chris gagged. "That's disgusting. Let's get out of here!"

━━◈━━

Sunday night, both Margo and Chris ate dinner in near silence, though Margo had a lot on her mind. The church had replaced her concern for Margaret, and the issue of her mysterious death dropped to the background. God had revealed something else to Margo, and she needed to discuss it with Chris, but the timing had to be right.

After eating, the two of them planned on discussing the recent events more in depth. Chris volunteered to help clear the table, and maybe even wash a few dishes. The two worked together side by side as they carried on a light conversation that helped ease the tension.

"You sure like to soak these dishes in a lot of soap," Chris commented.

"Do you like your dishes clean?" Margo answered for him. "Then you need lots of soap." As she finished the last word, she scooped up a few bubbles and tossed them toward him. In return, he delivered a huge spray of bubbles.

"Look at what you've done now!" Margo glanced down at her soapy shirt but decided not to complain. What was the use of staying annoyed when her husband was trying to ease the tension? After they cleaned the kitchen, Margo filled the teakettle and prepared to disclose her inner thoughts about the recent events. The two sat down together on the faded living room couch. Margo looked straight into Chris's eyes. "Something's going on. It's giving me the creeps."

He sipped his strong tea.

"Are you listening to me?" He seemed preoccupied with his own thoughts. Ever since he came home, he'd been acting strange. Quieter than usual.

He placed his mug on the end table and looked at Margo. "I think we're under spiritual attack."

"Why? What've we done?"

"I'm not completely sure, but I think it's the prayer meetings." Chris took another sip. "I don't know if this is related, but Mark and I found a disgusting animal buried near the cave I found."

"What! You didn't tell me about this. Is that why you've been so sullen?" Margo didn't understand why her husband didn't tell her about it when he came home. He kept things bottled up instead of getting them off his chest. She hoped their conversation could bring things into the light.

Chris answered, "Well, you say I tease you too much, so now I'm being serious, and you don't like that either?"

"No, it's just you change your moods so quickly, but that's a whole other bag of worms." Margo didn't want to hurt her husband's feelings, but his moodiness seemed worse lately. If only he'd talk more about how he felt.

Chris squirmed. "I'm not a puppet. I can't always control what I feel."

Margo hesitated. "I know, but we need to pray about it and everything else going on. But I don't think the dead animal has anything to do with what we've been up against. Do you?" Margo didn't want to try to figure out anything else in this jumble of events, so she dismissed the information for now.

"Now let me see, you've gotten me off track. Lately, I've been thinking—"

"That could be dangerous." Chris smiled.

"Can't you be serious?"

"Sorry. Just trying to lighten up."

"I got the strangest feeling the other night. Remember when I thought I saw a prowler?"

"Sure do."

"Well, I never told you this. I've been praying for the church, and God gave me a vision." There it was…out in the open. Now he knew she was getting visions from God. It was time Chris knew.

He answered with a slight Freudian accent. "What kinds of visions, my dear?"

Margo threw a pillow. "Okay, Doc, analyze this. I saw a wooden pier—"

"A pier? Umm, that might be very significant." He held up his finger in parody.

"You didn't let me finish."

"Sorry, dear. Go ahead."

"This pier…it had big wooden pilings underneath. Half of the supports were underwater…and they were rotten!"

"Hmm, what do you think it means?"

Margo closed her eyes. "I've been thinking about this a lot. I believe the pier represents a structure, like a building where people gather. The pilings underneath hold up the building, like the foundation beams. I'm not completely sure why they're rotten, but it may be connected"—Margo paused—"to those weird feelings I started getting after I did the grave rubbings."

"Hmm." Chris lowered his voice. "This may be important, but do you think it's related to Margaret?"

"Truthfully…no, though I'm not sure. It might be tied together in some way, but unfortunately, I felt it had something to do with the church."

"Wow! That's something else."

Margo scrunched up her face. "What do you mean?"

"Lately, things have started to be a little strained with the elders. People are taking sides, and there's been division. And on top of that, did you know the group from the other side of the river is considering leaving and starting their own fellowship?"

"I knew they planned on it eventually, but not so soon after we bought the new building. Do you think that's what the rotting piles represent?"

"It's hard to say. I think that would have more to do with the foundation of the church, which would impress the elders. I detect some kind of problem there. But somehow I think the rotten animal has something to do with it."

"That really makes this whole matter complicated. There's just too many threads to untangle."

"Yeah, we'll need some divine insight to understand this jumble. By the way, what happened to the pier?"

"I was afraid you'd ask." Margo shuddered. "It collapsed."

9

Margo watched the spectacular sunset from her studio window, glad summer had come to a close and the heat dissipated. Puffy cumulus clouds painted a rich red sunset over the hills of New Coven. Etched against the crisp black edges of the surrounding mountains, she studied the contrast of dark and light. A painter's dream, she thought. But in a moment, the bright colors faded and the sun descended behind the dark mountains.

Evening twilight settled on the scene, and Margo retreated from the dark window. Cool air rushed into the uninsulated room, and she grabbed a warm sweater. She felt chilled to the bone and buttoned her cardigan to the neck. Margo walked over to the shelves and counted the number of glazed pots on them. Picking up a cup with runny glaze, she fumed. *I can't believe all the bad luck I've had lately: glazes running, pots breaking...just terrific.* She realized all these problems had started just after she'd discovered the note and Margaret's grave site.

Hoping to unearth some other clue, she walked over to the clay jar where she placed the photocopy of the letter. She read it over. Several words stood out: *hateful, evil men, scheme, diabolical evil,* and *one of our ancestors.* It plagued her. *What was the diabolical evil and who was the ancestor? Could this evil possibly have been responsible for Margaret's death?*

Frustrated, she put down the letter, drawn to the rubbings posted near the door. She walked over and studied them once again. Certainly, someone had tried communicating about someone's death. No doubt "kil—" stood for *killed*. Earlier, she entertained the notion it stood for *kiln*, but she soon abandoned the idea. She studied the rubbing more carefully. The next letters, N-b-s-h-b-s—u, seemed to be a code because they didn't make sense, at least not in English. However, the subsequent ones were now evident. After eliminating different solutions for "pri—": *private*, *primary*, *prince*, she concluded it represented *priests*.

If indeed she was correct…which ones?

<hr />

The small procession walked in silence, arms crossed, heads bowed down, following their leader. The full moon rose slowly and hung in the sky like a huge saucer. Its silver moonbeams danced in and out of the woods. The lead man, taller than the rest of the troop, stopped and motioned to the others. He pointed to a thicket, and the men obeyed.

As an important member of the higher order of a selective society, Bill enjoyed his position of leadership and power. He was on his way to becoming a Third Degree Master Mason and would earn much more respect. Hungry for the power of this position, he acted the part well. Everyone stepped aside for him as he led them to a small field while the moon spilled its beams on their destination—a rock ledge. When they approached, he noticed something askew outside the cave. He stopped and motioned for the others to proceed. He waited until the group trailed inside and then investigated the situation. Sure enough, he found someone had tampered with the unmarked grave site. He fumed and kicked at the soft earth. *If Paul did this, I'll have his head.*

His companion trailed behind, and Bill motioned for him to hurry. "What's the problem, boss?"

Bill spun around and aimed the flashlight at the ground. "What the hell kind of job is this?" The two looked down at the disgusting sight and nearly gagged. Bill kicked the dirt and uncovered a disembodied goat's head. He grabbed his partner by the shoulder and dragged him away from the site. "What a lousy job," he snapped. "Are you crazy…digging a shallow hole like this?"

"Sorry, boss, but I didn't leave this mess. I'm not that stupid. Somebody must've been poking around here and dug up the stupid animal."

The boss inched closer to his partner's face. "I know. And that's what I'm concerned about!" Pointing to the gruesome remains, he half growled, "You didn't dig deep enough. Now some idiot found it, and who knows what's going to happen?"

"Whoever it was…probably got more than they bargained for."

"Yeah, but he better not come back again." Bill took out a rolled cigarette and lit it. He inhaled, and the ember glowed in the dark. "Get rid of it…now! You'll be in deep trouble if you know who finds out." Tossing the remains of the cigarette on the ground, Bill ground it into ashes.

As he proceeded into the cave, a wall of cold air hit him in the face. Bill watched the flickering candles cast strange shadows on the walls. A profound darkness fell upon the scene as a low monotonous chanting changed in pitch. He breathed in the atmosphere. The smell of candle wax and incense intermingled with the sounds of the chanting filled him with a heady intoxication. He smiled to himself and thought about the ceremony to come.

As the chanting grew in intensity, Bill sensed the worship would begin soon, and he stepped into the circle. At the right moment in the ceremony, he stepped aside, turned around, and took several long strides to a boulder blocking a small alcove. He braced his strong arms against the rock and pushed sideways with all his strength. He strained a little. It was harder without Paul, but he knew he could move it. Drops of sweat glistened on his forehead as his muscles flexed. Little by little, the rock rolled away. Then one of the priests broke off from the rest, stepped into the alcove, and pointed to a round stone tablet that bore engravings.

Bill squatted down to one side, and the priest knelt on the other. Together they raised the carved stone off the floor then positioned it sideways and carefully maneuvered it though the small opening. He felt the electricity in the air as two other hooded figures approached. They took the stone wheel and placed it in the middle of the table on a black cloth.

In the bright candlelight, he observed the etched writings and soon recognized the ancient symbols. Bill had made it his business to know anything of value, and he believed this to be a costly object. No wonder his *associates* wanted it so much. Bill smiled at their cleverness and cunning. Money was no object, and he was the perfect man for the job. An inside trade.

The light intensified and illuminated the surface, revealing dried red drops of blood splashed over symbols Bill knew well. The chanting stopped. Anticipation filled him. The high priest opened a vial with a white powdery substance and passed it around on a glass tray. There were so many advantages to this job.

Bill stood up tall and moved into his place around the table, completing the number—six in all, with the high priest and priestess at either end. When all inhaled the white powder, the priestess slipped off her black robe. She began to twirl and gyrate. Her actions fascinated Bill, but the others remained emotionless. Picking up a white scarf dipped in blood, she fluttered it through the air, high above her head and naked arms. Her long black hair swirled about her body. At that point, he would have done anything to have her, but he must learn to master himself so he could control others.

His eyes never left her. After several incantations, she dropped the bloodstained cloth carefully on the stone and let out a piercing cry. The chanting stopped, and all eyes were on her, including Bill's. He felt the electricity in the air.

The beauty stepped up onto the table then placed her foot on the stone. Bill's desire grew, and he felt he could barely contain himself. He watched the high priest open a book and recite the familiar words. With a wild look in her eyes, the priestess recited the same invocations but in a higher-pitched voice. Each time a name was added, she cut a chord—symbolic of division and death. Before each new "spell," Bill saw her point to the stone. As she did this, her eyelids fluttered and her lips twisted so her face was screwed up grotesquely.

Bill turned away for a moment, disgusted. *Wow, what a change.* A high-pitched scream shattered his thoughts, and he spun around to look. For a moment, even he was surprised. He saw the embodiment of youth quickly take on a horrifying and deathly appearance. He listened intently as curses spewed from her distorted mouth. She repeated the same incantations the required six times. Finally, the priestess fell exhausted to the ground in front of him, her figure a limp, lifeless form. When she looked up at him, her face returned to its enticing beauty, and an inviting smile spread across her lips. In that moment, he realized she had great powers and would be very useful to his cause.

10

Just outside the cave, blue-and-yellow flames glowed in the dark. Paul paced back and forth a distance away from the tongues of fire licking the mutilated body of the goat. He stopped for a moment and stared at the consuming fire, satisfied with his method of disposing of the carcass, though anxious his boss might not agree. He sometimes resented the fact Bill was top dog and that he had the big connections and the brains, but Paul had the brawn.

Paul continued to pace up and down away from the flames. The smoke smelled horrible, and he had to keep his distance. Boss took longer than last time, and he wanted to get out of the place. The whole scene gave him the creeps—all that chanting and mumbo jumbo stuff. Suddenly, he heard a piercing scream that made even his flesh crawl. He would have beat it out of there if he hadn't just spotted a tall figure emerging from the cave—Bill!

Even in the absence of daylight, he knew his unmistakable gait and long, confident strides. He watched as Bill checked his appearance and combed his hair. Paul wondered why he cared at a time like this with no one around to see him. But then again, Paul didn't really care. He didn't think about a lot of things and had everything he wanted, except a steady girl, though he had enough women.

Bill sauntered over and slapped him on the back. "Good idea...burning the carcass. There'll be no evidence this time, but it sure stinks." Bill took out another cigarette, bent over the flame, lit it, and inhaled deeply. He smiled and patted Paul on the back again. "Thanks for sticking around and cleaning up this mess."

Paul grinned and nodded. "I know I've got to stay here, but the place gives me the creeps."

"Don't worry, city boy. Nothing's going to jump out of the woods."

"I'm not frightened of no woods, it's those guys in there." He pointed to the cave.

Bill sauntered back toward the cave while Paul watched the consuming fire.

Later that night, thick clouds moved in from the south and covered the moon like a shroud. Occupied by his thoughts of Margo, Chris unconsciously drove along the river road even though the drizzle had changed to torrents. As he rounded a corner, he saw water spilling over the creek's banks creeping up to street level. Startled by what he saw next, Chris stepped on his brakes. Up ahead, it looked like a car had smashed into a tree. He grabbed a flashlight and jumped out of the car. "Dear God," he prayed, "let no one be hurt."

As he approached, he saw the strangest sight. Some kind of bird of prey had crashed into the windshield, and part of its body stuck out from the glass. The car lights cast an eerie glow and illuminated the silhouette of a gnarled tree. Chris flung open the door. A young lady sat slumped over the steering wheel, blood dripping from her head. He punched in 911 on his cell phone. The phone chirped while he checked her pulse. Nothing. He listened for a heartbeat. Nothing.

"Nine-one-one. What is your location?"

"Get an ambulance pronto to the end of Hawk Drive. Near Route 23. Now."

"What is the nature of your emergency?"

"A young woman bleeding to death in a car accident."

He threw the phone in his pocket and examined the girl. *Why didn't I get here ten minutes earlier? Such a young life.* He shined the flashlight on her face. Though bruised, her features were unmistakable. "Dear God, no, please don't let this be true!" The whirring of the ambulance shattered his thoughts and the silence of the night. The flashing red lights painted the treetops.

The paramedics rushed from the ambulance carrying a stretcher. Chris dashed out of the front seat.

One of them greeted Chris as they rushed to the vehicle. "What do we have here?"

Chris stammered, "I-I used to be a m-medic, so I stopped." Just then blue flashing lights and sirens split the night. The paramedics ignored them. "You take care of the police. We'll handle the girl." They maneuvered the young women onto the stretcher then into the ambulance.

The policeman strolled over to Chris and flipped his wallet badge. "Sergeant Thomas. I'll need to ask you a few questions."

The sergeant glimpsed down as the stretcher whizzed by. He looked back at the vehicle and spotted the strange sight. "What the heck happened here?"

Chris just shook his head. "I really don't know, Officer. I wish I did." The siren from the ambulance made a high-pitched *whoooop, whoooop, whoooop*, which pierced the night.

Chris felt his heart break as he stared at the taillights of the ambulance disappear, carrying Mark's sister, Ashley.

—◦◇◦—

Margo couldn't believe Chris's story. She felt things were getting weirder every day. Staring in front of her on the front page of Monday's *New Coven Monitor* was the picture of Ashley.

How could this be true?

She'd just seen her a week ago when she helped Margo take pictures of the stone houses. Ashley had been spooked going to the cemetery. Now this.

Margo folded the page and read the report. "Twenty-year-old Ashley Dart, daughter of Frederick and Martha Dart, was pronounced dead at 11:56 on Sunday night, October 16. The autopsy cited internal bleeding as cause of death. No foul play is suspected. Police investigated her whereabouts before the accident occurred. She had been returning from a party at a friend's house on Sawmill Road. There was liquor there, but the autopsy showed no traces of alcohol or drugs."

"Thank goodness." Margo read on, "Chris Pierson, a former paramedic, arrived on the scene at eleven and immediately called 911. On approaching the vehicle, he found the front window smashed and, of all things, a dead owl stuck into the windshield. Mr. Pierson surmised, 'Evidently, Ashley was so frightened she slammed on the breaks, and the car spun out of control into the apple tree.'"

Margo called. "Chris, come here, I need to ask you something."

No one replied, and Margo went to look for Chris. She found him in the garage, tinkering with the car.

"Is it true?"

Chris stood up from being hunched over into the car. "What?"

"Do you think Ashley died because she hit the apple tree or because of the bird?"

Chris rubbed his chin. "Well, yes and no. I think the owl crashed through the window first, startling her and sending her head-on into the tree, which may have killed her on impact, but only an autopsy will reveal this." He hesitated for a moment. "Anyway, she did crash into the apple tree."

Margo's hands trembled. Something inside her stirred. She felt the same way when she had read about Margaret's death.

But it didn't make sense.

"Chris, this is weird, but I feel there might be some kind of connection to Margaret's death. I don't know how, but something inside tells me they're related."

Chris had resumed his work on the car, and Margo tried to get his attention.

Annoyed, she tapped him on the back "Please answer me. Do you see a connection?"

"Yeah, this hose is connected in the wrong place."

Margo thought Chris got just a little too wrapped up fixing his car. "No, no, I mean about Margaret. Guess who was with me when I discovered her gravestone?"

"Ashley?"

"Right. And who was with you when you discovered a dead goat buried outside that cave you found?"

"Mark."

"And now who's dead?"

"Mark's sister."

"It's the strangest car crash I've ever heard of." She looked straight at Chris. "It seems odd, but I think these events are interconnected."

Chris's muffled voice questioned, "But how?"

Margo shrugged her shoulders. "I don't know." She walked over to a wooden box sitting on a tool table in the garage, fumbled around, and pulled out an old piece of paper from an envelope. She read the disturbing words and handed it to Chris. "Maybe this could provide some answers, if I could just figure out what it all means." Chris shook his head and whistled. "Where did you find this?"

<hr />

Margo overheard people talking in the church foyer before the funeral service began. "Isn't this a terrible tragedy?" one woman commented. An old man in a gray suit adjusted his collar and shook his head. "Makes no sense, no sense at all." Margo figured they were relatives, but she didn't know where they stood about spiritual matters. As she walked past the strangers, she heard a young woman comment, "Now I know why Ashley stopped going to church. How could God do this to her?"

Margo held herself back from explaining the situation to this young lady. People had such misconceptions about God and what He did. She didn't fully understand either, but she knew God didn't kill people. Instead of jumping into a heated conversation, she looked around for other members of the New Way Fellowship. She saw the pastors and a few others like Lance, who attended not only as an elder but as a cousin of Ashley's. Mark sat upfront with his parents and his wife, Jessica. He looked tired and upset.

She and Chris sat down near Rich and his wife. Melanie stared straight ahead and didn't look at anyone. The family's pastor began the ceremony. "We are gathered here together to honor the memory…"

The congregation stood up. Margo heard some people crying in front of her. She wanted to comfort them but wondered what she could say to help. When they sat down, Margo held Chris's arm close to her. She couldn't imagine the horror of finding Ashley in a puddle of blood.

Margo struggled to erase the picture from her mind. As the ceremony progressed, Mark gave the eulogy. He talked about his sister. "Ashley was a beautiful and loving person. This is a terrible tragedy." Mark shook his head. Margo glanced over to Mr. and Mrs. Dart, who clung to each other.

Then Mark changed gears. "I know this is difficult for some of you to understand. It's been tough for me…and the family. Sometimes events happen in life, which don't make sense. You may ask, how does this fit in with God's plans for us? Or, what kind of God would allow something like this? We can't always understand why God does something or why some things happen. Ashley's life may have been snatched from us, but why? I don't know. For now, I'm just as confused as you, but I intend to find out why this happened." He looked right at Margo for a long moment. Glancing away, he resumed. "One thing I do know, this is only temporary. We'll meet her again where there are no more tears, only shouts of joy."

Margo agreed. She didn't understand what was happening in her life either, but God did. She hoped He would show her what she needed to know. When Mark had looked at her before, it was as if he were questioning her. Even if she thought it might be loosely connected, how could she know why this happened? For the moment, she felt very uncomfortable. Complete silence fell when he walked down the steps from the podium. Margo watched as he joined his parents. His mother squeezed his hand.

Tears flowed, and Margo felt some of the tension break. Before the service, Margo could almost read people's minds— their anger, questioning, and wondering. Now she felt a sense of release. Though people may still think her death was tragic, at least they knew Mark's family believed in heaven and weren't blaming God. But she wanted to know what Mark thought as he glanced at her. Did he think she knew something he didn't?

11

After the funeral, Chris drove Margo home. Although physically present, her mind wandered far away from the little town of New Coven.

Chris jolted her. "What are you thinking about?"

Margo's reply was less than eloquent "Huh?"

"Something troubling you?"

"Yes, Ashley…and the letter."

"Yeah, it's a real shame, but I don't know if the letter has anything to do with it. Evil is a broad category these days."

Margo's thoughts flooded to the surface as she struggled to make sense of what she was thinking and feeling. *How does evil get hold of someone?* "Do you think God put down His hedge of protection because Ashley was beginning to backslide a little, to party here and there?" She put her head down. "Does God really hold us to a straight and narrow path? That's not the God I know."

"Me either."

"He certainly could have zapped me on several occasions. And how about Mark? He can be a bit immature at times, but I'm sure he prayed for his sister."

Chris nodded. "Yeah, he was praying. Mark said Ashley was dating a strange guy who wasn't a Christian. He thought maybe… this guy might—"

"Might what?" Margo demanded.

"Might be involved—in some kind of cult." Margo jumped. "Wow! Maybe that was Ashley's problem…and ours."

⟹◆⟸

That evening, Chris set the table while Margo made dinner. During the meal, Margo didn't say a word. Several times she sat with a forkful of food poised in the air and stared out the window.

Chris asked, "How's the pottery coming along?"

Margo smirked. "Lousy."

Chris decided no conversation was better than trying to pry stuff out of his bride of five years. He thought she was overreacting to Ashley's death, but he didn't completely understand his wife. One day chatting away, the next as silent as death, but Chris knew Margo wouldn't keep her feelings bottled up for long. But then again, he'd never seen Margo act so unusual as in this last week.

While Chris finished cleaning up in the kitchen, Margo plopped herself on the couch. He soon joined her. She sat staring at the TV, watching a show she didn't like. Maybe she needed some breathing room, so he sat on her other side. It felt strange. She wasn't laughing or talking or getting up to do something in between commercials.

When the show was over, Margo clicked off the set with the remote and sat silently. Chris ventured into dangerous territory. "Do you want to talk about this?"

She stared at him. "I just can't believe this. I just can't believe it."

"Can't believe what?"

"The owl."

Chris admitted. "That *was* strange."

"Beyond strange. You ever heard of something so weird? An owl breaking a windshield…"

Margo pulled the blanket off the couch and wrapped herself in it.

"Accidents happen."

"Like this?"

"Not often."

She pulled the blanket tighter. "It's cold in here."

Chris fiddled with the remote. "You're cold a lot lately."

Margo jumped up and gestured toward the remote, blocking his view of the television. "Put that thing down. We're not watching the boob tube tonight. Don't you see—"

"No, you won't let me."

"Don't be a wise guy. Can't you understand? There's some kind of connection."

"Connection to what?"

Margo threw her hands up in the air. "I don't know, but somehow Ashley, her boyfriend, and all this strange stuff going on sure seems evil to me!"

"Yeah, but I don't see the connection," Chris mused.

Margo poked her finger in the air, gesturing toward the pottery barn. "I don't know, but it has something to do with what I felt... in the studio, in my nightmare, and in church."

"You think it's related to Ashley's death, and the evil indicated in the note? It seems far-fetched."

"Maybe. Deep inside I feel it was no mistake an owl hit her car. I just know it. Something's wrong, but I don't know what."

"Wrong with the church, her unknown boyfriend, or Ashley?"

Margo hesitated and shrugged her shoulders. "At this point, I'm not sure."

"Do you think it has anything to do with the vision?"

"I've been thinking more about this." She leaned closer to Chris. "Maybe the pier represents the church, not just any building. But what would that have to do with Ashley?"

Chris furrowed his eyebrows. "I don't know."

"This whole incident smacks of the same spirit that's been harassing me lately—and it's definitely *evil*." Margo stood up. "I intend to find out how all this is connected."

The next day, Margo decided to visit Jessica. She wanted to stop in to say hello and drop off a meal. When Margo arrived, she noticed Mark's car wasn't there. Maybe he went back to work already, but it seemed strange. Margo rang the doorbell, and Jessica opened the door, wearing her bathrobe.

"I brought dinner over, thought you could use some help." Margo handed the dish to her but didn't ask to come in. Jessica's eyes looked red and puffy.

"Do you want to come inside for a minute?" Jessica took the dish Margo offered.

"Sure, if it's okay with you." Margo walked into the living room. Piles of clothes lay scattered around, as well as papers and books.

"Sorry, the place is a mess. We haven't had time to get anything done since Ashley's…passing." She put the meal in the refrigerator.

Margo felt guilty for not volunteering. "Sorry, I should have called and asked if you needed help."

Jessica ignored the comment. "Want some coffee? I've got some here." She pointed to the coffeemaker pushed in front on the counter. It usually sat stuck in the back.

Margo preferred tea, and she didn't recall Jess being a big coffee drinker either, but she didn't mention it. "Sure. I can get it." She poured a cup for herself and a mug for Jess. She placed them on the kitchen table.

Jessica moved some books and papers aside.

Margo sat down. The tension in the air hung heavy. "So how are you and Mark doing since Ashley's accident?"

"Funny you should ask. Right now, Mark's up at that blasted cave looking for that awful dead animal he found the other day."

Margo raised her eyebrows in surprise.

"He's looking for clues. For some strange reason, he thinks his sister's death may be related. Can you believe it?"

Margo wasn't ready to express her opinions yet. "Does he have any idea how?"

"You know Mark. He always rushes into things without thinking. He came up with some weird explanation. Something about rituals and mind control. Like you could radio control an animal. How stupid can you get?"

Margo never thought of it that way. Maybe Mark was on to something, but he shouldn't have left Jess all alone. "How are you?"

"Truthfully, Margo, I've about had it with him. Six years together and he still doesn't have a good job. I can't live like this. I need someone to help me."

Margo sipped her coffee then placed it squarely between them. She thought of Mark as somewhat impulsive but all in all a nice guy. "I know Mark can be immature at times, but he loves you, Jess."

Jess dropped her head into her hands. "Well, I don't know if I still love him."

Margo couldn't believe her ears. She knew they had a few problems...who didn't? But she never heard Jess talk like this before. What next?

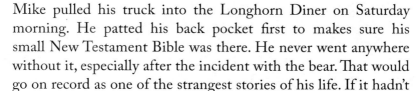

Mike pulled his truck into the Longhorn Diner on Saturday morning. He patted his back pocket first to makes sure his small New Testament Bible was there. He never went anywhere without it, especially after the incident with the bear. That would go on record as one of the strangest stories of his life. If it hadn't happened to him, he would've bet it was a tall tale.

He climbed down from his pickup truck wearing his pointed leather boots and warm flannel shirt. The air felt brisk as he walked toward the diner. Funny how the weather changed on a dime in these parts...nothing like his home state of Texas. Inside, Mike tipped his cowboy hat to one of the waitresses then looked over people's heads, searching for Pastor Dave, as his friend's called him. Mike spotted him and, in a few strides, was by his side.

Extending his hand, Mike grinned. "Glad you could make it here, Pastor."

Dave returned in kind. "Nothing like a good breakfast and great company."

Mike sat down, and a waitress came over right away. "Coffee as usual?"

He looked up and smiled. "Yup." He turned back to Dave. "Sure was something else you told me about your dream and prayin' for me. It surely was no ordinar' dream. That bear nearly tor' me and my partner apart."

"I'd like to hear more about it."

"Sure, but let's order first. The Western omelet and hash browns are the best this side of the Great Divide."

The waitress returned with two large mugs of coffee and took their order.

Dave closed his menu. "God sure works in mysterious ways. I've never heard someone calling me in a dream…and to find out later it was real."

"Well, in the six months I've been a Christian, I've been saved by an angel and from the jaws of a bear." He gulped his black coffee. "I never thought someone like me would've been helped by something I didn't believe in, and now by a pastor's prayers."

"So you weren't a believer?"

Mike shook his head and thrust out his jaw. "Not until I almost drowned one day. My boat got overturned in the spring rains, and I almost went over the falls. At the time I wouldn't admit it, but it had to be an angel that helped me reach a high branch and hang on for dear life."

Mike supplied a few details, and the waitress delivered their orders.

Dave poured ketchup over the hash browns. "So what happened with the bear?"

"That's a long story. It all started when my friend Bob threw fish heads out behind our tent and this ornery bear went after them." Mike suspended a forkful of omelet in the air.

Dave listened as Mike told the whole incredible story from the bear ripping apart their tent to the bright light Mike believed was another angelic appearance.

"The strangest thing was that brown bear transformed right before my eyes into the meanest looking grizzly I ever saw. I thought I was losing my mind…a grizzly in the Northeast. But the beast had a look in his eye like the devil himself!"

Margo moped around for a couple of days after the funeral, thinking about her last encounter with Ashley. Her mind bounced back and forth from the "freak" accident to the image she concocted of a mutilated goat. Her spirit sensed something uncanny about the owl's precise timing. Deep down she sensed it wasn't an accident. As crazy as it seemed, she thought it all related to the note she found…and Margaret, but she didn't know how or why.

She didn't feel clearheaded enough to focus on decoding the inscription further. But of one thing she felt assured. It was no suicide. Margaret was killed. And she had the notion somehow her death related to Ashley's. But what could she do? She had an important craft show to prepare for and pots to be fired. She resolved to pray and get on with her work.

Early Saturday morning, she snapped out of it. She sprung out of bed early, and by eight o'clock, she opened up the studio's back door. Now three days behind schedule, she had a lot to do. Chris was a doll and unloaded the kiln. When she went into the back room to get the clay, rows and rows of cups, plates, and vases greeted her. She longed to linger, to hold each pot, turn them over and admire their color, but Chris told her he had checked to make sure the glazes didn't run. They all looked so beautiful, so original. The colors were magnificent! They came out better than expected. Looking around, she couldn't locate her big beauty. Did Chris forget to fire her?

Margo didn't waste any more time in the kiln room. She grabbed her bucket of clay tools and a large wedge of clay to throw a few small cups. As she stepped into the open space, she gasped. "Oh no." In the middle of the floor rested the remains of a large clay pot. She dropped her bucket and ran over. Turning over several pieces of the vase, she cried, "Who could've done this?"

12

Chris couldn't believe the rash of bad luck they'd encountered lately in the studio. First, the supposed prowler frightened Margo a couple of weeks ago then the problems with the clay Margo insisted he didn't mix correctly and then runny glazes. Now someone had broken in and smashed one of Margo's valuable vases. *What's happening around here?*

Margo made Chris look for signs of entry. She thought this too must be connected to all the strange events. He thought she was going overboard in trying to relate everything together. But he hoped to find evidence of the robbery and report it to the police. He had checked the inside window sashes but found no clues. Outside, he walked around one side of the barn and saw nothing. He circled around to the back window. Some bushes grew nearby and would make a good hiding place. Chris made a mental note to remove them. As he approached, he looked down on the ground between the bushes. Something caught his eye.

Chris pushed back the foliage. His face drained white. Two animal bones placed in an *X* beneath the window glared up at him. It seemed like something out of a bad B movie or a practical joke, but this wasn't funny. Things were getting stolen, lives interrupted, and even a very strange death happened.

He bent down and turned one over with his foot. Bits of flesh still clung to them. The odor smelled putrid. His stomach turned.

They came from a small animal, maybe a sheep. He looked closer. Could it be...a goat?

Why hadn't a wild animal carried them away in the night? Chris didn't know what to make of the whole situation. He'd heard about things like this but never thought it would happen around here in their small town. What could it mean?

He debated about whether he should tell Margo. He didn't want to scare her any more considering everything that's happened lately. She had enough trouble sleeping, and this would frighten her even more. He didn't like all this talk of evil.

Chris stood up and decided he would discreetly remove the carnage without Margo's knowledge. After all, he reasoned, he could tell her at another time when all this had blown over, which he hoped would be soon.

<hr/>

On Sunday morning, Bill and his companion drove up the long driveway to the Carsons' home. He'd been invited to church and looked forward to the opportunity. As he stepped out of the sporty black Jaguar, he caught his reflection. He loved the James Bond look and his car. It exuded money and class. From the looks of Rich's house, it seemed they liked similar things.

As he stepped to the door, he noticed a young-looking woman peeking through the curtains. He smiled and rang the doorbell. She scampered away. He turned to Paul. "This should be fun."

Paul grunted, and Bill laughed. He loved games, and this looked like it would be a lot of fun.

Rich opened the door. "Glad you could make it. C'mon in, boys. We're just finishing getting ready." He called out to his wife, "Melanie, hurry up. The two guys I told you about are here."

As Rich's wife entered the room, she straightened out her tight-fitting dress. All eyes were on her.

Her husband whistled. "You look terrific, babe." He quickly walked across the room and grabbed her around the shoulders, hugging her tight. Turning toward the two, he announced, "This is my wife, Melanie. Am I not lucky?"

Bill nodded. He looked her straight in the eye, admiring all her best qualities. In a deep voice, he agreed. "Yes, she's beautiful and sophisticated."

Melanie looked up at him, and a spark of electricity passed between the two. Bill liked what he saw—the curve of her throat, her full breasts, and her dark red lips. He extended a hand.

"Pleased to meet you." He couldn't wait to get to know her.

As the foursome headed out the door, Bill brushed Melanie's thigh. Her face flushed, and while she looked down in embarrassment, her body spoke another language. Bill read it and smiled.

Rich decided the foursome would take Bill's car to church. "Hey, Mel, let's arrive in style."

She didn't protest when Bill suggested she sit up front in the comfortable bucket seats, which were heated.

Bill looked at Paul and said nothing. He climbed in the backseat. His muscular frame barely fit. Melanie sunk into the warm seat and glanced over at Bill. "I've always wanted heated seats."

"Yeah, they're great"—he patted the seat near her—"especially in winter." Bill grinned.

Rich leaned forward. "So how's the deal shaping up, Bill?"

"Great. Yeah, the town board was thrilled with the idea of getting rid of that sleazy place."

They talked business for a while, but Bill stole glances at Melanie as she stared out the window. He acted uninterested so as not to alert her husband. He wanted Rich on his side.

Before long they arrived at their destination in New Coven, a brick building that doubled as a church on Sundays.

Rich politely opened the door for his wife. "Wasn't that the best ride of your life?"

Melanie smiled. "Yes, dear." She exaggerated the last syllable. As he led her into the church building, Melanie glanced behind her and met Bill's approving gaze. She didn't look down this time. Bill watched her shapely form.

Paul smirked. "Don't mix pleasure with business. Remember why we're here."

Bill laughed. "Don't worry. I'm good at both."

Inside, Bill studied the worship service and the people. The lively music touched their emotions, and a few were dancing. While some might think the church too emotional, Bill knew better. He knew the power of worship. He had experienced it for himself, just from the opposite end of the spectrum: from power and wealth—what counted in life.

The shrewd businessman had a plan. He already had one ally, Rich, and he wanted to be careful not to move too quickly. If he played his cards right, he could gain a place of trust where it counted and plunder his enemy's treasure and a few trinkets, like that gorgeous wife of his.

But for now, he had to move slowly and draw them to himself; then he would enjoy the spoils after. He closed his eyes for a moment, as many others were doing, and thoroughly enjoyed his fantasy.

Paul leaned over and whispered to Bill, "I'm outta here—" But Bill didn't let him finish. He simply looked at Paul and placed his hand firmly on his leg. He could practically read Paul's mind. "Not yet. Be patient and you might enjoy yourself. Look around. There's plenty here for the taking. Just be careful."

"Yeah, nothing I want…except maybe over there." He gestured to a pretty young woman just a few rows ahead. Bill removed his hand. "Well, maybe that can be arranged."

Smiling, Bill faced forward and turned his mind to the preacher's words. It was of paramount importance to understand the people in the church, especially their beliefs. He knew the requirements of his craft and the degrees of knowledge and power in the illuminated Masonic structure, and he must learn theirs too.

Paul's ears perked up at the mention of blood. One of the guys in front of the church spoke about the blood of Jesus cleansing people from sin. Recalling having to deal with the goat's blood, Paul thought the pastor crazy. He groaned as he recalled the night he buried the goat. Blood covered him everywhere and made him—

His thoughts were interrupted by the preacher's words. "The blood of Jesus has power. Power to heal, power to change you, and power to overcome the enemy." A chill ran down Paul's spine. He looked over at Bill, who sat unflinching in the seat, calm and cool. His dark-blue suit perfectly in place, and his shirt unbuttoned at the collar showed off his broad chest. The expensive Rolex watch glistened on his wrist. Bill glanced at Paul and then leaned over. "Bingo, this is the right place."

Paul shook his head no. He couldn't wait for the meeting to be over. He jangled the change in his pocket, but he found himself listening.

"Come to the fountain of blood and be washed clean of sin," the pastor proclaimed, looking around at the congregation.

Paul wondered about this idea of blood-possessing power. *Maybe the goat's blood has—no way.* He interrupted his own thoughts. *But then again…*

The pastor stopped speaking, and Paul jumped up. A few people stood up and said they had messages from God. Embarrassed, Paul sat back down.

Then the pretty woman shot from her chair. "Be careful how you walk for the days ahead are evil. Do not walk according to the flesh, but according to the spirit…" He watched her every move—who wouldn't, with that dynamite figure and long shapely legs. Her long, silky hair cascaded down her delicate shoulders as Paul eyed her up and down.

"Watch out you don't fall into…"

His thoughts trailed off in a different direction, but Bill kept his eyes straight ahead.

After church, Bill and Paul were introduced to Rich's small circle of friends, which included Chris, Margo's husband. Bill acted friendly and cordial. He knew with his charismatic personality he could win over the devil himself to his cause.

He engaged Chris in conversation. "Your lovely wife seems to be quite spiritually aware."

"Yes. She seems to know things before anyone else." He looked over at her.

This interested Bill even more, and he wanted to meet her. Margo caught her husband's glance and walked over. Rich introduced her to his two new friends, and Margo acknowledged them with a smile. Paul straightened his tie. "Pleased to meet you." He didn't shake her hand.

Bill used his rich, deep voice. "This is a very nice church. I enjoyed the service. People here seem closer to God." He hoped she would respond to his statement, but she didn't, so he added. "Wouldn't you agree?"

"Yes and no. Looks can be deceptive. It's what's on the inside that counts."

Bill knew she sensed something. He would have to put out the best vibrations and aura he could. He would not conquer her as he did most women, so he tried a different tactic. "I'm new in town and trying to clean things up a bit. I've bought that old run-down bar on the corner of Main Street, and I plan to fix it up into a restaurant."

"That's nice." Margo hesitated a moment then continued, "The place is such an eyesore."

"I agree. I plan on remodeling it and giving it a whole new look." Bill tried to impress her.

"That's good, but folks around here don't like change. They don't like outsiders messing around with their town."

He knew this, but wondered why she mentioned it. The conversation lulled for a moment, and Chris held Margo's hand.

Paul tapped his boss on the shoulder and whispered, "Let's get outta here."

In a moment, Rich jumped in. "Margo's got a pottery business just across from the college, and she makes some nice pieces."

Bill smiled and felt like the Cheshire cat from *Alice in Wonderland*.

"I might be interested in some pottery for the plants and other items in the business. Do you sell to businesses?"

"Yes, but I make only hand-thrown ceramic pottery."

"Well, I might want to purchase a few pieces. I also have contacts with shops in the city that might be interested—"

Chris interrupted. "Doesn't sound like a half-bad idea. Maybe Bill can stop over sometime and see your work."

Margo frowned. "Right now, the shop's a mess, and I don't have a lot of finished pieces for sale. I can send you some photos."

Bill knew she was making up an excuse, and he tried to read her mind, but couldn't.

"I'll be seeing a lot of Bill these days, so if you give me the pix, I'll get them to him," Rich chimed in.

"Okay," Chris answered. "We'll do that."

Bill nodded to them in agreement, and then the little group disbanded. He smiled as he watched Margo and Chris walk away. Too bad she was off-limits, but there was more than one way to skin a cat.

Paul interrupted his thoughts. "I wouldn't mess with those two."

Bill shot back. "Don't worry. I'm in control. I've got more than good looks in my back pocket."

"We'll see," Paul said as he opened the church door and walked though to the other side. "There's something different about that girl."

"She's exactly what I'm after." Bill smirked, and Paul joined him.

13

Chris walked into his favorite local coffee shop and scanned the tables for his friend Mark. Only a few people occupied the tables, drinking fresh brew and reading the paper. He liked it here much better than the chain store variety. You could carry on a conversation here without interference. After what Margo had told him about what Mark had done to Jessica, Chris hoped to hear his side of the story.

Mark sat in a corner, staring down at the table, drinking a mugful. Chris joined him. "Glad you could make it. How're things?"

Mark looked up from his coffee. "Great, just great." He plunked the mug down on the wooden table, and it thudded. "This is a lousy cup of joe."

Chris felt the bitterness roll off Mark's tongue. "So, it's that good."

Mark shook his head. "Ever since Ashley's death, life has taken a nosedive."

"How's Jessica handling this?"

"We're not doing good. She's spending more and more time at school. Says she's planning projects for her preschoolers, but I don't believe her." He looked over to Chris. "We've been arguing a lot."

"About what?"

"Everything under the sun. She stayed at her mom's a few times. I went over the other night. She wasn't there. She came home late. Said she went to the movies because I've been leaving her alone. The next day, we had a big blowup."

"What happened?"

Mark plopped his head down into his hands. "I got really mad at her. I slapped her in the face because I thought she lied to me."

Chris closed his eyes. "Don't you see what's happening? We have to call the elders and pray about this."

Mark shook his head. "I did, but she won't forgive me. I told her I wouldn't do it again. She wants me to go to counseling, but I said no."

Chris stared at his friend in shock. "Then go to counseling to save your marriage."

Mark whispered, "I think she's having an affair."

A group of squawking crows woke Margo from a restless sleep. She felt groggy as though she had wrestled all night long with an evil being…almost like a monster from one of those kids' video games! *Ugh!* She'd tried to put this whole ordeal about Margaret on the back burner for now, but a sinister presence lurked in the shadows and even invaded her sleep.

Trying to wipe the cobwebs away from her mind, Margo stretched her arms and yawned. Her warm feet hit the cold floor as she peered out the window at the noisy intruders. They fought over a large piece of stale bread Chris probably had thrown them.

It was Monday morning already and a lot to get done. Margo made note of everything needed for the fair. *There's going to be some stiff competition this year with all those well- known craftspeople.* She padded down the hallway and continued talking to herself.

"Chris, where are you?" she called as she stepped into the cold kitchen. "We've got our work cut out for us today." Silence greeted her. She sat down and ran her fingers along the rim of one of her mugs. Its clean, smooth edge stood as a testimony to her fine craftsmanship. She poured a cup of coffee since she needed the caffeine. As she gulped down the dark java, she hoped he didn't forget the work they planned to do. Margo threw on an old flannel shirt and a pair of jeans and headed for the studio. "Somebody's got to do some work around here," she remarked.

Margo lifted the latch of the barn door and spotted Chris by the huge mixing vat. "There you are! I've been calling you. I thought you forgot about today and went for a prayer walk around town."

"No, I couldn't sleep too well after what Mark told me yesterday. Do you know he thinks Jessica might be having an affair?"

"What? She never mentioned it to me, just that he slapped her."

"Yeah, well, there's always two sides to a story. I want him to go to the elders about it. I know I'm going to pray about it all."

"While you're at it, pray we can get some work done around here. So many interruptions and weird things happening."

Chris walked over to the mixer and dumped the powdered clay into the water in the steel vat and put the motor on slow. "Yeah, we don't want any more temperamental clay."

"I know how you feel. I want to help them, but I'm not sure what to do other than pray. Everything is coming at us at the busiest time of year."

Chris knotted his eyebrows in a puzzled look. "I thought we finished the conversation about Mark and Jess and were back at work."

"I'd love to forget for just a couple of hours, but I had another horrible dream last night, but there's no time to get into that now." Margo tried to dismiss the thought about the Darts' marriage and the hideous monster in her nightmare. "Thanks for mixing this batch. I'll start kneading the porcelain I made on Saturday for the more delicate work."

She opened the clay barrel and stuck her hands into the pale-white clay. It felt so different from stoneware, so refined. She gathered a good-sized piece, filling up both hands. Then she plopped it down on the kneading table.

Good, this is perfect. I don't need to wrestle with stubborn clay. After working it to the desired consistency, she shaped them into seven smaller balls. Then she lined them up at the potter's wheel and gathered all the tools she needed.

Slapping the first ball down on the plaster disk, she began turning the wheel with her foot. As her hands cupped the pale-white matter, it easily conformed to the shape she wanted. *Porcelain is perfect…it's so easy to form.*

Margo's hands worked adeptly, but then a wisp of hair fell in her face, and she accidentally brushed it aside. Her hand left the clay for a split second, just long enough to unbalance it. The clay bulged on one side and wobbled as it spun around.

She responded quickly. "Come on, Lord," her voice pleaded under her breath. "Help me with this one. I can't have another flop." She focused all her efforts on pulling the clay upward, forming it into an elegant vase. The clay responded.

"Looks pretty good," she called across the room. "I almost lost it but got it back."

As Margo sat resting, she thought about the vase. Even though she'd been throwing clay for years, it took an incredible amount of concentration and effort. One glance away could ruin it. She realized how this paralleled her own life.

"Lord, help me keep my eyes on You. There's just so much to do that pulls me away, and I just don't have time."

Margo didn't realize she prayed aloud and Chris responded, "Is everything okay?"

"Oh, I wasn't talking to you. The Lord just showed me I need to focus more on Him, but I have so many irons in the fire to keep track of, and more stuff keeps coming my way."

Chris walked over. "Maybe God's trying to get your attention."

"Yeah, that's for sure, but I'm not quite certain what He's saying."

"After the craft fair, we'll have to spend more time together praying. But for now, I'm here to help." He patted her shoulder. "I think He sometimes shows us through everyday things. So how's the porcelain?"

"Good, but it can be tricky."

"Did it have any lumps?"

"No, smooth as silk."

"So it yielded to your hand with no problem?"

"Yeah, sure." Margo turned around and looked at Chris. "So what's your point?"

"Well, don't you recall the story about Isaiah and the potter?'

"Of course. I love that story. It reminds me...I need to be malleable—just like clay."

"So, then let Him be the potter."

Margo threw her hands in the air. She knew God was trying to work with her, but she felt frustrated. "I just don't understand what kind of clay pot God wants to make me. Am I a porcelain vase or a stoneware coffee mug?"

Chris shrugged his shoulders. "Only time will tell."

"Time, that's another problem. Who's got enough of it to get everything done and have a slice for the Lord?"

"Well, maybe you don't have to get everything done...just listen to what He wants."

Margo threw a clay tool and just missed Chris. "That's what I'm trying to do."

"Yeah, I know. You've been hearing and seeing in stereo."

"But I don't know what it all means."

Margo fished around in her pocket for a cutting wire and found it. In one swift motion she sliced through the clay like butter, releasing the form from its foothold.

———◆———

A few hours later, someone tapped on the window. Startled, she jumped. "Who is it?" A familiar feeling slid down her neck. She met two sets of eyes peering in the side window and recognized one of them. He pointed to the locked door and waved. She unhooked the black iron latch.

A cool waft of air swept into the studio. Margo wrapped her arms around her chest.

"Can we come in?" Rich grinned.

Margo shrugged. "What are you guys doing sneaking around here?"

"I was driving by the college with Bill, and I told him your studio was nearby, so he wanted to see your work. Remember, you said it was okay to drop by."

Caught off guard, Margo hesitated. "Yeah, but I'm in the middle of throwing some pots, and I can't let them harden."

Bill flashed a big smile, and his eyes glistened like diamonds. "Yes, we were watching you. You certainly know what you're doing." Scanning the shelves, the businessman added, "These aren't just pots. These are works of art. You've got creative talent just like the Creator."

Margo blushed and noticed how strikingly handsome Bill's tanned features looked against the dark-blue suit. At least he has some belief system in God, she noted.

"Yeah, well, thanks, but I better get back to work."

Rich directed his question to Chris. "I just wanted to show off Margo's work to Bill. I thought I'd drum up some business for you guys."

"I've got a lot to do. I can't make new pieces."

Bill looked directly at Margo. "Of course not. I'm interested in what you've got here."

Margo pushed back a wisp of hair with the side of her hand. "Listen, I've got to get back to work. Talk to Chris."

Chris gave her a reassuring look. "That's fine, we'll just talk and let you know what's up before we decide anything."

"Okay." Margo slipped into her red flannel shirt and returned to her work. She overheard snatches of their conversation. Phrases like "stores in the city" and "much better quality" came up several times. The tall, handsome enigma faced Margo, and she stole a few glances at him, managing to avoid his gaze. Despite his cunning eyes, he might be okay. She felt torn in two opposite directions. Was he a phony or not?

Rich sauntered over to Margo. "Bill wants to buy a few of your bigger vases, and he's willing to pay a good price."

Margo wondered what a fair price was to them. It took her many days to make this piece. "Did he mention a price?"

Rich shook his head.

Bill made eye contact with her again, and she studied him for a few moments but then looked down. She recognized the look—the guys at the craft fair trying to cut a deal. She wondered what he was up to. "Excuse me, Rich, but I better see what Chris is willing to get for my work."

Margo slipped out of the potter's wheel and walked over to the side office where Chris worked. She had so much work already, could she take on more? She hoped Chris would know what to do, and she asked him to join them.

"I'm flattered you like my pieces, but I don't think I could produce for the city and markets up here."

Rich cut in, "That's just it Margo. You could make more money by doing less. Get better prices and do less production work."

This sparked Margo's interest. "How?"

Bill explained, "I've several friends who own gallery shops in the city—looking for pieces just like this urn."

Chris wrapped his arm around her. "You could do more of what you like."

Margo warmed to the idea of making more of these.

Bill continued, "A piece like this would go for $1,500 in the city, and you would get between $1,200 to $1,300 for it."

Margo stepped aside and spoke with Chris. "What do you think?"

He looked over toward the office.

Margo knew he was thinking about the stack of bills on the desk.

"I say, let's give him a try."

"Okay." Perhaps she had judged Bill too quickly.

Margo wiped clay from the palm of her hands and pushed aside her annoying wisp of hair that fell from her ponytail. Looking intently at Bill, she tried to figure out what he really wanted. She attempted to probe beneath the surface of his good looks and firm physique, but instead she unconsciously was attracted to him. They could do a lot with $2,000 in one shot: more clay, more beautiful glazes, some more shelves. Chris seemed to think it a good idea. "So what's the deal?" Turning around to face Bill, her arm swept across the table and knocked over several mugs that fell to the floor.

"Wonderful, there goes two hours' work." Annoyed with her clumsiness, she bent down quickly and scooped up the deformed pieces. She handed them to Chris.

Flustered, she regained her thoughts. "Okay, it's a deal."

Bill's face softened right before her eyes, and the darkness she had felt about him before melted away. For the next ten minutes, they discussed the details. By the time they were finished, Margo felt ecstatic. She held $1,000 in her hand. This would help them a lot. Maybe Bill was an answer to prayer.

14

Dave Light prayed long and hard in his study at the Kingsland church. The small room—surrounded by books and furnished sparingly with a comfortable armchair, a modest-sized desk, and wooden chair—provided the ideal place to pray. He prayed on his knees, his tall but thin frame bent over the seat of a wooden chair facing the spindles, hands clasped together. "Dear Lord, please help this small body of believers. Encourage Joy and Ray in their efforts to restore harmony in the church. Thank you for their willingness to help." His strong frame shook with fervency. "Lord, please don't let this incident bring more division. And please mend the broken hearts." He knew God wanted to bring healing to the members of the congregation, especially after the recent split in the church. Dave saw the obvious solution to the problem—prayer.

"Dear God, I plead for Your mercy. Please help these sheep not to gossip. Help them to overcome bitterness in their lives and turn their eyes on Your Son, Jesus."

He knew in his heart many who left the church were deceived by their own desires, and he prayed they would return. Today, however, he focused on the potential danger that could arise from gossiping, backbiting, and anger. Although he heard none of it up until now, he knew how subtly these things could start: a slight twist of the truth here and there, a word whispered in unrighteous judgment, a statement of pride. Dave saw how easily a Christian could stray down the path of natural inclination to find themselves deep in the mire of anger, bitterness, and worst of all, self-righteousness.

So on this Monday morning, he earnestly sought God to protect the church from all manner of evil, from both the inside and the outside. He didn't want to attribute more power to the enemy then he had, but neither would he be ignorant of what the devil could do in a situation like this. It could rip a church apart.

He stood up. "Dear God, you know how easily the enemy can get a foothold if the sheep start wandering from Your Word. Please guide them through this valley." He thought about the man who had led some of them astray. He had once been a brother, but he erred and believed Christians could not sin, no matter what they did. A powerful preacher, he twisted the Word of God to ultimately fulfill the lust of the flesh.

Dave paced back and forth as he thought about him. "Dear God, I loved him like a brother. How did he allow himself to get so deceived?" Dave already knew the answer. "Dear God, keep us pure in your sight and let us never take our eyes off You!"

As the senior pastor of New Way Fellowship, Vince had called a special meeting for the deacon board and elders to discuss the threatening situation. As his wife rushed around the room vacuuming the new blue carpet, hanging up clothes, and putting magazines away, he prided himself on his house and new furnishings. He enjoyed living in a nice middle-class neighborhood in a roomy split level at the end of a cul-de-sac. But if the truth would be known, he hoped for something even bigger. But for now, this would do. They would meet in the newly renovated basement.

Within half an hour, the first man arrived. Rich, who was newly appointed as a deacon, walked into the room and greeted Vince.

"Glad you're here first, brother." Vince slapped him on the shoulder. "We've got some important issues to discuss. I need to talk about one of them right now." He ushered Rich into his private study and the two spoke in hushed tones.

Within fifteen minutes, all four men had arrived. Three of them—Mark, Matt, and Lance—sat on the couch his wife had purchased for the entertainment room. On each side, Vince and Rich sat in the two matching wing-back chairs.

The meeting opened with a short prayer, but Vince wanted to get right down to business. He sat up tall and spoke. "As all of you already know, a number of members from the other side of the river approached me about starting another church over there." He looked around the room and added, "But what you don't know is—they want to start within a couple of months. I hope you realize if we let them go just like that." He snapped his two fingers together to make his point clear. "Then we'll be losing their much needed support."

The church could not afford to lose their money. They needed it; he wanted it to prove their success to the mother church. This particular group was composed of the fortunate couples who lived across the river—college grads who landed good-paying jobs. Unlike the struggling young couples who composed the rest of the church, their tithes were more generous.

Vince stared at the other men, hoping they would agree to his plan. He did hold one ace up his sleeve, Bill. The man had tithed over $2,000 this week alone! Yet they needed to make sure he'd continue coming to their church, befriend him, and draw him in.

Lance broke Vince's train of thought. "You guys know they planned this over a year ago. They wanted to start their own church as an offspring of New Way Fellowship."

Vince countered. "If we let our brothers and sisters leave us now while the church is still so young, it will ruin us."

Rich jumped in. "Yeah, it will look like a church split."

"But that's not what this is all about," Lance interrupted. "And you know it. They don't want to divide, they want to multiply." He looked each and everyone straight in the eye. "If they meet across the river, then they can impact the people living there, and they'll grow and flourish. That's what's important here. Not what other people think." Lance looked down at the carpet and pointed. "Look at the traffic patterns our shoes have made on this new carpet." Everyone looked down.

"What does this have to do with anything?" Vince spat.

Lance got down on his knees and brushed the carpet with his hand. The shoe imprints disappeared quickly. "Even though the carpet pile was momentarily affected, all it took was a brush of my hand to restore it to its original look."

"So you're making an analogy that the church is merely a carpet. And if a whole group of our congregation leaves us, we will spring back in no time, just like that." He snapped his fingers again.

"Of course it's not that simplistic, but if this is God's will, then He can pull us through."

Vince smiled as he thought of Bill. "Yeah, maybe God has already provided. Rich brought a rather generous guy to church last week. He tithed a considerable amount. Of course, I don't know exactly how much, but the secretary was impressed." Vince cleared his throat. "If Bill continues to attend church and he brings others who are as generous, we might be able to make the budget."

Rich agreed. "Yes, Bill has many contacts, and he's a believer. He told me himself."

"Well, that remains to be seen," Lance concluded. "Anyway, how do we know he'll continue to attend church and give money each week?"

Vince knew Lance would be the hardest one to convince. With his position as an elder, he stood only a notch below Vince. He'd have to be subtle in his suggestion and give it a spiritual spin to get past Lance—not that his own concern wasn't moral, but Lance took things to the extreme. He drummed his fingers on the table and answered. "We'll just have to make Bill feel appreciated."

Rich agreed. "We could invite him to some of our meetings and make him feel like an insider."

"Not a bad idea," Vince concluded.

———◇———

After Dave poured out his heart for his congregation, another prayer began to take shape. At first he was aware of it as a feeling that arose in his chest and expressed itself in a language of its own that flowed from his spirit. Then he saw a picture in his mind of a number of people—some he knew, others he did not. They seemed to be standing in a circle around a young woman. Mike was one of the people. "Dear God, I don't know who all these people are, but protect them and especially be with Mike and this young woman."

Dave thought of Mike and recalled their luncheon at the diner. He was so different from the rest of his congregation: ex-hippies from the sixties, recovered alcoholics and drug abusers, a number of musicians and artists, some single parents, and a small smattering of middle-class baby boomers. Mike continued to come week after week, and Dave thought about their conversation and the interesting story about angels.

The pastor knew the appearance of this Texas-bred cowboy in the Northeast would hold significance for the church. Maybe he would get the members' attention and help them to focus on what's important, not their image as an alternative church. Dave laughed and enjoyed the mental picture of a bunch of rednecks mixing with a group of ex-hippies. One thing's for sure, this Mike was not your typical redneck. He was sensitive, intelligent, and spiritually aware. Maybe they'd learn a thing or two from him. "Anyway, God, this may be an answer to my prayer. You just might have something up your sleeve."

———◇———

The discussion about the finances ended and they moved on to other concerns. Mark, one of the younger leaders, looked over at Lance, who then spoke. "Mark called the other day and has something important to tell us."

"I'm not sure if all of you are aware of the strange goings on around here in New Coven and its surroundings."

Rich furrowed his brow. "No, what's up?"

"Well, the other day after the Saturday-morning prayer meeting, I was wandering around. I decided to go for a short hike, and guess what I discovered?" Mark looked around the room and blurted, "A dead goat."

Silence followed. Vince thought about the ramifications. The others didn't seem as concerned. "Tell us more about it."

"I tried calling you, but you were all too busy." No one commented.

"Anyway, it was strange that by the time I got to go back there a couple of days later, the goat was gone. Vanished, disappeared."

Rich laughed, and his blue eyes brightened. "I know why you didn't call me. You know what I'd say. What's it this time?"

"What do you mean *this time?*"

"Oh, come on, according to you, there's always a conspiracy brewing." Rich lifted his arm in a sweeping arc. "It must be some master plot to destroy all Christians in New Coven and the Northeast. Last time it was some crazy vision of two huge burning buildings. Okay, out with it, what demon is trying to get us now?"

"I don't think any *demon* is trying to get us, and I don't think there's a conspiracy in town, but are you ignorant of the fact goat's blood is used in satanic worship?"

"I just knew you'd have some demonic explanation for all of this. You're so paranoid about being a Christian you think everyone is out to get you."

Mark ran his fingers through his shoulder-length hair. "I didn't say they were after us. But I'll tell you something." He leaned in closer to the group. "After I discovered that goat, weird things have been happening: Ashley's death, Margo's strange visions, and now Jessica's behavior. She's been staying away from home, and we've been fighting a lot."

"And whose fault is that?" Rich leaned forward in his chair.

Lance raised his arms to separate the two. "Okay, guys, that's enough."

Vince realized he better take control of the situation. He turned toward Rich. "You're new here, and we don't speak to each other that way. I understand you two don't see eye to eye on these spiritual matters, but let's at least have the courtesy to consider what Mark has to say."

Rich sat back in his chair. "Sure, Vince, whatever you say. But nothing Mark has to say will change my mind."

"Just listen, okay?" Vince wondered why Rich had to be so opinionated. He was a good businessman and could help them financially.

Lance continued. "I don't think Mark believes there are demons everywhere attacking—"

"But we shouldn't be ignorant either!" Mark stood up.

"Mark, please sit down." Vince didn't like all this tension and focus on demons. With talk like this, he'd wind up losing the whole congregation. "We need to be open to each other's views."

After a few more comments, the two backed down. The men decided Lance should investigate the area. The meeting ended abruptly at nine o'clock when Vince's wife came downstairs with an important call. The guys all shook hands and promised to pray for each other and their families.

15

Before she washed her work jeans, Margo turned the pockets inside out. Pottery shards, clips of artwork, and pieces of clay fell onto her hands. What lay there mirrored her feelings. A detective might be able to piece all the scraps together to form a conclusion, but to her, it just seemed like a big mess. How Bill and Margaret and these visions fit in she didn't understand.

As she went to toss the pants in the machine, a small business card protruded from the pocket.

She pulled it out and stared at the name.

Should she really follow through with Bill's proposition? The thousand dollars would help, but she could cut things off anytime she wanted.

Chris snuck up behind her and grabbed her by the waist, the card waving as she struggled to get free.

"Let me go," she said.

"Only if I get a kiss." He drew her close.

"I'm not a kid, and I'll make no such promises."

Chris spotted the business card. "What's in those tiny paws of yours?"

"Oh this, it's nothing." She held the paper away from him.

"Yeah, I can tell, but it's different…black with gold lettering. Let me see it."

"No. Now, let me go."

Chris jumped to get it. "Not until you let me see who it's from." She struggled to get away and dangled it beyond his reach.

Chris caught a glimpse. "Is that the name of the shop Bill owns in the city?"

"I don't think so. He said it was one of his associates who might be interested in my work. Truthfully, I was just about ready to throw it—"

Chris seized the card. "Oh no, you don't. Didn't we agree if the first piece worked out, you'd give him another?" Margo nodded.

"Don't you see what's before you? God just handed you a double blessing—make some money for the shop and find out more about this Bill guy."

"That's true, but I don't want to get involved with him." She feared the momentary attraction she felt for Bill back in the studio, even though it passed quickly. She wasn't sure of his intensions. On the other hand, maybe Chris was right. Stretching on her tiptoes, she nearly reached the business card, but then Chris hid it behind his back.

"Can't you see this as an opportunity? If you can work for him, you can watch him more closely and see what he's up to."

"But is he interested in me or the pottery?"

Chris hesitated. "I don't know, but this might be the key to finding out. Besides, he's at least ten years older." He tapped the card with his finger. "He's a businessman, and I think he's in it for the money. Just tell him I'm your manager, and wherever you go, I go."

Sighing, Margo gave in. "As long as you're in on all the dealings, I guess there shouldn't be any problems. He just gives me the creeps. Yet if you're willing to get involved, then okay. But let's see if the vase sells."

"I sure hope so. It could mean another $500." Chris handed the business card with the gold lettering back to Margo. She studied it for a moment. It was the most striking one she'd ever seen.

She wondered at its significance. Was it black merely to stand out from the crowd of hundreds of others, or did the owner mean to imply something else? That would be too blatant, she decided.

The phone rang and interrupted her thoughts.

She picked it up and called for Chris. Mark—again. He probably wanted to get Chris back to that cave. Chris took the phone, and she snuck into the living room and listened ' on the extension.

ng for some moral

on the mountain.

into this spiritual

whole thing."

?"

ne had to find out

he mountainside.

Hey, slow down.

...you're sounding like Jess. I can handle these roads…know them like the back of my hand."

Chris thought for a moment and ventured into the subject. "Did you ever consider Jessica might be right?"

Mark quickly turned his head around and faced Chris. "Don't tell me you're on her side now just because I did one thing wrong."

"Easy, boy, settle down." Chris didn't expect this reaction. "No, I'm just giving you my honest opinion. It's what you've wanted in the past, right?"

Mark eased up. "I guess so. Just stand by me on this one, all right?"

Chris nodded. He didn't want Mark to get riled before their monthly prayer meeting on the mountain, especially this one.

Mark pulled the car over into the pebbled parking lot, and gravel spit from the tires. Chris didn't comment; he realized

Mark was nervous. Chris looked around, but no one else had arrived yet. They waited in the car in silence. Mark drummed his fingers on the steering wheel.

After a few minutes, Chris spotted Lance's vehicle. Mark jumped out of the car and greeted Lance while Chris stepped out into the frosty air. It wasn't usually this cold, but today, the autumn winds slapped at his nylon jacket and penetrated his bones.

Chris sauntered over to Mark and waited as he talked. At least Lance supported their position.

One by one the others showed up. Finally, Vince, the senior pastor, arrived. "Sorry to hold you guys up. I had to help rearrange the new furniture for the den."

Chris noted Vince's preoccupation with material possessions had increased lately. He hoped it would pass. It seemed like so many different issues were attacking the individual members of the church: Margo's nightmares, Ashley's death, Mark's problems with his wife, financial problems in the church, and now this whole business about the goat, which might be nothing.

Chris pulled Mark aside as Vince greeted the others. "Just play it cool for a while. Don't jump right into prayer. Let others lead."

Mark smirked. "Sure, I'll keep a lid on it for as long as I can."

The group gathered, and Vince opened the monthly meeting. "Dear Father, we ask for your guidance here today. Let us not be rash and jump to conclusions about things we think we see or don't. Let us wait for you."

The words sounded guileless on the surface, but Chris interpreted them as a warning to Mark. He wondered what Mark thought.

Lance prayed next, more cautious than usual. He asked for God's wisdom in working with the community and the other members across the river. The other deacons prayed about various concerns including membership, finances, outreach to the college students, and so on. One of them asked for God to comfort Mark's family concerning Ashley's death.

Mark took this as an opening. "Dear Lord, I pray You will reveal the reason behind my sister's death, how that owl was able to crash through the windshield and kill her." No one said anything, so he continued. "Please show us if this is related in some way to the dead goat I found near the cave in these mountains. Reveal the presence of darkness and..."

As he prayed, Chris noted a number of turkey hawks circled above. He watched as one dove into a clearing in the woods near the area of the cave. When he focused on the prayer again, he heard Mark's voice gain volume. "We command you, spirits, by the authority given us in Jesus Christ, that you will reveal yourselves to us..."

"Hold on a minute." Vince held up his hand. "I don't think any of us want spirits to reveal themselves to us right now. They can be powerful, and we don't know a lot about this. I think you better just wait and—"

"Wait?" Mark questioned. "That's exactly what I've been doing here for an hour as you spouted your anemic prayers."

Suddenly, a hawk screeched, and the cry echoed off the rocks. The hair on the back of Chris's neck stood up. Something strange was happening.

Vince leapt at Mark. "How dare you accuse us of weak prayers! I'm the one who started these special meetings. Get out of here right now!"

"Yeah, he thinks he's cornered the market on spirituality," Rich agreed.

Tension rippled through the small band. Chris witnessed the visible change in Vince's demeanor as anger flashed in his eyes.

Right then, a large cloud covered the sun. Chris felt the presence of something dark and sinister. Now he understood how Margo felt.

Margo looked at the clock once again, impatient for Chris to return. She paced up and down the kitchen and peered out the window looking for his car. *Where in the world is that guy?* Without warning, an urge to hunt for her husband consumed her. Not questioning it, she got into her car, her hands shaking so badly she nearly dropped her keys. Between her feeling someone was following her, the visions she'd been having, and now this urge to find Chris, her world seemed to be slipping out of her control. If ever she needed God to lead her steps, today was the day.

Margo raced past the flats outside of town, her mind occupied with Chris. From the corner of her eye, she spied movement in the rows of corn. At the same time, a deer bound in front of the car. Her heart jumped. She slammed on the brakes and swerved onto the other lane. An oncoming car leaned heavy on their horn. She jerked the wheel back and straightened out the car.

Trembling, she pulled the car off to the shoulder for a moment. She picked up the items thrown to the floor. Thank God she hadn't hit the deer or the other car! Checking her rearview mirror, a black flash streaked across it like an apparition. She saw a figure. *What could it be?* She felt its presence.

Dark, oppressive, and choking. It sucked the oxygen out of her. Panting, she rolled down the windows, and the cold air assaulted her lungs.

The letter…an evil presence…

She gasped. But she couldn't linger. She needed to find Chris.

Pulling the car back on the road, she spotted the black dot again in the rearview mirror. To her surprise, it crept closer to the road. As the figure vanished, her eye caught the glistering sunlight on several blond strands of hair.

Something about it made the hair on Margo's arms stand straight up.

The flaxen-haired woman opened her black book of incantations and chanted, "Yenna, yenna yenna." She called to the north and stretched out her arms, pleading. Then she fell to the ground. After a few moments, she slowly rose; her hips swayed as she lifted her robes and discarded them. Leaping, she danced naked along the secluded banks of the river—singing.

She knelt and prayed to the river, waving her arms to change its flow. The Madkill could change course at will. For this reason, legend said it held special powers, especially for those who knew its secrets. She stood as one among twelve others who acknowledged its power. They believed certain rituals performed in sight of it could bring a curse or a blessing. Hexes were given extra potency. If one wanted to add power to their incantations, the river would grant favors to the obedient.

She chanted "In can della divi riva divi" over and over. She stepped into the water and swirled it around. Once the car passed, she stood up and danced, twirling in a circle till dizzy. She halted. Steadying herself, she moved closer to its banks, under the bridge. There she lifted her arms upward and closed her eyes.

The priestess let the river's power fill her. She drank it in. The cold caressed her body. She became one with the cold.

Unrobed, she walked deeper into the chilled water, submerging herself to the waist. The cold stabbed at her body, but she ignored it. Instead, she soaked in its power. The priestess would sacrifice her own body, except she would not want her dead corpse found. Never would she want to alert the enemy to her presence. Not yet.

Let them sleep.

Turning to the south, she basked in the warmth of the Egyptian sun god Ra. Her golden hair gleamed in its setting rays. She lifted her arm, and it sliced through the chilly air in an effort to divide the bonds of matrimony, especially those of Christians. Then she repeated the same ritual and faced east and then west to the great god of the pharaohs, Horus, represented by the all-seeing falcon. From this ancient civilization, she and her cohorts drew great power and learned their black magic and sorcery. And now they joined forces with the power of wealth. The annihilation of the enemy was eminent!

Facing the north, her arm met with resistance, and she struggled to perform the rite. This meant only one thing: resistance.

Her heart began to beat wildly. Something was wrong…very wrong. Somehow, they had been alerted. She must stop them in their tracks!

16

Mark furrowed his eyebrows. He turned over every rock and leaf outside the cave. The goat had disappeared! Not a shred of evidence. Somehow he had convinced the group to help him investigate inside the cave, though they barely agreed. They tramped inside, and Mark watched as Chris inspected a large rock that protruded from the back wall.

Chris called to the reluctant crew. "Hey, guys, I think I may have found something, but I need help."

Mark was there in an instant; the others sauntered in at will.

Chris explained, "There's a rock wall in the back over here, which is covering an opening. I tried to push it myself, but it's too stubborn. With a couple of us, we could do some damage."

Mark jumped. "Yeah, I see what you mean. " He fingered the huge rock.

The others joined them. Vince took command. "Chris and Mark, you grab on to the side and push while Lance and I will push at the face of the rock."

Everyone took their places. At first, the rock wouldn't budge, but then it slowly began to move enough to allow someone to squeeze through.

Mark slipped in before anyone else. Darkness engulfed him. Chris squeezed in next and flicked on his flashlight. Elongated shadows covered the walls. Immediately, they both spotted a small table up against the back.

Mark grabbed the light from Chris and swept it around the small room. "Nothing much but this table," he announced to the others. "Let's drag the table out into the cave to look it over thoroughly." His hands were on it before Chris responded.

Then Vince stepped inside and accidentally blocked his way. "Okay, bring it out."

Mark frowned at the nondescript table. He expected more than just a smooth wooden surface and four legs—no marks, no insignias, nothing. "Why in the world would someone go through so much trouble to store an ordinary table behind a—"

"Someone's gone through a lot of trouble for a reason," Chris interrupted. "We just have to find out what."

"Yeah, most likely some college kids." Vince laughed.

Lance cut in. "You're right, sometimes college kids do crazy things, but I think this is beyond them. They can play cards in their own dorms. They don't need to come all the way up here. I think we should keep this a matter of prayer and—"

"We got to do more than pray," Mark demanded. He was tired of just praying. They needed to take action and investigate further.

Chris responded, "Prayer is always a good place to start, but action can also be required. We don't want to act foolishly or irrationally, Mark. We are to be men of prayer, right?"

Mark agreed. "Of course." But he didn't feel convinced. Prayer took time and trusting God. Something he wasn't so sure of lately.

⬤

A band of three large grotesque creatures stood overlooking the cliffs. The largest of the three, His Eminence Pride, spread his wings and cast a dark shadow on the mountain. "They have played into our hands. They think themselves more spiritual than others and have been blinded. Soon we will completely win them over." A bone-chilling screech echoed in the canyon.

The Prince of Division stepped forward. "I too have been working relentlessly. I will soon demolish that puny excuse of a...of a...church." He spat out the last word. "I will destroy their marriages, and they will be left in shambles!"

"But," the third announced as he cloaked himself in his black robe, "I have not wasted my time on those who hate the master as their numbers diminish. My efforts are turned toward those who worship the only Great Dragon of Old, from the beginning of time, Lucifer. We have infiltrated all levels of these human's squalid society, and we grow stronger and darker every day. We will soon obliterate the mention of that detestable name above all names!"

More than the usual crowd gathered for the Wednesday-night prayer fellowship held at the Hopelyns'. As Joy ushered each one into the living room, she felt glad more than just a handful had showed. Ever since the visions she'd experienced and her dream about Mike, she felt an urgency to pray. She hoped he would come tonight. Joy liked the cowboy side of him. He brought a fresh perspective with his tales of simple faith and angelic rescues. He helped others to drop their pretense and open up.

As the doorbell rang again, Joy rushed to the door and opened it. Mike stood in the shadows, and she showed him in. A short muscular man accompanied him. He introduced him simply as Paul.

As Joy walked them to the meeting room, she couldn't help but notice the huge muscles popping out from under Paul's short-sleeved shirt. She disliked being suspicious, but she sensed something dark and foreboding about this fellow. Wanting to make new people feel comfortable, she went out of her way to foster an open atmosphere, but she wondered where Mike had found this guy.

When she ushered them in, heads turned. Their eyes spoke volumes. She sensed curiosity mixed with fear.

Ray stood up and smiled. "Have a seat right here, guys." He pointed to a pair of comfortable chairs where the Hopelyns usually sat.

Ray moved over to a folding chair, and Joy sat next to him. Once everyone was settled, Ray started the meeting. "I'm glad everyone has gathered here tonight for prayer."

Joy watched Paul squirm in his seat. He obviously didn't know what this meeting was all about. As introductions began, Joy's thoughts wandered to last week's sermon. While in Tanzania, the pastor saw an actual deliverance from demonic forces take place. Troubled men and women renounced their demonic practices and burned hundreds of magical arts books. David told the couple he was struck by the fact the deliverance was spontaneous. As the Word of God was proclaimed, the demons fled.

Joy knew that more than half of those who professed to be Christians in the US didn't even believe in Satan. But the more they examined the modern-day culture, the more they saw evidence of demonic activity; and tonight, she felt their presence. She wondered if her husband did too.

Ray began with a general prayer of thanksgiving. Others followed with prayers for healing of people's ailments: Sam's back, Mary's tumor, and Pastor Dave's headaches. One woman prayed for her depressed husband who'd lost his job.

An anguished mother cried out, "Dear Lord, have mercy on my son and deliver him from drugs." Tears sprung from her eyes, and a few women gathered round to comfort her.

Then the room grew quiet. Joy thought she saw a shadow pass.

Ray must have sensed something, and he prayed for their protection. His voice started off quietly but gained volume. "By the authority Jesus has given his children, we command you, Satan, to get out of this house." Joy watched as the visitor fidgeted in his seat.

Ray finished his prayer. "You have no place in here. In Jesus's name, I command you to leave."

The visitor's face twitched. Then he hissed. "You have no authority over us."

Ray shot up. "By the blood of Jesus and His authority, I command you to loose this man."

Several people began to pray fervently. The stranger let out a long, deep, frightening moan. Everyone opened their eyes. Mike leapt to Paul's side. He held him down. Ray got down on his knees and prayed aloud.

Paul's face screwed up, and his eyes fluttered. The moaning grew louder. It changed into unintelligible syllables gushing like a vile stream, flooding the atmosphere with guttural punctuated sounds. "Ag...da...ba...ahhh!" Then it stopped.

The man's body quaked. Mike held him in his seat. The visitor didn't attempt to leave.

A whiny, high-pitched voice burst from Paul, "Leave me alone, this is my house and you can't kick me out."

As he spoke, the strong man flailed his arms and legs, like a child having a temper tantrum. The demons spoke. "No, no, you can't kick me out!"

A few others got down on their knees.

Then Paul coughed several times. His whole body shook from head to toe. He tried to stand up but fell back in the chair. Joy felt the Bible was being reenacted before her eyes. The whole event took on a dramatic, unreal quality. She prayed—hard.

Mike held Paul down, pressing on his shoulder. "Who are you?"

Paul flinched and jerked away from Mike, but the cattle wrestler quickly grabbed him. Three other men shot to their feet and surrounded Paul. Two seized his arm.

Twisting and writhing, he hissed, "None of your businesssssss." A few people exited the room.

Mike wrestled his guest to his seat. A demonic voice shouted, "Leave us alone!"

Before it could speak again, Ray countered, "Anyone who is held captive by Satan is *my* business."

The strong man's body trembled.

"But he chose to be a captive, so you can't kick us out."

Ray bent over and looked directly into Paul's eyes. "I am a son of the Most High God, and by the authority of Jesus Christ and His blood, I order you to leave."

"Nooooo," they screamed. The air grew thick with a sulfuric stench.

Joy burst into song. "There is power, power, wonder working power in the precious blood of the lamb." Others joined in. Paul's body spasmed and fell to the floor. People cleared the area as he writhed, and some ran into the kitchen.

Paul foamed at the mouth, and the demons inside wailed, "He's ours."

"No, he's not. He's under our roof and under the blood. Now get out, in Jesus's name."

The sound of beating wings filled the air. "We'll be back soooon." The lights flickered, and a rushing wind surged though the room.

Joy felt something crash against her chest, and she jumped backward. The curtains swayed. Everyone watched them flutter back and forth, and then they stopped. Complete silence followed.

Paul went limp. His arms dangled at his side. His face relaxed, and the foul odor cleared. The man returned to his normal demeanor. Paul opened his eyes, sat up straight, and looked around the room.

He shook his head. "What was that all about? I just felt like someone ripped my guts out."

Everyone faced Ray. He hesitated. Not wanting to scare Paul, he asked, "What brought you here tonight?"

Paul cleared his throat. "You want the truth."

"Jesus does."

"Mike invited me. I saw him in town the other day, and he told me all about his big change. I've been getting spooked by my boss's activities lately, so I figured I'd give the other side a try." Mike verified the story.

Paul continued, "I've answered your question, but you haven't answered mine. What happened?"

Ray looked him straight in the eyes. "You were just delivered from some very dark forces in your life. Did Mike talk to you about Jesus?"

"Of course."

"Did you accept what he said as truth?"

"I'm thinkin' about it. Not sure yet."

"Well, you better make a decision real quick. Did you hear what those demons said as they left? They'd return soon."

"You believe that?"

"Not only will they return, but they'll bring more," Ray warned.

"That's crazy." He turned to Mike. "You're sounding like my boss. I'm outta here." He strutted out the door and banged it shut.

Ray let him go. "He's got a lot to learn, and he can't do it all in one night. God has His hand on this man. We'd better pray for him."

An engine revved and he pealed out of the driveway. Joy peeked out from the curtains and saw a car tear up the street.

"I hope he's not heading for trouble."

17

Margo's car screeched into the gravel parking lot, sending a spray of small stones flying. She flinched at their sight and reprimanded herself for driving too fast. Turning her attention to the primary reason for the trip, she nervously scanned the assortment of vehicles then spotted Mark's car. She carefully maneuvered hers into a small little space on the edge of the lot. In the rearview mirror, Margo glimpsed her husband standing with a group of men. She breathed a sigh of relief; then her temper flared.

He's got a lot of nerve keeping me waiting all afternoon.

She grabbed her small backpack and jumped out of the old Chevy. As she drew closer to the group, the appearance of the men's faces concerned her. Frowning, she wondered what they were discussing and thought about what could be so important that her darling husband forgot to call home.

As she approached, Chris met Margo's eyes. His looked troubled, and his face was pale. She hoped he was okay. Moving closer, she overheard Vince say, "I don't think it's our place to get involved."

"We might not want to, but it's our town, and we need to protect it," Chris added as he faced Margo. She pointed to the backpack and summoned him. As he walked away, it looked like Vince was making some weird gestures.

Chris approached.

"Where in the world were you?"

"I'll tell you later." He swiped the backpack offered to him and tore it open. He grabbed a couple of sandwiches, keeping one for himself while passing the others around.

Margo had the reputation of piling on the sandwich meat, mayo, pickles, and lettuce, and she knew Chris loved to brag about it.

Men and their appetites.

She watched the group devour the food in silence. Holding back her anger, she attempted to reason with herself. Obviously, something important had consumed their time—and their brains.

After they finished, the group disbanded and said nothing more. Margo sensed the tense atmosphere, but she realized this wasn't the right time to discuss the situation. *Lord, you sure know how to keep me dependent on you.* Patience was not one of her virtues.

On the ride home, Margo drove as Chris stared out the window at the towering cliffs. He turned to his wife for a moment and spoke, "We'll talk later."

Margo nodded and kept her eyes on the road, knowing the descent down the serpentine road was sometimes more dangerous than the ascent, especially at dusk. The cliff's mysteries lay behind her, and she struggled to leave them there forever. Yet she also believed some answers begged to be discovered. The question was, what? Was Margaret tied up in all this? Pondering this, she rode in silence. Had the young woman been murdered…there?

⊰◆⊱

A shining blade glistened in the sun, radiating enough light to blind a human.

The prayer warrior, Zuriel, placed it back in its sheath and peered over a dark cloud. "They see so very little."

The gleaming Veritas, removed his scabbard and let the light play on the surface of the sword, illuminating the darkness. "That is why we must hold up the truth before them. We must help them to see the light."

"But they are so blind," he cried. "What are we to do?"

"We must wait for the Master's orders. He has a plan."

The smaller angel mumbled, "But these humans are notorious for missing it and doing things in their own strength."

"Ah yes, these humans often wait until they are on the brink of death to lift their eyes heavenward."

Veritas flicked his wing. "'Tis true, 'tis true. But it only takes one who is willing to ask for God's help."

Zuriel lifted his sword high and shouted, "When they learn this, nothing will keep us from storming the gates of hell!"

<hr />

During dinner, Chris didn't say a thing. Margo made his favorite meal—breaded pork chops with chunky applesauce—but Chris wouldn't eat. She reached across the table and clasped Chris's hands. "I can see something is troubling you."

Chris sighed, "Yeah, I know."

"Do you want to talk about it?"

"Not really, but I will."

Margo thought about her husband's response. Men, they're just so different. How can they keep things pent up inside so long? She cleared the table and wrapped up his pork chops and put them in the refrigerator for leftovers. He still said nothing. Then she brewed him his favorite coffee and brought the steaming cup into the living room. Chris reclined in his favorite overstuffed chair, and Margo sat on the soft couch. "Maybe this issue is just too hot to deal with at the moment."

Margo said a quick prayer. "Lord, give us direction and discernment. Show us what to do. We need your help."

Silence followed. He bowed his head and said, "Amen." Then he opened his eyes and looked up at Margo. "Margaret

Bernadette, you know I intensely dislike gossip, but lately I sense there is a definite problem in the church."

Margo knew Chris meant business. He never called her by her full name unless there was something really troubling him.

"I tried to talk with them today, to bring it before the brothers, but only Lance understood. I've tried to talk to Vince, but he seems too wrapped up in the church's finances."

"I was so disappointed when I overhead the snatch of conversation this afternoon. I was hoping you would be able to iron out a few problems."

"Believe me, I tried."

Margo inched closer to the chair and whispered, "It appears to me division is creeping in all over the place. First, there's the problem with the members across the river wanting to leave."

Chris objected, "But you know that's because of the distance they travel."

"Okay then, how about this. Every time I turn around, there's another Christian woman wanting to leave her husband. Jessica even mentioned divorce! Did you know about that?"

"It doesn't surprise me, but no, I didn't—"

"Now there's trouble with the prayer group, and it's bringing division among the church's closest members. It just isn't right. Then all of the dreams, premonitions, and prophecies—"

"Which started right after you found the letter and Margaret's gravestone."

"Yeah, Margaret. Somehow it's all linked, but how?"

"I don't know."

Margo's voice rose in intensity. "And today I felt an evil presence down by the flats, just like the night at the studio. It gave me the creeps. Just like Bill. But I can't totally figure him out. He's hard to read. He's all business with me, but have you seen how Melanie moons over him when he's around?" Margo held Chris's hand. "I know you thought he could help us, but I'd rather avoid him altogether."

"Since he gave you the $1,000, I thought we should give him a chance. Vince thinks he's okay, but I agree with you. I don't trust Bill."

She hesitated a moment before continuing. "I've been feeling a little uncertain about Vince's intentions. The way he handles certain situations makes me feel uneasy. He always wants to be in control."

Chris hesitated. "I'm not sure I agree, but you have to admit he's a dynamic speaker."

An awkward silence followed.

Margo dropped the subject. She had to admit Vince was dynamic in several ways. Good-looking and smart, he knew how to captivate an audience. Most of the women in the church wondered why he married plain Jane instead of some knockout. At first, Margo attributed it to his spirituality; but lately she felt something wasn't right about Vince.

Chris resumed the conversation and summarized the afternoon's events. "Another thing that troubled me was Vince's attitude. He trivialized what we found."

"That doesn't surprise me. He doesn't want to give credence to anything you do."

"How could he think college students would go through so much trouble to put a table in a cave—just to drink?"

"It doesn't seem like a very logical conclusion." Margo shrugged her shoulders.

"My same deduction, Sherlock."

Margo picked up a couch pillow and hit Chris on the shoulder. "Well, Dr. Watson," she faked an English accent, "you're certainly a bloodhound when it comes to finding clues. So what does this all mean?"

"You've got it all wrong. You're Sherlock, and you're the one who comes up with the conclusions. I just observe and write about it."

Margo laughed. "Okay, how's this. Vince's trying to hide *something* because he knows *something* we don't know. Or he doesn't know *something* we do, and he doesn't want to look like a fool."

"Well, you've certainly covered your bases with enough somethings, but you might have an idea there. It might be a little of both."

Margo thought before speaking. "Maybe he just doesn't want to get into this spiritual warfare stuff because the parent church has warned him."

"That's exactly what I was thinking." Chris fumbled. "Oh, sorry, I mean—precisely, my dear Watson."

"No, Sherlock," Margo corrected. "I'm Sherlock, and you're Watson."

"Whatever, but how did you figure it out?"

"Well, I know the church will lose money when the group across the river leaves, and Vince is very concerned, so he doesn't want to step on the elders' toes, spiritually or financially speaking."

"Very clever, Sherlock." Chris pointed a finger. "I think you're on the right track."

Margo threw down a couch pillow for emphasis. "So it all comes down to money?"

"Not all, my dear. I think there's more involved, but money is a definite factor."

"And what else is involved, my clever Dr. Watson?" Margo inched closer toward Chris.

He put his hand to his chin and rubbed it as though tugging on a beard. "Power, Sherlock. Power, that's been the problem from the beginning of mankind."

"Yes, men always seem to have a problem with that—power and pride." Margo poked him in the ribs. "Don't forget about that one. The two seem to go hand in hand."

"Yes, power, pride, and wealth. They are mankind's issues."

"And they're a problem both outside and inside the church." Margo thought a moment and continued, "But inside, the desire for power isn't as obvious. Its spiritual strength mixed with pride gets people into trouble—striving for position and recognition while manipulating others."

Chris moved to the edge of his seat. "Then the inward sins are followed by the outward: lying, cheating, covering up the truth…"

"Yeah, it all starts small, like yeast in unleavened bread, and then it continues to grow and gets out of hand."

"Just like Jesus said in His parables."

"Yeah, and like a cancer, it spreads quickly."

<hr>

Margo tossed and turned, waking several times during the night. She hated when she couldn't get back to sleep. When she couldn't take it anymore, she stole into the living room and read. Drawing back the living room curtains, she peered out into total darkness and closed them. In her Bible, she read the familiar verse, "Yea though I walk through the valley of the shadow of death, Thou art with me." *Not again*, she complained. *Why do I keep reading this verse, Lord? I know it doesn't just relate to those who have died, but does it have anything to do with Margaret? Please show me, Lord. I'm not getting it. Could you make the message a little clearer?* Margo fell asleep on the couch and the Bible slipped from her hand.

<hr>

The first rays of golden sunlight filtered through the living room curtains and crept across Margo's sleeping form. She sensed the warmth as it caressed her cheek, and she awoke to the brilliance of a Sunday morning. Stretching her arms, she yawned and noticed the Bible on the floor.

She picked it up, walked across to the picture window, and drew back the curtain. It revealed a glowing orange ball surrounded by bold red brushstrokes painted across a pale-blue canvas. Margo admired the breathtaking scene. She looked toward the mountains and the silhouette of the Mohawkin Tower and sighed. *I used to love this place, but now, everything's going haywire. I have to find out what you're trying to tell me, Lord. So I'm sorry, but today, I have to miss church to find out the truth.*

18

Margo Pierson stared out the window as Chris drove and wound through the side streets. Her thoughts turned to her college days when she first saw the small town and fell in love with it, especially the mountains. She looked up at the watchtower perched on the east side of the rock outcroppings. Lately, the whole area felt ominous as if someone or something watched her every movement. It gave her the chills.

Although the sun shone brightly, the air seemed heavy as the car drove upward. The higher it climbed, the more Margo felt trapped. Watching several big birds—possibly hawks or turkey vultures—spiral upward on an airlift, she began to feel light-headed, as if she couldn't breathe. Maybe those birds have all of the air she thought and then shook her head at her stupidity.

She asked Chris, "Do you sense the heaviness?"

"What do you feel?"

Margo let out a shallow breath. "Like I can't breathe."

"Hmm, can't say I feel like that, but I do sense something out of the ordinary. Try not to let it affect you so much. Maybe you're hyperventilating. Breathe deeper."

Margo breathed in and out, but the heaviness on her chest would not go away.

As the car labored up the mountains, she pointed to the vultures.

"What do you think they're doing up there?"

Chris glanced over. "Probably just riding the currents. They love to do that."

"I think they might be looking for something to eat."

"That's possible, but they're not social birds. They usually hunt by themselves."

Margo didn't respond, and Chris carefully negotiated the hairpin turn. A mixture of dread and expectation came over her like a cloud. She hated encountering anything with such power as she'd wrestled with lately, but she was also filled with expectation. Margo believed they would find something important.

Chris hoisted a small backpack. "Just in case we need some assistance."

His wife nodded, but her thoughts were elsewhere. Margo stepped out of the car and watched a line of clouds move in from the north, threatening to engulf them.

Chris interrupted her thoughts and spoke. "Let's get this show on the road before it starts raining." Together they crossed the gravel parking lot.

He directed Margo to the first path, which led to the cave. It was well traveled and easy to hike. Usually, Margo liked to stop and take in the breathtaking views, but today, she hurried along with Chris. She stopped on the ledge for a moment to locate a few familiar sites, but they were hidden. How quickly things change, she mused.

At the end of the main path, Chris came to a halt. He directed Margo to a clump of scrub pines, vines, and overgrown brush and pushed back some branches with one arm. "You first, madam. These are the finest trails in all the Northeast."

Margo threw her head back and laughed. "And you, sir, are a perfect coachman." She knew Chris was hiding his own nervousness.

Surprised, she stepped into a world that looked liked the imagined forests of the *Grimm's Fairy Tales*. Vines wrapped themselves around short pine trees and their branches overhung what little of a path existed. Brambles grew everywhere although flattened from recent traffic.

After fifteen minutes of slow navigating, Margo asked, "How much more of this incredible journey, Prince Charming?"

"For you, sweet damsel, fifteen minutes, for everyone else, only five." He picked her up in his arms.

She kicked her feet back and forth. "Can't you ever take things seriously?"

Chris put her down. "C'mon, gotta move fast. I don't want to get caught in a storm."

They quickened their pace. Within five minutes they were out of the woods and into a clearing. Chris led the way to the cave. As Margo jogged, she noticed the grass ahead was flattened. She stopped and found a set of footprints. Bending down, she examined them and called for Chris. They looked like loafers almost twice her foot size. She called again to her husband, but he didn't answer. Just as she was finishing her investigation, Chris appeared. "Hey Sherlock, what did you find?"

"Okay, Detective, take a look at that." She pointed to the footprints.

"Good going, so we know people have been here."

"Look more closely." Margo smirked. "I think it's a man's shoe."

"Fine, but look at those clouds." He pointed. "We've got to get a move on."

Margo stood at the cave's threshold, hit by a blast of cold air and an all-too-familiar feeling. She stood erect as a stone while Chris explored inside. Waiting, she glanced at the ceiling, which gave her about a foot of clearance. She reached absentmindedly to touch it. Black soot covered her hand. Disgusted, she wiped them off.

Chris returned with the flashlight, and Margo stepped farther inside. Darkness engulfed her. He grabbed her hand. Stopping in the middle, he bent down to shine the light. "Did I tell you about the bloodstains I found here?"

"How could I forget?" Margo whispered. "It frightened me to death."

"Well then, take this and I'll investigate." Chris handed her the flashlight while he searched the floor for fresh bloodstains. The dim light made it difficult to distinguish the normal surface of the rock, and several times, Margo gasped. What she saw next confirmed her fears.

"Oh no. Look." She pointed, stifling a scream.

Chris jumped over and rubbed the stains. "Just as I suspected. These are new. Something's going on here, and it ain't just a bunch of college kids having fun."

"What's up?" A voice resounded.

Margo screamed. A figure stood in the shadows. *Oh no, he's got us now.*

The perpetrator stepped from the shadows.

Margo gasped. "Mark, what in the world are you doing here?"

After a few rounds of banter between him and Margo, Chris interrupted. "Okay, guys. Listen up. Now that we have some manpower, let's move the rock and take another look at the table."

While the men rolled up their sleeves, Margo moistened and blotted the stains with tissues yet obtained only a trace of blood. Discouraged, she stood up and watched the guys.

Chris's face turned beet red, and Mark groaned as they pushed the heavy stone blocking the entrance to the alcove.

Margo wanted to help, but knew they wouldn't let her. An idea popped into her mind, and she stepped outside. Returning with a long, sturdy stick, she handed it to Chris. He wedged it between the two pieces of stone.

"Good idea." Chris thanked Margo.

She smiled and directed them. "Mark, why don't you come over here." When the three of them were in position, he did as instructed. Everyone strained and grunted. Chris's muscles glistened with sweat. At first the rock wouldn't budge. Then it creaked against the wood and moved aside. Margo slipped though the passageway, illuminating a small alcove with a low ceiling.

"I found it," she coughed. "A table."

Margo inched forward, breathing in the stale air mixed with an unidentifiable odor. It grew more pungent.

"Whew, it smells in here." She erupted into a coughing fit.

"I'm coming in," Chris demanded.

"No. Stay there." She dropped down on one knee to examine its surface.

"What do you see?"

"Blood—everywhere."

Margo's hands shook as she pushed the table toward the opening. She bumped into a large round object on the ground. Holding the flashlight, she gasped. "Oh my God."

She bent over and traced its circular shape. "Chris, I found it. I found it!"

"Found what?"

Margo's head swam. Visions and dreams blurred together as she fought to separate the two. "The, theee…st-stone, the stone…"

"What stone?"

"The stone in my vision, the stone in the cemetery. It's here!" Margo cried.

Chris pressed closer. "Stay calm. Now which stone is it?"

"It appears to be both."

Chris peered through and illuminated the stone with his flashlight. "You're right. It looks like some type of millstone."

Margo examined it carefully with the light, searching up and down. She gasped.

"What's wrong?"

She ran her fingers over its surface. "It feels and looks like… dried blood."

"Blood? Are you sure?"

"Yeah, from the looks of it. I know it's not paint." She ran her hands all along the surface and on the side. Her finger caught on an edge. "Wait a second." She lit up the side with the flashlight. "Looks like there's another thinner stone melded to the bottom."

Chris maneuvered to inspect it better. "I can't see too well, but don't you think we should get the heck out of here?"

Mark interrupted. "I'm glad you found the stone, but what about the table?"

"Forget the table," Margo insisted. "It has little significance. It's the stone you should be after."

Chris didn't continue to argue, so she proceeded to work on moving the stone. It lay flat, and Margo tried to prop it up. She failed. Then she remembered something. "Chris, pass me the stick I found for you." He passed it though the opening, and she managed to wedge it under the stone. She pushed hard and it slid farther.

The stone yielded, just a little.

Margo wedged her foot under its weight and managed to lift it just enough to thrust her leg against its side. With all her weight, she pushed against the cold object. It stood up and wobbled. Too heavy for her to keep upright, it fell against the cave wall. She let out a sigh. *If ever I need you, Lord, it's now. Please give me wisdom and strength.* A thought occurred. In this position, she could possibly roll it through the opening.

"I've got a plan," she announced as she struggled to push it out. The stone wouldn't budge.

Chris declared, "I'm coming through."

The slab leaned against the wall, blocking his entrance. "You won't be able to fit," Margo insisted.

"Let's try working together," Chris offered.

While Margo pushed, Chris pulled. It began to roll and wobbled halfway though. Mark joined in the effort. The stone emerged and fell facedown, along with Margo.

The cold air felt refreshing, though she wanted to get out of there as soon as she had the strength.

Mark inspected it. "Whoa! Look at those funny inscriptions here." He pointed to the underside that hadn't been facing Margo. "They look like something out of a high school social studies class."

Margo raced over and gasped at what was on the other side.

"Oh no!" She couldn't believe her eyes. Encased in a ring of open rectangular designs stood bands of stylized symbols. "Hieroglyphics?"

19

"You bungling idiots!" the Dragon Master seethed. His nostrils flared, and he exhaled a glowing flame of fire. "Agghhhh!" Deception screamed as he fanned his scorched wing.

"Every one of you received my commands to delude the girl and keep her away from the cave at all costs!"

Pride did not flinch, though his chest burned red hot.

The Master, known by many different names, lifted a scaled appendage and swiped the air with his sharp claws. A great gust of wind ensued and knocked over the Prince of Division and those surrounding him. "All you accomplished so far—stirring up arguments, division, and lust in the faithful—can be vanquished by the foe if we are not careful. She must be eliminated!"

Deception turned his face to reveal his other side. "Sire, we had a plan in place, but he bungled it." He pointed an accusing finger in the direction of Pride.

Puffing out his chest, he stepped forward.

"Go no farther." The Dragon of the Dark Abyss breathed a fiery warning.

He turned his head and faced Deception. "Please continue."

"Pride has spent so much time preening himself over his successes in New Coven that he blinded himself to the workings of the northern kingdom, puny as it is in number." He bowed low.

"You know, Division and I worked overtime in Kingsland and had great success there."

Division stepped forward. "And I've been working relentlessly in New Coven."

"Just as I have been." A falcon-like figure flew from the shadows.

"Silence!" Smoke steamed from the dragon's nostrils. "Do you take me for a fool? I know your plans, for I hatched them myself! Continue on, Deception."

"Pride did not work hard enough in the overzealous pastor in the northern realm. He has been spending long hours in prayer."

"Rrrrrrr." The Dragon Master, Abaddon, slapped his tail against the ground, and the fiery pit beneath them quaked.

The demonic powers were knocked off balance.

"Don't you mention prayer again! That is one of the enemy's sharpest tools."

His beady eyes glowed as he opened his cavernous mouth and shot a streak of fire at Pride.

"Ahhhhhhhh!" Pride's chest burned, and he pounded on it to quench the flames.

Deception smirked, and the others repressed a snicker.

"Yes, scoff at Pride, but not for long. Now it is my time to laugh. Since you have been so inept, I will bring out a troop far smaller than you for assistance." The Dragon Master bellowed, "Come forth, my little ones."

A thousand irritating fledglings blanketed the air. "They have been at work behind the scenes. But now, it is time for you to join forces." He pointed a bony finger toward the horde. "Disperse now, you little distractions."

A thousand winged creatures blackened the abyss amid deafening cries. Hundreds of them surrounded the demonic lords. Their claws ripped at each commander's chest, and venom spurted high in the air. A raucous erupted, and Captain Anger wailed. The Prince of Division and His Eminence Pride slapped as the beings attacked but could not resist. The creatures burrowed into them, diffusing into their spirit bodies.

The falcon from the shadows, now in full view, screeched, "It is complete, my lord."

"Yes, you have done well, Lord Witchcraft, in further empowering my legions, and you shall be duly rewarded." He surveyed the scene and nodded in approval. "These Christians who fear such grave sins as lust and pride will surely bend their knee to these many distractions." He cackled. "They will have no time for"—he spit the word out—"*prayer!*"

After some arguing about what to do with the stone, Margo conceded. They would return it to its place. Mark and Chris grunted and groaned as they pushed the circular stone back through the opening. She had to admit, the men were right. It would be impossible to bring the stone with them, and its disappearance would alert the owners. Once the men finished the task, Margo lingered in the cubicle with it for a few minutes.

Chris called to her. "C'mon. Let's get out of here!"

"Okay, hold on. I'll be right there." She folded a piece of paper and stuffed it in her bag. Margo always carried drawing paper and soft pencils for rubbing, which turned out decent though rushed.

As she walked out of the dark cave, the light blinded her eyes. She wanted to follow up on this discovery as soon as possible, but it would have to wait. Her work at the studio took priority over some tenuous evidence of foul play anyway. Nevertheless, on the hike back, she couldn't expunge the picture of the tablet sprinkled with blood. What could it all mean? Did it have anything to do with Margaret? Maybe it was just a coincidence the stone with the code and this one had some similar markings. Something told her it wasn't mere chance, yet with so much on her mind, and with her plate full, she really couldn't sort it out just now.

As they walked back, Mark departed for his car, and Margo watched the mist lift and give way to a beautiful, sunny, crisp autumn day. The view from the lookout point resumed its natural splendor—enhanced by the crimson and bright-yellow leaves. On other days, it looked homey like a patchwork quilt; today it gave her goose bumps. How innocent and peaceful the town looked on the outside, but inside, a cauldron churned.

Bouncing along in the car, she stared out the window and fell into a contemplative mood. Her pottery beckoned to be priced and packed up for the show, but the letter echoed in the recesses of her mind along with their latest discovery…a millstone of sorts. Without warning, her heart started pounding furiously, and then the walls of the car began to expand and disintegrate. Margo looked through the roof into the clear blue sky. The sunlight blazed so intensely she could not see at all, and then it appeared—water spilling, overflowing, and swirling into a vortex.

An ocean appeared; waves roared and crashed, battering against the wooden pylons. The scene panned below: polluted water ate away at the wooden foundations, rotting the very insides. The scene burned into her brain and then disappeared. The car walls came crashing in.

Chris was calling her name, "Margo, Margo, are you okay? Should I stop?"

She shook her head and rubbed her eyes.

Margo looked around at the familiar surroundings.

"Nothing really, it's just…" She wasn't sure she should tell Chris, but she couldn't keep this to herself. "The very same vision I had in my dream appeared in the sky."

Chris wanted the facts. "Which one? You've had several lately."

She described the whole scene as she contemplated its meaning. Her hunch was that it involved the stone, but how? Who could she trust besides Chris?

Who could help her understand? Vince? He didn't want to acknowledge such things in fear of losing the support of high-profile members. Rich? Far too full of himself. Lance? He's understanding but conservative on these issues. Though lately, he'd been more open. "I guess the only likely candidate is Lance."

Chris asked, "What about Lance?"

Margo blushed. "He's the only other one we can confide in."

"Yeah, I was just thinking the same thing," Chris affirmed. "But we have nothing to prove our point—"

"Don't worry," Margo interrupted. "This time we have evidence." She rummaged through her bag and triumphantly held up a rubbing of the stone. "I got this while you and Mark were arguing over what to do."

"Wow, you're amazing!" He gave Margo a quick hug. "You did a great job. Let me see." He knit his eyebrows as he inspected it carefully. "This will make great evidence, but I have no idea what any of it means."

⸻⬧⸻

Margo stared out the window, deep in thought. There was a reoccurring theme in all these.

Wood and stone—the symbols of her vision, the contents of the cave and the etched code.

What could it all mean? As soon as the craft fair was over, she vowed to decipher more of the letter, the millstone, and this new rubbing. Thinking back to her Bible study, she recalled the Old Testament prophets used stones as markers to record an important place or event, and in the New Testament Jesus was called the chief cornerstone.

Of course, she wasn't sure how all these related, if at all. Her thoughts wandered to events in which stones were involved. Margo imagined what the engravings would look like written in Hebrew and got an idea. Turning to her husband, she asked, "Did that stone remind you of anything in the Bible?"

"I'd have to think about it for a while."

"Well, here's a hint: tablets inscribed by God's hand."

"That's too easy, but what does the Ten Commandments have to do with an engraved circular stone?"

Margo shook her head and leaned over to him. "Don't you get it? Satan is a master of imitation, but he never gets it quite right. He's an imitator, but it's not the real thing."

Chris hesitated. "Hmm, so let's see where you're going with this. The Ten Commandments were a code of law. Do you think those inscriptions are some spiritual code?"

"Possibly." She shrugged her shoulders and threw her hands in the air. "I'm no expert on this subject. It's just that engraving is so...definite, so lasting."

"Of course there's the blood too," Chris added.

Margo lowered her voice as her husband pulled into the church parking lot. "That's the most potent aspect of all. We know the power of *His blood* to cleanse us from sin and save us."

Chris raised his eyebrows. "So maybe the combination of the carving and the blood is meant to be...a double whammy."

"Exactly."

——⋙◆⋘——

The service started before Margo and Chris arrived. A few heads turned, but for the most part, their entrance didn't disturb the singing and dancing. The music played loudly, too much so for Margo's taste, but today, she enjoyed the lively worship. "When the enemy presses in too far, the battle belongs to the Lord. When the enemy forces come in like a flood, the battle belongs to the Lord."

The words rang in her head. *Yes, this is the Lord's battle*, she affirmed, *not mine*. Margo felt the power of the Spirit coursing through her, and she focused wholly on the Lord. She stood and danced, which sometimes embarrassed Chris; but today, he understood. The stone became a blur as she beheld the Lord, high and "lifted up."

Rays of sunlight shone through the roof of the church—a brilliant, radiant white softer than the radiance in the car. Margo was glad she wasn't having another vision. She thought she was just imagining, and she pictured herself wearing a beautiful flowing white dress as her fluid movements danced across her mind. Then she saw herself glide up a hill, twirl on top, and then run down the other side till she reached a body of water. She stopped short.

Looking all around her, she then stepped carefully onto a wooden dock. She danced on the wharf with controlled, graceful movements. A swirling vortex appeared, like the one from the other day, though it moved more rapidly. It threatened to suck her in. She tried to run. She couldn't. Her legs were caught. An edge collapsed. She clamped her eyes shut. Frightened, she jumped off the pier and sailed through the air.

Dropping like an anchor in the water, she thrashed her arms. Was she about to drown? When she opened her eyes, she found herself underwater. Margo faced the submerged wooden pilings head-on. Several of them were rotted to the core. The pier sagged terribly. Soon it would collapse on top of her. Kicking her feet, she swam away from the danger up to the water's surface.

She reached the top and broke through, gasping for air. The water around her streamed backward like a tide wave rewinding. Then the vision dissipated. She looked down and was back in church. Her arms remained outstretched. Then the music stopped.

Margo shook and bit her lip. *Lord, what are you trying to tell me? I want to follow, but I don't get it? Please help.*

Mark's voice startled her as he announced the weekly events. Shaken, she leaned toward Chris and whispered, "I thought he wasn't going to come."

"You never know what he'll decide to do. I guess he was lonely."

Margo drummed her fingers on the Bible. What was going on here? Was she merely overtired, or was this another revelation from the Lord? They were coming faster now than she could decipher. What was she to do? Now, more people were getting involved, and the vision grew. She didn't want Mark to blow everything and tell Lance about their discovery at the cave. Mark didn't know how to explain things clearly, and she feared they'd lose the elders' support. This was all getting too complicated and convoluted.

She glanced around the room. Bill wasn't there. Good. Margo relaxed until she realized Melanie and Jessica weren't there. She tried not to be suspicious. She supposed everyone had a right to a Sunday off, but those two were gone more than they were there lately.

Suddenly, Vince stood at the keyboard. Shoulders back and head straight, he approached the podium. He smiled with confidence. His cold, distant eyes seemed to address subjects rather than a congregation.

Vince stood firm on the truth as he saw it. "How can we know the true place of worship?" A few heads looked up. They knew the question was rhetorical. "If the place of worship does not adhere to all the truth, then it is not a true place of worship."

He lifted his Bible. "It's important, *my people*, that you know doctrine so you can know the truth. On Wednesday night, we will be discussing important foundational truths. Do not be ignorant..."

Margo's mind wandered. She disagreed with Vince's staunch adherence to dogma. He had a long list. Some were fundamental, like accepting Jesus as your savior and the forgiveness of sins, but Margo felt issues on church organization and the Holy Spirit were open to some interpretation. She was tired of differences that divided churches and kept born-again Christians from each other.

Vince ended the sermon. Margo closed her eyes. A message formed in her spirit. Butterflies filled her stomach as words broke like waves on the shoreline. Margo swallowed hard. She wanted to keep her mouth shut, but she knew this was a word from the Lord.

Her voice sliced through the silence. "There is a spirit of division present here." Margo's hands trembled. "You appear to worship in unity, my children, but division is lurking in your heart." She didn't want to continue, but the words spilled out. "Some of you are true worshippers, but others worship at a different altar—"

Vince shot up from his seat before Margo had delivered the full message. "I think this Word from the Lord is a warning to those who want to start a new church. There is division in your heart. You might need to heed this Word and stay and worship here."

Margo stood dazed for a moment then sat down.

Chris comforted her. "I can't believe he's doing this. He's twisting the prophecy to meet his own needs. He knows the others have been faithful and are ready to start a sister church."

Margo felt embarrassed. "Maybe I was wrong...maybe I got my wires crossed." She stuttered, "I-I'm not...infallible, or p-perhaps, Vince's right."

"Let's just wait and see what happens."

Margo's mind swirled. She felt like she was on a sinking ship, but no one else seemed to notice. She couldn't help but see the similarities to the *Titanic*. Though a magnificent ship, strong and beautiful, it plummeted into the depths of the ocean. They ignored warnings of danger ahead, thinking the ship invincible. Plunging confidently into the dark night, it headed straight for disaster.

20

Bill Guiles inconspicuously studied Margo Pierson from the foyer as she walked down the aisle toward the church exit. She was a beauty: long, honey-colored hair, big brown eyes, and a good set of legs—though he wanted her for other reasons. He realized he would have to do something about her soon; however, first he had to gain her trust.

When Margo caught him staring, he quickly turned away and acted embarrassed. "I wonder what he's up to?" She tilted her head in Bill's direction and then rubbed her arms.

Chris asked, "Are you cold?"

"No. Bill gives me the willies. Sometimes I think he's from another realm."

"So you believe in aliens?"

"Sure, why not?" Margo playfully punched her husband's arm as they neared. "I'm just a visionary nutcase."

Bill Guiles overheard Margo as she drew closer and didn't agree. Margaret Bernadette Pierson, he discovered was smart, too smart for her own good. As she and her wimpy husband passed by, he turned from his conversation and greeted her warmly. "Sorry about the staring before, I just wanted to get your attention. I've been so busy I haven't had the chance to let you know one of your vases sold."

Margo stopped dead in her tracks. "Already! When did you get down to the city?"

"I actually own another shop across the river and took it there on Thursday. It sold on Saturday." He fudged the truth.

"Really? You never told me about that place. You said you'd bring it to the city."

"So I did, but it looked like you needed the money now when I saw that stack of bills—no pun intended."

Margo didn't laugh. "When did you see them?"

"When I went in your office to discuss the terms."

"I don't like to discuss business on Sundays. I'm sure you kept your part of the bargain. You can contact my husband about the money."

Margo took Chris's hand and exited the building.

Bill smiled as she strutted away, admiring her spunk and a bit more than just that. *Perfect, another chance to go to her studio.*

※ ◇ ※

Monday morning, Paul woke up early feeling different. He didn't have a hangover and wasn't grumpy. He didn't even want to beat up someone! Weird. Ever since that strange meeting last week, he felt peaceful. He jumped out of bed. *Man, that felt good.* He looked down at his hands. They weren't shaking. *How about that?*

Paul filled a coffee pot with water and waited. *What in the world's happened to me? One day I'm living on the wild side, the next I'm clean as a church mouse—or is that poor? Whatever.*

He sat down. A familiar feeling tugged at his heart. Being lonely without a female, his thoughts spun in circles. *I gotta get me a babe. But where in this hick town? Boss is sure slick. He can get them anywhere, even church.* A dark cloud spread over him, and he felt frightened. *Boss isn't gonna let me work for him if I wimp out. I can't change like this. I gotta be mean. It's my job.*

Paul poured some brew and walked into the living room. He picked up a magazine from a stack of *Playboys*, flipped through the pages quickly, and then paused, looking more intently.

A voice commanded, "Put the magazine down."

Paul whirled around. "Who said that?" He got up and scanned the room. He saw no one. "Okay, whoever you are, get outta here. Now!"

173

An inner voice spoke softly, "There isn't anybody here."

Paul looked under the couch. "Where are you hiding?"

The voice spoke again, "It's Me, Paul."

"Who's Me?"

"Jesus."

Paul laughed. "Are you kidding? Your sound effects are great, but you're dead."

"For three days, Paul, but I was dead in your life much longer—since you were eleven."

"Eleven?"

"You know, Paul. That's when your mother died. You thought I killed her, but it was a drunk driver, Paul. I didn't plan it."

"How did you know that?"

"I'm Jesus, Paul. I saw you cover your pain with alcohol and drugs. You hated your father too and wanted to beat him up. Then he killed himself, and you felt guilty. You hated me even more."

Paul punched the table. "I hate you!"

"You don't hate me, Paul. The demons convinced you of that."

"Demons? You're nuts. I don't believe in them."

He started to shake and sweat. Paul fell down on his knees and wept. Heavy sobs reverberated within his chest. He thought about the girl he wanted to marry. She broke it off because of his drinking and drugging. Now he was involved with Bill and that group's crazy rituals. He made good money, great piles of it. He liked that. Plus there were always plenty of girls. Yet he felt lonely and miserable.

"Oh God," Paul cried out. "I'm going crazy. I gotta see Mike."

———⟫◇⟪———

Later that night, Paul followed close on the heels of an old pickup truck as he pulled his black Camaro into a parking lot. He felt out of place at the Longhorn Diner.

Mike walked over and shook his hand. "Sure great to hear from you, pal."

Paul nodded. He rattled the change in his pocket. "Yea, sure." He looked around suspiciously. "Let's get inside."

While Mike motioned to the waitress to seat them in the back, Paul checked around. He didn't want anyone ratting to the boss. Bill hadn't called yet, and he hoped nothing was lined up for tonight. He didn't want to deal with that strange group tonight. He could handle alkies and druggies, but those robed guys were totally weird—with their chanting and bloodbaths. He thought about the woman with the long black hair and high-pitched scream. She was almost as scary as what happened the other night. *Yea, the other night, that's the whole reason I'm here.*

When the waitress took their orders, Mike had his standard charbroiled steak and thick home fries. Paul ordered a mega burger plate and Coke. The two of them ate their dinner in silence and engaged in a minimum of conversation.

Paul was relieved when Mike finally broke the silence. "So I'm glad you called, Paul."

A few awkward moments followed as Paul drained his Coke and ordered another. He put his glass down with a clunk. "I bet you are. You know it's all your fault. You're the one who brought me to that blasted meeting."

"So you don't like being clean?" Mike put down his fork.

Paul shot back. "Don't be a wiseass. Being clean for a while is okay, but I can't be a wimp. Not with my work. I want to know what happened."

"First, tell me what you think."

Paul thought for a minute. "I was getting really angry, and I felt like I was going to explode. My head felt like it was spinning, and then *wham*...I fell to the floor. Then some guy jumped me, and we were wrestling. I'd like to know who it was."

Mike looked for a long time at Paul. "It wasn't a person who jumped you."

"Don't lie to me." Paul felt like swearing, but something inside him stopped him. "I know when I'm fighting."

"You're right, Paul. You were in a fight, but not with a person."

"So what was it, someone's pet lion?"

"No. Something stronger."

"Stronger?"

Mike nodded. "Stronger, but not of this world…of another."

"Oh no. Don't tell me you're in league with the chanters?"

Mike looked puzzled. "What chanters?'

"That group—" Paul was about to explain but then he interrupted himself. "Oh no, I'm not that stupid. I came here to ask you questions. Not to answer yours."

"Okay, no more dancing around the issue, I'm going to shoot straight from the hip. You were wrestling with a demon."

"You mean a funny little green-eyed man," Paul snickered.

"No," Mike stated flatly. "I mean a demon, a fallen angel, a supernatural being who torments human beings at the request of their leader, Satan."

Paul stood up. "That's it. I'm outta here. You're just like the other weirdos." He pointed his finger. "You're strange, the town's strange and—" Paul was about to leave when he remembered his encounter with the voice. He hesitated for a moment and sat down.

The waitress came over and asked if everything was okay. Paul nodded and noticed Mike did too. She cleaned the table and scurried to the kitchen.

Paul leaned forward. "Do you really believe in demons, or are you setting me up?"

"Up until a few months ago, I would've said the same thing, but not in the same way." Mike put his hand on Paul's shoulder. "I'm not joking. If angels can stand on a log and save me from drowning, then I'm sure demons can pull us under—or at least try."

"So you believe in angels too?"

"Yeah, one saved my life. I never would have believed it myself." Mike told the story of his angel rescue.

At first, Paul couldn't believe, but he found himself listening. The story engaged him. He relaxed. He thought back to his early childhood when his mother took him to church. Paul recalled studying the stained glass windows with angels on them.

"I think I'll be needing one of them angels. Soon. If Bill gets wind of this."

"Before you get involved in requesting heavenly beings, you need to talk to someone about Jesus."

Paul jumped up but then didn't say anything. The name Jesus struck a nerve ending.

"Have a seat. I'm trying to help you."

Paul sat down. "Maybe you should talk to Ray, the guy in charge of the meeting," Mike suggested. "He knows a lot."

Paul hesitated a moment. He wanted to say forget it, but couldn't. "Sure, why not? Now I'm in this up to my neck. Just tell me when and where."

Paul couldn't believe he gave in so easily, but lately, everything surprised him. He hadn't gulped down a cold brew or shot of tequila in over three days. And he hadn't even cursed once. Then this morning, he put down one of his favorite magazines. *Before you know it, I'll be saying, Praise the Lord.* Paul laughed at the absurdity of it all and wished his thoughts would stop dragging him all over. *Yea right, a hardened city boy like me praising the Lord. What next?*

⋙◆⋘

Paul felt uncomfortable in the smoky bar where he normally met Bill. It was Tuesday night and the place was quiet, except for the two in the corner puffing away like chimneys. The summer crowd was gone, and the college students had already arrived, but Paul didn't care about any of this. He made his way through the smoke and found his boss.

Bill drank a martini. Paul hated martinis. He was partial to vodka and tequila, but tonight, the smell of the liquor turned his stomach. He ordered a beer instead.

"Hey, my man, what's up with you?" Bill slapped Paul on the back. "You haven't gone straight on me, have ya? I haven't seen you at the local club taking in the sights." Bill laughed. "You should have seen the girl there last night." Bill outlined the girl's figure with his hands. "She was hot. It could have been a threesome, but you weren't there."

Paul groaned. "I haven't been feeling good lately."

"Why, you look great, especially those muscles."

"My stomach feels awful," Paul lied.

"Well, I hope it doesn't interfere with what I have planned."

"I'll be okay."

"Good, because tonight, we're going to have some real fun."

Paul winced in disgust. For the first time since childhood, he actually felt a pang of remorse. He felt dizzy and confused. *What should I do?* Paul hoped he could pull the wool over Bill's eyes for a little while longer.

<hr>

In another part of town, Margo was busy getting ready for the prestigious Autumn Harvest Craft Show. She had five days left to fill the studio shelves, fire up several loads, glaze pottery, decorate plates, and box them up. If she hadn't gotten involved hunting down clues about Margaret, she probably would've had everything glazed by now.

She felt divided. On one hand she had her business to consider, on the other, she felt prompted to find the connections between the letter, the grave rubbing, the vision, and now the stone with the hieroglyphics. Evidence was mounting, but what it all had to do with each other, she didn't know.

Was Margaret the common thread? The correspondence warned of an evil that stalked the town. Evil was alive and well back then, just as now. But what specific evil did it mean? Something diabolical according to the letter. Did it have to do with Margaret's death and possibly another one of Margo's ancestors? The questions nagged her. She had to figure out the name on the first rubbing as soon as possible. Yet how could she do more research now?

As it was, she stayed up late every night turning out pots, plates, mugs, and vases. Tonight, the studio was filled with things to do, clay tools strewn about, bags of powdered glazes, mixing utensils, and bowls. Greenware needed to be fired. Pottery needed to be glazed.

Margo rushed around. Chris had mixed the glazes, but it was past midnight, and he went to bed. She needed to do the finer work. Chris just didn't have a clue when it came to decorating with glazes.

Margo stood by the sprayer and spun the vase. She stopped the spray gun and looked over her work. It passed her inspection, and she moved on to the next one. This took a great deal of concentration, and she actually preferred to work alone.

As she finished up a batch, she passed by the rubbings stuck on the wall and stole a glance. She wiped her hands on her smock and grabbed a pencil. Maybe she could look at the letters while she worked. She jotted them down: N-B-S-H-B-S. Obviously two of the letters repeated themselves.

She tacked the paper on the side of the glazing booth and continued her work. She ran though the alphabet in her head, *L-M-N-O*...Maybe the first letter could be either letter on the side of *N*, which would be *M* or *O*. If she followed through with this line of thinking, the second letter *B* could actually be *A* or *C*. The third letter could be *R* or *T*. She stopped for a moment and retrieved a pencil from behind her ear. Scribbling down both alternatives for this method proved rewarding. Suddenly, the simple code became clear. Just one letter removed from what it stood for: N-b-s-h-b-s easily became M-a-r-g-a-r.

179

Margaret! A piece of the puzzle finally slipped into place.

A blast of cold air gave her a chill. She shot up and looked around to see if a window was opened, but all seemed secure. An evil presence filled the room. The same oppressive feeling overwhelmed her. What could she do? She stood up, and secured the door latch. Everything appeared normal, so she returned to her glazing.

Her thoughts turned to Bill. So mysterious yet great-looking. Why did he creep her out? He had stopped by yesterday with the money from the vase. *I wish I hadn't sold him my pottery, but I got this new sprayer out of the deal.* Margo looked around at the other things she needed—more stacking shelves and glazes were next on the list. She didn't want to do more business with him, but she had a contract. *After this, it's curtains, baby.* She laughed at her own silly remark from an old-time favorite movie of Chris's.

As she continued to twirl the greenware around on the sprayer, she couldn't get Bill out of her mind. She thought about his handsome features, his strong chest and broad shoulders, but those eyes…There was something about those eyes—so appealing, smiling, and beckoning. Margo drifted into a daydream then awoke from her reverie. *That's it,* she realized. *He hooks you with his eyes. He's what my mom would call a lady-killer, that's why Melanie and Jessica swoon around him.* Margo shuddered.

It was past midnight. Time to quit. She cleared up a few tools and closed the glaze containers in the back. When she walked into the main room, she heard the door latch rattle. At first she felt frightened but then realized it must be her husband. She called for Chris as she approached the door.

It flung open wide, and Margo stood there speechless. Instead of Chris, a short muscular man blocked her way. Realizing it was Mr. Guiles's helper, she demanded, "What are you doing here this time of night? If you're here on business for your boss, tell him to come here himself during normal business hours."

Paul approached her as she spoke. He reached out and covered her mouth before she knew what happened. "Be quiet and I won't hurt you." He pulled out a kerchief and gagged her. Then he wrenched her arm back so she couldn't struggle free and put her in a headlock.

Margo twisted and turned, struggling to free herself, but his powerful arms constricted her movement. Her eyes were full of fear, and he stared into them.

"If you stop struggling, you won't get hurt. I promise."

She detected a hint of concern in his voice and relaxed a little. *Oh God*, she prayed, *please don't let him hurt me.* The panic subsided. Margo stopped short as he tried to push her outside. She stalled for time and wouldn't budge. He scooped her up into his arms.

Margo punched his chest and kicked her feet, slamming her boots into his thighs. The brute seemed to barely notice as he walked to his vehicle, his arms holding her tight against his body. Then he released one arm for a moment and opened the car door. He held her in check and pressed her thighs against the cold metal of the door. Then he tossed her in the backseat like a sack of potatoes.

He bent over her, and she had a second of freedom and lunged to escape, ramming her head into his tight stomach. He barely flinched and grabbed her wrists. Slipping a piece of rope from his pants pocket, he then wrapped it around her wrists.

Margo attempted to kick him in the face or jab him with her knee, but the backseat was too cramped. *Dear God, where's Chris?* Her eyes wandered to the area where the house stood, set back behind the trees. *Great, he parked so the trees hid him from the house. How in the world would Chris hear me all the way out here anyway?* But Margo didn't give up and continued to kick her feet like a two-year-old having a tantrum. Her shoes made nary a sound against the leather interior.

Within a few short moments, the man tied her ankles together like roping a steer. Funny, *he doesn't look like the cowboy type,* she mused. *But what a stupid thought to have when I'm being abducted.* She stared at the car window trying to lift her body up and hoping Chris would look outside, but he didn't. The engine purred quietly. No chance of him hearing them taking off.

Paul jumped in the front seat, kept the lights off, and carefully backed out of the short gravel drive that led to the studio. Margo banged her head against the window hoping to get some attention from anyone, and he turned around. "Relax, lady, you're gonna hurt yourself. If you don't stop I'll have to…never mind." The guy never finished his sentence.

Her mind raced. *What can I do? Help me Lord.* The car wheeled slowly unto the pavement and he straightened it out. He still didn't turn on the lights. As they passed the house, she banged her head again on the door window. *Chris, pleeease*, she pleaded.

Paul didn't say a word this time but drove away slowly. Margo collapsed, exhausted from the fight. *Dear God, where is he taking me? And why?*

<hr />

Margaret Eltin Dubier looked down from heaven upon Margo and nearly wept. She recalled a time long, long ago when a similar thing happened to her. The taste of pain and fear almost whelmed up again within her, except the Savior had healed the terrible memory with His love. Though her death was made to look like suicide, her family knew what happened. Now Margo was caught up in similar circumstances to unveil the truth. She had finally put some of the pieces together. Just like she herself had. Margaret whispered a prayer, and within a moment's breath, a company of angels surrounded her. She hoped they would help the young lady and entreat others on earth to lift their voices in prayer.

The angels knew, as time drew closer, they would need to be vigilant to keep Margo safe, but they could not interfere with freewill. Paul was being drawn into the light, but he still had choices to make. Bill was a true threat, yet he had his limitations.

The beating of angels' wings was like music to Margaret's ears. She knew they could help and would grow stronger as the saints prayed more. The leader of the group, Zuriel, dispatched a small band of angels to surround Margo. He would have to wait to send more until more believers prayed or the Father dispatched them. For now, though, he would do what he could.

21

A mixture of excitement and repulsion coursed through Paul's body. A good-looking young woman lay helpless in the back of his car. In the past, the rush of adrenaline from such excitement would've given him a high, and he'd have pulled aside for a little fun. But tonight, he felt sorry for the girl, sorry for what he had to do—sorry...he felt sorry. He knew he had to deliver the girl to the boss. *You don't cross the boss, ever, not if you wanted to stay alive.* Paul snapped back to reality. *What's the big deal anyway? What's wrong with me? I've done this a million times before. Anyways, the boss promised me he wasn't going to hurt the chick, didn't even want her body, just wanted some information. That's his business.* Paul stepped on the gas pedal harder. *Well, the boss does whatever he wants, and no one ever stops him. That's why he's the boss.*

Margo's mind reeled back and forth, her thoughts swimming in a fog. She faintly remembered a needle prick her arm, and she tried to resist, but the strong man easily overpowered her.

"Where am I going?" she kept repeating, but got no answer. The car sped along a winding road, and she felt tossed around like a roped calf. Later, when they came to a bumpy stretch, she bounced up and down like a ball. A warm, uninviting sensation coursed through her veins and washed over her mind. She felt suspended between consciousness and oblivion.

Margo fought to stay awake but quickly lost ground. Her eyelids fluttered up and down, until she succumbed to an intense drug-induced sleep. Specters of grotesque creatures with bulbous eyes haunted and attacked her. As she battled to free herself from their suffocating presence, she grew weary and gave up. Just as a serpentine figure was about to push her off into an abyss, she was startled awake. *Where am I?*

Her head ached something awful. She pried one eye open. The room spun as the blurry image of a man appeared in front of her. She tried to focus on him but couldn't. Her heavy eyelids dropped. A deep voice spoke as if from far away. But it sounded familiar—Bill?

"How are you, Margo?" The voice floated on air.

She forced her eyes open again. This time she got a better look at him. He wore a charcoal-gray suit, and he had jet-black hair. Though she despised his voice, she struggled to answer. No words came out.

"You're not a very polite guest, young lady." He chuckled. "But don't worry, I'll pardon your bad manners for today. You'll be talking soon enough."

Margo attempted to stand, but her legs wouldn't move. The man saw her plight. "I'm sorry it's taking you so long to recover, but you must not be used to…uh…pharmaceuticals. I'll give you something to pep you up."

Bill motioned to Paul. "Give her these." He dispensed two tiny red pills then pushed one away. "No, just give her one. I don't want her to be too aware. And get her a glass of water."

Paul returned with a tall glass and gave it to Margo. She gulped it down but spit out the pill.

"I knew you would be a difficult case to handle," the man spoke, and Margo now recognized his voice. "But this is for your own good." He shoved the pill into her mouth and clasped her mouth shut. "I can't hypnotize you and get what I want while you're in such a drugged state. You must be partially aware of what I'm doing."

So that's what he wanted. She tried to hold on to the thought and struggled to get free.

"I admire such passion in a woman." He eyed her trim figure up and down. "Too bad you're so misguided. I could have put that passion to work for you. With me as your boss, you could be living in a penthouse instead of playing with mud." He leaned over and put his hand on her knee, inching it upward.

Margo kicked him in the shins as hard as she could and prayed for God's help. Bill pushed her back on the chair, hurting her shoulder while he pressed his hands closer to her chest. "I could take you by force if I wanted, but your body isn't my main concern. I can have a real woman whenever I want. Right now, I want your mind, but if you decide not to cooperate, I can always resort to other tactics." He stared at her long and deep, his eyes as black as coal through Margo's blurry eyes.

"We're going to find out what you and that goofy husband of yours have been up to lately. I think you've been meddling where you don't belong, but I'll discover that soon enough." He tossed his head in Paul's direction, "Get me the—"

"Hey, boss," Paul called, "phone call for you. Sayz he's a VIP from the city. Wants to talk to you right now." Bill took his hands off Margo, but not before he let them slide across her chest. "There's more of that in store for you, honey, if you try any funny business." He called to Paul, "Get over here and keep her company."

Margo screamed inside. *Why is God allowing this to happen to me?*

Bill spun around and took the call while Paul walked over to watch her.

"Hey, cool your jets," Paul spoke from the side of his mouth. "You'll be dead meat if you don't cooperate. Get my drift?"

Margo heard what he said, but she tried to tune in to Bill's deep voice coming from a corner in the room, arguing about something. She strained to hear something…a word or two, but Paul was talking.

She stared at him and shook her head, pleading for him to be silent, but he didn't understand. *Where is this guy coming from? Whose side is he on?*

When Bill returned from the phone call, his eyes looked like steel bullets that could pierce her with one look. A look that spelled murder.

He approached her and sat down on a leather chair. "Let's get down to business."

Margo tried to stand up, but as much as she commanded her legs, they wouldn't budge. "What have you done to me?"

Bill laughed. "The wonders of modern medicine, a drug for every need. Just what the doctor ordered." He leaned his elbow on the arm of the chair and leaned in closer. "You're like a rat caught in a cage. You can't move, but your mind is aware, so I can operate."

"Operate?" Margo's voice registered panic.

"Not with scalpels, my dear, but…"

He leaned back on his chair. Folded his hands together. "I'm sorry." He chuckled. "But really, I can't tell you any more."

Margo's mind began to clear a little. She realized the room was expensively furnished, and paintings hung on the walls. They looked like originals. Bill had a lot of money. The wheels in her brain began to spin. *So he wants to know what Chris and I have found out…what we've meddled in.*

While Margo was thinking, Bill sauntered over to a small table. He opened the drawer and pulled out a large piece of paper. "Does this look familiar?" He held it up for Margo to see. "You already know too much, and that's the problem we're going to clear up tonight. So let's begin." He unfolded it.

Margo's eyes grew wide. "Where in the world did you get that?" She struggled to stand up and grab it, but her legs collapsed beneath her. "Give me it."

Bill waved his hand like a politician. "It was our good fortune to find this crumpled, seemingly insignificant work of art in your pocket. And I think as the expression goes, "finders keepers, losers weepers."

Bill strolled behind Margo and rubbed her shoulders. She hit his hand. "Leave me alone."

He slapped her across the face and growled. "If you want to play tough, then we'll play tough," he roared. "I can get whatever I want from you. Whether you survive is up to you." He grinned and held up her rubbing of the hieroglyphics. "Now be good and tell me all about this, or I might just have to get intimate with you."

Margo flinched and tried to pull away. Her mind raced. So that's what he wanted. Thank God she didn't know what it meant. "I don't know what it means."

"Don't get smart with me. I don't care about that. I want to know what you do know."

"I don't know about it."

Bill's arm shot from his side and tore her shirt. "I'm tired of playing nice guy. I'm in charge here!"

Margo's body trembled. Her face turned beet red. *No, you're not.* She prayed, *God, get me out of here!*

She watched his eyes grow even darker. "Listen, don't make this more difficult on yourself. You're at my mercy. I can…"

Margo saw his face change right in front of her eyes. His handsome, beguiling features took on a ghastly, beastlike quality. His voice deepened to a growl as he spat out the words, "You don't know what I'm capable of. I'll hand you over—" He stopped short and sprung from her side like a wild beast and began to pace.

Paul spun around, and in several steps, he was right beside her. He twisted her arm and whispered in her ear. "Hey, listen, you gotta stay cool, you don't know this guy. If you don't cooperate, forget it…I'd hate to see what he'll do to you."

Margo leaned toward Paul. Why did he want to help her? "You don't understand. I can't cooperate with evil."

Paul stalled for time. "Just be quiet, and I'll get you halfway out of this." He pinned Margo's shoulder to the chair, pretending to hurt her. "Okay, boss, I've got everything under control."

Bill leapt upon the two, pouncing like a lion. He scowled and pushed Paul aside. "You fool, I could do the same thing. I wanted her to be willing. I can't force her to be hypnotized, but since she's too stupid to watch out for herself, bring me the needles."

Paul obeyed.

Bill waved them in front of her. "This one is a truth serum, SP-117." He plunged it into her arm. "Now you'll give me what I want…and more." He jabbed another one in. Margo jumped. "And this one is to teach you a lesson."

Her body quivered, and she fought back tears. *Lord, be my rock and my fortress.* No way would she show Bill her inward fear. Her eyelids fluttered as the edges of the paisley wallpaper blurred. The room pulsated. She felt like she was floating. Weightless. Her body separated from her.

My child, though you walk in the shadow of death, I am with you.

"Who said that?"

Bill looked at her and snickered. "Hallucinating already?"

She heard it again. *I am with you.*

Was she going insane? Or was that the voice of God? She felt His peaceful presence. *I will be with you.*

Her mind swam but remained in a semiconscious state. Two men moved about the room, and she watched them as though they were in a movie—their actions slowed, their voices muted. They seemed far away—in another time and place. A voice beckoned her attention. Pausing, she listened. It was calm and even. Alluring. But something inside her didn't trust it.

She felt in a trance. In that strange state of mind between sleep and wakefulness. Another voice called. Margo recognized it. She was running. Running for her life. It called her back. Was she dreaming? She wasn't sure. Her eyes closed, and she couldn't open them up again.

Pray, she told herself. But the words wouldn't come.

The strange voice beckoned again. She floated toward it and followed its command.

"Tell me everything you know about Margaret and the stone. Everything..."

—————>◆<—————

Bill smiled like the Cheshire cat. Even though he didn't get all he wanted, he got what he needed. He felt smug thinking about the cover-up story and the alibi he invented. Suggesting to Paul to bring Margo to the hospital for observation relieved his nagging feeling about him—that his confidant may have abandoned Bill's allegiance.

During the hypnosis, he planted a lie in Margo's mind about her disappearance and then selectively removed what he wanted. Ah, the power of suggestion. He told her she received a call from a friend who was in need of prayer. Bill knew people in church who would verify that. On the way to her house, she had a small accident. Bill took care of that—witnesses, dent in the car, etc. Paul had seen the accident, and instead of calling 911, he brought her in to the ER himself.

The hospital did a routine check and found she had a slight memory loss. They concluded she must have bumped her head in the accident, but there were no other bruises. She appeared to be mildly traumatized and under the influence of drugs. Bill planted several pills on her for evidence. Of course he removed his own fingerprints and put Margo's on them.

Under Bill's hypnotic power, she admitted to a problem with amphetamines to help her do her work. He would have liked to go for something stronger, like cocaine, but he didn't think anyone would buy it, so this would have to do. Anyway, Paul confessed to be her supplier. Bill loved it! No one from the church would believe a word she said anymore. Even if her stupid husband refuted it, Bill had her convinced. This would tarnish her shining reputation and teach her a lesson about refusing him, Bill Guiles, the lady-killer par excellence.

22

Paul drummed his fingers on the steering wheel. Why did he feel guilty over kidnapping Margo? She didn't get hurt, so...no worries. She needed to forget all that dangerous information anyway.

As he drove his car down the highway, he thought it over. Maybe this bad rap about the drugs would keep her away from things she should avoid. Still, guilt ate at him. *Imagine that...me feeling this way. I didn't do nothing bad to her.*

The vehicle hugged the side of the road, and Paul easily took the curves. He loved the feeling, racing his sports car, but he usually had a couple of beers in him. He hadn't had a strong drink in over a week, and his mind felt clearer than it had in years. *What the heck is wrong with me? Ever since that meeting, I haven't touched a drop. And here I am, going back again.* He looked down at his watch. *I'm even on time. I'm changing...way too fast!*

Paul drove into the neighborhood and slowed down. He came to a stop outside a small white house. As he climbed out of his car, he caught a reflection of himself in the side mirror. He thought he looked cool with his black leather jacket, but he wondered what these people would think.

His short legs stretched to their fullest gait as he bounded up to the front door with his hands stuffed in his jacket pockets. Out of habit, he scanned the area. When he felt the coast was clear, he rang the doorbell. His feet shuffled back and forth on the wooden porch flooring as he waited. Finally, a woman answered the door. Paul remembered her kind smile, soft brown hair, and joy-filled eyes. She glanced at his leather jacket and smiled. "Come on in, Paul." She ushered him into the hallway. "My husband has been waiting for you."

Paul crossed the threshold and stepped into the house. He felt awkward, standing in the hallway of this nice little house, surrounded by others. It was just the type he often made fun of in his younger years but secretly wished his family had owned.

As he walked into the living room, Paul recognized Ray. He looked up from his newspaper then quickly rose and walked over to him. Ray stuck out his hand, and Paul took his hands from his pockets, then gave Ray a firm handshake.

Squinting, Ray commented, "That's some grip you got there, Paul."

Paul grinned.

"Ah yeah. I work out a lot."

"That's evident."

"Would you like some coffee?" Joy asked.

Paul took his other hand out of his pocket and tried to relax. "Sounds great." He breathed in the familiar smell of fresh brew and sat down at the kitchen table where Ray indicated. Paul put his hands on the table and looked down at them.

Ray broke the ice. "So, Paul, where are you from?"

Paul wasn't sure how to answer and replied, "Do you mean now or before?"

Ray smiled. His kind eyes pierced Paul's being, but at the same time they held something that lured the young man to him. Paul studied him for a moment.

Ray replied nonchalantly, "Either."

"Well, I'm originally from the Bronx, but I moved upstate about"—Paul hesitated and wiggled in his wooden seat—"a couple of years ago." The truth was Paul had lived up here only a few months ago and hadn't really moved, but he didn't want anyone to know the truth.

Joy poured the two men a cup of coffee and placed the steaming mugs on the kitchen table along with a tray of cookies. "There's cream and sugar so you can fix it the way you like."

"I take mine straight up—black, that is."

Paul looked around the pleasant kitchen. Homey. His mind momentarily slipped to his childhood. They never had a nice kitchen or pretty flowered curtains, but there was always plenty to eat. His mama was a great cook. Always something cooking on the stove.

Paul inhaled a familiar smell. "Is that chicken soup?"

Joy smiled. "Why, yes, would you like some?"

He couldn't remember the last time he had chicken soup or had spent time at home. He grinned sheepishly and politely refused.

Ray watched as Paul drank his coffee. After Joy had asked him about the soup, Paul kept his eyes glued to the coffee mug and gulped down the brew.

Waiting for the right timing, Ray then posed a direct question, "So, Paul, how are you feeling lately?"

Paul sat up. He looked up and stared directly at Ray then relaxed. For some unknown reason, this guy made him feel at ease. "Well, part of me feels much better than—" Paul stopped midsentence. He wasn't accustomed to being truthful with people, and he wasn't ready to spill his guts about his whole life—at least not here, not yet. He continued, "I mean, I feel good, but part of me feels…well, so different."

"In what way?"

"It's hard to explain, but, uh, I'm the real nervous type. Ya know, always jangling the change in my pocket. My stomach usually feels tied up in knots, like a pretzel."

"Yeah."

"Well, it's weird. I feel better, a lot calmer."

"That's really great, Paul. Do you know why?"

Paul shook his head. "That's why I'm here." He leaned over the table, closer to Ray. "What happened to me here last week?"

The doorbell rang, and Joy went to answer it.

Ray explained, "I invited someone here who can explain to you more clearly then I can...and I think he's here."

The man walked into the kitchen. Paul broke out in a sweat.

Ray looked up at him and motioned for him to sit down. Then he introduced the two. "Paul, this is Dave Light. He's one of the pastors at the church we attend."

Paul sprang out of his seat like a caged tiger. "Church! I ain't going to another church."

Dave laughed, not the vicious kind of laugh Paul was used to, but an inviting, warm laugh. "That's up to you, Paul. We don't force anyone to do anything they don't want to. I'm just here to help you understand what happened to you. So why don't you have a seat and you can be the one to ask me the questions if you want."

Paul hesitantly slipped back on the kitchen chair. Joy served some more coffee, and Paul held on to his mug like a security blanket. His mind conjured up images of the big stone church with stained glass windows. At first, Paul liked it. The way the colors on the windows lit up when the sun shined through them. The image of his mother enveloped him. She would always stay after church and light a candle for each member of the family then kneel and pray.

As a child, Paul loved to watch the candlelights flicker in their glass cups. His mother told him the flames were like the love of God shining in a dark world. He held on to this image for a long time, but then it slowly began to fade. As he got older, the priests in their long black robes scared Paul, telling him he would go to hell if he didn't go to church every week and say confession. Paul vowed never to go to church again, and he kept it that way. He only recently went again, just once, the other day because it was part of his job and Bill's plan.

The sound of Ray's voice brought him back to reality.

"Sorry, Dave, I forgot to fully introduce you. This is Paul Cambio."

The pastor looked at Paul and responded warmly, "If I've got my Spanish right, your last name means *change*."

"Ah yeah, you're right. How'd you know? Do you speak Spanish?"

"No, but I've picked up a few words here and there. So, Paul, I hear you had an incredible experience last week."

"Yeah, it was somethin' else," he replied. "I sure feel different."

Ray and Dave looked at each other. "That's great, Paul. You interested in knowing more about it?" Dave asked.

"Yeah, I am. One day I'm Paul Cambio, and the next day I feel like some kind of saint." He wanted to reach for a cigarette but didn't have one on him.

Dave pulled the chair closer and put a leather book on the table. Paul had grown quite fond of leather. It made him feel strong, powerful, and envied. Leather showed off Paul's muscles and made him look sharp. Women were attracted to him in his leather outfits, especially his tight leather jacket. When he was dressed in leather, women were easily attracted to him.

Paul looked at the black book with the gold lettering. It said *Holy Bible*, in embossed letters. There was something remotely familiar about it, something about the lettering, but he couldn't remember where he saw it before. He was waiting for this guy to do or say something.

Finally, Dave spoke. "Let me ask you, Paul. You look like you're a strong guy. Are you strong enough to hurt someone?"

Paul laughed. "Yeah, I can cause a lot of pain."

"Can you beat someone up bigger than you?"

"Sure can."

Dave opened his Bible but continued to speak, "Are you able to beat up someone stronger than yourself."

Paul thought. "It depends. If he's having a bad day or if I know his weakness."

"How about under ideal conditions for the strong man?"

Paul shook his head. "No. Of course not." He wondered what this guy was leading up to.

Dave flipped the pages of his Bible and looked up. "Well, basically, that's what happened the other night."

"I don't get it."

"Don't feel bad. There's a lot of Christians who don't understand it either. But I think I can explain it in a way you'll understand. When someone stronger than yourself challenges you, of course you don't take things lying down. But once you recognize they are stronger than yourself, you either surrender to them or get beat up."

"Yeah. So what?"

"Well, Paul, you have an opponent, a strong man who was living inside you, trying to destroy you through whatever means he could, but mainly with alcohol."

Paul laughed nervously. "Wait a minute here, Pastor. You've completely lost me. I don't have anyone living inside me but myself." He pointed a finger to his chest.

Dave flipped through the pages of the black leather Bible and found the verses he was looking for. He read from the gospel of Matthew, "'How can anyone enter the strong man's house and carry off his property, unless he first binds the strong man?'"

Paul digested the idea and spoke slowly, "Okay, I get that. You gotta tie up the strong man if you wanna get his goods—like his fifty-five-inch screen TV. But I'm not a house, and I don't have anyone living inside."

This time, Paul thought for sure the guy was stumped.

The pastor didn't seem troubled. "Jesus used stories, called parables, to help people understand truth. Of course there wasn't a man living inside of you, but there is a spirit world, whether you believe in it or not. Evil exists—just look at the world today. Sometimes evil gets a strangle hold on people and fills them up with it. That's the strongman. But Jesus is stronger." Dave looked directly at Paul. "For some special reason, Jesus chose to kick evil out of your life, even before you let Him into yours. There are examples of this in the Bible."

Paul avoided the pastor's penetrating gaze, but he thought about his words.

Ray stepped in. "This might sound crazy, but I have a feeling if you think back over your life, you'll remember a time when you no longer felt like you were in control. At first when you started drinking and…well, carousing, you felt you were in charge. Did you ever feel you lost control?"

Paul kept his head down and thought about his life over the last several years. Images of smoky bars and nightclubs crowded his thoughts. He loved the attention he got when drunk. Everyone laughed at his jokes. In a bar, he was the life of the party. He lost his inhibitions and knew how to talk to women. Paul pictured himself at a barstool, slyly checking out a beauty. She would fall for his sweet talk, his masculine bravado. He also loved the power he felt when he was drunk. He could smash a wall down if he felt like it.

Then he met this guy Bill. He was impressed with Paul's strength and ability to manipulate people. He paid Paul a lot of money to intimidate and beat up people. Life just kept getting better and better—more money, more women, more alcohol. Then Bill introduced coke to him, and life began to get out of control. He started getting drunk and drugging more often then he cared to admit. Women were no longer attracted to him the way they were before. His anger grew. He thought if he worked out more, he could beat this thing, but it was no use. He was hooked on the drugs Bill so freely offered in the beginning. That only lasted for a while, and then it was payback time for Paul. In order to pay for the good stuff, Paul had to do whatever Bill demanded. Paul picked up his head when he finally realized what had gone on in his life.

"Yeah, now that I think about it, things started to go downhill for me after I met B—" He stopped short. *Did they know Bill?*

Better not spill the beans. "I could handle the liquor, but the drugs got hold of me." Paul thought about how Bill screwed up his life. He stood up. "I'll kill that guy."

Ray stepped in and spoke calmly. "Paul, steady now. Your accomplice, let's call him B, was only a puppet himself. He is bound by the strongman too, even though he doesn't know it."

Paul sat down, his face drained. "Well, I still feel a lot of anger." Paul hesitated. "But ya know what? The strangest thing has happened to me. I don't have an ounce of desire for another drop of liquor or cocaine. It's weird. One day I'm hooked and the next, bingo…nada."

Ray and Dave nodded in agreement. "The reason you don't have the desire anymore is because something, or more correctly, *someone*, stronger than the desire to drink or do drugs drove that strongman away. It doesn't often happen that people are instantly delivered of addictions, especially if they haven't accepted Jesus into their life. There must be a reason why, but I don't know."

Paul put his elbows on the table and rested his head between them. "I don't know what you mean by letting Jesus into your life. I used to go to church, and I know who Jesus is, but, man, he's not living with me!"

Dave laughed. "Accepting Jesus means you want to try to follow him. You realize you're a sinner and want to change, but you need the Holy Spirit to help you do this. His Spirit can live within you, Paul."

Paul shook his head. "Now you want ghosts to live with me! This is weird."

"Paul, all this may sound strange, but if you stay for the meeting, I think you'll understand better. Why God chose to deliver you on the spot, we don't know, but God's ways are not our ways. Maybe He has something He wants you to do. One thing's for sure: it's important for you to accept Christ, or else, these demons could return and make your life a living hell."

The meeting began with prayer. Paul looked around as people started talking about all kinds of things going on in their lives. The guy next to him leaned over and explained they were sharing prayer concerns and asked Paul if there was anything he wanted prayer for. Paul sunk lower into the seat and shook his head. "No…thanks," he managed to reply.

He felt better when Ray began to pray for the church and its work with the homeless and poor in the area. Relaxing in his chair, he let go of his strangle grip. Just when things seemed like they were coming to an end, Dave stood up.

Paul cringed in his seat. *Please don't let him mention anything about a strongman.* Dave began to speak and thankfully didn't say a thing about him. Paul listened so as not to be caught off guard. The guy who sat next to him told him Dave was talking about how God answered his prayer. *Good, no spotlight on me or the strongman.* Paul settled back into his seat and nearly fell asleep. He hardly heard anything else the pastor mentioned until he heard his name. Paul nearly bolted out the door, but he stopped himself. After a minute or two, he realized Dave was talking about someone in the Bible. At this point, Paul decided he might as well stay. It would look weird for him to get up and leave now, so he decided to hang tough and even listen.

Dave quoted from the Bible again, "But the tax gatherer, standing some distance away, was even unwilling to lift his eyes to heaven but was beating his breast saying, 'God, be merciful, to me a sinner!' I tell you this man went down to his house justified rather than the other, for everyone who exalts himself shall be humbled, but he who humbles himself shall be exalted."

Paul liked the idea that the sinner was the one who was justified, whatever that meant. He thought about the other guy for a moment. *Boy does Bill ever act like that dude, always thinking he's so great.* Dave continued with another example. All this talk of humility made Paul feel a little uncomfortable—he and Bill were just the opposite. Paul was lost in thought and wasn't listening anymore when Dave looked up and directly faced him.

"The centurion had authority over a hundred legions of men, yet this Roman knew his military authority could not compare to the authority Jesus Christ possessed. This example shows the centurion's faith. He knew Jesus need only to speak a word and his servant would be healed. It is faith mixed with God's authority that healed the centurion's servant."

Paul sat back in his chair, contemplating what Dave had just said. He thought about Bill's authority and how he used it to manipulate and harm people. Would Bill ever realize a higher authority? He doubted it, but what about himself? He ran away from God at an early age when his mother died. Some good all her going to church did her. He blamed God for her death and grew bitter and hateful, even violent. *Could I really ever change*, he wondered. *Do I want to change?*

While Paul was wrapped in thought, the group got into a discussion about something else. He couldn't help but think of the events of his mother's death. Some stupid drunk hit her. How ironic, he thought. She never even touched a drop of the stuff herself, and then a drunk driver ran her over. Was that fair? What kind of a God would allow something like that to happen? *How can I understand God if He does things like that?*

Ray spoke up, and Paul recognized who was speaking. His smooth yet strong voice broke through Paul's thoughts. He nearly jumped out of his seat when he heard the verse, "Even the demons are subject to us." Paul had no idea what the Bible meant by this, but something struck a chord within him. Maybe those weirdo chanters are demons, but then he dismissed the idea as they were real people. Ray had definitely gotten his attention, and for some reason, Paul actually wanted to understand. He had never cared for the Bible or anything religious, but now he wanted to know how God could kick out a strongman.

Ray explained, "Jesus had sent the disciples out with nothing but a cloak and sandals, the bare essentials. The disciples had to be completely dependent on God and not their own resources. With the power of God within them, they were able to cast out the demons." Paul looked up when he heard the word *demons* mentioned again. Ray continued, "But look what Jesus had to say to them. 'Rejoice not that the demons are subject to you, but that your names are written in the Lamb's Book of Life.'" He looked straight at Paul and asked, "Now what do you think of that?"

Paul hesitated. He wanted to answer, but he wasn't sure of himself. On the other hand, he wanted to know whether he was on the right track or not. He stammered, "I think, umm…well, put it this way. The apostles were pretty powerful dudes, but they got their power from God."

Everyone smiled at Paul and a few nodded their head in agreement. Encouraged by the group's response, he continued, "I don't know what this Book of Life is, but Jesus thought it was even more important than casting out…demons." Paul hesitated. "I don't know much about this Christian stuff, but that's what I think."

Joy, Ray's wife replied, "We're all learning, Paul. Just open yourself up to God, and he will show you what you need to know."

Paul looked down at the floor. Regret settled in his stomach like a heavy stone. He should've known Bill would do something underhanded. He said he wouldn't harm Margo. Yeah, right. Now she wouldn't be able to remember Bill had twisted her mind. *But could God restore her memory?*

23

Margo woke up with a splitting headache that pulsated right above her temples. She'd been feeling terrible the last couple of days, but she hated to take the medication. She fumed, and her head hurt more. *I can't believe I confessed to using amphetamines at first when they found them in my pocket. That car accident must have really rattled my brain. Good thing Chris vouched for me being clean. It still seems like it was all a dream!*

Lord, things sure have taken a turn for the worst. I hope you clear my name and my head! I can't remember a thing lately…Chris said I took some pencil rubbings of some stones, but I can't find them anywhere, and why were they important?

Earlier, Chris had tried to convince her of the significance of the stone, but Margo hadn't felt good enough to really care about anything. The doctors told them it would take time.

Time to remember.

What day is it? Margo scratched her head. Wednesday or Thursday, two days after the incident. Or three? The setting sun cast a rosy glow through the curtains, and she figured it was early morning. She picked up her head to look at the clock: 9:00. *Wow, time to get up. The craft show is only a few days away.*

Margo lifted herself up carefully out of bed. She slid her feet into her cozy bear slippers, a present from Chris, and tramped down the hall to the bathroom. As she opened the medicine cabinet, she caught sight of herself in the mirror, and nearly screamed. *Is that what I look like?* She shook her head.

Good thing only Chris will see me for the next couple of days. First, I've got to get rid of this headache, so I can help him unload and load the kiln. Margo furrowed her eyebrows as she swallowed the pills. *We've got to finish everything. This is the big show that will make or break us for the winter.* Then another thought came to her.

Margo's head spun as she thought of him. *There's always Bill. He can sell a few big pieces for me in his store. He's such a nice guy, and sooo... good-looking, but I don't trust that associate of his, Paul. What a creep!*

⟹◆⟸

"What's on your mind?" Dave asked Paul.

He looked up and propped his elbow on the arm of the sofa chair. "So what's this Lamb's Book of Life?"

A familiar voice sailed across the room. "Thought you'd never ask," Mike's cheery voice answered. "Paul, the Book of Life is a book you want your name in."

Paul looked in his direction. "I didn't see you here. When did you sneak in?"

Mike laughed heartily. "When you weren't lookin'."

Paul grinned. "Which was about half the time I've been here."

"Yep."

"Okay, Mike. Shoot straight from the hip. Why does my name need to be in that book?"

"'Cause those people with their names in the book know Jesus and are going to heaven, that's why!"

Paul jangled the change in his pocket. "I gotta think this over, but tell me, how do I get my name in there?

Dave stepped up to Paul. "If you'd like, a few of us could pray for you so you could make the decision real soon to accept Jesus."

Paul felt confused about this accepting Jesus stuff. He wasn't sure he was ready for that, but he actually wanted the prayer. "Okay, what do I have to do?"

"Nothing for now," Ray explained, "until you want to pray along with us."

He hesitated, and Mike put his hand on Paul's shoulder. "Don't worry, boy. I was in this same position about a year ago. I wasn't no saint either at that time. I could tell you a colorful story or two, but now that's all changed, and it feels good, real good."

Paul figured he better listen to the cowboy. Something he said made sense even though he couldn't figure out why. So he sat back in the comfortable chair and listened with one ear as the small group prayed for him. He heard snippets of words, "Open this young man's heart to you Lord and…" But his mind was occupied with another thought. *I wonder who is stronger, this God they're talking about or Bill?* Then he stopped for a moment and felt a stirring of hope deep within his soul. He prayed silently. *God, I hope you're there 'cause I'm really gonna need your help after Bill gets hold of me.*

⋙◆⋘

Bill Guiles leaned over the barstool and gloated over his success in both hypnotizing Margo and adding just a little bit of tarnish to her reputation. His associate at the hospital, the doctor who had supposedly treated Margo, advised Bill he shouldn't make a case about the drugs. "Just say she took some amphetamines to keep her awake at night while she prepared for her art show. Let people construe what they want." Bill knew just the people to tell to get it all blown out of proportion.

He laughed at the thought of Margo's helplessness. Confident he would see her in that position again, he hoped he would have further opportunities. He loved having control over her thought life. He admired his ability to reshape someone's unconscious mind. It was out of the ordinary, and he knew it. The power surged though him when he wanted it. It came at his beck and call. So he thought.

Yet he felt troubled. Now he would have to take care of Paul—of all people! Ever since he abducted Margo, he was getting increasingly religious…on the other side! He even asked to have Sunday afternoons off, but Bill flatly refused, especially since he gave him Wednesday night off. *Paul wouldn't be an easy one to put under the influence,* Bill mused as he put down his shot glass on the counter. *Maybe he wouldn't need to after all. Wasn't there an old saying, There's more than one way to skin a cat?*

The bartender, a surly old cowboy with a number of deep cuts on his face, refilled Bill's glass. He slugged it down in one shot and continued with his train of thought. *Maybe Margo would make sure Paul stayed away from any church activities.* He hoped that the negative image he tried to implant in her mind of Paul had taken effect, as well as Bill's suggestions of his stellar looks and character, but there was only one way to find out. The craft fair would be a perfect opportunity, but until then... he would have to keep a careful eye on Paul.

The night before the Autumn Harvest Craft Fair was colder than usual. Margo had stopped getting headaches from the car accident, stopped mistaking the time of day, and only suffered memory loss about certain things. She and Chris put all their time and energy into getting ready for the big day. They had stayed up a few nights in a row until 3:00 a.m., glazing pottery and loading pieces in and out of the kiln. Tonight, she went to bed relatively early, 11:00 p.m.

Physically exhausted, Margo fell immediately into a deep sleep. She was sleeping soundly and peacefully until...*crash...tinkle, tinkle.* The sound of breaking glass startled her awake. She shot up straight in her bed and shook Chris.

"Hey, wake up, you dead man. Didn't you hear that?"

Chris yawned, "What?"

"Are you deaf? You didn't hear it?"

Chris rolled over. "No."

Margo jostled him awake. "Please, Chris, just go outside and check the van. Make sure no one broke in and destroyed all our hard work."

Chris turned to her. "Okay, okay, I'll check the van." And he rose like a dead man walking.

Margo listened carefully as she watched Chris struggle into his bathrobe. She felt guilty, but she stayed frozen in bed, fearing the worst.

Chris returned within a few minutes with a favorable report. "No sign of a broken van window." He turned off the light. "Now let's get some more sleep."

Margo sighed. "I don't know what's wrong with my brain lately. It's doing weird things. Maybe I heard a crash in my dreams... but it sounded so real."

She scrunched up her pillow and attempted to go back to sleep, though she tossed and turned for a good portion of the night as though on a ship. In her dreams, she heard the sound of the ocean waves lapping against the shoreline. Peaceful.

She saw herself standing on the edge of the shore; then a voice called to her, *"Margo, come here, come here to me...come."* She walked deeper and deeper into the water. The waves washed up around her, first to her knees then to her waist then over her head. It felt peaceful, alluring, and she welcomed it.

Death?

Suddenly, a gentle but firm hand pulled her out of the water. She was transported to another scene. This time her mind zoomed in on a wharf. Someone stepped onto the dock, and Margo squinted to recognize the person. She couldn't see their face. As the figure walked down the dock, it stood silhouetted in a black robe. Margo panicked as she frantically tried to discover the person's identity.

Then the scene flashed over to a woman walking on the opposite side of the dock. As she strained to see her...*bam.*

The picture went black.

This repeated itself. Each time it was almost the same, except with each progression, the cloaked figure turned more toward her. She couldn't quite distinguish the face. The woman fought to move closer to Margo. She'd seen her face before—in a book, a magazine…a portrait.

That was it!

Was it her mother? No, too young. Her grandmother? Maybe. The woman broke free from the shadows and ran into the light.

Margo saw her features.

The woman called to her, "Margaret?"

The Father of Lies from ancient times assumed his other favored form and hissed. "What is thisssssssss I hear? She called out her name!" The whole underworld stopped and listened.

"There will be repurcussssssssions for this, you bloody fooolsss! Deception, come forth."

Light streaked across the abyss and turned his dark side to his father.

The Master of Deceit bellowed. "I told you to give him the power to erase everything in that pea brain of hers that was reminiscent of the plan!"

Prince Deception bowed. "My lord and liege, I have done as you requested. He has extraordinary powers. Bill is ours. While she, on the other hand, belongs to—"

"Don't you dare mention His Name!" He pointed a long finger at the prince

"Sir, I would never consider such an atrocity. May I continue?"

A group of lesser demons twittered at his groveling.

Deception spun around and snarled with his blackened face. "Shut up, you imbeciles!"

The Master of Disguise, who some referred to as Satan or Apollyn, nodded in reply.

"Our servant on earth has done well and erased all of her memory of this. What remains is only a trace. She knows not what it means. She utters words with no understanding."

The master swept his long black cloak to his side, revealing a glowing-hot celestial body. In the process, he scorched an entire legion of lesser warriors. A few new recruits whimpered. The furnace demolished them.

Turning to Deception, he addressed the important matter at hand. "This better be the truth, or you will find yourself stripped and thrown into the vast gulag of a frozen wasteland." He laughed in an uproar. "Or trapped inside a teenage gaming machine."

Lucifer, also known as the god Horus in Egypt, made an about-face. "Begone, all of you. To your stations! I have better things to attend to." He stretched out his arm and gave one last charge. "Next time, I want to hear an evil report. Perhaps I will send Lust along with you this time to move things along more quickly."

Deception shuddered at the thought of the Master wanting someone to work with him. "As you wish, sire, but I will execute all my powers. Just wait to see what I have in store for her. You will be pleased."

Laughing, Lust appeared from the shadows. "Perhaps I will be too!"

Deception hissed, "You think yourself so clever, but you are only a passing pleasure. I, however, last for eternity!"

24

The fairground swelled with artists and craftsmen scurrying around carrying boxes, unloading vehicles, and arranging displays. Margo's booth sat in a fairly visible area, and she brought some beautiful, rich velvet to drape over the wooden crates for her display. While Chris unloaded the boxes of pottery, Margo darted here and there trying to put up the tent's framework for her exhibit. Her idea of the stone house backdrop was an unfinished project due to Ashley's untimely death, and this troubled and confused Margo to no end. She couldn't make up her mind how to place any of her work.

In frustration, she kicked a crate over.

Chris put down the cardboard box he was carrying. "Need a little assistance there, young lady?"

Margo slumped down on the ground. "I just don't know what's wrong with me. I can't seem to concentrate on anything, and I feel so bad about Ashley." Margo put up her hands in exasperation. "But in response to your question, boy do I need help."

Chris bent down and stroked Margo's shiny hair. "It's understandable with all you've been through plus losing a friend. You tossed and turned a lot last night. Did you sleep at all?"

Margo shook her head. "I've got to start feeling better. I have a lot of people to deal with today. I'm sick of not feeling right. This has got to go beyond a simple car accident." She stood up. "Could we please spend a moment in prayer?"

Chris nodded yes, and the two of them walked behind the booth. He closed his eyes and began. "Dear Lord, we need your help right now. We don't know what's going on here, but you do. For now, please strengthen Margo for the task ahead."

Margo agreed and prayed. "Dear God, help me. I need your strength to face this day." After a moment, she added, "In your timing, please restore my memory, and if possible, show me why I don't feel well. Amen."

She opened her eyes at the same time as Chris, and he hugged her. "Feeling any better?"

Margo managed to produce a weak smile. "A little." Actually, she felt like her brain was whirling around like a washing machine on the spin cycle, but she managed to steady herself enough to walk.

She meandered around to the front of the booth when suddenly, she heard footsteps running away. Chris ran over to one of the boxes, and Margo trailed behind. He rummaged through it. "I think we just got robbed!"

Margo ran up behind him and saw the vacant hole left by the missing pottery. Just what they didn't need, but it could've been worse. "Thank God whoever it was didn't take off with the whole box."

Chris stood up and looked around the booth. "I think we'll need to keep a watchful eye on things today. If vendors are stealing, then there's a real problem. We can't trust anyone!"

Margo agreed. "My best pieces will go here behind the cashbox. We'll need to be vigilant." She barely felt able to manage herself, never mind watching out for suspicious characters. But she had to do what she had to do.

"And we won't be able to leave the booth unattended. We'll have to take shifts when we want to get something to eat or look around," Chris chimed in.

"That's okay by me. I intend on spending the whole day right here." She plopped down on a folding chair and prayed her head would stop spinning. "I'm only getting up to help customers." Margo hoped she could do just that.

Chris put his arm around her. "Sounds like a good idea to me."

Margo feared she wouldn't know how to ring up a sale properly, but she didn't tell Chris. She shook her head. How could she forget something like that? She felt older than her years.

The morning and early part of the afternoon passed in a blur of faces parading before Chris and Margo. They kept busy with customers, ringing up purchases, helping people choose the *right* color or the *right* piece for their dining room, packing the pottery carefully, and making correct change. It took everything Margo could muster to handle the cash properly, but she managed.

Once in a while they got a breather, and the two collapsed on their stools, recharging for the next flux of customers. Though Margo had more energy, she still didn't feel well inside. Some of the other craftspeople came by to look at her work like they did every year. "Very nice glazes. Look at this cool one," a fellow artist pointed to a cerulean-blue vase with puffy clouds trimmed in gold.

Margo shrugged. "Thanks."

"Burned out?" Another inquired.

"No, just..." Margo searched for an appropriate word. "Just not up to par."

Margo wasn't lying. She wasn't exhausted, just disoriented, detached, and far away. Every once in a while, she felt like she couldn't breathe. The air was being sucked right out of her.

Then the world around her faded, replaced by another reality. Water surrounded her. She felt like she was struggling to keep her nose above the surface so she wouldn't drown. Would she soon join Ashley?

Drifting, she stood by the edge of the sea, like in a movie, and watched the waves rise up over her and drown her. The odd thing was she didn't move, she didn't cry or run away. She let the waves engulf her and take her away.

Far, far away from herself and her mind.

Somehow the scene felt familiar, real, as if she'd really experienced it. But that would've been impossible, right? Still she couldn't shake the feeling her mind was engulfed, but by what?

By midafternoon the weather had grown quite warm for an October day. Business lulled for a while as Margo gazed across the valley. A forest of brilliant red and orange leaves stood in rich contrast to the deep-green evergreens.

Margo nudged her husband, and his sandy-colored hair fell over his eyes. "Look at that gorgeous tree there, handsome."

"Over where?" Chris pushed aside his locks. He indicated the vast array of trees.

"C'mon." She slapped his shoulder. "You know which one I mean. The brilliant-orange one that looks like it's on fire."

He pretended to take a snapshot of the tree. "Yeah, the leaf peepers will be out in droves on a day like this. I bet that tree will be photographed a hundred times today and posted on Facebook at least fifty! And then they'll line up over here to buy one of your leaf plates."

Margo didn't care about selling any more of her pottery today and making money. She felt so tired and wanted to go home. Something inside told her she needed to examine those rubbings Chris told her she'd made. She'd completely forgotten about them, though she finally remembered the name Margaret. But what did it mean?

Margo turned to Chris. "I need to use the restroom. I'll be back in ten minutes."

"Could you just wait five more minutes?"

Margo stared up at the cliffs as though the mountains held some magnetic attraction.

Chris interrupted her staring. "Hello! You have some customers interested in some wares over here, and they have some questions." Chris cleared his throat. "Would you mind reporting back to earth?"

Margo didn't respond at first. The mountains held a key to her memory, and she wanted it unlocked, though now wasn't the time. She shook her head and replied. "Sorry, I just thought about something." She walked over to answer the customer's questions.

"How can I help you?" Margo asked with a wooden smile. She felt like she was selling them her soul.

Several times during the afternoon, Chris heard Margo mumbling to herself, and he asked what she was saying.

The young potter simply replied, "Nothing."

As the sun began to sink lower in the sky, Margo grew increasingly distracted and disturbed. She paced back and forth, rearranged what was left of the pottery several times, and wouldn't talk. Not like Margo at all. Something was going on in her brain.

Chris figured it was time to pack up the bowls and plates, and he began wrapping them in bubble wrap and placing them in the boxes they'd brought to the fair. Even though a chilly wind swept across the field, he didn't feel the need to wear a jacket.

Margo shuddered several times and zipped up her light parka. "Did you feel an icy wind slash across the cornfield? It feels like winter already."

Since he was working hard putting away all the pottery, the cold breeze felt refreshing to him. "Yeah, I felt it, but it feels good to me. Maybe you should go get in the van and turn on the heat. I'll pack things up."

"No, I'll help."

Chris wanted to get her home. He resumed packing the items, increasing his pace. Margo stood there staring at the cliffs, and he let her. Maybe it would jar her memory. He tried to tell her a couple of times what they'd discovered so far, but she couldn't remember any of it. The doctor said it would take some time to recover, and only a few days had passed since the strange accident. She hadn't regained her memory yet about the stone or the visions, though she did remember about Ashley's death. It confused him. He'd have to look into getting her tested after the show. For now, he needed to concentrate on packing up the pottery.

A gust of wind blew through the display area, but Chris ignored it. Margo shivered again. "You felt it, didn't you?"

"Truthfully, no, Margo, I didn't, but it doesn't matter." Chris struggled to maneuver an awkward box under the table to store for the night. "We need to get you home, and to bed." He wanted her to feel safe once the memories started to return.

Margo's lips thinned to a weak smile, and she stared at him. Vacant.

<hr />

That evening the wind whistled through the trees while the branches creaked and groaned, lamenting their condition. Margo tossed and turned throughout the night, rising and falling on the gusts of the wind, riding them as though they were invisible waves threatening to sink her, but never quite succeeding.

Her dreams alternated between vague nightmares of impending doom and vivid images. Candles flickered against a cave wall, casting ghoulish black shadows. Shadowy forms in black robes swayed to chanting—echoing and bouncing, resounding to a deafening pitch.

Margo thought she saw a familiar face. She strained to see, but the face turned away from her, and she couldn't distinguish the image. As it melted away, the chanting changed tones, rising in pitch. Margo's heart raced wildly in the dream, and she saw herself in a long white gown fleeing through the woods. Running, running, running over rocks and sticks, pushing aside branches. Panting.

Breathless.

She paused. Terror filled the dark woods.

Where am I? she screamed in her head.

Stop. Rewind. Reverse. Going nowhere backward. The sequence repeated itself over again with the keening cries driving her insane.

Suddenly, the chanting stopped. The haunting spirits stopped pursuing.

Somewhere, somehow, Margo's spirit reached into the night, into the shadows of a cave. She saw something familiar hiding behind a rock wall in an alcove. She peeked through a crack.

Disappointment.

All she saw were the elongated eerie forms of black-robed figures, flickering in the night.

She waited.

Margo held her breath.

She caught a glimpse of them struggling with a heavy object. She strained to see more. They lifted the object up onto a low table. A group of robed forms surrounded it.

Fear gripped her heart.

She turned away. Someone said her name. Frightened, she spun around, and then she saw it. The object of her fears lay in the middle of the table.

Margo screamed in terror.

"The stone!"

Chris awoke and held her tightly, stroked her hair, and spoke in a soothing voice as she sobbed. She gasped for breath in between heavy sobs.

He loosened his grip and looked into her swollen, red eyes. Her words sounded like a hysterical jumble. He attempted to calm her as she repeated, "The *stone*, the *stone*, *the stone*."

"The stone we found—"

"Yes, yes, yes. I saw *the stone*, and I heard my name. It was real, it wasn't a dream. I was there."

"So you remember?" Chris was thankful.

"Of course. Did I ever forget?" Margo sobbed.

It wasn't the time to rehash the last week. And there was no use trying to convince her it was only a nightmare.

Chris smoothed her hair. "No, no. You never really forgot. It was just locked away."

She moaned. "No, I didn't. I was there." Chris listened to her recount the terrifying dream while he rocked her in his arms.

"Margo, my sweet Margo, you've been through so much." He kissed the top of her head.

After a long while, she fell asleep in his arms. Totally exhausted.

Never had he seen her in such a state. He worried about her. *How could she ever handle the Craft Festival tomorrow?* What a stupid thought, he decided. *I'll do it myself.* He lovingly laid her down on the bed and covered her with a warm blanket.

He carefully slipped under the covers so as not to disturb her and attempted to sleep. Though he couldn't help thinking of how insistent Margo was about the nightmare being real.

Her words echoed in his mind: *I was there.*

He hoped she wasn't becoming delusional.

<hr />

Beams of light streamed from behind a black rain cloud as Veritas stood beside it, dispersing much of the darkness. Other angels followed in his wake, and he turned to face them. "The battle over New Coven and Margo has intensified. The enemy has launched his attack on many fronts. He is using all of his old weapons: pride, witchcraft, lust, power, and, worst of all, division among the believers. Yet hope has lifted its head!"

The small host of angels rustled their wings.

"Though Mr. Guiles erased much of what Margo discovered, he could not eradicate it from her spirit!"

A song of praise rang out among the ranks. "Holy is the Lord. He is worthy to be praised. All glory and honor belong to Him."

As the song subsided, one of the smaller angels inquired, "What are we to do next?"

Veritas's face shone as if he had just been in the Lord's presence himself. "He will make his will known to us in his timing. Right now we need to minister to Margo and those who follow the King's way."

"But what of all this trouble with the saints in New Coven?" asked another.

Zuriel, who was silent up until now, chimed in, "They must learn to pray, rest in the shadow of the Almighty, and resist the enemy." He spread out his wings, preparing for flight. "And I must go when the Lord bids. I hear His voice now."

Some of the host alighted with him, but a few remained. The smallest of them shook his golden halo. "I fear for these humans. They are so very weak in their own strength. What shall become of them?"

25

Melanie Eltin-Carson sat across from Bill Guiles and stared admiringly into his eyes. She smiled coyly. His dark eyes penetrated hers and thrilled her to the core. *What a hunk…and such a gentleman. How nice of him to bring me out for lunch when I had nothing to do…just because he's my husband's new business partner.*

She fixed her tight red dress and smoothed out the wrinkles.

"Is everything okay?" Bill asked in a concerned tone of voice. "Do you feel comfortable?"

Melanie folded her hands on her lap. "Oh yes, it's wonderful. I've never been here before."

She stared at his handsome features—his eyes as dark as deep pools, the aquiline nose, and the strong cut of his chin. She tore her gaze away and looked around the room. It was decorated with several bold-print wallpaper designs, one of which seemed to dance and swirl along the surface of the wall. Melanie liked its carefree design and the bold, colorful strokes. It made her feel free and happy inside.

"I love the décor. Is it Mexican?"

"Why yes, and it has authentic cuisine. I hope you like the selection."

She opened the menu. "Oh yes, I love Mexican food. Sometimes it's a bit hot, but today…"

Bill gazed into her eyes, and she liked what she saw—glinting dark pools filled with mystery, a strong chin, black wavy hair, and broad shoulders. Someone you could lean on without them falling apart.

He put his hands on the table and reached out for her. "I hope the food isn't too hot for you. You could order one of the milder dishes."

Melanie blushed and fingered her necklace around her throat. "No, I feel adventurous today. I think I'll try something with jalapeño peppers. Rich doesn't like Mexican food, so I don't really get a chance to eat it." She lay her menu down and put her arm on the table.

Bill reached across and patted her hand. "Yes, Rich does seem to be a bit conservative when it comes to his taste in food. We always have to eat American when we got out to lunch. He just forgets his wife has different tastes."

Melanie's eyes darkened. "Yes, he seems to forget what I like and focus on himself."

Bill locked eyes with her. "Well, now that we're business partners, I'll have to teach him how to treat a woman."

Melanie smiled and thought *I bet you know how to treat a woman,* but instead she said, "It won't be an easy task. He doesn't like to try new things." Melanie sighed. "People probably think I'm happily married because Rich is successful."

She leaned closer to Bill and lowered her voice. "Truthfully, I'm bored. While Rich is out running around making money, I'm sitting at home arranging pictures on the wall and picking out color schemes."

Bill smiled. "Some women love to do that."

"Well, that's not enough for me. I need some…excitement in life." She lifted her hands up slightly.

Bill raised his eyebrow and stared at her V-neck dress as it lifted her chest. "Oh, an adventurous type."

The cocktail waitress waited for Bill to finish speaking and walked over. "Can I get you another glass of sangria, miss?"

Melanie looked down at her half-finished glass and said, "Yes, I'd love another." *It's been too long*, she thought, *since I've had a little fun. I'm thirty-five years old, and look at me. I haven't had a glass of wine in years. It's time for me to start making some changes.*

The waitress took Bill's order. He watched her sashay away then picked up his glass and proposed a toast. Melanie held hers midair.

"To Rich and me, a new partnership and a new friendship." He smiled.

Melanie looked straight into his eyes as she clinked her glass against his. "To *our* new *friend*ship."

"Yes, to friends." He reached over and touched her hand again.

She felt a chill run up and down her spine. *Finally, some excitement in my life.*

⇒•◆•⇐

Jessica picked up the heavy suitcase and slammed the front door shut. She felt sick and tired of her husband's outbursts. *Man of God, yeah right, he can't even control his temper.*

She informed him if they didn't see a marriage counselor soon, she would leave, and that's exactly what she was doing. *If his pride wants to get in the way of our marriage, then it's his problem.* Her mom completely understood Jessica's position and the direction she was heading. Jessica lifted the cumbersome bag into the back of the car and slammed the trunk door shut. She hopped into the front seat and backed up out of the driveway.

It was a hot autumn day—Indian summer—and she wore shorts. She hadn't noticed the dark clouds thickening on the horizon. Her mind was filled with the last couple of month's events—the fighting, the yelling, and now his preoccupation with that stone and hunting for evil.

She just couldn't take Mark's anger and neglect anymore. Her feelings for him changed so much since this whole cave incident. It took this for her to see clearly just how self-absorbed he was, and he was unwilling to recognize he had a problem. She'd seen things clearly and wanted a divorce.

Divorce.

She had never thought of it much before. Now, it seemed it was her only option. If he wasn't willing to see a counselor, he'd never change. She wasn't going to stay stuck in a marriage with a lunatic.

A light drizzle began to fall, and Jessica turned on her windshield wipers. She sped down the country road, taking the curves just a little too fast.

With her mind preoccupied with last night's argument, she didn't see the approaching danger. Leaves were strewn across the road. Coming into a curve, the car slid on the slick surface.

Jessica gripped the wheel and stepped on the brakes.

The tires screeched, and the car began to spin. She jerked it in the opposite direction and overcompensated. The car swept into a tailspin.

Jessica cried, "Oh my God, Oh my God. Help—"

Another car was headed her way. In her lane. She stepped on the gas and pulled out of the spin.

Head-on with another vehicle.

She jerked the wheel in the other direction and screamed. The tires spun in the dirt and rocks on the shoulder of the road. Out of control, it careened, sideswiping a telephone pole.

Crunch! The door handle flew off. Jessica rocked back and forth, thrown about by the impact.

The car slowed and veered off into a ditch. It jerked to a halt, and Jessica's chest thrust into the steering wheel, and her head hit the dashboard.

Knocked unconscious.

Bill's Jaguar approached just as the blue car landed in a ditch. He stepped on the brakes, and stopped his vehicle. He recognized the car and instantly knew what he was about to do. Turning to Melanie, he registered concern in his voice. "Stay here. I need to see if anyone's hurt."

As he opened the Honda's crunched door, he looked in on Jessica. The poor girl. She'd given up so much to him. He felt for her pulse. Unconscious but alive. He whispered in her ear, "Can you hear me?" His voice penetrated, and she nodded.

Perfect.

She moaned.

"Just lie back and relax." He patted her shoulder. "Count backward from twenty to yourself, and I'll take care of everything."

As she obeyed, Bill stepped out for a moment, pulled out his cell phone, and punched in a number. "Listen, Melanie, someone's been hurt here. I'm going to stay with her until the paramedics come. Just stay in the car. I'll be with you soon. They should be here any minute."

He opened the door and slid next to the unconscious, but impressionable, Jessica. He'd call 911 as soon as he finished with her. "Now my dearest," he used his smoothest voice. "Remember I'm your savior, and your husband is a very evil man. You can trust me." He snapped his fingers and called 911.

Melanie got out of the car but stopped when Bill waved her away. She turned back, disappointed. She hoped this wouldn't put a crimp in their day. The ambulance sure was taking longer than she thought it would. What could Bill possibly be doing?

After almost half an hour, she heard the alarming cry of the ambulance when it approached and watched as the red lights flashed. She observed the scene from the car window, wondering how long much longer Bill would be delayed. He appeared calm and directed the paramedics to the young woman. Unlike her husband, Bill knew when to step aside and let someone else handle the situation.

She studied his broad shoulders and tall, lean figure. Bill was both strong and gentle, two qualities Rich did not possess. Melanie hoped his partnership with her husband would rub off. She also wondered if Bill was married, but she hadn't seen a wedding band, only a handsome gold ring with a large square diamond. He was a man with good taste and money.

Melanie watched as the paramedics took care of the injured woman, and Bill assisted. She looked down at her watch. *What was taking so long?* She got out of the car again and walked toward Bill. "Can't we leave yet?" she called across the street.

"Please go back to the car. I don't want you to have to get all involved in this. I'll only be a minute more. Then we can go wherever you want."

Melanie brightened at his answer. He returned within five minutes. As he slid into the front seat of the car, she felt her face flush. "Do you always help someone in need?"

He laughed and scribbled something on a pad of paper. "Sure, if I can be of help. Isn't it the Christian way of doing things?"

"Yes, but so few people actually take the time to be of help to others."

Bill revved the engine. "So where to?"

Melanie thought for a moment and took a deep breath. She couldn't bear to go home and be alone for the rest of the afternoon. "How about the park across the river?"

He smiled broadly and pulled the car out onto the road. "Just tell me the way."

26

Margo lay flat on her bed with yet another headache. *Dear God,* she prayed, *I'm getting a little tired of this. Can you please do something about it?* She looked up at the clock: eight o'clock already. "Hey, Chris, where are you? We've got to get the van packed up." She heard him in the kitchen and forced herself out of bed and into the kitchen.

He was making coffee when she asked, "Have you loaded up the van yet?"

Chris looked up, puzzled. "I never unloaded it. It's all ready to go."

"What day is it?"

"Saturday. Remember how busy yesterday got?"

Margo searched her memory files. "Oh yeah. I forgot. I've got another of those dozy headaches. Could you get me an aspirin?"

"Sure thing, but do you feel well enough to go? You had another really bad night last night."

Margo poured milk into her coffee. "I don't remember."

"Are you sure?" Chris knitted his eyebrows.

"I'm sorry, but I really don't."

"You were really upset about the stone. You had an awful nightmare, but you kept insisting it was real."

Margo blew out a long breath and clenched her fists. Yet another incident she couldn't recall. And it involved some crazy stone. "After this craft fair, we've got to go back to the cave and see what's so important about that hunk of rock."

Chris wrapped his arms around her waist. "Until then, promise me you'll try to concentrate on just your work?"

She kissed him on the cheek. "I'll certainly try my best."

When they arrived at the fair, a long line of people waited at the ticket booth. Yesterday, she would've groaned, but now she felt better. She rubbed her forehead. The headache was finally gone. "Thank you, Lord," she whispered. Once Chris parked the van, she practically flew out of it.

She took control and started setting up. "These are some of my best pieces, and the dealers are coming this morning, so we don't have any time to waste. Please, please get a move on and don't just stand there." Her mind flooded with everything she needed to do, and she bounced around from one thing to the next.

"Okay, Sergeant." He saluted her and unloaded some boxes. "Where do you want these?"

She pointed, and he jumped.

"Yes, sir." Chris put them down. "Is that okay…sir?"

"Stop calling me sir," Margo snapped. "This is not the army." It felt good to be back in the swing of things, and she didn't want Chris teasing her, but she also realized she acted a bit jumpy.

He moved closer. "I know you are a woman of many different personalities, but lately, you have a few more in there." He pointed to her head. "You don't usually go from Soft Sally to Sergeant Sam in five minutes. I'm just trying to figure you out."

Margo threw her arms around him. "I'm *so* sorry. I don't know what's wrong with me. One minute I'm outraged, the next minute, I'm frightened to death. Help me, Chris, I'm just not myself!" She dropped her head into her hands and muttered. "But we've got to pull the show together, or we'll be in a financial mess."

Chris rubbed his chin. "Well, there's always Bill."

Margo spun around. "That guy's an enigma. One moment I think he's Prince Charming, and the next I think he's a slimy, conniving snake. My mind feels like a Ping-Pong ball. I just don't know what to think. When he's around you, he's charming. The only problem is, I don't know if he's the charmer or the snake!"

"Okay, we'll forget about Bill for now, but didn't we do well yesterday?"

"Yeah, but we sold a lot of inexpensive stuff, nothing big. I've got to attract dealers today."

Chris laughed. "You're usually quite good at that. One look at you and they'll fall in love...with your work." Chris stroked his chin. "Can make a guy like me feel downright insecure."

Margo gave him a love tap on the arm. "Don't worry, I'm hooked on you."

She placed one of her beautiful blue-and-crimson platters on display and unpacked some gold-rimmed vases. Several prospective customers walked over, and one engaged Margo in lively conversation. Their comments drew attention from a businessman.

He picked up the dish. "Good application of multiple glazes and layering." He pointed to the vase. "Did you refire this one with gold?"

"Yes, it's genuine."

He looked at the price sticker. "In that case I'll take it. Wrap it carefully."

Margo jumped up and down on the inside though her outward appearance remained calm. The extra money for the gold glaze came from her sales to Bill. *At least he did some good*, she mused.

The morning went well. Margo and Chris worked busily, showing off pieces, ringing up purchases, and wrapping them in tissue and newspaper. A man in a lightweight blue suit inspected everything critically, but only bought one small piece. She thought she recognized him, but couldn't place him.

Margo and Chris fell into a rhythm together and worked well as a team. Margo didn't feel as distant or as remote as yesterday. Though her memory about the stone and Margaret were still foggy, she felt at home being the businesswoman again.

Bill never showed up as he had promised, but Margo felt relieved. He had a way of knocking her off track and making her forget things. Even though most of her larger pieces remained, she hoped they would sell in the next few hours.

Business slowed down in the late afternoon, and Chris announced it was time for dinner. He grabbed a $20 bill out of the metal box posing as a register. "I shall return, fair damsel, with vittles for the evening meal." After yesterday's little incident, neither of them left the booth unattended.

"What a gallant knight you are, sire." Margo batted her long eyelashes.

Exhausted, she plopped down on a lawn chair behind the register. She looked over at the empty shelves next to her. *Boy, what a rush hour, but we really needed it. Thanks for coming through, Lord.* She noticed most of the mugs had sold, but she really wished a few more of her artistic pieces would sell.

Margo's lids fluttered shut for a moment. When she opened them, the man with a blue suit was looking at her work. Startled, she asked. "How long have you been here?"

"Only a few moments," he replied flatly as he looked around.

Margo recognized him as the same guy from before. *Why had he returned?*

"I see you still have your Chinese style vases left. Am I correct or are they spoken for?"

Margo stood up. "Yes. That's correct, sir."

"Very beautiful, but a bit pricey, wouldn't you say?"

Margo felt embarrassed because Bill told her they were underpriced. "Not according to some businessmen. I was advised on these prices."

"Oh, I see. Then you wouldn't be interested in striking a deal?"

Margo didn't want to undercut herself. "Yes, but I do have one buyer who is willing to pay $1,700 for this one."

The man cleared his throat. "And where is he, my dear."

227

Margo detected an English accent, but she wasn't sure if it was real or phony. "He's not here today, but I have his business card."

"Well, you can have my card too." He reached in his jacket pocket to get the card out.

Margo looked at it and hesitated.

"Of course I have the money, cash, which is much better than merely a card, but it's up to you."

At that point, he took his wallet out from his back pocket and showed her a roll of hundred-dollar bills. "I'll give you fourteen of these for the two vases and not a penny less."

Margo corrected him. "You mean, and not a penny more."

"No, I mean what I say. I wouldn't want to cheat you."

Margo's heart rushed, but she didn't want to appear too anxious. She looked down at the artwork and ran her hand down one of them. "You'd be getting a good deal. You do realize this vase is done in the Cloisonné style, which takes several firings and is quite expensive."

He took off his glasses and inspected it more carefully. "Ten-K gold leaf?"

Margo nodded.

"That's a tremendous amount of work. I'll give you two hundred more for it."

Margo extended her hand. "You have a deal."

The tall thin man cracked a smile for the first time. "You drive a hard bargain, young lady."

Margo shook hands with him to seal the deal, but his clammy hands prompted her to pull away quickly. Yuck. They felt like a wet fish. She had to control herself from wiping them off.

"I'll need those packed for shipping," he instructed Margo. "I'm traveling quite a distance."

She wrapped the pieces in two layers of bubble wrap and placed them in a box full of packing peanuts. Looking around, she wondered what was taking Chris so long to get dinner. Maybe he got caught talking to someone.

As she handed the customer the box, he refused to carry it himself. He complained of a bad back.

He looked down at his watch. "I'm sorry, miss, but I'll have to forgo the transaction. I have a plane to catch in three hours for Great Britain, and I must be leaving now."

"My husband should be back any minute." She looked around, but Chris was nowhere in sight. What could be keeping him?

The man demanded his money back.

Margo wrung her hands. Why did Chris leave her all alone? Then she realized he went to get dinner. She wished her brain would function like it used to, or at least closer to normal. Finally, she asked, "How far is your vehicle?" She decided the frail-looking man wouldn't pose a threat.

He pointed. "That way, about a three-minute walk."

She decided to volunteer and help with one stipulation. "I don't like to leave the booth by itself. We had a robbery the other day."

The man replied in an understanding tone of voice, "Then why don't you get one of these other chaps to help you?"

Margo conceded. "Okay, I'll do that."

The woman next to her booth was happy to help her. She wasn't busy at the time and wouldn't mind watching the booth for ten minutes."

"Okay, where's your car? I hope it's not too far. These boxes can get heavy," she muttered under her breath.

The man led her through a shortcut, but they wound up on the outskirts of the fair. Margo looked around, uncomfortable. She wanted to put the box down, but the man pointed. "It's right over there. The black van."

Margo sighed. "Good thing."

When they arrived, the gray-haired man immediately opened the door for Margo. She quickly placed the carton down on the floor and turned away. "Leaving so soon?" A hand reached out from behind her and grabbed her arm, twisting it in back of her. She cried out, but no one was in earshot. Margo tried to scream, but the businessman quickly gagged her. She kicked and tried to hit him, but a strong arm pulled her inside the van. Kicking and thrashing, she fell onto the backseat. As she struggled to get free, she caught a glimpse of her assailant from the corner of her eye. Moving closer, he bent over and breathed heavily on her as he tied her legs together and began stroking them.

She cried in horror. *Bill?*

When Chris returned, he didn't see Margo. The woman in the next booth explained the situation and pointed in the direction Margo had left. He ran in that general direction, looking all over for her, but she wasn't there. He cupped his hands to his mouth, calling. "Margo, where are you?" *Where could she be?* His heart began to pound in his chest. *I never should've talked with that guy who stopped me.* He ran over to another seller and questioned them. They said she passed by, carrying a box, while a man in a light-colored suit accompanied her.

The thumping in his chest grew stronger. Where could she be? He rushed over to the next vendor and, in the process, knocked over someone's dinner. The catsup from the hamburger and fries spattered on his pants, but he didn't care. The annoyed painter asked, "Hey, buddy. What's your hurry?" Chris apologized, handed him a $10 bill for his ruined dinner, and quickly explained the situation.

"Yeah, I saw the pretty little thing go down that way." He pointed farther on.

Chris dashed off in the direction indicated and prayed. "Lord, help me find her!"

Margo rolled around on the floor of the van attempting to sit up. Her gaze fell upon the face of another man who emerged from underneath a plastic drop cloth. Terror filled her body as he slapped a black cloth over eyes and tied it with a jerk. Another knee jammed her back. Stinging pain radiated through her body. She collapsed on the floor.

Just when she thought she could take no more, he wrenched her arms behind her and tied them so the rope cut into her skin. Hot tears ran down her cheeks. *Why God? Why? What have I done to deserve this?*

Then a voice sliced though her darkness. "Hello, Margo, it's me."

Margo knew it was Bill. She froze. Terror gripped her heart as he placed a hand upon her shoulder.

"Don't you remember the other night?" Bill kissed her ear.

In repulsion, she thrust her head back as far as possible. *Dear God, what did he do to me?* "I guess you don't. I did such a good job hypnotizing you."

She furrowed her eyebrows in anger.

His hand slid down her arms. "Don't look so mad at me. I'm the one who should be angry." His voice lowered. "You refused me, but tonight will be different." He laughed.

Her body stiffened.

He falsely comforted her, "Don't worry, *my love*, not here, not now. That's Paul's game, not mine. I have other, umm, let's say more suitable and enjoyable—"

Margo twisted her head away.

He grabbed her head and kept it from moving. He hissed, "You're mine, and you will do as I want. Just see."

He kissed her lips, and she jerked her head back, banging it against the van door. He grabbed her arms and pulled her two inches away from his face. "You're mine." He sputtered a sinister laugh.

A putrid odor clouded Bill, a sulfuric, nauseating smell. She nearly gagged. Then suddenly, out of nowhere, a needle jabbed into her right arm.

"Ouch!" She looked around in terror.

"So sorry we have to do this again." Bill laughed. "But it's so efficient in achieving the desired effect." He snickered.

An accomplice drained a cool liquid into her system. It seemed all-too familiar.

She tried to pull away from the wrenching pain. Tears sprung to her eyes.

Margo feared the worst. *Dear God, please protect me from this beast...*

She bent down and sobbed. The van lurched forward.

Her body fell into Bill's waiting arms.

———⟫◆⟪———

Chris searched frantically for Margo having followed the path the painter had indicated, but Margo was nowhere to be seen. He stopped at several booths from jewelers to engravers, but so far, zip. He couldn't believe people were so blind. No way had she disappeared into thin air. Finally, he stopped at one of the last vendors and asked a long-haired guy who sold tie-dye T-shirts.

Chris stopped and caught his breath and asked, "Have you seen a young woman with long, honey-brown hair?"

To his surprise, the guy replied, "Yeah, man, it was a weird scene. This beautiful chick carrying a heavy box for this weird-looking old man."

"How long ago?" Chris asked, hopeful.

He scratched his beard. "Maybe five or ten minutes. Not really sure."

"Did you see where they went?"

He pointed to a narrow passageway.

Chris patted him on the shoulder "Thanks, man." He took off, praying he'd see Margo around the next bend. As he ran past a tangle of generators and an assortment of vehicles, he didn't see anyone. He turned around in a slow circle but saw nothing unusual. *Where could she have gone?* Perhaps she'd dropped off the package and was on her way back. As the dusty road opened up into a grass field, fresh tire marks indicated a vehicle had taken off in a hurry. Chris prayed Margo wasn't in it.

27

Vince's wife, Jane, watched her husband as he paced back and forth in the kitchen. His shoes slapped the newly installed ceramic tile and jarred her senses. She fought to squelch the growing fear and conquer it. Since she knew where his worries lay, she began to calculate a solution. Gliding over to the coffeemaker, her silk bathrobe swished against her body. She reached for an oversized mug and poured him a cup of the aromatic brew. "Here you go, darling, your favorite—macchiato."

He stopped for a moment and took the cup. "This will do for now, but don't think this will take my mind off the finances. I don't know how the church is going to survive."

Jane cocked her head to the side and thought for a moment. "Hmm, we'll just have to recruit some new members, maybe a wealthy businessman." She slid closer to her handsome husband. He was so much better looking than her, which made some people in the church wonder if he married her because of her father's money. "Look, we already have Bill, and didn't you say he wrote a check for $2,000 just last Sunday?"

"Yes, but how many men like him can we attract? We're not exactly a traditional church, and anyway a few new members won't make up for losing half the membership."

Jane looked confused. "What do you mean half? I thought you made it clear that—"

Vince interrupted, "They decided it was time for them to leave, even after last week's sermon. Lance let them go." Vince sat down, his face taut with lines. "And on top of it, a few deacons are having marital problems, if you know what I mean." Vince looked straight into his wife's eyes. "There's going to be a lot of changes around here from now on."

Jane looked around her beautifully furnished living room and faltered. "I thought you were the head elder and called the shots here!"

"Not when the board unanimously voted to let them go."

"Unanimously?" His wife acted surprised. "Have they turned against you?"

Vince laughed nervously. "Sure looks like it. We might need to find a new church ourselves."

"But...but everything was going so well." She wrung her hands.

Along with her husband, she enjoyed being in a position of authority and didn't want to let go. Money could always be found. Her father had enough of that, but position was another story. She stood up quickly and nearly knocked over her husband's cup. "Those deacons are just plain rebellious. We'll have to get some new ones. Imagine that Lance, the nerve of him! He never was very spiritual anyway. We've done so much work in the church just to throw it all away in one day."

Vince didn't look or sound very invincible right then as he hung his head. "I don't know. Maybe I should have listened to Chris more. Maybe there is something to this stone they found and—"

Jane interrupted. "Whatever are you talking about?"

Vince sighed. "It's a long story, though. Ever since Chris and Mark found some weird stone up in the mountains, things around here have gone haywire, but I don't want to get into details tonight. I'm just going to bed."

Jane paced the floor; her bathrobe whooshed as she walked. A plan brewed in her mind. "Okay, darling, you go get your sleep and don't worry about anything. I'm sure everything will work out just fine for *us*. You know there's always my daddy."

Later that night in Kingsland, Bethany Light felt her husband, Dave, tossing and turning in the bed. Since it was past midnight, she didn't know if she should wake him. *I think all this commotion lately is finally beginning to get to him.*

Suddenly, Dave cried out in his sleep, "Help her, Jesus, help her." He moaned several times and cried out in a loud voice.

For an instant, fear gripped her. She didn't know what to do. "Dear Jesus, be with us," she prayed. Finally, she shook him awake.

Dave stared blankly at Bethany. "What's going on?"

She sat up on the bed. "You're having another nightmare...or premonition. This one seemed worse than any of the others. Do you remember what it was about?"

Dave looked disoriented and sat up then switched on the light. "Remember last time I felt like someone needed help, and I prayed for him?"

His wife nodded.

"Well, this is about ten times worse. Some poor woman was crying, actually screaming for help."

Bethany thought about his other dream. "Do you know where she was?"

"It was all dark and gloomy, but there were a few flickering candles. That's all I can recall." He stopped and thought for a minute. "It's frustrating I can't place who this woman is, but she seems vaguely familiar."

His wife sat back and closed her eyes and tried to imagine what her husband was telling her. "Do you know why she's screaming?"

Dave strained to remember. "No. There was so much darkness it was hard to tell what was going on."

"I don't know if these *nightmares* are visions from God or not, but the last one turned out to be true. Maybe God *is* trying to tell you something again."

"Yeah, I'm not sure what he's saying, but I definitely think we should pray."

Both of them closed their eyes, and Dave began. "Dear Lord, we come before you united together, my wife and I, to pray for a woman who might be in trouble right now."

They waited to hear from God. Slowly, a figure in a dark cave-like atmosphere appeared in Bethany's mind, and she prayed. "Lord, you have placed this woman before me, whoever or wherever she is, please minister to her. I sense a very urgent need in her life."

"I come against the powers of darkness overtaking her life." Dave quickly responded. He was a little surprised at his last statement, but he continued in the boldness of the Holy Spirit. "I come against this evil by the power of His blood shed at Calvary. I command this spirit to loosen her. Not by my might or my power, but by His Spirit."

Bethany rose up in her spirit. "Lord, we pray for her protection. Whoever she is. Lord, send people to help her, to rescue her." With a womanly sensitivity she added, "And, Father, help her not to feel abandoned. Help her to know You are there with her, seeing her through this."

"In Jesus's name. Amen."

She laid her head back on the pillow, and Dave followed suit. Though she had stopped praying audibly, a spirit of prayer remained in her heart for this troubled young lady in her husband's dream. But was she real?

<hr />

Just outside the city limits of Kingsland, another couple, Ray and Joy Hopelyn, had a similar experience. Joy's spirit felt deeply disturbed within her, like a black cloud had passed over her. Ray told his wife he sensed a sinister presence. Ever since the prayer meeting last week, Joy had several harrowing dreams and strange revelations.

She shut off the blue glow of the TV. "Let's pray. My spirit feels so heavy."

Ray got up from the couch, sat next to Joy, and hugged her. "I agree. Let's start right away. I sense urgency." He cleared his throat. "Lord, we come before You this day to lay claim to what is Yours and to take back what the enemy has stolen from us. We bring before you Paul Cambio. We know he was a child of Satan, but now You have called him. We pray he will respond to You, oh Lord, bring him to know You as Lord and Savior."

Joy waited and then prayed, "Dear Jesus, help Paul to change, to make the right decisions. Give him both the strength and grace to do Your will and to turn away from a loveless life. Soften his heart even now and help him to turn his back on darkness."

"Keep him from the spirit of death and give him courage and wisdom to choose life. Cover him in the blood of Jesus. Amen." Ray concluded the prayer.

Joy jumped at the mention of the blood of Jesus, and her arms broke out with goose bumps. A dark void swirled together with pinpricks of light.

Her husband opened his eyes and saw her shivering. "What's wrong, Joy, are you okay?"

Rubbing her arms up and down, she replied, "I'm not sure, but when you mentioned the blood of Jesus, I got chills." Little by little, the picture became clearer.

"That's an unusual response." He put his arms round his wife. "Did you happen to *see* something to make you feel that way?"

She raised her eyebrows. "How did you know?"

"Just a hunch. So what was it?"

She closed her eyes. "I saw a dark cave and what looked like a hundred little flickering lights. In the middle of the cave there was...there was..." Her eyes fluttered open. "A l-large round stone," she stammered, "w-with our names written on it!"

———⟫◇⟪———

Margo struggled to open her heavy eyelids. Her mind felt fuzzy, like a scrambled TV channel. Muffled voices and scuffling feet alerted Margo. Yet she did not sense the presence of human beings. Something else surrounded her.

Something dark and foreboding.

A sinister evil surrounded her. Her thoughts drifted like clouds. At times she felt she was just having a terrible nightmare. Then the painful throb of her head awoke her to reality. This was no dream.

Footsteps scraped in the distance. Within moments, terrifying images loomed in front of her, like specters in the night.

She gasped for breath.

A man's voice glided toward her. It sounded slow and garbled. "Maake suuure sheee cooperrrates." Her mind drifted farther and farther away. She tried to reel it back in, but it floated away.

Suddenly, two strong hands clasped her, and she jumped back into her body. Then another pair held down her legs. Her mind screamed, *Fight!* But her body would not move. Arms seemed to come at her from everywhere and lifted her up and away. Another pinprick jabbed her, similar to what she felt at the doctor's office. But the pain was only momentary.

Within a few minutes, Margo felt like Alice in Wonderland—falling, falling, falling down a very, very long tunnel.

———◇———

At the house of Joy and Ray Hopelyn, the doorbell rang almost nonstop. Their pastor and his wife, David and Bethany Light, were among the guests. Joy greeted everyone with hopeful anticipation. Ray had to go down the basement several times to drag up whatever chairs he could find. The seats were arranged in a large circle and ranged from a comfortable blue recliner to a wooden plank stretched out between two chairs. Each one was occupied, so others milled about looking for a piece of carpet to sit on.

Amongst the bustle, Joy found a place for everyone and sat down next to Ray. He stood up, looked around the room, smiled, and then cleared his throat. "First, I'd like to—I mean my wife and I would like to thank you all for coming." He bent down and gave his wife a quick hug.

A hush fell. The shuffling of feet stopped, the buzz of conversation ended, and all heads turned to face Ray and Joy.

"Most of you already know this is a pressing matter for prayer, so I will speak little and pray much." He shuffled his feet back and forth.

"Truthfully, I know less about this matter than Joy, so I'll let her do the talking."

Several people let out a nervous laugh at Ray's comment, but when Joy stood up, a hush descended again. All eyes turned in her direction. Everyone wanted to hear the reason for the emergency meeting.

As she looked out to the anxious audience, she closed her eyes for a moment, and saw the same vision that woke her from her sleep. She dropped her head. Ray reached over and took her hand. She fought back tears.

The circle of believers bowed their heads and prayed silently. David prayed aloud for their protection.

Joy recovered. "Just a few hours ago, I had *a very* disturbing experience." Her voice faltered, and she opened her eyes. As she looked out over the faces of people, she thought of how much she had grown to love them.

Regaining her composure, she continued. "But it was much more than just a strange experience. I believe it was a *vision.*"

She closed her eyes again. "A vision not only of spiritual things, but of something that truly exists...in the here and now. In this particular place, I felt enclosed, engulfed in darkness, and surrounded by the coolness of stone, like in a cave. In the distance I saw lights flickering, casting shadows upon a rough-hewn wall. Then I heard chanting, and I felt my spirit lifted out of my body and carried toward the flickering lights."

Opening her eyes, she looked upward. "At first, it felt freeing, like flying through the air. Then as I approached the scene, a cold draft hit my spirit and knocked me to the floor. The chanting stopped, and darkness suffocated me. An overwhelming, sickening stench wafted though the air, like the smell of rotting meat and blood."

One of the ladies in the group cried out, "That's disgusting!"

Bethany went over and comforted her.

Joy grew more upset as she recalled the scene. She continued, stopping and starting at several different points. "Then I felt my body slammed against a rock, and my hand slammed against a cold stone surface. I opened my eyes, and in the candlelight, and I saw a cave."

A hush fell over the gathering.

"Then as if from nowhere, a dark-robed figure with a hood over his head appeared, carrying a stone wheel. From the walls emerged a band of black-robed figures with hoods. Then believe it or not, I saw the stone wheel floating in the air, heading right toward me."

By this point, her voice strained and cracked as the words became a great burden for her to utter. "I saw the stone loom right before my eyes...carved with symbols and letters."

Several people gasped.

"The letters of my name and Ray's were engraved on it!"

Her head dropped to her chest. The horror of the scene overtook her. The vision of the stone seared her consciousness.

Several of Joy's good friends, as well as the pastor and his wife, got up and laid hands on her. The small group prayed. "In the name of Jesus." They repeated several times.

Then one voice rang out clearly and distinctly. "Get outtaaa here, Satan."

Immediately, Joy recognized the voice and opened her eyes. She looked up, surprised. Standing above her, grinning from ear to ear, was one of the new church members, Mike.

Joy smiled and thanked him. "You learn quickly."

The lanky cowboy bent over and whispered, "I recognized the scoundrel right away, and I just couldn't keep my mouth shut."

Several people nearby heard him and laughed. The tension broke for a moment; then silence fell once again on the intimate group. More needed to be said.

Ray continued the story. He took his wife's hand and held it tightly. "We did not call you to this meeting solely because Joy had a vision in which she saw her name engraved on a bloodstained stone. She also saw…" Ray turned to her for confirmation, and Joy nodded her head.

"She saw more names. Those of several other people, here tonight, drenched in blood!"

28

Aloud rapping on the door interrupted the heavy silence in the Hopelyns' living room. Mike lifted his head, but stunned by the recent news and feeling burdened, he ignored it just like everyone else.

The knocking persisted. Ray asked Mike to answer it, so he gathered his strength, stood up, and walked toward the impatient caller. As he dragged himself past each one, he wondered—was he a marked one? Was she?

He opened the door. No one. Looking out into the darkness, he saw a brawny figure emerge. Recognition dawned. The man across from him looked tortured, especially in the glow of the porch light that accentuated the shadows on his face.

"Got to talk to Ray," he demanded as he burst through the door.

Mike blocked his path and looked him straight in the eye. He questioned the intentions of the intruder, especially after the recent turn of events. "What can I do to help you, Paul?"

The muscular figure stepped back and gave him a hard look. Mike watched his tense face soften just a little. Paul laid his strong, heavy arm on Mike's shoulder. Breathing heavily, he answered, "I need your help…desperately."

"Okay. Come in and sit down. Joy and Ray are busy right now."

Paul yanked his arm away and spat out, "Too busy to save someone's life?"

Mike stroked his chin. "What do you mean?"

Paul didn't waste any time and shot into the living room. Mike followed.

All eyes faced forward as Paul stepped over the threshold. "I gotta talk to Ray."

Ray stood up and walked directly over. He put his arm around Paul's shoulders and tried to coax him out of the living room.

Paul would not budge.

Mike moved closer. He hoped Paul wasn't drunk. They could drag him down if they must, but he prayed this wasn't the situation.

"I need your help…and as a matter of fact"—Paul scanned the living room and pointed to a few other strong-looking men—"I could use their help too."

Ray took his arm off Paul's shoulder. "As you can see, we are in the middle of an important—"

"Important? Don't you think a young girl's life is important?"

Mike watched as everyone began praying silently, some with their eyes open. He joined them.

Several puzzled faces looked up as Ray questioned him. "What do you mean?"

"I mean someone's life is at stake, and we're standing here like a bunch of politicians debatin' whether or not to help."

A few people smiled at his comment.

Mike sensed Paul was telling the truth.

"Don't you get it?" Paul threw up his hands. "You don't understand, there's no time for questions. I already tried to contact her husband, and he wasn't there. I had nowhere else to go, so I came to you." He looked at Ray. "If you want to save a life, then you better gather up a few of these guys, right now!" Paul pointed again to several men.

They waited. The pastor, Dave, volunteered to go.

Ray shot a glance at Mike, and he nodded in ascent. "Okay, you'll get what you want, but if there's any trouble, I'm going to call the police."

Mike watched Paul flinch at the mention of the word *police* and then replied, "Okay, let's just get the h—— out of here. I only hope they haven't done her in."

Ray and Mike grabbed their jackets, and three other men accompanied them out the door.

Mike gobbled the ground with his long legs and climbed into the driver's seat of Ray's Jeep. He called to him. "I know the area—real well. I'll drive, if it's okay."

Ray threw him the keys and ran around to the passenger's side.

Paul gestured to the others. "You two guys, come with me!"

They obeyed.

"We're goin' up the mountain," he shouted from the front seat of his red Triumph. "Just follow me."

Ray rolled down the window. "This better be legit, Paul, or I'll have you—"

Paul gunned the engine and lurched out of the driveway.

Mike turned over the ignition and followed suit. He stepped on the gas and squealed away. Mike hoped the police wouldn't arrest *him*.

⋙◆⋘

Chris stood in the small booth at the fairgrounds, wanting to scream. "Yes, she's only been missing for less than an hour, but you don't understand, she was abducted once, and it might have happened again!" He stared straight into the cold eyes of the policeman. He needed his help, and he wasn't going to let the guy intimidate him. "Sir, if you don't send out some troopers now, I'm going to the chief."

"Now, just hold on there, boy. We need to do a sweep of the grounds before we send out anyone."

Chris apologized, "Yes, I understand, but could you please get on it right away? I've been standing here for over ten minutes."

"Well, boy, it's a busy place." He swept his arm in front of him, indicating the fairgrounds. "You're not the only one with problems. You need to wait your turn."

Chris understood, but he felt the cop was stalling, wasting time. Only one other person was present, and she had reported a theft. Chris tried to keep his tone even. "Yes, I understand, sir, but I think my wife is more important than a few items of missing jewelry. Could you please send someone out now?"

The cop lifted his arm slowly and pressed the red button on a walkie-talkie. "Hey, Sam, Could you send two guys over? We've got a missing person, and a *freaked-out* husband."

Chris didn't exactly like the term the cop used to describe him, but at least he called someone on the job. Maybe she's on the grounds, he tried to console himself. *Dear Lord, please be with her.*

<hr />

Margo's head throbbed with the staccato beat of the chanting voices stabbing the darkness. Sharp pain shot up and down her legs, though she could not move them. Her arms wouldn't budge either. They felt like dead weights.

A tight blindfold cut into the bridge of her nose, adding to the pain. A stone cold slab pressed against her back. Straining, she tried again to move. With concentrated effort, she managed to wiggle her toes. Her whole body ached, yet at the same time, it felt like it wasn't completely there. She had no control over it; the feeling frightened her to death.

Muffled voices muttered in the background. Eerie, faraway, like a nightmare. In silence she cried out in her anger and her pain, *Oh, God where are you? I don't see any angels coming to my rescue. I don't even know where I am.* No one there heard her inner cry.

Suddenly, the chanting stopped and a dead silence fell.

She held her breath—for a moment. Suspended in time.

Whrrrrrr, whrrrr, whrrr. A fluttering sound sliced through the air with a putrid smell following in its wake. Margo's stomach turned sour. She felt like retching but controlled the impulse.

A cold breeze hovered over her body, lingered for a moment then disappeared. Margo tensed in anticipation. *What's going to happen to me, God?*

Guttural sounds interrupted her prayer. She listened. No. It was gibberish.

Margo tried to decipher the syllables. She followed their cadence, up and down, then it broke into a feverish pitch. Another voice joined in.

Cold droplets rained down upon her body, scattered from head to toe. She shivered. It reminded her of being sprinkled with holy water like she saw the Catholic priests do in a mass.

Dear God, what is this about?

Her mind flashed with pictures from her childhood—a priest walking down the long church aisle shaking holy water on everyone, another swinging an incense pot with a smoking heavy fragrance. What connection did this have?

No sooner had the image formed than the pungent, though more pleasant, odor of incense wafted through the air.

Then another fragrance wafted though the room. Margo recognized the scent immediately, an interesting mix. Very strong.

Where, where, where did I smell this before? She raked her brain to recall.

Wait a minute. Images drifted by. She struggled to patch the details together. The scent grew stronger. Margo flinched.

A cornfield...the sun setting...not long ago.

She stopped to watch...to watch what? *C'mon, Margo,* she urged herself. *Yes, yes that was it. I stopped to watch a young woman.* The smell of corn, strong and hot, mixed with a pungent perfume.

Margo shivered as a cool, silky cloth fluttered overhead, touching her bare legs. The familiar fragrance hit her nostrils more powerfully than before. A warm body stooped over her, a hot breath blew into her face.

The vision of the memory, the recollection, the scents, the current ghastly moment, and her past experiences all merged in a flash of recognition.

She groaned at the realization of the ritual. Satan's perverted imitation. *Dear God, I don't understand what this woman has to do with me, but please, help me!*

Margo's simple prayer shot heavenward. Its power mobilized forces under the command of one greater than the evil force surrounding her.

"His strategies will prove successful."

"Yes, our troop is much smaller than theirs, and so we must listen carefully to the Master's orders," Zuriel insisted. "We must descend one level at a time, for there are many captains of evil hovering high above the cave and in it. Only through the prayers of the saints, which have ascended, will we break through."

29

When they reached the overlook parking lot, Paul joined forces with Ray and Mike in the Jeep. He felt like a third wheel, but his Triumph would never negotiate the trail. He also conceded to Mike driving, since Paul didn't know the area as well as the cowboy. His stomach flipped as Ray's Jeep bounced over branches, rocks, and every form of mineral on the forest floor. Paul braced himself against the bumps and his head almost hit the vehicle's roof several times. Dave followed with the others in a rugged but small SUV.

As they pitched and swayed, branches and leaves slapped against the side of Paul's window. Paul had wondered when he hiked this trail with Bill if a vehicle could make the trip, but his boss would not hear of it. Tonight, the urgency of the mission drove all of them to extreme measures. Time was of the essence.

Paul's mind raced ahead. Earlier he convinced the men of the importance of their intervention. He omitted the part about the grave danger they faced.

In the backseat, heads bowed in a state of intense prayer. His eyes were fixed on the washboard trail as Mike drove. He had only been up this way twice before, when Bill ordered him to—

Paul trembled at the thought of Bill. His strong square shoulders and handsome features lured many females. He conquered them all.

All but Margo.

Paul recalled how this infuriated Bill to the point of near insanity. Paul knew his boss's thoughts. Now she would pay. She would be the prey in a game of cat and mouse.

Mike interrupted Paul's thoughts. "We need to discuss a plan." He turned and faced Paul. "Do you know how many we'll be up against?"

Paul stiffened. "At least ten or more."

The four-wheel drive unpredictably jerked to a stop, and the small caravan of men lurched forward. Those trailing in the other vehicle halted.

Ray jumped up. "I'll take a look and see what the problem is."

Paul shook his head. "No need to do that. We've probably hit one of those blasted boulders. We'll have to walk the rest of the way."

Dave stuck his head out the window then pulled it back. "We're better off walking at this point."

Paul hopped out and inspected the area. Pitch-dark. He had hoped the moon would light the path, but clouds quickly gathered.

"Just our luck," he mumbled.

Meanwhile, the other men, including a friend of Dave's from New Coven, joined them, and they gathered in the darkness. With bowed heads, they prayed silently.

Paul looked around and tried to get his bearings. He knew the cave was not far, but he wasn't sure where. The path headed in two different directions. He faintly recalled bearing to the left. "I think it's this way, guys."

He started walking. "Yes, this is it. C'mon, let's move quickly," he urged them. The rocky path was slippery with evening dew and moss. He picked his way through the brambles and hoped the other men could navigate as well. It could hardly be called a path. Paul knew few hikers traveled this way. If he was right, in a few moments, it should open up to a small grassy field. He prayed it would.

Within a few minutes, he reached the clearing and stopped dead in his tracks. The distant chanting of voices carried in the night air and eerily echoed off the stone walls.

The others approached. Paul waved his arms, indicating everyone should stay put.

He whispered, "I have a plan. The cave is not far from here, just around that corner." He pointed into the darkness illuminated by a pinprick of light.

"We'll have to break into two groups. Mike, you lead around to the right, and I'll take the left." He hesitated and shuffled his feet for a moment, loosening a small rock. He stooped down. "And while you're at it, each one of you pick up as many rocks as you can. We'll need them."

The small circle of men nodded in unison.

Paul instructed them further. "Wait until both groups meet at the entrance to the cave. Then we'll rush at them and throw rocks at their feet. They're probably barefooted, and that will kill their toes."

One of the guys, Lance, laughed with a nervous twitter.

Another added, "That will get them hopping for sure. But will there be guns?"

Paul nodded. "One or two. Don't worry. I've got my bases covered."

Mike interrupted, "We better get a move on, or we'll be the ones getting the surprise."

Paul pointed to the side of the cave, indicating where he wanted them to meet. "Move along quickly and don't make a sound. We've got to surprise them, or we'll be dead meat."

No one questioned Paul or the choice of his words.

Before the two groups split up, Paul leaned against Mike and whispered, "Leave the head honcho to me. He's probably armed and dangerous."

Mike nodded then signaled to his group. They separated and somberly set out into the night, praying for God's protection.

Paul looked up as an eerie glow penetrated the darkness. The clouds broke into wisps, but no moonlight was visible. The hooting owls and other night creatures made him tense and overly aware of his every move. His neck felt tight. He thought it might snap at any moment.

Suddenly, the chanting stopped, and a shrill voice split the night. The hair on the back of Paul's neck stood up. He stood glued to the spot. Frozen.

Tension hung in the air like a cleaver waiting to drop on the head of its victim.

A small band of angels gathered in the woods disguised as woodland creatures. They rejoiced at the cover of darkness for the moonlight would betray their positions. Undercover, they could lead the mortals who surrounded themselves in prayer. With moonlight, the men may have relied too heavily upon their own resources. In prayer, they had much greater strength and allies of the King's realm.

Dark forces gathered in the cave, cackling with glee. The Overlord, Witchcraft, took the head seat and wrapped her garment around her. "You thought my methods too outdated, but look…" She pointed upward toward the cave. "I've done better than all of you."

His Eminence Pride stepped up. "If it wasn't for me working in their hearts, you'd be in the hot seat."

"And how about me?" A host of other vices cried. They began to quarrel.

"Silence!" The Prince of Division pronounced. "Our Master of the Dark Abyss approaches."

————⟫◦◦◦⟪————

A chilling breeze blew down from the north in the direction of the rock-faced wall. The dampness penetrated Mike's jacket and made him shiver. He prayed for their protection. Up ahead he watched as one of the others stumbled along the path, almost tripping over long clumps of field grass and small stones. Several of the men near him couldn't stop shaking. Despite the fear, Mike sensed a growing sense of confidence rising within.

As the men approached their destination, an oppressive heaviness fell on him like a dead weight. It seemed as if the whole rock wall was about to fall down, pulverizing him and the rest of the small troop. At first he struggled under its crushing weight.

Mike realized the spiritual battle. He dropped to his knees on the wet ground. The other men hurried to his side. Pastor Dave laid hands on Mike and prayed. The cowboy recalled the time just a few short months ago when he and his friend, Bob, went fishing. He remembered how God had come through for the both of them, though he regretted Bob never saw it that way. *A man's gotta make his own choice,* he concluded.

"I choose Jesus," Mike proclaimed out loud.

Liquid warmth surged through his body, crushing the oppressiveness. He heard a rustling of leaves and turned around.

Nothing.

Motioning to the other men to continue, Dave got up and followed the lanky cowboy into the night. Mike thanked the Lord for lifting the awful weight. He hoped his proclamation hadn't alerted the enemy.

By this time, the two groups had split. Mike led the right flank to the outer wall. The small group proceeded cautiously as they approached the cave's entrance. Mike thought he saw something hover around them, but he wasn't sure if his imagination was playing tricks on him.

He prayed for the blood of Jesus to protect them.

The small band of men proceeded toward the unknown, but they no longer shook with fear. Mike hoped they would not falter.

When they reached the side wall, he had them rest for a moment and pray.

"Dear Lord, guide us through this valley of the shadow of death."

Mike stuck his hands in his pockets and pressed his shoulder against the rock, sliding cautiously along the edge. The others followed suit.

The darkness engulfed them. As they inched closer to the entrance, strange noises erupted from the cave. The sounds disarmed them—otherworldly and unnatural.

Deep, unintelligible sounds rose as from the bowels of the earth.

The owls' hooting mixed with the cries. Searing-hot and freezing-cold sensations coursed up and down Mike's skin.

He feared they would all soon be dashed upon the rocks, bewitched by the sounds. He tried to ignore them. Knowing the others needed encouragement, he looked back, trying to spur them on. They forged ahead. *Yeah, though I walk...*

He watched Paul's group as they neared the entrance ahead of him and his men. It took great self-control for him not to leap ahead. He quickened his step until they were a few feet away. His heart pounded and threatened to push its way up to his throat as they reached the entrance. *Through the valley of the shadow...of death!*

The chanting stopped.

A chilling scream reverberated off the cave walls. Mike fell down on his knee and prayed, "Deliver us from evil."

Margo prayed for God's protection like never before. She felt like she weighed a thousand pounds as she tried to resist the urge to sleep, but her body wouldn't move, and her head swooned. Her last breath before she lost consciousness was a plea. *Lord, please send someone, anyone. Soon!*

30

Paul's arm shot in the air. He held up three fingers, signaling to Mike. Then he lowered one finger, mouthing the word *two*.

Mike's men got into their positions, taking the rocks and sticks out of their pockets they had gathered as they hiked.

Six men crouched, waiting to spring into action; eyes fixed on Paul.

"One!"

He leapt into action.

The left and right flanks united and rushed into the mouth of the cave, throwing sticks and stones onto the floor and sides of the cave.

The noise reverberated throughout, startling everyone, especially the robed priests. Paul spotted one of them clutching a small black book to his chest. He quickly hid it in the folds of his robe. Several others froze in place temporarily startled by such a rude interruption.

The young priestess sprang into the air, like a cat springing off a roof. She dove for the nearest one and attacked. Her nails ripped into soft flesh and drew blood.

Paul spotted Bill. His ex-partner drew a gun from his side pocket but couldn't get a fix on Paul. He barreled forward and slammed into Bill, toppling him. The gun clattered on the rock floor.

It came to a dead stop.

Paul wrestled Bill away from where the gun lay. He wrapped his legs around Bill's so he couldn't get up. Then he punched the creep square in the chin. One powerful blow after another. He was the stronger of the two, but Bill was quick. His ex-boss delivered a couple of quick punches to the side of Paul's face, but he retaliated with precise jabs to Bill's stomach.

"You lousy—" Bill sputtered as he feverishly tried to pry Paul off him, but he clung with all his strength and more. With God's help, he would bind this *strongman*.

<hr />

Paul yelled and signaled to Mike. "Over there, get Margo out of here, pronto! I'll take care of Bill."

Men were engaged in hand-to-hand combat, but Mike managed to avoid them. He followed Paul's pointing finger and found the young woman inside near the far wall, stretched out on a slab of stone. Her body lay limp; her long light-brown hair clung to her sweaty neck, and…Mike almost gagged. Margo's body was lying in a pool of blood. He prayed it was not her own.

He turned away from the hideous sight. His eyes darted about the room.

Searching.

He spotted a white sheet spread over a smaller table and he grabbed it. He spun around and lifted her body into his arms, wrapping her in the cloth.

During the few minutes when Mike was occupied with Margo, he'd hardly been aware of the raucous fighting raging all around him. Then the noise and confusion that had blurred into the background jumped to life when he picked up the young woman.

Two men attacked him, grabbing at his arms. They pawed at the girl, trying to pry her from his hands. Mike kicked them in the shins with his pointy cowboy boots. "I knew they'd come in handy," he remarked as he avoided their bodies. They doubled over in pain, giving Mike just the few moments he needed to elude them. He picked his way across the ground as carefully as possible, trying to avoid the men rolling around on the floor.

He felt like he was in a bubble of protection. The fight consumed everyone, like a barroom brawl, except for him and Margo. He wasn't sure which side was winning. All he saw was a tangle of black robes and bodies tumbling. One thought loomed uppermost in his mind: he had to get the young woman safely out of there.

As Mike inched his way past the tumbling mass of bodies, a woman hurled her body at him, nearly knocking the two of them over. She clawed and scratched at him with her long red nails and dug into Mike's face, drawing blood.

He puzzled at her incredible strength for such a skinny, weak-looking thing. She attacked with such ferociousness like a wild bear defending her cub. He tried to fend off his attacker by shoving her, but he couldn't use his hands if he wanted to keep Margo in his arms.

Not wanting to kick the young "lady" the way he had done to the men, he waited for just the right opportunity to back away and put some distance between them.

The moment came. As she surged forward, he stuck out his leg, and the enraged creature tripped over him. She sailed through the air and plunged to the stony floor.

He quickly jumped over the two men directly in front of him and dodged others who were engaged in combat. He yelled back to his comrades, "Code red," and shot out of the mouth of the cave like a salmon flying upstream out of water.

Outside the cave, Mike's eyes adjusted to the lack of light. It was physically darker there, but he felt lighter as the oppressive weight, which had nearly crushed his insides, slowly lifted. He shook his head and looked up to get his bearings.

The moon was still nowhere in sight, engulfed in clouds. Mike strained to orient himself in the right direction. *A city boy would be completely lost in the darkness of the night, but thank God I know my way around this place. I'll take the woods over the city any day.*

Mike adjusted the young woman in his arms and took off in the direction of the truck. His long strides gave him an advantage and his innate sense of direction supplied the edge he needed to outwit the band who would soon be at his heels.

He prayed his strength would hold, and he hoped his plan would work...not blow up in his face or worse yet...in Margo's.

Bill lay pinned to the cold stone floor as he wrestled to free himself from the traitor's grasp. Though Paul proved to be a strong adversary, Bill possessed more cunning. He had greater powers on his side and knew it was only a matter of time before he'd be released. As soon as Paul tired, Bill broke free and lunged for his gun. His fingers lay within inches. Stretching to reach it, he clasped the cold steel...like an old friend. In one fell swoop, he shot to his feet, brandishing the revolver.

His anger raged within as he steadied his pistol. Just as he aimed it, Paul attacked again, hurling his entire body into Bill's torso. The man was strong, but Bill felt the surge of strength stir in his veins. He appealed to the all-knowing eye, and a rush of power coursed through him. The assault temporarily pushed him back, but his lackey couldn't bring him down.

Bill shot two bullets against the cave wall, announcing the acquisition of his weapon. They ricocheted, and the noise exploded, catching the attention of those around him. He hoped to scare the intruders, if only for a few moments. Soon he would have the decided advantage. If he could corner both Paul and the man's inexperienced assistants, the victory would be his.

Calculating his moves from the corner of his eye, he spotted Paul on the other side of the cave, preparing to charge him again.

Bill moved like a cat.

He spun into position and aimed his gun at Paul's head and shouted, "You're mine, boy. All mine." He trapped Paul. "Put your hands behind your head." He smiled, knowing he was in charge. He felt his master's pleasure.

Paul obeyed. "I don't care, go ahead and kill me."

The master braced his weapon. "You moron. Did you think you could outsmart me, a high-ranking Mason?" He rammed the gun against Paul's temple. "Now you will pay—"

Booomm!

From a shadowed corner of the cave, a figure shot out of the darkness. The hefty frame, curled up in a ball, charged against the lady-killer's legs. Startled, Bill swayed and his arms shot straight up in the air. His trigger finger accidentally released another bullet. It hit the low ceiling and shot back down, grazing his own thigh.

Pain seared through Bill's skin. Crouching over, he checked his leg. His hand shook as he waved the gun and cursed, "You idiots."

Bill bent over to examine his wound. It was bleeding. Suddenly, another guy lurched at him from behind. "Why, you no-good—" With the impact, he doubled over and crumbled like a rag doll.

The gun clattered to the floor, spinning like a bottle in a child's game.

Paul and a robed figure dove for it.

Bill shot up. "What the devil are you doing?" His voice echoed in the dark chamber.

Everyone froze in their place.

Paul gained control of the gun. He felt the powers of darkness waiting for his move. "Give me that, you fool," the master demanded.

Paul shook his head and kept the gun steadily pointed at Bill's chest. "No," he replied through clenched teeth.

His old boss inched forward. "Who do you think you are?" He didn't respond, and Bill, looking like a demon, sneered. "You're a coward and you'd never pull the trigger."

Paul emptied the bullets from the gun and threw them helter-skelter. He shoved the empty gun in his pocket.

"You're a fool!" Bill turned around and signaled for help. Slowly, a few robed bodies stiffly stood up and fought to resume their threatening positions.

Then two other men, Lance and Dave, rose out of the dark shadows and attacked Bill full force from behind. He was unprepared, and Paul got in a hard blow to Bill's stomach. He doubled over and went down hard, crashing onto the floor.

His head slammed against the hard rock—out, stone cold!

"You bungling idiots!" the ferocious commander yelled. "Where were all the troops when the enemy masterminded this rescue?"

A group of drooling serpentine demons faced the edge of a fiery abyss, shaking. One particular contorted figure among them spoke. "Sir, we were standing guard over the church as you ordered."

"You fools! Our man Bill had taken care of them. You should have been helping him. Many will suffer for your fatal mistake!"

Satan stood up and lifted his enormous wings. He fanned the furnace below till the flames were licking their feet. In one swoop of his segmented wing, he sent a thousand hurtling off the precipice into the fiery inferno below.

Screaming and cackling echoed through the dungeon as thousands fell writhing into oblivion.

The master retracted his wings and glared. "Would anyone else like to join them?"

A thousand bulging eyes stared in silence.

"Good, now off to your posts...all of you!" he bellowed. "And don't let them slip through your hands," he snarled. "Or you'll all be burnt toast!"

31

Margo struggled to release her heavy eyelids. They opened for a moment, and the sight startled her. The corners of the room shifted positions back and forth, overlapping, creating a geometric pattern in her head like a kaleidoscope. Margo groaned and shut her eyes. The dizziness drove her crazy. She clenched a fist and opened her eyes again. "Why won't the room stop spinning?" she moaned.

She addressed a man in white who looked like a Picasso painting—several images of the same face multiplied themselves in profile. She couldn't stand it anymore and closed her eyelids. The whirling didn't stop.

The voice responded to a question she must've asked. "Are you awake now? Just blink if you can hear me."

Angered, Margo obeyed. *Of course I'm awake, can't you see I'm in pain?* she screamed inside. The man in white bent down, next to her, but Margo closed her eyes at the rapid movement.

"You're in the hospital, young lady, recovering from an overdose—"

Overdose. Margo's face turned beet red at the insinuation, but she didn't have the ability to form a coherent answer. While she thought, another voice sailed from the opposite corner, as from another planet.

"From the looks of things, you're lucky to be alive." The voice bombarded Margo's senses.

Oh, real luck, Margo thought. *Why was God allowing this to happen to her...again? She was trying to listen to Him, but had she missed His voice?* In her head, she cried out with all her heart, *God help me!*

Margo opened her eyes wide and stared up at the multiperspective face, not quite properly aligned. She tried to focus and make the images come together, but it hurt too much.

The hurt didn't go away. She tossed and turned while holding her head to make it stop spinning. Grotesque figures danced on the screen of her mind, appearing like vapors and disappearing again. They frightened and maddened her at the same time as she tried to place them in context. They looked familiar, like in a nightmare but more real. *Where had she seen them before?*

In the midst of her duress, the first voice spoke and told her to relax. "With the dose we've detected in your blood, you will probably suffer from hallucinations."

Hallucinations? Was that her problem now on top of everything else? She didn't know what they were talking about. And where was Chris? She missed him terribly.

Her mind swam in different directions though she summoned enough strength to ask. "Why am I here?"

"You were brought to the hospital a couple of hours ago by several men who said they rescued you from your murderers, but that's for the police to decide. I found quite a few drugs in your system."

She struggled to ask. *Murderers? Drugs? What are you talking about?* She held her head down. "And where is my husband?"

"I'm sure the hospital has notified him."

Margo's speech trembled. "Then why isn't he here?" She knew Chris would come no matter what. Something didn't seem right.

The calm tone spoke again, "I'm sure he'll be here soon. It's three o'clock in the morning."

The doctor gave her an injection and she flinched. "Now just relax. This will help you to sleep...and take care of everything else."

261

Margo's tense body relaxed a little. She hoped sleep would overtake her as she fought to erase the haunting images that plagued her mind. *Were they real or just a terrible, terrible nightmare?* She hoped the latter.

⋙◆⋘

Paul's mind raced down the highway as his car sped away from the hairpin turn. Mike sat as his side, quiet, most likely recovering. Bill lay in the back of his car tied up in knots while Paul wrestled with what to do. If he notified the police, then his former boss would surely implicate him in many other crimes. If he let him go scot-free, then he would surely wind up on his doorstep someday.

Paul vowed never to live under Bill's shadow again. Patting the gun in his left pocket, he contemplated taking care of the situation himself. He'd gone that route many times before.

Paul felt like a kid again, watching a clip from an old cartoon. On one hand, an angel perched on his shoulder whispered in his ear "Paul, do what is right." However, the other side pulled Paul in the opposite direction. "You know what you need to do. Just get rid of your problem, forever!"

Bill rustled about in the backseat. Mike turned around to check on him. "Still unconscious. Thank God." He slowly shifted in his seat and looked at Paul. "So did you come up with a plan?"

Torn up inside, Paul shook his head and avoided answering the question. "Just make sure the belt and rope are tight around him." He gestured toward the backseat. "Or we'll be the ones who'll be tied up in knots." He added, "If we're lucky, that is. Be ready for a fight if he wakes up sooner than expected."

He stepped on the gas pedal, and his car quickly responded. They were doing seventy in a fifty-mile speed limit road. Though accustomed to speed, Paul laughed nervously. "Hey, this is one time we could use a cop."

Mike turned and faced Paul without smiling. "No joke, son."

Chris paced the floor of the hospital corridor with his head drooped down, looking at the green and white specks on the floor. "I want to see my wife," he demanded, but no one responded. After all evening searching for her, scouring the streets and back roads of New Coven, calling all her friends, and dying for any information about her whereabouts, he got a late night phone call from the hospital and raced over. Now that he knew she was here, they wouldn't let him see her...not yet.

He'd been told the doctors weren't finished examining her. Yet how could they keep him from seeing his wife for over an hour? He felt like busting open the doors. But what good with that do? Instead, he turned to prayer. *Dear God, please let her be alive and show us why all this is happening.*

Jessica sat by herself in the newly renovated bar turned pub restaurant and ate the last bite of her sandwich. She drained her Coke and found herself daydreaming about Bill, her rescuer from the other day. Hearing he now owned this place, she hoped to get a glimpse of him to thank him for helping her out. The thought of him made her tingle all over. He was nothing like her lame husband, Mark, and his divided attention. Bill's eyes looked straight into hers and read all her desire. She hoped to get to know him better as soon as she was free of Mark. *But where was that handsome devil?*

After a long wait at the hospital, and a lot of red tape, Chris and Margo finally arrived home. Chris put his head in his hands and wept at the sight of Margo in her own bed. He stroked her tangled cropped hair with his damp hand and thanked God she was resting peacefully. He had almost lost her...again. He looked at the clock—four thirty in the afternoon, exactly twelve hours after Lance told him, to the best of his ability, what she had faced.

Ritual murder.

Waves of nausea struck him. He'd suspected foul play up at the cave site, but never, never did he think they—whoever *they* were—would stoop to such measures.

Blood sacrifice!

To think that Margo narrowly escaped this fate made Chris sick. This can't really be happening, he argued, but it was as real as the hand in front of him, balled into a fist. His mind swam with the details. His vivid imagination kept replaying the rescue scene Lance had reluctantly told him. The jumble of recent events began to fit together. They started to form a picture—not a very pleasant one at all, especially for Christians.

Chris wanted to know the whole truth. This was only a part of it. Margo had gotten caught in the middle of something terribly evil...like a fly trapped in a spider web. But thank God, He freed her.

Kneeling, he prayed. *Dear God, thank You for protecting my dear Margo.* He stroked her hair once again, then continued. *Please protect the men who rescued...* the images loomed in his mind, and his face fell flat on the bed...*Oh God, thank You, thank You, thank You that...she is alive!*

⇒◆⇐

Lance rang the doorbell to the Piersons' house and waited. Chris answered, and the elder embraced him in a show of brotherly love and concern as he'd never felt before.

"How's she doing?"

Chris shook his head, and Lance studied him for a moment. The young man looked liked he'd aged a decade.

He motioned Lance to the living room. "Sit down and I'll tell you. We really need to pray for her. But first tell me about this ordeal and how you got involved. I forgot what you said. When you called, I only wanted to hear about Margo."

Lance sat. He didn't want to give Chris more gruesome details about the ritual, so he chose to focus on explaining how he got there. "You know I'm friends with the senior pastor of the Kingsland Church, Dave Light. He called me about an important prayer meeting, and he thought I should be there, so I went. When we started to pray, Paul the guy who came to church with Bill one day, burst in and told us someone needed our help 'real bad.' That someone turned out to be Margo."

Chris dropped his head. "Strange. Paul looked like the last person to help us. He seemed more like a gangster who'd mow us down if we got in his way."

"Yeah, it's strange how God works sometimes. His plans certainly aren't ours. But this whole incident with Margo unearths a much bigger problem. One which affects the whole church and not just us."

"Yeah, I thought about that."

"It's a subject not too many people—even Christians—want to believe, even though the Bible talks about it." Lance leaned toward Chris. "It has to do with demons and satanic worship right here in New Coven."

Chris shot up. "What? People worship that deceiver right here in the middle of our pleasant little valley! No wonder Vince wants to keep this under wraps. Imagine that in our statement of faith!"

"Yes, he wanted me to keep you quiet, but I said no. We need to let the church know what we're up against. Especially since Bill had become one of our lead contributors and had penetrated into the church. A real wolf in sheep's clothing."

"Yeah, and I was fleeced, but Margo sensed there was something wrong about him the whole time."

"Well, the Kingsland Free Church has been praying against the plans of the evil one, unknowingly praying for us—and others, no doubt."

Chris paced back and forth. "This must relate to everything Margo's been experiencing—the nightmares, the visions, and when she can remember, the stone!"

"Yes, the stone is very much a part of it, but I'll tell you more about it later. Let's pray now." Lance opened up his Bible and turned to a scripture from Ephesians. He read it. "For we do not wrestle with flesh and blood, but against principalities, against powers, against the rulers of darkness of this age against spiritual hosts of wickedness in heavenly places."

32

Bill sat on the regulation cot issued in jail, scheming his way out of his situation. An orange uniform replaced his gray tailored suit, but he didn't plan on staying in this atrocious costume for long. He cursed under his breath, outraged by Paul's audacity to betray him. Bill's superior, a Thirty-Third Degree Master Mason of the Ancient Royal Order, would take care of Paul. *He'll pay with his life for this one.*

The passing of a correction officer on his rounds interrupted Bill's thoughts. He turned his back to the guard and snickered. *This won't last long.* He had connections—big connections, like the rich and powerful Illuminati. Though he had not attained to this height, they would arrange his bail, no matter how much it was. On top of it, his crime connections could spring him out of this lousy two-bit jail or hire a crafty lawyer.

When the heavy-footed jail guard passed, Bill stood up and paced the floor, running his fingers through his hair. Bill wanted out soon, if not now. His mind raced through all sorts of scenarios from the last couple of weeks. He was so near to infiltrating the church, had a few women in the palm of his hands, except for that infuriating potter. Now he would have to skip town. *Too bad. Anyway, she won't be long for this world, and neither will Paul.* Bill laughed again, a sinister sound that started in the bottom of his throat and bubbled up until it grew into a loud guffaw that took total control.

One of the inmates yelled from another cell. "Shut up or I'll punch your lights out."

But Bill wouldn't stop. He continued all the more, pacing back and forth on the floor, laughing hysterically. Within a couple of minutes, the laugh turned into a high-pitched snicker.

The other prisoner rattled the bars. "If you don't shut your trap, I'll personally wipe that grin off your face. You won't eat for weeks."

Bill snickered all the more and yelled across the corridor. "You don't know who you're messing with, little boy."

A dark slimy shadow passed over the jail cell and oozed between the bars. The other guys shut up.

———◆———

Margo bolted upright in bed, squinting from the rays of light filtering through the bedroom curtains. Glad that morning had dawned, she stretched her arms out wide. It was a terrible night indeed, tossing and turning from horrifying nightmares, one right after another. But something good came out of it. She felt like the Holy Spirit purged and purified her body, mind, and spirit of a terrible filth. The taste of their bitter presence was gone.

Slowly the reality of what happened to her came to light. Images from the ceremony taunted her. The thought of the cold slab table bought goose bumps to her flesh. Indeed this was a terrible evil, as the letter forewarned. But what could she have done to ward it off? Thank God she was spared. To think she had almost lost her life. She cried out, "Chris!"

Weeping, Margo flopped down on the bed. She heard his footsteps running in the hallway and looked up. He rushed into the bedroom.

"Chris, I saw it. I saw it all!"

"Saw what, Margo?" He moved closer to the bed.

She sobbed even louder. "The whole horrible ceremony."

Chris sat down and held her in his arms. It felt so good to feel the warmth of his embrace. Margo buried her head in his chest and sobbed for a few more minutes and let it all out. He stroked her hair, and she gained enough composure to speak.

"It's not just the terrible things they did to me that I'm crying about, but it's what they've got planned for other Christians. Oh, Chris…" A sob caught in her throat. A torrent of words spilled out about the ordeal. "They tied me up and drugged me, but they didn't knock me out all the way, but just enough so I couldn't fight back. They bought me into a dark chamber, lights flickering, chanting, the smell…oh, the putrid stench of blood, mixed with a heavy incense. I nearly vomited." She choked out the words.

Chris held her and stoked her head of cropped hair. "You don't need to say anything more if you don't want to."

Margo's body shook. "I'm freezing. Give me more covers."

Chris wrapped the blankets tighter around her.

"It was worse than a nightmare. The chanting, over and over again, the candles flickering, shadows passing in front of me." Margo spread out her hands. "Something touching my body. "Then," she screamed, "blood dripped on me, and then they dripped it on—"

Margo slumped down on the pillow in exhaustion. "It's so frustrating, I can't remember. I'm missing an important piece of the puzzle. I just can't figure it out, but I saw names floating by somehow, some way."

Chris held his wife's hand. "Is it the stone?"

Margo drew a blank. "What stone?"

Bill stayed up half the night thinking over what his lawyer had told him, to hang tough until he could see him.

He didn't want to wait. Waiting meant trouble. The longer he sat in jail, the longer Margo had to recover. Anyway, he hated it here. The animals next to him kept him up half the night, rattling their bars and banging them with their shoes. He couldn't even shower without permission. He hadn't been bossed around since childhood when his father—if you could call him that—barked at him and packed a mean punch.

He shook his head and dismissed the image of his cruel father. His thoughts were interrupted by the sound of a correction officer's shuffle. He shouted to him, "Hey, you in the blue, I demand to talk to my lawyer. *Now!*"

The overweight man approached slowly and grabbed hold of a bar with one hand. He turned his large bulldog face around and glared at Bill. "Well, buddy, you're in jail now, and you don't get what you want when you want it." He laughed out loud. "This ain't the Ritz or the Hilton." He turned away and called back over his shoulder. "The food's even worse."

Bill sneered and narrowed his eyes as the heavy-framed man sauntered down the corridor. "Okay, wise guy, wait till I get ahold of my lawyer again. I'll sue you for maltreatment. You don't know who you're dealing with. Just you wait." Bill vowed to prosecute the jerk for what little he was worth. He'd also change lawyers if his present one didn't get him out on bail today. It didn't matter that bail was set at $250,000. Chump change for his boss—that is, the master.

Though he didn't give a rat's tail, Bill was curious why bail was set at a quarter million. No murder took place. A trial would have to prove motive and intent, so why such a big fat sum for such a crummy little county pokey? Whatever, it didn't matter. *Once I get out of this two-bit hole, there'll be no witnesses left to testify against me by the time I get to trial. That's already in the works, thanks to Sal.* A grin spread over Bill's face as he thought of a plan. *I'll just help speed up the process and rat out a few of them in the meantime.*

Margo awoke the next day to the noonday sun streaming through her curtains and warming her face. She opened her eyes and looked into the face of her concerned husband. She smiled. Her mind felt clearer than it had in days. Puzzle pieces nudged into place.

"How are you doing?"

"Much better, but I have a headache again."

"I'll get you some aspirin."

"No, that's okay. Stay here with me. There's a lot I need to talk to you about. I'm so sorry how I've acted toward you." She leaned over and put her head on his chest. "I really haven't been myself ever since I laid eyes on Bill." Margo shivered. "I knew I should have gone with my first impression of him, but he bewitched me."

Chris reached out and held her hands. "I hate to admit it, but you were right." He paused. "I must've come under his spell too."

"Chris, we have to find that stone. You know, the one we found up in the cave." She looked up at him for recognition.

His face lit up. "You remember it now?"

She frowned. "What do you mean?"

"You haven't been able to recall anything about if for almost three days."

She bolted upright. "Oh, Chris, this is far worse than we thought. Someone knows we know and is trying to destroy us." As she looked into her husband's eyes, he seemed to understand everything.

Another piece slipped into place.

Tears streamed down her face in streaks. "This is the terrible evil that the letter spoke about. Now I understand. We are not the only ones in danger. We have to act soon before someone else gets killed."

Chris knitted his eyebrows. "Someone else?"

"Yes, someone named Joy."

"You mean the woman who had the prayer meeting in Kingsland the night of your abduction? But you never met her."

Margo bit her lip. "Ahhh…I saw her name on…the stone."

Like always, Bill Guiles managed to get his way, at least for the time being. His lawyer did some wheeling and dealing, and the bail was met. The $250,000 came from various businessmen in and out of town, but the largest contribution came from another source. Bill didn't really care who came up with the money as long as he was free. Though he was a little bit curious about the mysterious contributor, he didn't dwell on it long. He was just glad to be out of that stinking dive.

Before he left, he made sure to get his Rolex watch back. He turned it over and looked at it carefully to make sure the idiots didn't scratch it. Before he left the place, he also got the name of the correction officer who laughed at him. Someday he'd get even, but for now, he didn't plan on staying in the area. Once Bill stepped through the doors and into the fresh air and sunshine, he didn't care what his probation officer told him.

He jumped into his shiny black Jaguar, revved the engine, and peeled out. "Sorry, baby," he patted the leather steering wheel. "We gotta make time and find Paul."

Chris was instructed to notify the police as soon as his wife was feeling well enough to provide a coherent story regarding her abduction. She'd been questioned before leaving the hospital, but her story sounded more like a sci-fi novel than reality. If it hadn't been for Lance's explanation, he wouldn't have believed it himself.

Chris tried to clarify some details for the officer on the phone, but the man asked him to bring Margo down to the station. She would need to identify the suspects from pictures. The police informed Chris that Mr. Eville had been released on bail, but he was confused. They knew him as Bill Guiles, not Eville.

"Is that Mr. Guiles you're talking about?"

The guy on the other end went to check. "Yup, Guiles is his middle name. His last name is Eville."

"Are you kidding?" While he absorbed the new information about Bill's last name, Chris shouted into the phone. "You let him out on bail after what she told you?"

"Sorry, but he met bail. We don't have a very coherent testimony from her. That's why it's vital for her to come down to the station."

The ring tone from Bill's cell phone startled him as he headed south out of town. He wasn't going to pick it up, but he recognized the number as the Master's. He touched the screen and answered. "How goes my fellow brother's craft?"

The smooth voice on the other end laughed. "Well, my brother, well. So how does it feel to have such good friends?" Before Bill could respond, the other added, "You know, we had to pull some strings to spring you."

Uncharacteristically, Bill swallowed hard and loosened his collar. "Thanks, you know I'm good for it."

The voice came in loud and clear as if he were next door. "Yeah, we know that, boy, but we're just making sure you don't skip town before you consult with us. By the way, don't you want to meet your mystery savior, I mean…client."

Bill knew he meant the other bail contributor. "Sure, name the day and place."

The husky voice chuckled. "Tonight at our favorite restaurant… by yourself. Be there. Remember, big brother is watching you."

Angered, Bill slammed the phone down and punched the leather car seat. He wanted to get out of this one-horse town before the effects of the drugs and his hypnotism wore off Margo.

Most patients of his would stay under his hypnotic suggestions until he signaled, but this sassy girl was strong-willed and had a deep relationship with that God of hers! He had hypnotized and mesmerized other religious people in the past, but Margo stood out from the crowd.

With her, the memory loss and power of suggestion might last for only a few more days. She knew enough information to incriminate him and several other people. *Wait a minute, that's it!* Bill smiled and chuckled to himself. The guys would probably want to find out just how much this Margo chick knows. *When I tell them everything, she'll be on their hit list.*

Bill pressed on the gas pedal and sped happily along.

She was good as gone.

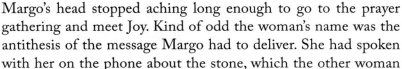

Margo's head stopped aching long enough to go to the prayer gathering and meet Joy. Kind of odd the woman's name was the antithesis of the message Margo had to deliver. She had spoken with her on the phone about the stone, which the other woman had also seen in a vision. But how could Margo tell her she saw Joy's name etched on it?

When Margo arrived, Joy hugged her warmly, and tears filled her eyes. "I'm so happy to meet you." She looked Margo in the eye. "You seem well for all you've been though."

Margo hugged her back. "Yes, thank you for all your prayers."

Joy led Margo to a cozy kitchen lined with floral wallpaper and porcelain teapots. She prepared a cup of fragrant Earl Grey.

It was one of Margo's favorite, and after a few sips, it helped her feel more at home. She could talk about it now knowing prayer would follow. She broached the subject. "So what did the stone look like in your vision?"

Joy sat down and told her. "It was round and had two different sides. One side had inscriptions that looked like children's simple drawings of animals with a big eye in the middle and a birdlike creature. Along the edge were some odd rectangles. Oh yeah, and some of them had dots in them."

Margo didn't remember about the rectangles, but so far, the rest of what Joy described hit the mark. *But did the woman know what they meant?*

After half an hour or so, people began to trickle in for the meeting. As soon as everyone sat down and introductions were made, Margo related bits and pieces of her life over the last few weeks. She provided as much detail as she could remember and which she thought necessary for everyone to be able to pray accurately. By the time she had reached the part of the story about the cave ceremony, many believers were already in prayer. Joy had told them the basics, but Margo gave them more insight into how it all related, though she skipped the gruesome details, which she herself had repressed.

She hesitated for a few moments then looked over at Joy, who walked over and gave her a hug, which warmed Margo inside. Ray stood up as well as Chris, along with others, and they formed a little semicircle. Three of them laid hands on her shoulders and prayed quietly.

Margo closed her eyes, and she felt a tingle course though her body. She saw herself clothed in white and blowing a trumpet as though sounding an alarm for combat, like the Israelites. By the time they had finished praying, a deep peace surrounded her in spite of the task that lay before her.

After the prayer, Margo took out a folded piece of paper. "This is a reconstruction of what I saw on the stone, first with my husband, then later when I was kidnapped."

She unfolded it, and the group looked at the maze of symbols and stylized pictures.

"The stone wheel is divided into twelve equal parts, called registers. I learned this term as an art student. This register contains pairs of different symbols, pictures, bars, and lines." She pointed to the appropriate sectors.

"Underneath each symbol, Joy and I filled in what letters we could." The crowd strained to see.

"Since I don't have the actual rubbings anymore, only what I copied, a number of the symbols are missing, which neither of us can recall. Therefore different letters could be inserted. However, it is evident these symbols make up names."

A few women gasped.

"We supplied various names, which could be constructed from each set. Since this is hypothetical information, I wrote it on another piece of paper." Margo produced another piece from her pocket.

"You may know some of these people. That is why you were asked to this meeting." Margo looked around the room. "Some of them may even be you."

<hr>

Bill thought through his options and punched in a speed dial number on his cell phone. He'd need to spend the day within the county line, and he saw no better place than the Carsons' home, as long as Rich wasn't there. When a woman's voice answered, Bill felt pleasantly surprised. He tried to sound businesslike just in case Rich was at home. "Hello, Mrs. Carson, this is Bill. I was wondering if your husband is home? I have some business to discuss with him."

The voice on the other end whispered softly, "No, he's not home right now. Is there something *I* can help you with?"

"Yes, there is, as matter of fact." Bill tried to feel out what she knew about the whole incident, but it sounded like she didn't know a thing.

"I don't know if you saw the paper today or not, but I'll be needing to discuss my business arrangement with your husband. I'll also need a place to stay until dinner this evening. Do you think he would mind if I stopped at your place and took care of some business?"

Melanie replied in an inviting voice.

"Of course *I* wouldn't mind. As far as Rich is concerned, if it helps him with his business, he won't mind either."

Bill chuckled. "Okay then. I'll be there in fifteen minutes."

Melanie greeted Bill at the door wearing a tight black chenille dress, which showed off her assets and very shapely figure. Bill approved. She seemed a little surprised at his appearance, so he tried to explain away his unkempt look. She nodded and didn't seem to suspect anything. He made sure everything looked very official and brought along his black leather business case. She invited him into the living room.

"So when will Rich be home?" He hoped not too soon.

"Not until five."

He opened up his briefcase and took out some papers. "I could explain all this to you now, or we could relax a little until Rich gets home. I wouldn't mind a cup of coffee." He stared in Melanie's eyes and felt her weakening, so unlike Margo.

Melanie smoothed her dress. "We don't have to deal with this right away. I'll make some coffee, or we could have wine instead."

"Sure, whatever you want." He didn't want to be too anxious. Wine would tip the scales in his favor, but he didn't need it.

She smiled, and a seductive look came over her. He knew the spirit well, and he would have his way.

As she left the room, his eyes followed the gentle sway of her hips and the curve of her waist and thighs. When she disappeared into the next room, he picked up the morning paper and noticed he wasn't on the front. *Good*, he thought, *hopefully the story is buried in the middle section somewhere.* He scanned the paper looking for any mention of the story.

Bill looked up as the appealing woman sauntered back into the room with two glasses of wine. He complimented her, knowing she needed it. "Did your husband ever tell you how ravishingly beautiful you look in that dress?"

Melanie giggled. "Who, Rich? Never."

She sat down next to Bill, and he took her hand in his and looked straight into her eyes. "Well, he's a fool."

The pretty young wife blushed, and the two of them toasted. "To a wonderful afternoon."

Bill moved closer to her, and he continued to stare straight into her eyes. He watched her chest move up and down as her breathing began to quicken. Within a few moments, he would get what he wanted. Who cared about Margo? She'd be out of his way soon enough.

The people surrounded Margo and Joy in a circle of prayer. Their husbands were petitioning God when one of the other men, Mark, spoke up. He startled Margo.

"In the name of Jesus Christ, we come against the spirit of witchcraft and idolatry, which has harassed these couples, especially this young woman." He laid his hand on Margo's forehead. "We come against a controlling spirit, and we break whatever power it has gained over this sister's mind."

Chris must have called Mark to come to the meeting, and though Margo didn't feel very comfortable with his prayer at first, she noticed the headache from before had disappeared.

Another man stood up and took off his belt and wrapped it around his legs. He prayed in a loud commanding voice, "We bind you, Satan, in the name of Jesus Christ and your spirits of division intent on breaking apart Christian marriages."

A hush fell over the small congregation. The man with the belt on his legs fell to his knees. One of the women prayed over him. "We break the spirit of division in the heart of husbands and wives. We come against the demonic forces that influence men to indulge their egos and women to follow their emotions."

The man on his knees spoke softly, "We repent of this sin, oh Lord, and the division in our heart, which keeps us from wholly following You. Bind us together, Lord, so we may strengthen each other. Help us to stand firm against the attacks of the enemy."

Margo examined her own heart. Her attitude toward Chris faltered lately. And hadn't she made remarks against Vince, adding to the division? She felt convicted.

She heard other people repenting.

One woman cried, "Forgive me for my infatuation with another man. Help me not to give into this temptation."

A holy silence descended. A few men lay down face to the floor. After the repentance, peace filled the air. It penetrated Margo's spirit. God's presence was so strong no one could move.

She felt a shift in her heart and in the heavens. Yet Margo sensed there would be an even worse battle up ahead and darker evil threatening these people's lives. Just like the letter said...*a diabolical evil!*

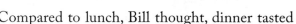

Compared to lunch, Bill thought, dinner tasted bland. The chef overcooked the lobster, and it lay half eaten on his plate. He pushed it aside in disgust. His companions didn't seem to notice. He drained his drink and loosened his tie.

With nothing to do, Bill fiddled with his fork. Previously caught off guard when introduced to the new investors, Bill struggled to regain his composure. He recognized the two men from the other night's activity—one the owner of a local newspaper and the other a cop. Neither acknowledged him. An awkward situation since Bill liked to be in control. Both men helped finance Bill's bail, and he knew absolute silence would be required of him.

Bill coughed and asked nervously, "So, where's my lawyer, brother? I thought we'd talk some strategy."

The head honcho of their 'illuminated' business associates, a heavyset man, impeccably dressed in a three-piece Oscar d'Lorenzo silk suit and tie, flicked a few cigar ashes on his cloth napkin, and smiled broadly. "No strategy tonight, Bill. Just wanted to make sure you know what's expected of you."

"Don't worry, I won't squeal on anyone."

One of the other members, a well-known psychiatrist, cleared his throat. "As you know, *Bill*, the power of suggestion introduced in hypnotism can be very powerful for those more easily swayed, but for the few strong-minded, it doesn't last long. Once this young potter regains her memory, she will begin to put some pieces together. Without a doubt, she will implicate you." He hesitated and looked straight at Bill. "But we are worried about the broader ramifications."

The off-duty cop spoke up. "Yeah, the little number was in the office just this morning, supplying more details than you'd like to know about, buddy."

Bill had never been referred to as *buddy* before, and he didn't like it one bit. If he weren't in this position, bailed out by their filthy money, he would have knocked that cop's block right off his shoulders. Instead, he coolly replied to the whole group. "You underestimate my powers, sirs. I can handle this little nuisance. And as far as being coerced into talking"—he leaned over the table—"I have superior powers that enable me to control my mind and others under the most severe circumstances."

The large man laughed heartily and slapped Bill on the back. "That's my boy. One thing you don't lack is ego and a way with women. You have our permission and whatever resources we can supply. Go get her, Bill."

33

Vince tossed the remains of the day-old newspaper into the garbage. The article he cut out didn't reveal a whole lot. Good thing. And the reporting, just plain poor—missing information, misquoted statements, in general full of editorial comment rather than facts. Better that way though. The reporter didn't pry too far into Margo's personal life other than stating she was a local businesswoman and owned a studio, the Pottery Shed. The New Way Fellowship, nor his name as head elder, hadn't been mentioned. Thank goodness.

On the other hand, he felt annoyed the article implied Margo's association with Bill was more than just business. The reporter quoted her as saying, "He visited my studio several times at night when I was alone, and I sold him some of my more expensive vases." It didn't take a genius to read between the lines. It wouldn't look good to other members of the church.

He paced back and forth in his living room. *It's a shame*, he thought. *Bill seemed like such a nice guy and gave generously to the church. I hope this gets cleared up and people will accept him back. Anyway, we're not supposed to judge those who don't know the Lord yet*, he rationalized, *but those who are already in the house of God. I'll need to confront Margo about this activity. I don't know what's happening to the women in this church.* Vince shook his head and continued to pace.

First, Jessica up and leaves Mark for some mysterious guy, and now Rich reports Melanie has been mooning over someone, but she won't admit to it. She had called him earlier to discredit the article and say Bill was a gentleman. Vince hoped she was telling the truth. He didn't think Margo got involved with Bill, but he may have fallen for her. After all, she had a dynamite figure along with good looks and brains.

Vince lingered for a moment on his mental picture of Margo and stopped pacing. His wife called to him, "When are you coming to bed?"

Startled, he yelled back, "Not until later."

⟶◆⟵

That evening, the prayer meeting didn't end until past midnight. Margo felt encouraged and refreshed as she went to bed. Now that she was able to remember and share what she knew, a great weight lifted off her shoulders.

Her disappointment over a small article about her in the *New Coven Messenger* also dissipated. The reporter had twisted almost all the facts and left out the information about the kidnapping. He'd tucked in a few lines about her business dealings with Bill Guiles, of all things. When Ray suggested she contact someone from a newspaper in Kingsland, she felt better.

"Perhaps they'll give you a little more truthful coverage," he encouraged.

She planned on contacting a reporter the next morning, though she wouldn't reveal all the facts, just enough to raise people's awareness.

Maybe the skimpy article in the *New Coven Messenger* worked out better after all. For one thing, she wouldn't look like a total jerk in front of the other members in the art guild. Maybe it would be best if a different newspaper not so close to home revealed a little more of the truth, though she planned on keeping the information about the stone completely confidential

282

to a small group of Christians. She didn't want to be branded a "kook" or "wacko." She just wanted to let the community know some dangerous people lived among them, especially one in particular—Bill Eville. Now she knew his real last name.

Paul stared at the picture on the front cover of the newspaper in disbelief. No doubt about it. He knew it all too well. Bill's black Jaguar, smashed into the side of the rock cliff wall!

The article indicated, "The brakes failed, while a man, thirty-two years old, identified as Bill Eville, had apparently been speeding down the mountain road when he was unable to slow his vehicle down on the hairpin turn. The car sailed over the railing and smashed into the rock cliff. Judging from the damage done to the car, the man must have been doing around 60 in a 15 mph zone."

"Whew!" Paul shook his head. "What in the world got into Bill? He knew that turn was a death trap for anyone going over thirty. He must have been infuriated about something."

Paul scanned the rest of the article. "Unfortunately, the airbag did not engage, and an investigation as to its failure will take place. The remains of the body were not found, though blood samples matching his blood type were recovered. The head of the EMT's force, Jude Rath, reports, 'With the impact of the crash and the damage done to the vehicle, it is highly unlikely that the victim escaped to safety.' The police suspect foul play."

Paul lowered the newspaper and swore under his breath. He knew Bill would be under surveillance from the society, but they sure wasted no time in eliminating him. But why would they steal his body?

A light dawned. He laughed nervously. *Would he be next?*

He'd moved away from the big city to get away from this garbage, and now look who's knocking on his back door, the devil himself. He needed to call Margo and warn her and then hightail it out of there!

Paul ran into the bedroom, grabbed some clothes, and stuffed them into his black bag. He threw open the closet door and took out the suit hanging in the closet. He slipped his pistol under his belt.

Feeling guilty, he looked up toward the ceiling and spoke. "Okay, Lord, I know you're my protection, but you just might need a little help if those guys are after us too. I thought I was through with this." He waved the gun. "But it looks like things are heating up around here."

Before he hopped into his car, Paul did a quick check of the brakes and other major systems. He didn't want to end up like Bill, if he really was dead. Although no really dangerous turns awaited him, he knew he'd be a target soon, especially since he recently changed loyalties. On top of it all, he organized Margo's rescue.

Fortunately, he escaped being mentioned in the papers, and he wanted it to remain that way. Before he left the driveway, he opened the trunk of the car. Everything checked out okay.

When he arrived at the Piersons' house, Paul decided to pull the car all the way into the driveway, close to the barn studio. He looked around first to make sure no one watched and removed the contents of the trunk. Weighed down with a heavy load wrapped under his loose trench coat, he lumbered to the backdoor. His muscles strained from what he carried, and he propped himself against the doorframe.

As soon as Chris opened the door, Paul shot into the kitchen. He lumbered to the bathroom down the hallway and left a lighter man. Rushing out of the washroom, he collided with Margo. "Sorry there, sweetie," Paul smiled sheepishly.

Margo brushed her sweater off and looked up at him. "Chris told me you called, c'mon, let's talk in the living room."

On the way there, Paul wasted no time. "I've gotta talk fast with you guys. They'll be after me soon." He burst into the living room where Chris waited. "I'm gonna skip town right away. I'll need you to do me favor and act like a decoy."

Chris sat down on the couch. "Wait a second, Paul. Who are you talking about?"

"The same people who did away with Bill. They'll be after me soon, and then…you guys next, or at least Margo."

"Are you saying Bill is dead?"

"The newspapers are sure making it look that way. Didn't you read about it?"

"You mean the article about me?" Margo questioned.

"No, today's news. Either he's out of their way, or they're playing a game."

"But why did they eliminate one of their valuable assets?" Chris wanted to know.

"I can tell you why. Bill knew too much. He was very powerful. The way he could manipulate people's minds was frightening, even to me. Maybe they were afraid he'd start controlling them." He coughed. "I dunno why for sure, but he's out of their way, and now there's me." He shook the change in his pocket like he used to.

Chris looked straight into Paul's eyes. "Who are they?"

Paul trembled. "Sorry, I can't take the risk of you knowing who. They have ways of extracting information from people, and I'd rather not have you tortured more than you've been already."

"But if they're out after me anyway," Margo interjected, "what does it matter? Wouldn't it be better if we knew who was out after us?"

Chris interrupted. "Paul, do you know who these guys are?"

He shook his head. "Not the big boss, some sophisticated wealthy guy. Bill called him illuminated or something like that. I never had to meet him, but sure, I met the guys at the cave before. I don't know 'em personally, but I'd recognize them in a lineup. They're out there, and they just might not like me knowing them, especially since I led the rescue." He turned toward Margo. "You gotta be careful. They know you saw them even though you were drugged and their faces were covered. They still might be worried 'cause you basically know 'bout their *secret society*, as they call it."

"Do you know their names?"

"No, thank God. Bill never let me know stuff like that. I was just his bodyguard." Paul laughed nervously. "Guess I didn't do too good of a job, huh?"

"Then why do you think they'll be hot on your tail?"

"Well, ummm, something important I took is missing."

"Took?" Margo queried.

"Truthfully, it was something *you* wanted." Paul stood up. "It's in your bathroom, but I'm telling you I've gotta get out of here."

Margo shot out of her seat and sprinted into the bathroom.

Chris stayed in the living room with Paul and put a hand on his shoulder. "You know God will protect you."

"I know I should have more faith in God, but didn't a lot of Christians die for Jesus?"

"Yes, Paul, they did, and they are still dying, but they don't run away. Besides, you could get police protection."

Paul laughed. "Police protection in a town that's in cahoots with the big boss? I don't think so."

"How do you know they're in league with each other?" Chris barely finished his sentence when he heard Margo scream. He didn't wait for Paul to answer but went running into the bathroom.

After a few seconds, Paul heard Margo moaning and crying. "The stone, the stone, he left the stone."

Paul couldn't stand the torment in her voice, but he had to do this. There was no other way. He had to leave the stone with her. Because of this, he might end up dead too, but someone had to destroy the power of the stone...and men like Bill!

⟫◆⟪

Chris shut the door, and Margo watched as he bolted it. They rarely locked the house when they were at home since they lived in a safe area. But now, they were dealing with men who would stop at nothing to destroy them.

Could God protect them now? What if these men got into the house and shot her and Chris. Did it mean God failed to protect them? On the surface, it might look that way, but Margo understood God didn't always shelter people from evil.

She believed God's protection went deeper than their physical body. He protected what no one could steal—their soul. So whether she lived or died in this ordeal wasn't the real issue. She didn't want the stone to fall into the wrong hands again.

Margo ran back into the bathroom to make sure the stone hadn't disappeared. It remained exactly as Paul had left it.

She couldn't believe her eyes. It looked just the way it had in her dreams. As a matter of fact, it appeared more vivid in her dreams than when she had seen it in the cave. Calling to Chris she asked, "Can you please get me my camera on top of the refrigerator? I don't want to leave this thing alone. I want pictures of it in its original state."

"I can't hear you," Chris yelled back.

Margo raised her voice, "My camera, please."

Chris burst through the bathroom door. "Taking pictures of the evidence, Sherlock? How out of character for you."

"Don't be funny. I want pictures just in case *this* or *you* or *I* disappear." Margo took several shots, and a couple of close-ups of the different registers. It was at a strange angle, but she didn't care about the distortion for now. Many of the symbols were still covered with blood. She knew the police would need samples to run DNA tests of it and hopefully lift some fingerprints besides Paul's. She decided to make a few sketches of the pictures in each register because a rubbing would not work. An Egyptian eye motif dominated the center and radiated outward. The other hieroglyphs, though covered in blood, were visible enough to decipher, and everything else was configured in a radial design. Falcons, lions, birds, and other stylized drawings littered the surface. She recognized them from the previous rubbing that disappeared—lost or worse yet, stolen.

Perhaps that rubbing was the very reason for her second kidnapping and near death. Margo held back tears. She could not allow herself to cry. Not now. Not when they were so close to solving at least a big part of the mystery.

She worked quickly. Her pencil outlined the basic design of each figure. She could provide details later. Working in a circular pattern, she duplicated the registers to prove authenticity. Margo decided to copy the strange open rectangles with dots along the perimeter of the stone, though they looked to be only a design. Yet she felt an urge to try to replicate the patterns as close to the original as possible. It would not be in their possession long, and she wanted as much information as she could get.

Chris had notified the police, and they would arrive soon. He told her they were given strict orders not to touch or move it before they took pictures. She wanted the photographs to be official, leaving no loopholes for lawyers.

With the last falcon sketched, Margo sat up straight, stretched her back, and stood up. Her knees wobbled, and her legs nearly gave out. She steadied herself and dropped the pencil. Shuffling into the living room, she went straight to the bookcase and pulled out a thick art history book. She and Joy had previously decoded three symbols using the monstrosity. Margo scanned the pages looking for more ciphers, but the art history pictures were not necessarily for translation purposes. Only a few symbols were assigned meaning. As she flipped though, she noticed the strange stylized eye and stopped to read about it. "The Udjat eye represents the eye of the god Horus. He was a sun god and was represented by a falcon."

Margo felt an electric shock course through her body as she recalled watching the turkey hawks circling near the cave. Certainly they were related to falcons, but what did that have to do with anything? This was getting more complex by the minute. Margo told herself to focus, and she let out long sigh.

Chris overheard and asked, "What's up?"

"I'm trying to unravel the meaning of these hieroglyphs and designs on the stone, but I keep running into more information, which I'm not sure is useful or not."

"Why don't you try researching on the computer?"

Margo looked up and shut her book. "Didn't I do that before?" She felt like her mind was swimming in a fog.

"Not that I recall."

Hmmm, now instead of forgetting things, I'm imagining them! She jumped on to the computer and typed in the search box "Egyptian hieroglyphics." A number of links flashed across the screen. Margo clicked on one. Pictures of various Egyptian hieroglyphs marched across the screen. *Not what I wanted.*

She clicked on the next link, though it sounded like it was for schoolchildren, *Write Like an Egyptian.*

The site instructed her to type in her name and it would inscribe it "the way an Egyptian scribe might have written it."

She followed the instructions, and in a few seconds, a tablet appeared with her name written in Egyptian. The first letter looked like a simplified owl followed by an arm pointing left. She wasn't sure about the next three symbols. One looked like the symbol for an eye, and another resembled an Egyptian-looking skirt and then a U-shaped rope.

She scanned the paper she copied from the stone for the same sequence. An owl, an arm, an eye, a skirt. Her heart nearly skipped a beat. They looked enough like the pictures on the stone, only minor differences. But she thought she had done this research before and it had come up inaccurate. *Why such different information now?*

The first four letters matched up very closely, but there were too many symbols after it. *Maybe they used my birth name?* She typed the name Margaret on the screen and waited.

The first four symbols were the same, followed by a series of other pictures, feathers, and a hill. She studied the sketch. They were the same!

But something didn't make sense. The etchings were in a whole different register. It appeared they'd been inscribed earlier. Margo remembered having difficulty deciphering some of these symbols since they looked worn on the surface. They were some of the first to be etched on the stone.

The first to be etched?

The paper slid out of Margo's hand onto the floor. Now she understood.

It wasn't her name but Margaret's.

Margaret Dubier's name was written on the stone! Her investigation had come full circle, and one more very important puzzle piece slipped into place. The mysterious woman whose name she uncovered first in the library and then at the cemetery.

The ramifications of this realization sent chills down her spine. Margaret had definitely been murdered! But why?

Lost in thought, she jumped as a young police officer walked into the computer room and picked up the paper from the floor. "This looks interesting. What are you doing?"

Margo hadn't even heard the doorbell ring, but Chris must've let him in.

She took the sketches. "Thank you."

"So what's that?" the officer repeated.

Margo stammered. "It-it's a copy of what you'll find in—"

"Our bathroom." Chris interrupted.

"Let's have a look." The police officer followed Chris.

Margo continued her researching.

She typed in Paul's name. The first symbol appeared on the screen and looked like reeds. The next she recognized the pointing arm again then a bird and a lion. She searched the drawing. One of the last hieroglyphs she copied spelled out his name!

⋙◆⋘

Margo sat at the kitchen table the next day, sipping her tea, as the sun poured into the room creating shafts of light spreading across the *Kingsland Chronicle*. She closed her eyes and rested for a moment. Her nerves began to settle as she approached normal for the first time in days. She'd just finished reading the article. Thank God it wasn't as slanted as *New Coven*'s sloppy reporting. After the grilling the police put her through, she needed some good news; but more importantly, she craved peace and quiet. She savored the silence.

So much had happened in three days—kidnapped from the craft fair, hypnotized by Bill for the second time, injected with mind-altering drugs, and then... She didn't want to face the truth, but she could now piece it together.

Stripped for a satanic ritual, she narrowly escaped with her life, and only because Paul had the guts to gather a rescue party. Margo dropped her head into her hands and cried deep, heavy sobs. Had Margaret faced the same awful treatment? And for what reason? What had she done?

Margaret Pierson saw her name on the same stone that condemned Margaret Dubier.

Covered in blood.

Her blood.

The very thought made her cringe. Up until now she would've called someone crazy to believe in such an archaic practice. But hadn't people today been murdered in even more brutal ways? Yes, but not for the same reasons. Not for sacrifice! This...this was evil personified. The very evil she'd been warned of in the letter.

34

Splashed in dappled sunshine, Joy and Ray's home radiated warmth and beauty. Margo stopped for a moment and basked in its tranquility. Though she and Joy had serious business to discuss, she hoped the worst lay behind her.

Ray ushered them into the dining room where they had a home-cooked meal of fried chicken, potato salad, fresh-baked bread, and soup. By the time dessert was finished, Margo and Chris felt refueled and a pound or two heavier, but renewed all the same.

As Margo retrieved the document with the sketched hieroglyphs, the back doorbell rang. Ray got up and answered it. A short muscular man with a long black coat and a small mustache stepped into the hallway. She felt puzzled at first until he opened his mouth and spoke.

"May I come in?"

Margo burst from her seat as soon as she heard the man.

He greeted everyone. "Hello everyone, it's me—Paul."

Margo needed no introduction. "I thought you were heading out of town."

Paul took off his coat. "I wanted everyone to think I left, but I needed to keep my eye on the situation. I didn't need any of Bill's or his boss's henchmen getting in my way." He looked directly at Margo. "I knew the *present* I left would make you vulnerable."

"Yes, but it gave us valuable information and the names of…" Margo hesitated and held up the sketches.

"You can show me later. Right now, I'm here to take it off your hands. I know it's in your trunk."

"We don't have it." Margo informed him. "The police do."

"The police?" Paul glared at Chris. "Do you think it's safe with them?"

Margo frowned. "What are you talking about?"

Chris turned to Margo. "Sorry, Paul warned me some police on the force are in league with Bill, so we staged the whole thing last night."

"Why?" Margo's eyebrows rose high on her forehead and her mouth gapped open.

"I didn't want you to lose another night's sleep over that blasted stone, and I didn't want it to fall into the wrong hands." Christ responded with vehemence.

"So where is it?"

"We put it in the trunk of the car. Paul's been guarding it all night."

Margo suppressed a laugh then got up and hugged her husband. "You're a doll, wanting me to get a good night's sleep. It worked, though I had my suspicions about the visit from the police. However, they will need blood samples."

"Don't worry about the blood. We took samples, though I think it's just from a goat, but we need to get the stone back in here quick."

Ray stepped in. "Drive the car into the garage, and we'll unload it there. We don't want any curious neighbors to wonder what's going on."

"That's for sure," Paul agreed. "Now get your muscles pumped so we can get that beast of a rock in here."

<hr />

The small group gathered round the table to examine the stone and look for some clues to its origin. Margo offered her insight. "It looks like it was styled after a piece I saw in my art history book. Of course the pictures were different. The original recorded the names of several pharaohs from the dynastic period. As a matter of fact, I think it's in a museum in New York."

"But why would someone go through so much trouble to make a replica and inscribe hieroglyphic names in stone?" Joy asked. "Did the original have religious significance?"

"Probably, since many of the Egyptian items we possess today revolved around their religious beliefs." Margo ran her hands around the edge of the stone.

"Okay, you two. You can conjecture all you want about the original, but we need to know where this one came from." Chris pointed to the stone. "This will help us unravel some of this mystery and maybe lead us to—"

Margo interrupted. "Hey, guys look over here." Margo inspected the area that was welded together. "I wonder if this was done more recently."

Ray examined it. "Possibly."

The wheels in Margo's brain began to spin "Could a blacksmith do this work, say one from the eighteenth century?"

Ray hesitated for a moment. "Yes, a good one with the right knowledge. Back then a first-rate blacksmith could make and fix an array of things, from horseshoes to nails. Welding would be right up his alley."

"I wonder if we could separate them."

"It might do some damage to the bottom and most likely destroy the top layer."

Chris reentered the conversation. "Why go through the trouble if it's just an imitation?"

Paul cleared his throat. "But it's not."

"How do you know?" Margo asked.

"One day I overheard Bill on the phone with the Big Boss, a.k.a. Worshipful Master, as Bill addressed him that day. It sounded like they was havin' a disagreement. Then Bill raised his voice when he answered, "Okay, okay, I'll get the blasted stone." I knew it had to be worth mucho bucks for the big cheese to want it, but I didn't know if it was a legal deal or a heist. Anyways, I started doin' some investigation on my own. I found out why. It belonged to one of the professor guys from the college in the weirdo group. Someone said he had gotten it on one of those *archeol—*" Paul couldn't pronounce the word correctly. "Well, you know what I mean, one of those digs where they find a bunch of old stuff. I think it's a duplicate of the one you saw in your art history book."

"I doubt it's that old," Margo offered her opinion. "But it could be a copy from centuries later."

"Is it valuable?" Chris questioned.

"It had to be worth a lot of money for the Big Boss to want it," Paul insisted.

"And you're sure this is it?" Margo needed to know. "The original Egyptian collections are in the hands of museums and curators, but copies, old ones, might also be valuable. I'm just confused how it got here and into the hands of a satanic coven."

Paul shrugged his shoulders. "All I know is Bill said it would bring us a bundle, and you almost got killed because you knew too much."

"But not enough." Margo sighed.

"Remember, though, with what we do know, we might be able to save some lives." Joy encouraged the group. "By the way, who is this big boss?"

"It's best if you don't know details, but I'll give you a hint." Paul smiled. "These satanic guys, as you call them, are only the tip of the iceberg."

"What do you mean by that?"

"That's what Bill told me. There's much more powerful, rich people running the country. I don't know any more."

Margo disagreed. "These occultists worship Satan and his demonic dominions, which is pretty scary and powerful to me!

God intervened and sent you to save my life, just in the nick of time."

"Maybe, but I don't know about this religious stuff," Paul answered.

"So what do we do next?" Chris demanded.

"First, we've got to get the stone out of here. With Bill gone, they'll send in others...direct from the top, much worse than Bill."

Paul walked over to the window and drew the curtain back just a little.

"Anyone suspicious?" Ray inquired.

"No one...yet...but we have to get the stone into safekeeping."

"Why can't we take it to the Kingsland Police?" Joy offered.

Paul shook his head. "We can't risk it. They'd probably call down to New Coven since the crime happened there, and it could get into the wrong hands."

"How can you be so sure?" Margo wanted to know.

"Just believe me. I know cops stick together, in a small town, maybe even more. Just let me handle it for now. If my plan fails, then we'll try another."

"So what's your plan?"

Paul shuffled his feet. "I figure we could hide out for a day or two in a hotel, disguise ourselves, then get the stone to some straight cops out of town." He looked up at the group. "What da ya think?"

After a few moments of silence Chris spoke, "I think it's worth a try, but we better get to it pronto."

They all nodded in agreement.

Paul's plan had some benefits, such as staying at a hotel with a pool and sauna, and Margo refused to stay the night without enjoying them. While in the car, she convinced Chris to stop at their house and retrieve a bathing suit and a change of clothes.

"Look, it's daylight. No one's going to try jumping us in the middle of the day. Anyway, we have Paul watching us."

Margo looked out the window. Paul followed in a rented car but kept a distance away.

Chris laughed. "Yeah, I guess we'll have Paul with us for a while. I wonder if he's going to get a room near us or sleep in his car."

Margo shrugged her shoulder. "I guess he'll do whatever bodyguards do."

Stroking Margo's hair, Chris comforted her. "Don't worry. Everything will work out in time. Look, even your hair is growing in nicely."

Margo playfully pulled his arm away. "Keep your eyes on the road mister." She held up a butchered end and wondered if she should go with a short hair style. "I know you're right. Things will work out. It's just so much more involved than I thought. I wanted to find a missing relative, and instead I opened a Pandora's box."

"You sure did, but good will come out of all of this. We already know the names of people they've targeted, and if Paul's plan works, we'll outsmart the bad guys."

Margo hoped they could pull this disguise thing off. When they arrived at the house, she jumped out of the car and ran to the porch. Everything looked in place on the outside, but when she went to turn the lock, the knob turned immediately. The door swung open. *Hmm, Chris must have forgotten to lock the house.*

She stepped inside and gasped. The couch was overturned, the legs stuck out straight like a dead animal. Chris's favorite recliner slumped to the side. Books from the bookshelf littered the floor. Her Bible lay thrown against the wall, pages torn out of it. *Who would do this?* Her anger mounted as she picked up her beloved Bible.

Margo scanned the rest of the living room. Books, magazines and papers were strewn all around. *Whoever it was wanted something—bad.* She stooped and examined the pile. Her art history book was missing.

She stiffened. Fear prickled the back of her neck. Glancing around the room to ward off the sickening feeling growing in her stomach, she discovered the TV and CD player were gone. Margo stood, taking in the destruction. She heard footsteps and spun around.

"What's taking you so—" Chris stopped dead short as he crossed into the room.

Margo ran and embraced him, letting her emotions out. "Oh, Chris, someone broke in," she sobbed, "and ripped my Bible apart and stole our new CD player and that old worthless TV, but I think they're after the drawings and the stone!" In between sobs, she caught her breath. "Soon they'll be after Joy and Ray!" Margo buried her face in Chris's chest.

"Well, at least we weren't here when they came. From what Paul says, they wouldn't think twice about doing us in."

Margo looked up and fought back more tears. "Yes, God protected us, and He didn't let those bimbos find the stone. I hope they don't know about Ray and Joy." Margo dropped her hands from Chris shoulders and tugged his hand. "C'mon, we've got to call them and go back there to protect them from these guys."

"Now just wait a minute. Let's think about this. What if they've bugged our phone or they're waiting for us to lead them right to the treasure?"

"Do you think they can trace our calls even on the cell phones?"

"I don't know, but those are things the FBI can do, so why not these guys?"

Margo sighed and then looked over at the computer. "It's odd they didn't steal this too. Too heavy, I guess. I wonder if Joy or Ray are online. I doubt they have a Facebook account, but I think I have her e-mail, but who knows when they'll check their e-mail."

"If you can't get through, we'll have to come up with a backup plan."

Margo sat at the computer and went to her e-mail account, though she didn't remember checking the box for staying logged on. She thought it a little odd since both of them usually signed out when they left the house. But time was precious right now, and she didn't say anything. She checked her Facebook page to see if the Hopelyns were listed, but they weren't, so she shot them an e-mail instead. "Keep on the lookout and protect our *investment*." Quickly scrolling through some messages from friends and an artists' e-mail list, she stopped at the one in caps: URGENT, READ NOW. "Hey, Chris, were you expecting an important e-mail message from Rich?"

Chris grunted as he turned his recliner right side up, "Not that I recall."

Margo clicked on the envelope icon, and the message appeared on the screen. It read,

> Dear Margo and Chris,
> So how do you like your living room? If you think that's bad, check out the bedroom.

Margo shouted across the room, "Come over here, Chris, this message isn't from Rich." She read the first two lines out loud.

Chris ran over, and they scanned the warning together.

> If you don't want more of this, you better hand over the goods. Don't think you can hide that stone forever. We have ways of finding and getting *whatever we want* without anyone being able to trace us. Notice whose name this message bears. And by the way, if you value your lives or your friends, you'll tell them to cooperate with us. Watching over you.

The last line startled them, *Bill and the gang*. Chris pounded his fist on the computer table.

Margo jumped. "What a rat, faking his death. Why?"

"That's easy," Chris volunteered. "To buy time to eliminate anybody in his way."

"That man infuriates me. He thinks he's got the whole world eating out of his hands. We've got to get back to Joy's without *Bill and the gang* knowing."

"And just how are we going to manage that?"

"I'm not sure." Margo hesitated, and a wave of inspiration hit. "Maybe we can put Paul's plan into action just a little sooner and disguise ourselves now."

"Not a bad idea. Okay, how?"

"I think I can pull something out of my wardrobe and..." She ran into the junk room in search of a box filled with outfits for the yearly Artist Party. Chris trailed after her. She tossed costumes aside and found what she wanted. "How's this?" She waved a disguise triumphantly.

"Oh no," Chris groaned. "Only if I have to."

Margo tossed it to him and dove back into the pile for herself. "Please, Chris, put it on. We don't have time to waste." She fit a long blond wig on her head. "For all we know, Bill's henchmen are on their way to Ray and Joy's right now."

35

The head elder of the fellowship nearly threw down his cell phone. Ever since the news about Mr. Eville, Bill Guiles, it hadn't stopped ringing off the hook. Vince had heard enough of people's complaints. All week long he'd listened to members of the congregation inquiring about Bill's involvement with the church. Now his sudden accident brought a fresh rash of calls. People voiced their concerns over Bill's entanglements with the law and how it might affect certain members' reputation.

He stood up quickly and spun the swivel chair around. *Great, just what we needed. Now our one hope of making some financial progress in this church is dead.* Vince slapped the chair's leather back and stopped it from spinning. *I don't know what's going on around this place, Lord, but whatever it is, it stinks.*

Bill pulled out his laptop from underneath the bed and plugged the cord into the phone line. He was glad this second-rate hotel had Internet access. He waited for the notebook to power up and then logged on to the net. As soon as he was connected, he typed in his phony screen name, RICH2 Million, and checked his e-mail messages. He laughed at his own ability to deceive whoever he wanted. He was excited when he saw his message to Margo had been opened. She had read his letter ten minutes ago.

Well, now she knows about my little deception. He smiled to himself. *I hope she acts prudently and leads us to that stone.*

Bill pulled out his smart phone and called an international number. It chimed a couple of times, and a sophisticated voice answered, "Is the new order progressing?"

Bill, who was one step shy of being a Third-Degree Mason, responded, "Worshipful Master, everything is in place. I sent the message, and it was received."

"Very well," the voice responded coolly.

Bill continued, "I'm sure she'll lead us right where we want to go. Have your apprentices ready with two vehicles and one for me. I'm getting bored hanging out in this dive." He looked around the shabby hotel and thought about that infuriating woman. "And of course, I want to participate. I need to eliminate this lower being. Then I'll probably depart from the country."

His Master answered in an affected tone, "I'm confident you'll succeed with the higher force's aid."

<hr />

From his vantage point parked behind a grove of pines, Paul spread two boughs apart and watched the Piersons' house for any suspicious activity, but he didn't see any. What was taking those two so long? Didn't they know they needed to get a move on?

He decided to check on them when he saw another vehicle drive by, stop at the Piersons' for a moment, then continue down the road and turn into a driveway. Paul figured he'd scope out the situation and ride by. He jumped into his car and drove down the road. Sure enough, two men sat parked in a car reading a newspaper.

Paul decided he couldn't take the risk of turning around and catching their attention. He'd have to go the long way. He hoped Margo and Chris wouldn't be foolish and leave without him or think he left them behind. Determined not to take a chance, he stepped on the gas pedal. He got there just in time. Margo and Chris were walking out of their house.

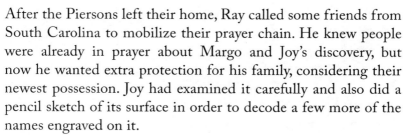

After the Piersons left their home, Ray called some friends from South Carolina to mobilize their prayer chain. He knew people were already in prayer about Margo and Joy's discovery, but now he wanted extra protection for his family, considering their newest possession. Joy had examined it carefully and also did a pencil sketch of its surface in order to decode a few more of the names engraved on it.

Since Margo discovered the symbols were principally Egyptian hieroglyphic code, entwined with newer engravings, she was more easily able to decipher the names. Yet the other strange markings had not been deciphered as of yet. While Ray made some phone calls, Joy studied the intricate work of the earlier symbols of a hawk, the unmistakable Egyptian eye, a cat in a sitting position, and different views of birds. She saw a marked difference between the older and newer engravings, which were more hastily inscribed and contained broken letters. Joy wanted to decode these as soon as possible.

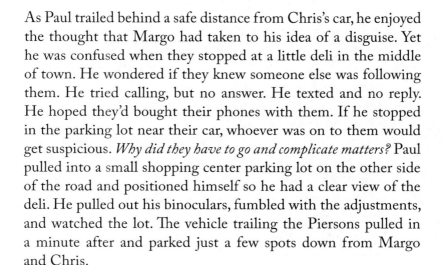

As Paul trailed behind a safe distance from Chris's car, he enjoyed the thought that Margo had taken to his idea of a disguise. Yet he was confused when they stopped at a little deli in the middle of town. He wondered if they knew someone else was following them. He tried calling, but no answer. He texted and no reply. He hoped they'd bought their phones with them. If he stopped in the parking lot near their car, whoever was on to them would get suspicious. *Why did they have to go and complicate matters?* Paul pulled into a small shopping center parking lot on the other side of the road and positioned himself so he had a clear view of the deli. He pulled out his binoculars, fumbled with the adjustments, and watched the lot. The vehicle trailing the Piersons pulled in a minute after and parked just a few spots down from Margo and Chris.

Margo had gone into the store, and Chris waited for her to come out. Then a young lady, who from a distance looked a lot like Margo, got into Chris's car, and he took off. The trailing vehicle waited so as not to be detected and followed behind. *What in the world is going on?* Paul wondered as his phone chirped, displaying Margo's number. *Finally!* He flipped the phone open, and her voice whispered, "Come get me at the store." Then she hung up. Paul figured out what was going on. *That Margo, she's no dummy.*

He started up his car, made sure he wasn't being followed, and drove into the deli parking lot. As he maneuvered the borrowed vehicle, he glanced in his rearview mirror. No one suspicious appeared.

Walking through the door, he was immediately on high alert just in case Bill's boss had somehow planted someone or got ahold of Margo's phone. He slowly looked around the store and found Margo bent over an ATM machine, making a transaction. He silently slipped next to her. When she looked up, she jumped back in surprise. "Don't ever do that again."

Paul stuck his hands deep into his pants pockets "Sorry, I couldn't resist the temptation. You scare so easily."

"So you've noticed. Well, thank God you're here."

Paul laughed nervously and then took her arm. "C'mon, let's go, wherever we're going." When they got into the car, Paul announced, "Where to lady? The Plaza or the Ritz?"

Margo shook her head and smiled, "Neither for today. The Hopelyns'."

Paul turned around to face her. "What, are you crazy? We just came from there. Remember our plan to lie low at some hotel?"

"Yes, but Chris is going there with my friend and whoever's following us. He's the decoy while you and I are the real thing."

Paul pulled the car into the street. "So I'm a Coke now, instead of a Pepsi?"

Margo thought about it for a second. "In a way, yes. We're the originals. Anyway." She swallowed hard and continued, "Our house was trashed, but they didn't find what they wanted. If they're as good as you say, it won't take them long to figure it out and trace our steps back to Ray and Joy's. We have to warn them."

"And you think they don't have more than just one guy on this case, trailing us this very moment?"

Margo frowned. "We didn't worry about that, but we did consider calls being traced, so we didn't phone them."

"That's good, but do you really want to lead them right to the booty if someone is on our tail?"

"Well, I have to warn them. Maybe you could drop me off, and I'll take a bus there."

"No way. They know what you look like. I guess I'll just have to take orders from you, *sister*, and keep my eyes peeled for, umm, suspicious-looking characters."

"And hopefully they'll be knocked off our trail by following Chris all around the county until he gets to the Johnson Hotel."

Paul looked in his rearview mirror before turning onto the main highway to Kingsland. Everything looked normal, so he signaled and turned. "One thing to remember, though, is that as soon as he gets to the hotel, they'll probably call for additional forces to aid in their search for the stone. They'll watch Chris, but they won't put their eggs all in one basket. We're not dealing with a bunch of amateurs."

Margo sighed. "Yeah, like me. But what can we do? We'll just have to pray and ask for the Lord's help and protection."

⟫◆⟪

Mike received a call from Ray only moments ago, and he immediately phoned Pastor Dave, alerting him to the newest developments. He then walked into the living room, knelt down and prayed. "Dear Father, You know we are wrestling not with flesh and blood but with powers and principalities...the forces of darkness in heavenly places. If ever someone needed your help, Lord, it's the Piersons. Protect and guide them. Keep them from evil."

In a simple yet powerful prayer, he humbly requested the assistance of angels to surround them with flaming swords and shields of steel. He hoped they responded.

Chris checked his rearview mirror to make sure his pursuer was hot on his tail. He made it as easy as possible for them to pursue him and look ignorant of their presence. But he couldn't ride around the county all day. He tried to delay his arrival at their destination for as long as possible. As long as the young lady who sat by his side, Lance's pretty young wife, was willing to help, Chris would continue to divert the attention of whoever trailed them.

He felt a little odd sitting so close to Heidi, a blonde by birth, but the golden brown wig made her almost a dead ringer for Margo. Her body type, size, and weight nearly matched Margo's; and every once in a while, Chris almost forgot she wasn't his wife.

A sweet young woman, Heidi told Chris she was happy to help, especially after her husband, Lance, had told her about the terrible mishaps Margo had endured.

"I hope your wife is feeling better. I'm glad she called me," Heidi said with a calm in her voice Chris envied. He couldn't believe she could be so sympathetic to their plight after all Lance had endured lately. "Yeah, thanks for being available. We sure appreciate it."

"Well, we value your help and support, especially after the death of Lance's cousin, Ashley."

Chris recalled Margo's concern that it was no accident, but he didn't want to mention it.

"Yes, what a terrible misfortune." He tried to offer Heidi comfort.

The closer they got to Ray and Joy's residence, the more Paul jangled the change in his pocket. Margo gently asked him several times to stop, and each time he apologized for being so nervous.

At one point, he took out a cigarette, tapped the filter on the edge of his knee, and was about to light it, but Margo deftly grabbed the lighter from him and protested. "I can't stand the smell of smoke in an enclosed area. It makes me sick. Besides, I thought you stopped."

Paul grinned sheepishly and put the cancer stick away in his jacket pocket. He sat up straight for a few moments with his eyes peeled to the back mirror and tapped his fingers on the steering wheel—*burrump, burrump*. The rhythmic sound was like a snare drum beating out the tension of the nerve-racking escapade.

"Will you please stop?" Margo implored. "It's beginning to drive me crazy."

"Sorry." Paul stuck one of his hands in his pants pocket and drove with the other. "I'm just jammed up. I know how tricky these guys are." Paul envisioned the two of them being sacrificed, and it wasn't a pretty sight.

Margo's voice brought him back to the present. "I understand, so am I, but after all I've been through, I thank God I'm alive."

Paul realized she had been through a lot, and some of it at his hands. "Listen, Margo, I'm not sure I ever told you, but I'm really sorry for kidnapping you before, I had to do what the boss told me, and I tried to keep you safe…really."

"Yes, you've apologized before, and I forgive you."

Paul didn't believe she really did. "Are you sure? I know I let the boss pump you with drugs, but I had to or it would've been… curtains. That's a lot to forgive."

"Paul, God forgives you, and so do I. It was a struggle at first, but God forgave me of my past and that helped me to forgive you. After all, you rescued me." She put her hand on his shoulder.

"Yeah, I figured I owed it to you after what I'd done." He looked down at his hands gripping the steering wheel and then glanced at Margo.

"Thank you," she whispered, recalling the horrendous incident and the struggle to forgive Paul. "Let's pray God will get us through this one."

He agreed.

Margo bowed her head. "Dear Father, we really need your wisdom and guidance now. Please outsmart the enemy and blind their eyes to our whereabouts. In Jesus's name. Amen."

Paul mumbled an amen, but as the car approached the small city of Kingsland, he began drumming his fingers on the steering wheel again. But Margo didn't say anything this time. He surveyed the situation, checked the rearview mirror several times; then he looked left and right to make sure nobody was in sight before he turned down the avenue leading to the Hopelyns' house.

The road was littered with leaves from the oaks lining the avenue and boasted large white houses with wrap-around porches. Margo pointed to them, and the huge Victorians that were once the home to doctors and lawyers were now relegated and subdivided into apartments and small offices.

Paul's mind was preoccupied. He shifted in his seat and surveyed the street up and down. A few children played by the side of the road, and a dog on a chain barked loudly in protest. Paul directed Margo to keep a close surveillance on everything while trying not to look suspicious, but she assured him all was well.

Instead of pulling directly into Ray's driveway, Paul decided to pass by it and then circle back around. If anyone was lagging way behind, he would spot them on the way back. But once again, the street appeared empty. The wind began to pick up and blow the dead leaves around as the sun slowly descended behind the mountains. Paul felt as if it sank into the pit of his stomach. He feared what he might find at their home.

Margo nudged him. "C'mon, the coast is clear, Magnum," she teased. He pulled the rental car all the way into the driveway and motioned for Margo to use the back door. "I'll stay here and keep watch. You go in and warn them. Signal me when you find the stone, if you find it."

Margo stood with the door opened for a moment. "I've got a better idea. I'll ask Joy to open the garage door, and then you can pull the car in there. That way no one will see us struggling with an awkward package."

Paul shook his head. "No. Wait a few minutes first so I can make sure no one is stalking us then open the garage door." Then he added, "Good thinking."

Margo grinned and jumped out. "Good idea," her voice trailed as the car door slammed shut.

36

After a nerve-racking ride, often looking over his shoulder, Chris arrived safely at the hotel with Heidi. So did his escorts. He hoped the plan Margo cooked up would work. For now, he'd have to act like Heidi's husband. Like a gentleman, he held the car door for her, unloaded one of her small bags and his then entered into the hotel. Chris had instructed Heidi to change in the bathroom and remove her wig.

Chris stuffed himself and his bag in a stall and quickly discarded his suit for a pair of jeans. He donned a wig and fake mustache he bought at the drugstore, thanks to the proliferation of Halloween costumes. They rendezvoused in a secluded alcove away from the bathrooms and went over the details. Chris watched as Heidi exited the front door. A shifty-looking character entered the hotel and passed right by her. She didn't look up, and Chris breathed a sigh of relief. He turned right and walked slowly past the hotel rooms and exited the side door.

A blue car, with Lance and Heidi in it, pulled up. Chris opened the back door and jumped in. "Thanks, Lance. I owe you…again."

"No problem. So where to?

Joy looked surprised to see Margo at the door so soon after they had just left their house. She invited her in, and Margo spilled out a torrent of words explaining the situation. Joy patiently tried to understand what the young woman was saying, and she laid her arm softly across her shoulder. "Slow down, honey, we're all right. We have half the Eastern Seaboard praying for us, and I can feel the presence of angels."

Margo hugged her. "But we have to get you and the stone out of here. I'm sure they'll be able to trace us here." Joy saw her great distress, and so when Margo asked her to open the garage door, she complied.

Within a New York minute, Paul barged through the side door that led from the garage and quickly ushered the three of them into the living room, "Listen," he said impatiently. "We gotta get a move on. It's not time for socializing here, ladies. Let's get that stone and move it."

Joy just stood quietly for a moment. "Now, let's not rush into things here. Remember, we have God on our side. Why must we move it from here? It's safely hidden and will serve as evidence for the police later on."

Paul tried to convince her that their lives were in danger, but she continued to protest. "At least let me examine it again. I need to figure out who the freshest engravings represent."

Paul conceded. "But only for a moment. Margo already made drawings and took photos." "Yes, but I need to pray as I look at the real thing."

The two women marched downstairs while Paul kept a look out upstairs. Joy moved to where she was working on the stone. "I want to pray about these symbols around the outer ring. I have a feeling they're not just a design. Maybe they represent something we need to know about. They don't look Egyptian. I also want to do a crayon rubbing on the inner area with your help." Margo bent down and inspected.

"Okay, but we need to be careful not to spoil the evidence, and we have to move quickly."

Ray thumped down the steps and joined them. "Paul said we need to hurry."

"As soon as we do this, darling," his wife sweetly replied.

They all watched as Joy took the paper and an unwrapped special crayon. Margo pressed on the paper, and Joy rubbed the middle section. A figure appeared that was barely visible.

Margo gasped. "I recognize that symbol. It's that elongated eye again with the falcon wing. The sign of pharaoh and the gods who accompany the dead."

Yet Joy didn't feel the need to rush, but worked quickly, though she knew God would take care of them. Ray supported her view. "I know, I feel God's divine protection, but Paul does know more about these people. How much have we dealt with dangerous criminals who think nothing of murder?"

"I guess you're right, but—"

Paul yelled down to them. "Time to go or we're dead meat!"

"Guys, we've got to get the stone to the car. How did you ever carry that rock down here?" Margo asked.

Ray explained as he handed her a wooden plank to wedge the stone. "We did what we're doing now and lifted it into a wheelbarrow and brought it here. If you didn't notice, our garage is on the same level as the basement, so we can roll it there now."

Everyone joined in to maneuver it off the worktable and onto its side on the basement floor.

Afterward, Margo ran upstairs to tell Paul to go to the garage.

Downstairs, Joy helped Ray roll the stone across the cement floor and up the incline into the garage. She helped as much as possible as Ray struggled to hoist the hunk of rock into the trunk. When Paul arrived, he dove in and braced the stone's weight against his chest. His muscles bulged with the strain. Everyone was present, except Margo, who was waiting upstairs for Chris to return.

Then she burst into the garage. "I'm not sure if this is anything to worry about, but I just saw a black limo with NYC plates drive by."

Paul frowned. "That's them. Let's get this stone in here and make a break for it before they call for backup."

He slammed the trunk and hopped into the driver's seat of Joy's blue Dodge. Paul grinned. "I'm driving."

The rest of the team jumped in, though Ray questioned Paul, "Shouldn't we call the police?"

He shook his head. "If they hear sirens, they'll break in, shoot us, and be gone by the time the police arrive. It's time to say your prayers now."

Joy hadn't stopped praying and assured them, "God is our refuge and strength, a very present help in trouble." She believed every word of it. She hoped Paul did too.

Melanie sobbed. She couldn't continue this way anymore. Rich just didn't understand her. She needed someone like Bill, even if he wasn't a Christian. He even offered to take her with him, though she hardly knew him.

But she wanted to know him more.

She stood up and looked out the bedroom window. At least he paid attention to her and admired her. More than she could say about Rich. Everything was about him and very little about her... except for the house. He let her reign there, but she didn't want to be a lonely princess shut up in a castle anymore. She wanted to live, and Bill made her tingle.

Her head ached, and she reached for the medicine bottle on the nightstand. If she couldn't have Bill, then she didn't want to live anymore. It would be so easy.

They shot out of the garage like a racehorse from a starting gate. The Dodge lurched forward, and he jerked the wheel to the right. The vehicle dug into the soft ground, tearing up great chunks of mud and grass, flinging them in all directions. Several hunks hit the gleaming black car parked near them. Before the driver knew what hit him, Paul charged past him.

The car on the side of the road had more time to react. Paul knew he would be on his tail in a second. The trick was to put enough distance between them so the tires wouldn't be blown out from under them. Sure enough, shots, silenced by mufflers, came streaking in their direction, headed for the wheels. A round of bullets bounced off the pavement, but one nicked a tire. It hissed slowly but wasn't completely deflated. Though the car wobbled, Paul didn't stop. "How far is it to town?"

Ray shot back, "About a mile."

"Good, then we're headin' there. Call the cops pronto. Let them know we have a high-speed chase with guns." He saw the car in the rearview mirror speed up. Paul wasn't going to let him crash into their trunk. He jerked the wheel to the right and onto a side street. The other car shot past them. "How do we get to the main drag?"

"Make a left here."

Paul jerked the wheel again. The girls rocked back and forth in the backseat like a pair of weebles.

"Get down!" Paul ordered.

Joy prayed. "Dear Lord, surround us with your angels."

Ray held on to the dashboard like on a roller-coaster ride. He tried to get his cell phone from his pocket.

Paul laughed. "Having fun yet?"

Margo piped up. "Where'd you get your license, from a cracker—"

Crunch! Margo heard the sound behind her.

The black limo hit the driver's side door of an oncoming car. It rocked back and forth like a carnival ride. Paul cheered. "Way to go, my plan worked!"

He screamed to Ray. "Where the heck is the police in this one-horse town? Didn't you get ahold of them?"

Before Ray could answer, the limo unleashed a fresh round of quiet fury.

It shot holes in the backseat window and sunk into the backrest.

Margo screamed. "Dear God, help us!" Joy continued to pray quietly.

"Stay down. It's their way of saying this isn't a game anymore. How serious are you about keeping this stone?"

Both women nodded and replied, "Very."

"Okay, well, let's get goin' then." Paul stepped on the gas, and the women crouched on the car floor. They brushed off pieces of shattered glass from their pants. The car rocked back and forth on three wheels. The limo gained on them again and shot at the rubber. Paul wove back and forth, miraculously missing the bullets.

"Make a right here," Ray yelled. "We're only a quarter mile from town."

Paul acted as if he would pass the street and then at the last second jerked the wheel right. He rode over grass and backtracked onto the street. Once again, the limo shot past them. It gave Paul a few seconds' edge while the black car's driver spun around and followed. They started entering the city limits, and a few houses lined the streets.

"The police station is right down the road!"

Paul thought for a second. "Hold on tight. Everybody down. You too, Ray." He slammed on the breaks and skidded.

Errrrrrrr!

Crrrash!

The black limo plowed into the back right side of the heavily padded Dodge propelling Paul forward. As he had hoped, it left the driver behind him with a flat front tire and a sputtering radiator. Paul regained his position and continued driving, though much slower.

Ray cried. "Is everyone okay?"

"No, Joy is hurt," Margo sobbed.

Joy popped her head up. "No, I'm not. I was crying to the Lord. I'm fine. How about Paul?"

315

"I'm a tough one, but I think I did in your car. Thank God it had a lot of padding, but I think it's—"

The sound of sirens and flashing lights filled the streets. For once in his life, Paul felt relieved at their sound. Two police cars moved in on the scene when the fury of hell was unleashed. Several black limos raced up the road and let out a torrent of bullets in rapid staccato. Paul felt trapped. Glass exploded.

A young cop gripped his shoulder and yelled as blood spurted from his fresh wound. Margo watched in horror. "Dear God, help us!" Joy yelled. Paul pushed her head down. The high-pitched whine of an ambulance screamed. Gunfire broke out between the two sides with them caught in the middle! Bullets whizzed by the Dodge and ricocheted off the metal.

With abandoned fury, one driver rammed into Paul's car again and smashed the trunk in, recklessly destroying his own front bumper and grillwork. Margo hid her head hard against the seat, "My poor brains."

As she rubbed her head, Paul groaned. Blood spurted from somewhere. This time, Joy yelled, "Paul's been hit!"

37

Ray heard the distorted *whoop whoop* of more sirens wailing toward them. The driver who'd been following them threw his car in reverse and tore out of there. He raced down the road.

Two state troopers responded to the local police call and screamed down the road heading into town. Seeing the black car speeding in the opposite direction, the officer spun his blue sedan around in the middle of the road, just missing a bystander's van, and screeched down the two-lane street in hot pursuit.

In a matter of a few minutes, enough police cars and emergency vehicles were attending to the smashed car and its passengers that it looked like a crime scene from a television show. Seeing the EMTs, Ray got out of the car and was nearly knocked over by one of them as he hurried to take care of Paul. In a few moments, they had him bandaged up and carried out on a stretcher.

Paul whispered to Ray as they whisked him away, "Don't take your eyes off your car. They'll be mad as the devil himself now we still have the stone." He coughed. "Don't think we're in the clear. This just made it worse. Now they'll send out their best, if you know what I mean. Professional assassins."

Ray nodded, and they loaded Paul into the ambulance. Despite the grim look of it all, Paul was the only one seriously hurt. As Ray walked back to the car, he overheard Margo explaining to the officer that he had called in the suspicious-looking characters, but they insisted she would have to file an accident report after they checked Paul into the emergency room. Joy was leaning against the car and said nothing. Ray knew she was praying.

Margo turned around and plopped on the trunk. Her brain felt fuzzy, but this wasn't anything new. She turned to Ray. "I wonder if the stone's still intact." He didn't have a chance to answer as the two EMTs ordered him to join his friend. They insisted she and Joy come too.

"We better call someone quick to keep an eye on the car," Margo said as she walked toward the flashing red lights.

Ray nodded. He flipped open the cell phone, the one that Joy insisted he get, and punched in the numbers. He prayed they'd answer.

Chris thanked Lance for the ride back to his car. "Don't worry, Margo will be okay." He assured them. "Nothing major this time. Just pray for her." He didn't want to get Lance further involved, so he tried to act casual as he pulled away from the curb.

The call from Margo unnerved him, and he was upset she was in the hospital again, even though she wasn't hurt. As he pulled onto county Route 23, he checked his rearview mirror to make sure no one tailed him. No cars followed directly behind him, so he headed north in the direction of Kingsland.

Margo had warned him to be cautious and make a few wrong turns here and there just to make sure. Even though he felt foolish playing this cat-and-mouse game, he followed her precautions and made a quick right off the highway into a small parking lot.

He checked his mirror again. A red car made the same turn, slowed down, then passed. Chris drove back to Main Street. He turned right once again, heading north, and felt safe. The red car wasn't behind him, and Chris relaxed as much as possible knowing he had to get to Kingsland as soon as possible.

Once out of town, he checked his rearview mirror less frequently and was moving along quite comfortably. A couple of cars followed behind him, but nothing suspicious, just a white SUV and a blue pickup. Chris stepped on the accelerator in a rush to get there fast.

The Kingsland police were finishing checking over the Hopelyns' Dodge, when a state trooper pulled up.

"Hey, what's going on around here?"

The local cop gave him a puzzled look then answered, "Well, for these parts, it's more excitement than we've seen in a while."

"Yeah, must be why I was radioed to help."

"Someone radioed troopers for help?"

"Yeah, thought there might be more trouble from the looks of things. Wanted me to assist you with the vehicle so you could take care of your buddy in the hospital." The trooper looked carefully over at the car and noted the license plate number.

The local guy frowned. "My buddy? You're mistaken. The main guy hurt here was someone in the car accident, though an officer took a shot to the shoulder, but they'll take care of him."

"Hmm, I was told an officer was badly hurt. Just wanted to help out. Since you don't need me, I'll be on my way."

"Well, thanks for stopping anyway."

"Sure, anytime, by the way, what wrecking company do you use around here?"

At first, the cop seemed hesitant to answer. "Just a local guy, Bob," he replied, eyeing the state trooper.

The state policeman moved closer and pulled out a business card. "Well, here's the card of our guy. Gives us a good kickback if you know what I mean, probably better than Bob's."

"Thanks for the tip, but our man will do fine."

"Well, it's your town. I guess you know best."

—————⊰◆⊱—————

Less than a quarter mile from town, Chris spotted a suspicious black Saab following him. There weren't any side roads until they were right in town, but he could pull a U-turn. He wondered if Ray's car would still be at the scene of the accident. Probably towed already, but he had to try. He didn't want to waste any more time, yet he also didn't want to lead a horse to water. So instead of going straight, he made a sharp right and practically flew down the hill. Then he jerked the wheel in the opposite direction and parked the car in the Boy Scout lot. Sure enough, the black car went careening down the hill too fast to stop and missed the hidden left turn.

Wasting no time, Chris spun the car around, kicking up sand and gravel. As he sped down the avenue, he met a red light. *Dear Lord, I've got to lose this guy*. Before Chris could think of what to do, he spotted the black car cresting the hill.

The only alternative was to gun it and try to lose him down some back street. As he spun out in reverse, he spotted the black car in his side-view mirror. Chris zipped into a driveway and made another quick U-turn. He knew the black Saab would be on him soon. But just his good fortune, the light turned red on the car following him. The driver looked like he would go through the light, but a turning vehicle stopped him.

Chris used the opportunity to turn down another side street and then back to the main drag. If the Saab got there at the same time, the police would be around, and the enemy's plan would be thwarted. Chris hoped and prayed his car was not only fast enough to lose the guy, but that it had enough power to allow him to escape with his life.

—————⊰◆⊱—————

Margo hated waiting in yet another emergency room. The black vinyl seats stuck to her legs even with the crisp autumn air outside. Her neck was killing her, but not enough to get her a grand entrance into the white-curtained room where Paul lay.

Although the surroundings were less than conducive to prayer, she petitioned the Lord for Chris's safety like she never did before. Where was he? It seemed like an eternity since she talked with him on the phone. Now she knew how helpless he felt the night she was kidnapped. It was a terrible feeling, but she was grateful God wasn't particular about where He met His family for prayer—an overcrowded waiting room gained as much attention as a beautiful cathedral. Although Margo's artistic nature had to admit she preferred the latter.

Ray interrupted her prayer as he walked out of the intake booth and sat down next to Joy. "So how's your neck feeling?"

"Not too bad. I think I didn't feel the impact as much because I was praying and didn't tense up."

He turned to Margo. "And you?"

"It's okay, but how are you? I'm sorry you got involved in this mess."

Ray rubbed his neck. "It hurts, but not too much to pray. Want to?"

"Yes, dear." Joy's voice sounded loving.

He scooted his chair closer to Joy, and Margo did too.

Ray looked around the room then bowed his head. "Dear God, we need you to send us some angels and blind the enemy's eyes. Please protect Chris. We come against this evil presence that's following us."

Joy nodded in agreement.

Margo lifted her head. "Yes, Lord. Please grant Chris the wisdom to know what to do. Surround him with your cloud of protection and hide him in your wings. Please keep *those* guys away from the trunk of the car. Thwart the enemy's plan, abort it, confuse them, and protect the stone from falling into their hands again. And by the way, please get us out of here ASAP."

Margo felt a tremendous power descend like a weight of glory. She saw a very bright light in her mind. It was too bright to open her eyes. She bathed in its peaceful presence.

While Ray prayed, his words seemed different and far away. Margo heard him binding the evil spirits of the occult, the supernatural and death, but she felt like the ceiling opened up and she was looking down from the clouds. She sensed she was beyond the dimensions of time and space, yet she couldn't see anything except an intense light. It wasn't heaven or what she supposed the face of God looked like. But it was the most incredible, beautiful golden light. She felt like she was floating toward it. If she had wings, she would fly.

But Margo still had the sense of being in the hospital waiting room. She felt it was an odd time to have a spiritual experience, in the middle of a stuffy, small room, but she didn't question God about it. If He chose that moment to show her His power, then it was His business, but she couldn't help wondering, why?

⬦

Stan's auto body shop wasn't the most honest or cleanest place in town, but he'd won the bid for hauling and impounding cars. Being the new guy on the block, Stan and his new partner, Bob, purposely underbid everyone else. Even though the place hadn't been functioning for over ten years, Bob began to make some minor changes. The lot was a converted hay field that wasn't paved over.

As Bob waved his flannel checkered arm and directed his men where to put the car, he wasn't at all surprised to see a couple of cop cars pull up to the shop. Mike had called and warned him that a blue Dodge, belonging to Ray Hopelyn, might be on its way. He told him to hang onto it no matter what.

Bob listened as the two cops argued over the car. It was probably a case of "jury-diction," as Stan called all that nonsense.

Bob didn't care whose car it was, state or local, but he wondered what Mike was all concerned about.

In the end, the state policeman won out, and the local cop tore out of the lot just as a sporty black Z pulled up. A tall, lean guy in a suit unfolded himself from the car. Bob was surprised he even fit into the vehicle. He watched from his vantage point in the lot as the man approached the state trooper. He saw the two of them talking, and then the suited man turned his back; but in doing so, he got a glimpse of what looked like a deep cut on his cheek.

Bob moseyed over and pretended to pick up an old tire lying on the ground right past the curious stranger. Maybe he could even make a little money on this deal, but he'd have to be sneaky. Mike warned him these guys could be rough. Maybe the cop was on the take.

"So," Bob coughed and took out the keys for the blue car. He dangled them in front of the two. "I guess I'll be locking these up for the night." Bob grinned like the Cheshire cat from *Alice in Wonderland* and put the keys back in his pocket.

The guy in the suit turned and faced Bob and looked him straight in the eye. "Well, you're quite the resourceful guy. Just the type I like to have around."

Bob shuffled back and forth for a second and then looked down. A cool breeze swept across the field from the mountains, and he looked up. Not knowing what to say and feeling unusually awkward, Bob just grinned with his mouth closed. This time he didn't show his black teeth.

The man in the suit pulled out some cash. "Would $200 cover the cost of those keys?"

The state trooper stuck out his arm, blocking Bob from taking the money. "That won't be necessary. The contents of this car are under investigation." He looked at Bob. "Hand over those keys, old boy."

"You got a warrant?" Bob asked.

The cop spit on the ground. "Don't need one." He pulled aside his jacket revealing a gun.

Bob spat. "No need for that, boys." He reached in his pocket and pulled out the keys. "Here you go." He threw them at the officer, and they landed on the ground. As the cop bent to get them, Bob forced his legs to run faster than they'd done in years.

The cop fired a warning shot. "These better be them or you're in trouble, old boy."

Bob waved. "Don't worry. Just got a call from nature." He felt his heart pounding like he hadn't in years. When he reached the office, he collapsed at the desk then rummaged through his papers. Now where in tarnation did he put Mike's number for that newfangled phone? Like his buddy said, *I sure could use some help here, Lord.* He reached into his pocket and pulled out a crumbled piece of paper.

38

That afternoon, a number of telephone lines across Kingsland were busy with the recent news about Joy and Margo. Ray insisted on calling Dave from Paul's cell phone, and the pastor had put the phone chain into effect. No less than fifty faithful warriors were either praying on the phone or down on their knees.

One woman in particular, a good friend of Joy's who was friends with a Christian counselor, had been talking with him about the recent events. The two had some long conversations together as he had counseled several former occultists who were now Christians. They suffered terrible nightmares over things they had done in their former life, and they also revealed some of the horrible and bloody rituals they had been involved in with animals. So the women knew just how serious all of this could be, and she dropped the phone when she heard the whole story. Her heart was heavy and burdened for Joy and her friends.

After the call, she fell to her knees; her heart grieved, and she started praying, "Dear God, please protect this young family and the Hopelyns with your Holy Spirit and surround them with your mighty angels. Cover them with the blood of Jesus. Confuse the plans of the enemy. Bring down the strongholds the enemy has established against you. Let your name be magnified and praised above all others."

The woman remained on her knees for over half an hour, pouring out prayers of protection and praise. As horrible and unbelievable as it seemed, she felt prompted to pray that Joy and Margo would not be one of the victims for the society's autumn equinox.

⸻◆⸻

Bill stepped around to the back of his sporty Datsun 280 Z and smiled to himself as he strolled over to the police. *Your little group of nobodies thought it was all over for me. How naive and foolish all of you Christians are, especially you, Margo.* Bill approached, and the policeman lifted the trunk. The stone lay wrapped in a blanket, and Bill unwrapped it. "Yes, this is the one." He nodded. With the aid of the state policeman, he hoisted the artifact into the trunk of his black sports car. He handed the trooper $5,000 and shook his hand heartily. "Thank you for all your help, sir. I'm sure my colleagues at the historical institute will be very pleased with your contribution to their cause."

He knew the officer probably didn't believe the story, but it was all a front. Outright graft sometimes left a bad taste in a cop's mouth, and Bill didn't want to risk offending and perhaps instigating a cop he didn't outright know or own, even if the boss said he did.

Bill slid into the front seat of the shiny vehicle, feeling a swelling sense of pride in accomplishing a deed even the boss botched up. *Boy, this will put me back in his good graces and even earn me some extra cash.* Touching the fresh scar on the left side of his cheek, he added, *Maybe even a whole new facial makeover.*

⸻◆⸻

Paul recovered quickly after the surgery and easily slipped out of the hick hospital once he was out of recovery. He urged the taxi driver to move it along faster and waved a twenty in front of him. The cabbie turned around, his white teeth gleaming, and stepped on it. Paul had got a mere seventeen stitches and a few hours of rest, but now he needed to attend to business again. Ray sat quietly and prayed as Paul churned out his plans in whispered tones.

They sped along doing 70 mph in a 55 mph zone, so when a car buzzed by them, it caught their attention. Sure enough, it was a black shiny Z, and Paul recognized it immediately. Not too many people knew the car, since it was the driver's personal pleasure vehicle and not a *company car*, but Paul did. He urged the driver to go even faster.

As the cab slowed down at the place Paul indicated, he looked quizzically at the two men. Paul handed him another twenty and hopped out before the driver even came to a complete stop. Paul urged Ray in the direction of the car and indicated to the driver to "get on outta here." He fumbled in his pockets for his keys as he headed for an old barn about a mile from the the Hopelyns's, where he had asked Ray to hide it. He hesitated for a moment and looked back at the driver.

The cabbie took off, and so did Paul with Ray trailing behind. As he ran across the field with his arm in a sling, Paul felt like a wounded soldier returning home after a tour of duty. It was the closest thing to patriotism Paul had experienced in a long time. It felt good, even normal, to be doing something for someone else, even risking his life.

As Paul neared the barn, he saw the grass nearby was matted down, and he worried some kid hot-wired the car. But as he entered, he saw it was right where it should be, though the rear bumper was dented in. He withheld a curse. *Probably just some stupid kids.*

He threw Ray the keys. "You drive. And make it snappy." Ray opened the car door, and Paul maneuvered his arm with the sling into the red Triumph and slipped in on the passenger side. His newfound friend jammed the key into the steering column, and it started. He audibly thanked God. Paul looked overly sheepishly and added, "Yeah, God, thanks…at least it's running." With that, Ray carefully negotiated through the bramble of bushes and entanglements of roots.

As soon as he reached the open field, Ray threw it into second gear; the tires spun for a moment and kicked up clouds of dust, but he didn't hesitate for a second as he stepped on the gas. The powerful engine shot the car forward tearing up chunks of field and grass as they rocketed toward the road. Paul shouted to Ray, "Where'd you learn to drive like that?"

Ray shot a quick look over his right shoulder. "You're forgetting this is my neck of the woods. I learned to a drive tractor at twelve."

Paul checked to make sure no cars approached. "Let her rip."

The vehicle hit the pavement full steam, practically sending the car into the air like the flying machine on the *Dukes of Hazzard*. Ray maneuvered the car onto the pavement, and they roared up Route 207. Ray prayed, "Dear God, temporarily blind the eyes of any cops that might be in the area, but more importantly, surround us with mighty angels of protection and power."

Paul laughed. "That's some prayer. You think God will do that?"

"I don't know about the blinding part, but the other, I sure hope so."

———⟫•◈•⟪———

Bob smelled something fishy with the story about the stone in the back of the car being stolen from the museum. And that guy with the cut on his face looked vaguely familiar. His cumbersome body shuffled up and down the small, cluttered cubicle of an office, and he racked his brain for over half an hour trying to remember where he saw that face. His mind, usually clouded with alcohol, was like tuning into a scrambled TV station, so it took a while to decipher what was actually going on. Often, Bob gave up and just lived in the haze of the moment, not worrying about the past and barely able to see into the future. Now that he no longer bar tendered on weekends, his mind was slowly beginning to recover, but huge gaps existed. He wanted to give up, but something nagged at the corners of his mind not to. *Dang, I know that face.*

Feeling exhausted, he sat down for a few minutes and shuffled idly though the stack of papers on his desk. Under some bills he found the channel changer and flicked the TV on. A theme song sounded like the tape had played too many times came on accompanied by the sound of choppers coming in for a landing.

Then all of a sudden, his mind lit up, like a circuit an electrician had been working on for hours. He pointed to the screen, "That guy," he mumbled half aloud. "The one down at the bar late one night," he shouted. That show had been on in the bar, and he remembered how much he hated it, and the two guys kept him there late. So late he almost missed his fishing trip with Mike the next morning.

Wait a minute, he furrowed his graying eyebrows. *That there was the fishin' trip when I damn near lost my life to that overgrown brown bear.* He pounded his heavy hand on the desk and reached for the phone. *I'm gonna let Mike know about these goings-on. I smell a rat, or is it a fish?* Bob laughed at how clever he was, as clever as a fish who knew how to steal a worm and not get hooked.

<hr>

Margo nearly fainted waiting for someone, anyone—a nurse or an aide—to see her. Finally they called her in and examined her. The doctor loaded her down with prescriptions: a neck brace and several different kinds of medicines, muscle relaxers, and painkillers. No way was she going to take all those.

She flipped her cell open and saw that Chris tried to call several times while she was talking to the doctor. Not wanting it to be traced, she hadn't been using the phone to call anyone, but she had to talk to Chris. He answered right away. "Are you okay?" He didn't wait for Margo to reply. "Ray called about the crash, and I tried calling you. Then Mike contacted me. I have some really bad news. They got the stone!"

Margo took a deep breath and regrouped. "It doesn't surprise me the way things have been going around here, but maybe God has another plan up his sleeve we don't know about. I heard Ray and Paul are on their way up the mountain, over to the garage where they towed the car. Why don't you wait for them and the two of you can join forces together."

"Hey, I'm talking to the owner of this garage, and he's got something interesting to tell me."

"Don't tell me you're listening to stories when our lives are at stake!"

"No, no, it's not just a story. It seems like this guy met Bill and Paul one night when he was bartending."

"Oh great, so know you're interviewing anyone who met them." Margo let the words slip out, but she wished she could take them back. She didn't know why she was being so nasty. "Sorry." Margo's voice was truly apologetic.

"You won't believe this. Bill was here! He was the one who took the stone away."

"That's impossible. I thought he went over a cliff?" Margo knew Bill was a trickster, but no one could have survived that accident.

"Maybe that's what he wanted us to believe. Anyway, the guy here said he had a long deep cut on the left side of his cheek, so he'd been in an accident."

"So where does that put us?"

"Probably back at the cave."

Margo groaned "Oh no, Chris. Please don't." She couldn't stand the thought of Chris going back up. There was such a strong evil surrounding the place, and she couldn't let her husband risk his life over the stone.

"Listen. This Bob guy is a friend of Mike's, and he gave him a call. Mike's on his way now, and we're going to head up the mountain."

Margo hesitated. "Then I'm coming with you. Pick me up at… what's the name of the pharmacy we go to?" Margo's memory for particular names still faded in and out since her hypnotizing ordeal and imposed drug overdose.

"Finns, Finns in New Coven."

"Yeah, I'll take a taxi there."

"*No*, Margo, you go home. You're in no shape to deal with this kind of danger. Mike and I will take care of this, and Paul and Ray can join us if they get here soon enough."

She took a deep breath and exhaled slowly. "You don't understand. It's me he wants. I'm sorry, but I've got to go up there and confront him."

Chris didn't answer for a few moments, and Margo thought she lost the connection. "Are you there?"

"Yes," Chris's voice answered. "I'm just worried. I don't want you to get hurt, but if you must, don't come alone. I'll see you up there."

"Okay, I won't." She hung up the phone and immediately dialed Lance's number. Margo wanted to listen to her husband's advice, she really did, but he didn't understand everything that had transpired in the cave. She had to meet Bill face-to-face and confront the evil. Nobody else could do this for her.

Nobody but God could help her, and hopefully Lance.

In Paul's estimation, Ray took several of the curves on the mountain road with only two wheels. The tires screeched and smoked, but miraculously, Ray stayed on the windy route all the way up. Unlike Bill, Ray slowed down for the most dangerous hairpin turn, but he took it twenty miles faster than the recommend speed limit of ten miles per hour.

"I guess you really know this road. You're driving it like a professional," Paul complimented Ray.

"Yeah, I've driven it a thousand times before at this speed when I was younger."

Paul nodded. He had other things on his mind…like Bill. The whole way up the mountain, he never caught sight of the black 280 Z again, and he wondered if they were on the right track. Would Bill be foolish enough to go back to the cave? Were they being stupid to confront a team of "occultists," as Ray called them, and maybe some hit men that big money could buy? Paul wasn't sure what to do. "Hey, you think we could pray?"

Ray shot him a sideward glance. "Sure…sure. Let's do it right now!"

Mike got Bob's phone call and immediately called Pastor Dave about the new developments. The pastor informed his wife of current events and asked her to call several other prayer chains in the Kingsland area. If he was going to risk his life, he wanted as much prayer as he could get for him and everyone else involved. This time he had a better idea of what he was getting himself into, and he knew they could certainly use the intervention of a legion of angels.

Margo phoned Lance at the Johnson hotel where he had rendezvoused with his wife. Just as she was about to hang up the phone, a groggy but sweet voice answered, "Hello, this is the Spears residence." Confused, Margo realized Heidi must have forgotten she and her husband weren't home.

"Hi, this is Margo. Aren't you at the hotel? Is Lance there?"

"Oh yeah, we're here. I'm sorry I just took a short nap. No, I don't see Lance. Is everything okay?"

"Yes, we're okay, but some of us were in a minor car accident, except for Paul. His was more serious. He got shot."

"Shot? Is he okay?"

"Yes, he took a bullet to the arm, but he's patched up. God protected us, but listen…I need you to help us again."

"Sure."

"Do you know where Lance is?"

"He's probably taking a swim in the pool. I needed to relax a bit, after—"

Margo interrupted, "Time is of the essence."

"Okay, what do you need?'

"Well, first I need the car and then," Margo hesitated and repeated, "then if Lance is willing, it sure would be helpful if he drove me up the mountain."

Heidi didn't reply at first and she took a long breath. "If that's what you need, I'll go tell him right away. Where are you?"

"I'm at the Kingsland General Hospital. The one on Main Street. At the emergency entrance. And don't call my cell."

"Okay, I'll talk to Lance about it and phone some of the elders for prayer."

Margo breathed a sigh of relief. "Thanks a million, but don't call Vince or Rich." She didn't want those two interfering with anything.

"Yes, I understand. How about Mark?"

"Sure." Margo hung up the phone. Hopefully Lance would come and get her, and then she could explain more fully what she wanted to do. It seemed crazy to go after Bill, but she had to confront him and somehow get the stone. How? She didn't know. That part of the plan wasn't arranged yet. Hopefully, God would supply the details if she supplied the faith.

Vince couldn't stand what was happening in the church and decided to take an inventory of the events over the last couple of months. First, Margo had some way-out wacky prophecy about divisions, and before you know it, the more prosperous members of the congregation had decided to form their own little group across the river. Next, she got mixed up in all kinds of trouble she didn't think he knew about, but he had ways of finding out. Then when a ray of financial hope appeared, he wound up dead.

Now to top things off, the members of his congregation were leaving each other faster than he could visit them. First, Jessica ran away from Mark, then Melanie went and had an affair, but Rich didn't know with whom. And now on top of it all, one of the most solid members of his congregation who has been married fifteen years was leaving her husband. Vince couldn't help to see that Margo was at the core of these problems. He hated to admit it. *Whatever she's gotten herself into is killing my congregation. She's got to be stopped before she does more harm.*

39

At Paul's insistence, Ray turned down an unfamiliar back road. He thought Paul might be bringing them on a shortcut to the cave, but he didn't see how, unless they went through the woods from a different direction. It seemed to him it would take longer. Ray decided to keep quiet and pray and then see what unfolded. He hoped they wouldn't be the only two confronting a group of muscle-bound, professional killers.

As he bounced down the path, questions plagued his mind. Maybe he was on the completely wrong track. Maybe they'd find nothing. Margo and Joy would have to accept the fact that it was in the possession of the enemy.

But then again, perhaps all the prayers they "offered" to the Lord would open the floodgates of heaven. He recalled the Bible story they read about Jacob and the angels who went up and down a ladder. He thought about the unlikelihood of such an event, though something new inside him stirred. Right then, Ray decided to pray aloud. "Lord, send us a legion of angels unseen by the enemy, so they will guide us in the way we should go. Amen."

Paul mumbled an amen and directed Ray to stop in an area hidden by large pine trees. He explained to Ray, "Hardly anyone comes this way. It's bordered on three sides by a state forest preserve and surrounded by fifty acres of private land. Only a select few have seen what I'm about to show you."

Ray agreed. "I've never been here before. How do you know about it?"

"Bill was in their inner circle and came here a lot. He even had an *office* up there." Paul told Ray to proceed slowly. Without an SUV, they bounced up and down along the rough dirt road for three sore miles. Then they stopped short.

"Park the car behind these bushes," Paul ordered Ray. He turned off the car and sat there for a moment. "So where are we?"

"Don't ask. The less you know, the better." Paul hurried him out of the car.

"Where are we going?"

"Just follow me. We're heading for their hideout." Paul prayed to himself. *Dear God, show me what to do.*

"Isn't that dangerous?

"Yes, but isn't that what all this faith stuff is about? Trusting God?"

"So how are the two of us going to do any good?"

"I'm hatching a plan right now. I'm hoping we'll beat Bill up here. We'll know when we sneak around the corner of the house and see if his car is there. If it's not, then we have an edge."

Ray raised his eyebrows. "We do?"

Paul slowly smiled. "Yeah, I thought you called on a legion of angels back there."

Ray looked sheepishly at Paul. "I guess you're right. I did!"

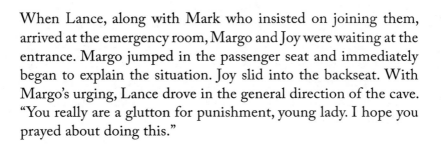

When Lance, along with Mark who insisted on joining them, arrived at the emergency room, Margo and Joy were waiting at the entrance. Margo jumped in the passenger seat and immediately began to explain the situation. Joy slid into the backseat. With Margo's urging, Lance drove in the general direction of the cave. "You really are a glutton for punishment, young lady. I hope you prayed about doing this."

Margo smiled coyly. "I've something to confess. We're not going to the cave, just somewhere near there. I know that much. I was familiar with the twist and turns from before, until we pulled off some side road. I just don't know where."

Joy, who had patiently listened to Margo for hours, interjected, "What are you talking about, dear? We don't understand."

Margo almost forgot Joy accompanied them. "It's complicated, but the night I was kidnapped, it took at least half an hour for the drugs Paul gave me to work." Margo needed to figure out where Joy could stay. She didn't want to put her life in jeopardy.

"Paul?" Lance interrupted.

That's it, Margo thought. Joy could stay with Lance's wife. "Yes, didn't you know he used to partner with Bill? He became a Christian just recently. Anyway, it's not important. Just let me continue. They took me up into the mountains by the hairpin turn, but little did they suspect I knew the area like the back of my hand. I recognized the twist and turns, except for the last one. I don't know where the road is, but I'm praying the Holy Spirit will show me. But first, do you think Joy could spend some time with your wife, Heidi?"

"Sure. It's on this side of town, only about five minutes out of the way."

"Oh, I see," Joy brightened. "Lance's wife and I can pray for the Lord's guidance while you're up there doing whatever you need to get done. I'll ask Bethany also."

Mark, who had been quiet till now, furrowed his brow. "Margo, what is it we're supposed to do when we get there?"

"I'm not sure, but again I'm hoping the Holy Spirit will show us, and with Heidi, Bethany and Joy praying for us, I'm sure He'll direct us."

Lance laughed. "I hope He sends you an instant message."

The Z zoomed up the mountain with no problem. It hugged the road like a gloved hand, and Bill loved the thrill of it all. Now that he had the stone in his possession, the bargaining power was his. He hadn't realized until recently just how much clout it possessed.

Now he understood why they were so cautious with it and wouldn't let just anyone touch it. It was the center of their rituals, and they believed it had power. And indeed it did. He already saw it working its division on those unsuspecting Christian couples. He thoroughly enjoyed the part he played in the whole scheme, enticing the female members. Bill loved what he did, and he was good at it. The best.

But even more important, the women were coming under his power and influence. All was going just as he planned, all but one little problem. *And that one I will soon eliminate, maybe even today.* He laughed.

Mike drove his truck up the backside of the mountain, heading south from Kingsland. As they sped down the twisty road, Chris stared out the window. He watched the leaves as they swirled around and hoped Margo wouldn't be swept away by this darkness closing in on them.

Chris wondered how far they were from their destination. He'd never traveled this way before. The area seemed unfamiliar, dark, and menacing, though it was practically right here in his backyard. The wind picked up and howled. The dark forces seemed to mount with wings and multiply.

The enemy had already made a number of inroads at New Way Fellowship. If only they could put an end to all of this scheming, but he didn't even know what the enemy was doing. He prayed they'd get there in time to help.

On the opposite side of the mountain, Margo, Mark and Lance headed north toward the cave, but Margo knew their destination lay just beyond. She closed her eyes and tried to recall that frightening night when she was bound in Bill's car, led to the mountain like a sheep to slaughter. She tried to feel every twist and turn, and she prayed, *Dear God, please help me to remember the way, show me Lord. Without your guidance, there is no hope.*

Paul and Ray edged their way around the back to the mountain house. The men hid behind trees when possible and kept a safe distance from the edge of a cliff. Electricity filled the air as they approached closer. Hawks swooped about, catching air currents

Ray shivered. "This looks like something out of a movie. How close is the house to the edge of the cliff?"

"Close, real close. Easier to dispose of intruders that way."

Ray put words to Paul's thoughts. "Then we better pray now, together."

"Yeah, we're a bunch of crazy fools to attempt this without prayer, 'cause that's the only thing that's gonna save our hides." He imitated a cowboy drawl.

Ray put his hands on Paul's shoulder. "Where'd you get that expression?"

"Come on now. You know who. Our friend, Mike. He might be a cowboy type, but he sure packs a powerful prayer punch. And that's what we need right about now."

Bill turned the Z down the approach road to the mountain estate. The car endured a few bumps and scrapes, all which could be taken care of later. A surge of energy rushed through him, along with a heightened sense of awareness. Like his car, he felt assured he would triumph. He felt in complete control.

Everything was going according to plan, even better since now he now knew the true value of the stone. Bill wasn't sure the Big Boss, the Thirty-Third Degree Master Mason, wanted it for the money it could garner or the power. But he didn't care as long as he got his take. For a moment, he wished the lovely maiden he had met several weeks ago at the cave would be present, but he doubted she had any significance in the scheme of things. Perhaps she was no longer even alive. The thought did not trouble him as he realized how close he was to catching his prize. *Margo, my dear, you're not going to slip away from me this time.* He patted his pocket. *You'll soon be mine.*

———⬩———

As the car climbed the mountain, Margo felt the same chilling presence she had whenever Bill was nearby. She fought to shake it off, but it clung to her like a wet towel draped over her head and shoulders. When she told the others about it, they immediately joined her in prayer. Their spirits became heavier the farther they drove into the woods. Margo closed her eyes once again and tried to remember. This time she felt Bill's presence even stronger, and she blurted out, "I believe Bill is up at the mountain house at this very moment. We will need to be very careful. I also believe God is orchestrating a plan."

Mark turned around and faced her. "Well, we're only about half a mile from the turn to the cave, so start looking for this side road you've been talking about. I hope the Lord lets us in on this plan pretty soon."

"Don't worry. He will, but I think we should continue to pray for His protection and guidance." Margo tried to sound confident, but she knew she was up against a very sinister evil.

Lance, who had been quiet the whole time, finally spoke. "God is protecting and guiding us. Many are praying. I called Pastor Dave and several prayer chains. We have people from all over the country praying for us."

"Thank God." Margo breathed a sigh of relief. "We'll need it. I think we stumbled upon this stone at a very important time."

"Yes, for such a time as this," Lance whispered the words of a familiar song.

"What did you say?" Mark raised an eyebrow.

"For such a time as this."

"Yes, yes, I remember that song from years back. I think you're right, for such a time as this."

Margo nodded her head in agreement, but she secretly worried she was jeopardizing their lives and falling into a trap. She had an uneasy feeling in her stomach that Bill wanted her to meet him at the mountain house, but she kept her doubtful thoughts to herself. *How could he possible think I could remember how to get there, unless…*

Lance interrupted her thoughts. "Well, Margo, here's the path to the cave. I'll go slowly from here so you can try to remember."

As she tried to recapture where they turned off, Margo closed her eyes and felt the bumps along the road. Just as she got a sense of where they were, Mark yelled. "Hey, there's Mike, along with Chris." Margo's eyes popped open and she thought aloud. "This feels like déjà vu. I've been here before."

"The Lord is guiding us," Lance said with confidence. "And he has brought us help."

Mike slowed down his vehicle and hollered in a friendly cowboy manner. "Well, fancy meetin' you folks up here. How about you all hop in my truck, and we drive up the road." He looked down at their car. "You'll never make it in that."

Lance nodded. "Okay, but let's get off the side of the road first."

Mike grinned. "Good thinking. There's a spot just about a quarter of a mile up the road on your left. Pull over there, and I'll meet you there."

As the car approached, Lance pulled onto a barely visible dirt road. Margo sensed something familiar again. They waited there for a few moments for Mike and Chris to join them. Then it hit Margo. "This is it! This is it! This is the turnoff."

Chris hopped out of the car and ran to his wife. "Are you okay?" he asked then jumped into the car and gave her a hug.

"So much has been going on I hardly remember what happened, but I'm fine, just a little whiplash." She tried to convince him as he rubbed her neck. "Hardly anything at all." She turned to Mike. "Do you know where this road leads?"

"Why yes, ma'am. This here is a poorly maintained park service road, so hardly anyone ever goes on it, but being the curious old goat that I am"—Mike scratched his head—"umm, I mean God's sheep, I've driven it to the end. About a mile up the road, it smoothes out, but then the road turns private and the most curious thing is—"

Margo finished his sentence. "It turns to paved road."

Mike looked at her, puzzled. "Why, how did you know?"

Before he could finish his thought, the other two joined him in the truck. Margo sat between the cowboy and Chris. "Listen, Mike, I've been here before, but not under the most pleasant circumstances. All I can tell you right now is that I'm pretty certain Bill is up there with the stone."

"Are you sure?"

"No, but I have the sense I'm right."

"Then we need to go there and not the cave."

"And we need to go right now," Chris affirmed.

Margo gave him a tight hug. She realized his fear for her had turned to courage once he knew she wasn't hurt.

"We'll need to be in constant prayer," Margo reminded them. "Let's get going."

Mike took the hint and stepped slowly on the gas pedal. "This part's rough going, so we have to take it slow, but only for a little stretch of road, then we'll be in the clear."

"As clear as mud," Margo mumbled under her breath.

Paul and Ray reached the edge of the woods bordering the eastern side of the mountain house. The air was damp and cold for October, and an icy wind blew across the mountaintops. From where Ray stood, he could view the entire southern portion of the Mohawkin Valley. It was breathtaking, but quite dangerous as there were no fences or guardrails to keep a person from falling to their death. Ray shivered as they passed and hesitated momentarily to peek over the edge.

"Someone could get hurt here," he commented dryly.

Paul turned around and nervously shook the coins in his pocket. "Exactly."

Ray motioned for him to be quiet.

They continued to walk along the edge of the cliff. Then Paul stopped and headed due east toward the direction of the house. Ray breathed a sigh of relief as they left the edge of the cliff. About five hundred yards away from the driveway, under the cover of thick pines, Paul stopped and pointed. "There's Bill's car parked in the driveway."

Not only did Ray see the Datsun Z but also two other vehicles—a black limo and a Mercedes SUV.

"How many do you think are in there?" Ray wasn't sure they could pull off Paul's plan.

"At least four or five, maybe more."

Right about now, it seemed the odds were stacked against them, though Ray believed God would make a way for them, even if they were outnumbered.

"Well then, God will beef up our side…somehow." Ray prayed God would show them what to do.

"Okay, you be the lookout, and I'll do the grunt work. Get as close to the house as possible without being seen. Give me thumbs-up for all clear and down for you know what. I'll rush out behind his car and wait for Bill to come out for the stone. I'll take care of Bill and a few others." He patted his pocket, and Ray knew he was packing. "You'll have to take care of whoever you can. Find yourself a big stick and—"

"Pray like crazy."

Mike knew the house Margo referred to as her abduction site. He'd driven down that road a number of times and even walked the edge of the property. The deer loved the area and wherever deer roamed, so did Mike. Since it was surrounded by state land, Mike could safely stay off private property without breaking the law. However, before he was a Christian, he broke the law several times and had actually snuck right up to the mountain house when there were no vehicles in the driveway. "It's a huge place," he told the gang as they drove up the paved section. "But I never saw what's inside. They always kept the curtains closed."

As they approached, Mike pulled the truck over to the side of the road.

Margo protested, "What are you doing? I don't see the house from here."

He smiled. "We'll just have to hoof it. We can't take the chance of announcing ourselves. I know a shortcut through the woods, which will take us right to the doorstep in about five minutes if we get a move on." So the party of four climbed out of the truck and followed Mike into the woods. *Show me the way, dear Lord,* he implored as they forged ahead.

40

Bill loved the thought of being in control, especially around so much money and power. He sat back in the comfortable leather chair and grinned. The Worshipful Master, as they called him—though Bill often referred to him simply as the Big Boss—sat behind a large mahogany desk engaged in conversation. Bill's attention wandered to the furnishings. Gold trimmed the edges of the armrests, and marble statues decorated the room. Rich brocade drapes hung from the walls, blocking out the sun. Everything spoke of money—Bill's language.

He recognized pictures of a few prominent, wealthy businessmen from the city, yet several photos of people he'd never saw before graced the walls. When Mr. Know finished talking, he turned to Bill. His dark eyes narrowed, and he reached over. They intertwined their hands in the Masonic handshake. Leaning over the desk, his raspy voice demanded. "Okay, so let me have it. How did you turn this all around?"

At that order, Bill shot up straight and explained how he executed his fake death after his release from jail. As he spoke, Bill sank back into the chair. He played the story out, making himself the hero. He also exaggerated his cunning and cleverness in recapturing the stone, which really wasn't very difficult. "I outsmarted the whole lot of them. They thought they had God on their side," Bill cackled. "They didn't know who they were dealing with." The room filled with a dark presence, and Bill fed off it.

The imposing figure leaned forward from the huge mahogany desk and listened intently. Bill knew he was more than interested. Normally, he would have cut him off and ordered him to deliver the goods, but he was probably in awe of the fact Bill had survived the car crash. The very *accident* they probably engineered, but Bill had used all his skill and power to survive. Willing himself to live, he called upon the great forces of the universe to come to his aide, and they answered. Any normal person would have died on impact, but not him.

Ten minutes into the story, the Worshipful Master gave Bill the signal, and he knew he had played it out. Bill grinned when asked for the goods. "Now, guys, you know I'm not stupid. You produce the money then I produce the goods."

A businessman in a gray Armani suit coughed and spoke in a deep low voice, "First we want to see what you have." He leaned back in his chair and grinned.

Another man spoke in a softer voice. "We are not concerned about monetary value, although," he cleared his throat and continued, "we are prepared to pay. However, this in itself is not our goal. We are only concerned about what is in your possession, Mr. Eville, it will be used for *our* purposes, purposes which have far-reaching consequences… purposes beyond your scope." He stared into Bill's eyes as if trying to reach into his soul, but Bill knew that game. He played it himself and put on an impenetrable mask.

Bill replied coolly. "I'm sorry, but Mr. Know acquired me for this job. It's not for me to negotiate." He turned to the stout man walled behind the desk but spoke to the man in the suit. "You, sir, must consult with the Worshipful Master." Bill knew this would curry favor with him, and he did it not to please the man but for his own purposes. Bill loved power, and he didn't really care where it came from. He only desired the title of a Third-Degree Master Mason so he could be in control. He had no allegiance to anyone, not even the so-called witches, warlocks, and occultists who gleaned their power from the dark side or even the Seventeenth-Degree Master Masons of their secret society and money. They too were caught in the clutches of something more powerful than themselves, but Bill played above it all, or so he thought.

He announced, "I will show it to one of you so you will know I indeed posses it. However"—he glanced around the room—"I am not ignorant enough to think you will not steal it if I bring it in here. So I'll let one of you come out and see it. You decide among yourselves who it will be. It can even be Mr. Know for that matter. I don't care, just decide who." After his speech, Bill stood up. "Before any of you pump me full of lead, you should know I've secured my trunk with a special lock only I can decode. And for added assurance, if you try to eliminate me, I'll press this little button, and the car will explode." Bill grinned and hoped they took his bait. He laughed at his own cunning. "And don't think I'm foolish enough to come here unarmed." He patted his jacket pocket and strolled confidently toward the door.

He stopped and turned around. "I'll wait outside for you for five minutes, no more, no less." As he hedged toward the door, Bill added. "And thanks for the great cover-up with the *accident*." He smiled and turned again to Mr. Know.

The powerful man, caught off guard for a moment, responded. "Of course, Bill, of course." A grin crept across his lips then grew full and broad.

Bill knew just what that meant. It was the master's way of admitting he'd been responsible for Bill's accident. But he didn't care. He was like a cat with nine lives.

⋙◆⋘

Zuriel rejoiced as he watched phone line after phone line jam with prayer requests. Friends of the Piersons and Hopelyns, respectively, gathered in small impromptu meetings. He felt the humans' sense of urgency as they poured out their hearts to the Father. Several captains reported some prayer warriors literally locked themselves in their prayer closets and petitioned the Lord for all those involved in this battle.

The Holy Spirit moved freely among them, and many called upon his kind to protect the small band of believers. Pastor Dave stood up and proclaimed, "Dear God, confound the plans of the enemy. Trip them up in their own schemes. Cause the division they called upon us, as Christians, to divide themselves. Grant wisdom to Mike and Ray and all his newfound friends. Give them strength and courage beyond measure. Anoint them with Your Holy Spirit for Your name's sake so the kingdom of darkness might be brought low this very day, even this very hour. By His shed blood, may they prevail over darkness. In Jesus's precious name. Amen."

This was the kind of prayer that mobilized their forces and brought angelic hosts to their aid. With prayer like this, the impossible just might become possible, if only the humans would continue to pray in faith.

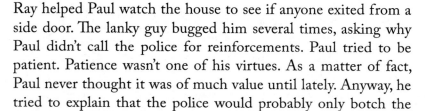

Ray helped Paul watch the house to see if anyone exited from a side door. The lanky guy bugged him several times, asking why Paul didn't call the police for reinforcements. Paul tried to be patient. Patience wasn't one of his virtues. As a matter of fact, Paul never thought it was of much value until lately. Anyway, he tried to explain that the police would probably only botch the whole thing. "Look what happened in Kingsland," he reminded Ray. "They were in on the deal."

"Yes. But now we have believers all over the county praying for us."

Paul looked him in the eye. "Yeah, I think this prayer stuff is good for your soul, but leave the body work to me." He pointed to his chest. "I know what's best. I want to leave the cops out of this." Paul didn't want any more crooked cops in on his stakeout. He knew how far Bill and his bosses influence reached.

"I can see you feel really strong about this, but not all cops are on the take. You've got to learn to trust people."

"I'm trusting you, isn't that enough for now?"

Ray slapped him on the back. "Thanks, buddy, but I'm not—"

Paul grabbed Ray's arm. "Did you hear that?"

"What?"

The rustling in the woods got louder. Paul squatted down and pulled Ray down with him. They brushed against the scratchy pine branches. "Maybe Bill spotted us a ways back and is prowling around after us. He must think I remembered these woods." Paul looked around. "Wait a second, he thinks I skipped town. And another thing"—he pointed toward the house—"I know he's in there."

No sooner had he finished his sentence when Ray exclaimed, "Hey, I think that's Mike."

"Mike? How would he know this place?" Paul looked in the direction of the rustling leaves. "Well, I see a cowboy hat, but I can't see a face. You must have x-ray vision to see through those trees."

"Oh, so now you're the jokester here. No, I didn't see the face, but I recognize the hat."

Paul laughed nervously. "What you recognized was a blur of tan and a cowboy hat like a million others. But don't stand up or signal him until we're sure. I'll keep my eye on the bushes and you watch the house for any movement.

But before Mike emerged from the woods, Paul heard an unmistakable voice floating on the air. He couldn't believe Margo would come out here after all she had been through.

"It's Mike and Margo," Paul announced. "I'm going to meet them, and we'll join forces. You stay here and keep an eye out. If Bill or anyone else steps foot out of the place, give a hoot. I'll only be away for a New York minute."

Paul took off for the woods, under cover. He prayed no one would notice the ripple in the bushes at the edge of the wooded area. When he came to the edge, he burst in on a party of not only two but four—Chris, Mark, Mike, and Lance had joined forces. Paul looked at them puzzled. "How in the world did you ever find this place?"

"It used to be an old hunting lodge they built on to," Mike answered.

Paul shook his head at Chris and Margo. "What are you two doing here? Trying to get killed!"

"No, we're the reinforcements," Margo said. "We're just trying to keep you alive."

Paul smirked and glanced over at Mark then Lance. "I guess you're here to give us our last rites."

"No, I'm not a priest. I'm here to—"

A shot echoed through the trees and startled Paul.

"Let's go!" he whispered in a harsh voice. They took off and followed behind him. As Paul charged through the tangle of branches, they lashed out against him, stinging his face. He didn't care. He'd left Ray by himself and was worried Bill's men had spotted him this time. If anything happened to Ray, he'd kill himself...or Bill.

As Paul neared the house, he stopped in an area shielded by bushes. Ray was just on the other side. Bill stood near the door, talking with another man, facing the other direction. Seeing his opportunity, Paul dashed from his spot and made it to Ray. He breathed a sigh of relief and slapped him on the back. "Glad you're okay, buddy."

"You were the one I was concerned about," Ray said. "I was praying that shot wasn't meant for you."

The rest of the party rendezvoused with Paul. Mike led the way.

"That sounded like a rifle, not a shotgun. Some old-timer might be huntin'," Mike conjectured.

"Great timing." Margo picked a twig from her hair.

"Let's stop this talk. I need a plan." Paul studied the scene. From his position, Bill's sports car was in view. He had parked next to an SUV. A few trees shielded it partially.

He turned to them. "This is my chance. I'm gonna make a run for it and hide under the vehicle next to Bill's." He hoped his large body would fit underneath.

Margo began to protest, but Paul darted away and into the bushes. He made it safely to the SUV and scooted underneath it. He positioned his legs onto the frame and hung on the other end with his one good, muscular arm. He hoped to surprise Bill when he opened his trunk without getting shot. It was a gamble, but it was a chance he had to take…for all of them.

———❖———

"So what do we do now?" Margo asked. She tried to think of a plan, something that would distract Bill if and when he came out of the building.

Lance looked up. "Whatever we decide, prayer needs to be included."

"That's for sure," they all agreed.

Margo hadn't stopped talking to the Lord since they got there. They needed a plan of action. So far they were just winging it, on the defense. They need to be on the offense. "Maybe one of us could create a diversion when Paul makes his move."

"Good idea." Chris nodded. "Lance, Mark and I could throw rocks and get their attention."

"It could work," Mark accepted. "But what do we do then, shoot them with sticks?"

"Of course not, I haven't thought that far." Frustrated, Margo didn't know what to do if they got shot at with real bullets.

"I can help Paul when he attacks," Mike offered.

Margo prayed again and waited for an idea. "I'd rather you help us navigate. You know these woods, right?"

Mike nodded.

"You could lead us around the back of the house and position us closer to the car, where we'll still be hidden."

He agreed, but added a caution. "It's dangerously close to the cliffs on that side. You need to be very careful and avoid getting too close."

"Can you see any other way?" Margo bit her nail.

"No, it's a good plan. Just risky."

Once everybody understood what to do, they crept through the woods. Chris volunteered to go around the western side of the house while Mike led Margo around the northern end. Thankfully, he steered her as far as possible away from the dangerous precipice. She hated heights and refused to even look down in that direction.

When they arrived at their destination, Mike ordered her to crouch down behind some shiny-leafed bushes near the hideaway. Their position offered maximum visibility of the car and house as long as they stayed there. But if needed, they would have no place to escape without being seen. The cliff formed a natural barrier to the back end of the house. Escape from the front seemed impossible in wide view of the windows.

Seconds ticked away.

Tension mounted as Margo heard voices arguing inside. A door banged open and shut. Feet scuffled on the wooden porch. A single shot exploded. It didn't sound like a hunter's rifle. Margo felt a lump in her throat. Were they on to them or fighting among themselves? *Dear Lord, what have I gotten everyone involved in? Please lead us and guide us safely.* It grew quiet. The air felt thick and oppressive.

Margo's muscles ached from squatting down on the ground in the same position. She rubbed her legs. All this waiting gave her too much time to think, and she relived all the pain this man had caused. If it weren't for the lives he put in jeopardy, she'd never want to face Bill again.

She leaned against a tree for a few moments then stood up to ease her tensed muscles. As she did, the front door flew open. Margo's heart jumped, and she dove back down. Bill strutted into the driveway accompanied by a rather large young man. Though she couldn't see his face close up, she felt as if his eyes bored a hole through her head. What was it about this man that made her lose her courage?

Margo watched Bill scan the woods and fields, checking for intruders. As she saw him walk toward his car, she broke out in a cold sweat. What would he do to her if the plan failed? She felt dizzy and nauseous, but she forced herself to watch and pray. When he neared his car, he walked around the side, facing away from the other vehicle.

How much longer could Paul hold on? If he fell to the ground now, Bill would have too much time to react. *Dear God, please help Paul know when to act.*

Bill clicked open the trunk, and he bent down to retrieve the contents.

Paul dropped from underneath the SUV.

Margo's throat went dry.

He charged out from underneath the vehicle.

Baam! Paul grabbed Bill's legs.

The sound of her heart pounded in her ears.

Bill wobbled back and forth…then fell to the ground.

The two of them struggled, rolling around on the driveway. At the same time, Mark and Ray created a loud diversion on the other side, and Bill's young companion looked in their direction. As he turned away, Mike charged from the trees. She hoped he could bring down the guy, but he looked like a tiger. She felt so small and helpless. What could she do but pray?

She watched in horror as one of the men in a suit turned around and fired at Mike. Margo stifled a scream as a bullet sailed over his head. "Thank you, Lord," she whispered. Yet what would happen if the men inside heard the shot? Surely they had.

But they couldn't lose now, could they? Didn't they have God on their side? Hadn't David killed a lion with his bare hands?

She recalled Joshua's battles. The odds looked grim against all their enemies, but the Lord gave Joshua battle strategy. *That's it! Lord, we need a plan, a really good one.*

In a flash, Mike attacked the guy, but he didn't go down easily. As Paul and Bill fought, he struggled to reach for something from his upper front pocket. Margo flinched. *God, no!* She mouthed the words.

Margo didn't know what to do. Could she help? She saw Chris run to the house, holding a spool of what looked like old metal wire. He and Mark unraveled it in front of the double doors and hid behind them as Lance stood poised with a huge stick in his hand. She wanted to scream. *Get out of there, run for your lives!*

She resisted the urge to run to her husband. Instead, she dropped her head in her hands. Fear crept up her spine again. How easily her faith crumbled. *How could they, a group of naïve citizens, fight against these experienced killers and hope to win?* It would take a miracle, like crossing the Jordan.

As she began to despair, someone tapped her on the shoulder. She felt exhausted and reacted slowly. When she saw it was her husband, she threw her arms around him. Relief washed over her. She never felt so happy to see him, to feel him next to her. Maybe this was her miracle. Chris was alive!

He pointed to the door. Ray had taken his place. As she watched, two huge guys wearing black suits threw open the doors, guns held high. They rushed out. Lance made sure one after another tripped over the unseen wire, and their weapons went flying. They took the fall hard down the stairs and lay sprawled on the ground. Ray and Mark pounced on what looked like automatic machine guns.

Mark jumped up and aimed the M16 at the two men. As the bodyguards slowly scrambled to their feet, Ray shot a round of gunfire over their heads and into the side of the house. The two froze. Margo rejoiced and wondered where Ray learned to use an automatic weapon. Perhaps this was the battle plan she asked for?

She revved into prayer warrior mode. "Thank You, Father, that You are in control. Your armies will have victory over the enemy. Please send heavenly reinforcements."

354

Though they weren't out of the woods yet, Margo sensed a tremendous weight lift. The burden felt lighter.

She sensed an angelic presence surround her, and she felt quite weak. As her legs wobbled and her heart pounded, she cried out to God. "Yea though I walk through the valley of the shadow of death, Thou art with me." Was there anything she could do? Margo surveyed the scene, and Chris seemed to be doing the same.

Over by the car, Mike had knocked the young man down, catching him off balance. The cowboy pinned him to the ground with David-like strength. Almost everyone was tied up in a fierce struggle. Yet the trunk remained open and vulnerable.

Mark and Ray held the two gangsters at gunpoint, but something had to be done soon. Where had they learned to handle such a deadly weapon? Apparently, they knew enough to keep these two at bay. The supposed hit men looked like stone statues. Should she notify the police? But what if the cops who responded were crooked? Maybe she should just trust God.

Perhaps something else aided them. Was it fear of the deadly weapons, or had God sent an angel?

Either way, she needed to help. But what should she do? Her head spun, and sweat dripped from her forehead in spite of the cold. *Show me the way, Lord.*

"Follow me," Chris yelled. "I've got an idea."

Margo tagged along as he ran toward Bill and Paul. The two men rolled around near the car, but neither side appeared to be winning. Did her husband think he could help Paul overpower Bill? What if he pulled out a gun? *Did Chris want to get them all killed?*

Instead, Chris bent down low and swept over the ground while avoiding the brawl. They reached the trunk of Bill's car in no time. Margo peeked in and was startled by what she saw—the stone. It had been cut in half! Not vertically but horizontally, like two sides of an Oreo cookie. Strangely, small sticks of dynamite littered the trunk.

Mike roped the guy he was fighting like a bull and came running over when Chris called for his help. When Chris reached in for the stone, he assured her, "It'll be much lighter now." As he pushed it, the top part slid apart, revealing the top half of the bottom stone.

Margo gasped.

It looked more recent than the top half and appeared as if a thin layer of wax or clear latex had been poured over it. Rather than hieroglyphs, a large Tree of Life stood in the center. From her study of art symbols, she knew this to be Irish or Celtic. Surrounding the tree were slithering serpents and symbols of broken branches grouped in threes, pentagrams with lightning bolts facing downward, and a large triangle with a stem resembling a champagne glass. Along with those, she saw several symbols of what looked like a compass, which she vaguely recognized. Once again, the familiar open and close rectangles with dots were present. "But what do these have to do with the others?"

Chris easily lifted up the top half with the Egyptian hieroglyphs. "Who knows? Maybe nothing, but that's what our lives will be worth if we don't get this out of here."

Margo bent down to lift the bottom stone filled with the strange symbols. As she brushed the surface, something inside Margo gave way. Her strength drained. "I can't move it. It won't budge." Margo's hands trembled as if she touched the very heart of a pulsating evil.

"Let me give it a try." Chris maneuvered the piece over the edge and flipped it out of the trunk. He leaned it against the vehicle "Here, you take the top half. It's much lighter. I'll deal with this one." He helped Margo get her stone on its end. "We can push these to Mike's truck and then call the police, that's if we can figure out which ones are honest." He lifted the heavier one and rolled it like a stone wheel.

Margo did likewise with hers. It rolled easy enough but needed to be kept under control. Chris's stone seemed more difficult to manage over the gravel driveway. It swayed back and forth and threatened to fall over. Sweat dripped from Chris's forehead as he moved the stone along.

They retreated to the woods, though Margo hated to leave everybody in such danger. Although miraculously, it looked like the three could handle it, as long as no one else was inside waiting for an opportune time. Yet they had to get these stones to safety, or more lives would be lost.

As they approached the edge, Margo glanced back over her shoulder to check on everyone else. She nearly fell over as she saw Bill wrestle a small revolver from his shirt pocket. She stopped and yelled. "Bill's got his gun!" Chris spun around.

Margo dropped her stone and screamed. "Paul, watch out!"

Drawing aside the drapes at all the commotion outside, Mr. Know watched the whole scene as anger rose and flooded his being. He should have brought more men, but he thought this would be between just Bill and him. If he stepped outside, he might be able to eliminate the whole lot, but that would soil his reputation as one who was to be worshipped above the folly of mere mortal men. Besides, he wasn't a trained shooter. Others did such dirty work for him.

A battle raged inside his soul, and he knew he was at war with spiritual forces not easily overcome. He watched as the amateurs trained their M16s on two of his prized apprentices. Drawing in a deep breath, he summoned the Great Architect of the Universe, Abaddon. He received an answer—a perfect plan. There was always more than one way to skin a cat.

Joy was praying in the spirit when all of a sudden she jumped. She bolted out of her seat and ran into the kitchen where Heidi and Bethany were fixing tea. "Something's happened to one of them," she announced. "I'm sure of it."

Heidi turned away from the counter. "What?"

"Something's wrong. I can feel it. We need to pray again, together."

Bethany, the pastor's wife, set the teacups down and accompanied her prayer partners back into the living room. Instead of sitting on the comfortable couch, they all got down on their knees.

Joy began. "Dear Father, we come to You this night asking for Your protection for those involved with this mission. Surround them with Your angels. Only You know what danger they face." A picture of the stone jumped out at her. Joy shivered. "Lord, nullify any evil effect of the stone. You are far more powerful than the devil's dominions."

"Yes, Lord," Bethany agreed. "Bring a host of angels to blind the eyes of those who have given themselves to evil. Confuse them."

"Please give our men wisdom. Show them the way." Joy stood up and walked around the room. "And give them the strength to do what needs to be done."

Heidi added a final note, "Lord, please make a way for them to accomplish Your will."

⟫◆⟪

Paul heard Margo's screech, though he didn't respond on purpose. As Bill turned to face her, his ex-bodyguard used the opportunity to punch the gun out of the hand of his former boss. It flew into the air then hit the ground spinning.

Bill scooped it up.

Paul shielded himself behind the car, thinking Bill would follow him. Instead, Bill took off toward Margo and her husband's retreating figures.

Paul's mind raced. He looked around. Who could help him? He yelled over to Mike. "Where's your guy?"

"I've got him tied up."

"Good, come over here and help the others. I've got to go after Bill."

Gunshots rang through the woods as Paul took off. He needed to make time. If he took the shortcut, he could overtake Bill, though he'd be out in the open for a few moments. He'd have to take another chance. Today he was gambling, big time.

Paul ran as fast as he could, but Bill closed in on Chris and Margo.

A spray of bullets rang out behind him, surprising him. The Big Boss must have sent out the rest of his henchmen, but these didn't come from the direction of the lodge. Paul forged ahead. Branches slapped in his face, stinging his skin. More gunfire followed. Sweat poured off his body as he closed the distance between him and Margo. He heard her footsteps and jumped into the clearing. "Over here," he yelled.

More gunfire erupted. A shot grazed his shoulder.

It stung.

Paul grabbed his arm. Though he kept on running, it slowed him down. Another shell sailed though the air.

Kaboom!

The bullet penetrated his flesh. Pain pierced his left side. Hot blood bubbled up to the surface. He continued to run blindly with searing pain. Then he stumbled and fell to the ground.

His world went dark for a minute.

As he sunk to the ground, footsteps approached. Paul balled up in fear as he expected to be shot in the head by one of the Master's "apprentices." Instead, a familiar voice asked, "Where did it get you?" Mike questioned.

Paul didn't have the strength to respond. The cowboy went to work and ripped off his shirtsleeve. Then he wrapped it around his shoulder. Paul suppressed a scream.

The sound of an automatic weapon exploded.

Paul feared they would all go down. *Please God, no,* he pleaded. Summoning the strength to talk, he whispered, "Get out of here."

Margo heard the commotion but didn't know what happened. Chris urged her on. "We've got to make it out of here and get this stone to the authorities." She needed to keep on running. Even though she'd dropped the Celtic-looking stone several times, she managed to keep rolling it. *Zing!* Another shot sailed thought the air.

"Bill's hot on our tail!" Chris yelled. "We've got to step up the pace."

Margo's legs trembled beneath her. She gasped for air. She had to do this for Paul, for all the Christians, and for Margaret. Her name was etched on that stone too. If she lived, she'd clear Margaret's reputation of the false suicide. But for now, both her legs and arms ached.

Could she keep running? Hopefully, the police would show up soon and put an end to this ordeal, but could they find them in time?

Bill and the rest of the group were gaining on them, and bullets whizzed in between trees. One thudded into the flesh of nearby pine. Margo's heart skipped a beat. They approached the edge of the forest.

Would they make it?

Chris pushed the stone over twigs and small rocks and maneuvered it around the larger ones. It began to gain a momentum of its own. Margo struggled to keep up with Chris as the stone rushed down the small incline, breaking twigs and flattening everything in its narrow path. They flew along with it, jumping over whatever was in their way. Exhausted, she lost footing and tripped over a rock.

"Eoyoww!" she yelled as she went down.

Chris ran to her side and rubbed her ankle. "Is it sprained?"

Margo put weight on it. "No, just a little hurt." She took off her sock and wrapped it around her ankle like an Ace bandage. She tested it again. "This will have to do."

She hobbled along for a minute, pleading for strength. The only way she could make it out of the woods was with His help. They were getting closer and closer to the towering rock cliffs. Margo prayed for wisdom. The two of them slowed down from exhaustion.

The gap closed.

"Dear God, it's now or never," she cried. Bill trailed behind less than five yards away. Margo ran closer toward the cliffs, and Chris followed. She kept running until she was only about a foot away.

Bill followed right on their heels.

Mike trailed alongside, out of view, and watched Margo stop dead at the edge of the cliff. "What is she doing?" Mike said aloud to no one but God. As he saw Chris position himself beside the other side of the stone, he figured out their plan. *But don't they know Bill has a gun?* he wondered. *Unless they have something else up their sleeve.* Mike crouched in the cover of the thick woods as Bill ran by, and the cowboy realized that their pursuer had run out of bullets as the gun dangled from his hands. He was pretty darn sure of the Piersons' plan now, but what to do to divert the others became his next challenge. Either he'd help them now or confront the evil on their heels. He decided on the latter.

Margo waited until Bill was in the right position. The two of them swung the lighter stone back and forth once and then pretended to hurl it over the deceptive rock ledge. Not knowing how steep the precipice, Bill went for the bait. Margo saw Bill's eyes open wide, filled with dark hunger and loathing as he approached them. Then as he got frighteningly close, she watched his eyes narrow into slits, and his whole demeanor contorted into a look of demonic hatred. A look of triumph rose on his face.

But then something went wrong. They had planned on only knocking Bill down to the ledge below, but instead he lunged at them. Margo scrambled out of Bill's way as his body flew through the air unimpeded. She turned away and glimpsed the back of Bill's torso as he flew over the edge like superman.

But he did not possess the power to fly. Margo flinched as she heard Bill's bloodcurdling screams.

41

Margo's mind whirled as she and Chris escaped into the woods. Desperate thoughts nagged at her like a thousand whirring creatures nipping at her heels. She had never encountered such evil before in a human being. Still, she felt terrible. Had she been responsible for Bill's death?

In a way, yes, but it was an accident. They only planned on hurting him. Besides, he would have eliminated her and many others to get what he wanted. Margo and Chris had to get the stone away from his killing hands, and especially those who sought its power. The thought gave Margo a shiver. It ran from her head to her toes, though her ankle burned as she put more pressure on it than she should.

She slowed down and limped as the path disappeared, and Chris struggled to maneuver the stone over limbs and rocks. What a pathetic-looking pair they'd appear to her sophisticated artist friends. Her limping like a three-legged dog and Chris with his dirty ripped shirt and pants. But didn't the Bible say God used the weak and frail things of this world? Good thing because she felt about as weak as a worm right now. She had gotten them into this whole mess, and now she couldn't even help get them out of it!

Chris grunted as they approached a fallen tree in their path, "The stone is getting too difficult to roll. I'll have to ditch it in the woods."

Margo bowed her head in defeat. "We can't go on—"

The sound of men's voices interrupted her. Chris hunkered down, bringing Margo with them. "They're in the woods, probably looking for us." He looked down at her ankle. "I'm going to have to carry you the rest of the way. Hop on my back."

Margo wrapped her legs around Chris's waist. It hurt, but her heart felt more bruised than her ankle. Could it get any worse? She'd dropped the Egyptian half of the stone when she twisted her ankle, and now they couldn't carry the other. "I'm sorry I'm such a burden. I've messed everything—"

"Listen, we're a team." Chris grinned and took off in a trot with his wife on his back. The voices of the men grew more distant as they made their way back to the road. Margo peered around Chris's head as his hair flopped up and down in rhythm. Nothing looked familiar. They must be backtracking a different way. Did Chris know where they were going?

If only she hadn't come back up here to get the stone. Now they had nothing to show for all the chances they took. Somehow she'd missed the Lord. Maybe she got her wires crossed. She'd thought He had wanted her to pursue uncovering the evil power behind the stone and Margaret's demise. Now, she wasn't so sure.

Chris cocked his head and looked up at the position of the sun. "Good. We're heading west, away from the cliffs and the house. The truck shouldn't be far off."

At least Chris was on the right—

Rat-a-ta-tat! Gunshots interrupted her thoughts and echoed in the woods.

———◆———

Abaddon, the Great Architect of the Universe, looked down with pride at all his legions and laughed. He turned toward his powerful horde. "You have done well, my lords and princes."

The high priest of the occult bowed. "Thank you, sire, for entrusting me with this most important assignment."

The Master Dragon lifted him up. "You have done very well these days, being responsible for much of today's worship of me, and for this I will elevate you even higher." He turned aside and summoned the prince of another powerful legion, Deception. "You too have done all I required of you. Come join us."

Power and Pride stepped forth and joined the others. "Our legions have worked tirelessly with humans and have made great inroads even in the enemy's camp."

"And for this I commend you." The lord of all darkness, Satan, spread his wings.

Prince Division broke rank and bellowed, "Yet without me tearing apart those followers of the way, you never would have gained the upper hand!"

Power swooped over and knocked Division to the ground.

The entire assembly of demons let out with screeches, howls, and the flapping of wings. Apollyn admonished them. "You are all my children. A house divided against itself cannot stand!" When they finally settled down, Division and the Overlord of the occult world smiled. "We have kept a powerful weapon safe. The stone will once again be in our possession!"

"Yes, that is our chief aim," Lucifer agreed. "Now, bow before the dominions so they may feed off us. There is still more to be done!"

Chris quickened his pace. He hoped they'd reach the vehicle soon. Although he had good stamina, tree roots sticking out here and there coupled with half-buried stones made it a challenging course. He stopped to take a breath. "The trees are thinning here, and I think we're close." He prayed aloud. "Dear Lord, please guide my footsteps. Confuse the enemy and make a clear path to Mike's truck."

"Yes, Lord, and please watch over Paul and protect all the others," Margo said flatly.

"Is something wrong?" Chris asked.

"No, absolutely nothing." Margo sighed. "Except for the fact I've blown everything, and who knows if we'll make it out alive."

Chris understood how she felt, but he didn't want to be negative. "Hey, cheer up. We're not beat yet. Just wait and see what God does."

Within a few minutes, Chris spotted a red truck through the trees. He picked up his pace and nearly tripped over a tree root, losing his balance. Margo slid off and landed on both feet. "Oooh, that hurts." She rubbed the foot with the sprained ankle, then hopped on her good one. "I think I can hobble over. Go get the truck started."

Chris ran ahead and reached the vehicle. He climbed into the passenger's seat and looked around for the key. It wasn't there. As Margo neared, he jumped out and helped her into the passenger seat. She winced as she climbed up. Chris hopped into the driver's seat.

"Why didn't you start it?" She looked at him and crinkled her forehead.

"Couldn't find the keys." He looked behind the visor, stretched his arm under the seat, and looked under the carpet protectors.

Nothing.

Margo leaned back on the seat. "Could anything else go wrong?"

Chris frowned. "Sure, we could be dead. It's time for prayer power." He bowed his head. "Dear Lord, we know we are in Your hands. You are aware of every sparrow that falls. We trust You even though things don't look too good right now. Please keep the stone safe. Blind the eyes of the enemy, and could You please send Mike back to his truck?"

"And please get someone to call 911. My phone has no reception out here," Margo added.

Chris put his hands on the steering wheel. "C'mon now, don't worry." He wasn't sure what to say to keep Margo's spirits from sinking, but he tried to sound encouraging. "After all we've been through, I don't think God will abandon us." Chris drummed his fingers on the steering wheel. *C'mon, God, help me out here.*

———⊰◆⊱———

Once Joy felt comfortable enough to trust Lance's wife with some of the details of their recent discovery, she revealed particulars about her own vision and the practices involved with the stone. She told her, "Margo has actually seen names carved on it with blood dripped on them."

Heidi's eyes widened. "Lance told me there might be some witchcraft going on up in the mountain, but we weren't sure. He was quiet about it. Didn't want to make any accusations." She sighed. "But maybe that's why there's been havoc in the church. We think the main target might be marriages."

Joy raised her eyebrows. "Has this been a problem in your church?"

"A problem?" The young woman threw her hands in the air. "It's been devastating. Three couples in the last several weeks have had major marital issues. And on top of it, the church is going through a split."

Joy contemplated her last remark. Not only did the enemy want to destroy Christian marriages but unity in the church as well. Division of a different sort was a problem in their church, but Dave had dealt with it. Still, the thought was disturbing. Maybe the enemy was at work in their church too. If this was going on in their small community, imagine what could be happening in the cities. "This may have far broader ramifications then we ever contemplated. Let's petition God about it."

She lifted her hands. "Dear Father, we thank You for hearing our prayers, and we praise Your mighty name. We thank You for watching over them, and we ask for further assistance for those engaged in this battle against evil. 'For we do not wrestle against flesh and blood, but against principalities, against powers, against the rulers of darkness in the heavenly places,'" Joy quoted the Bible. She knew in her spirit the battle was heating up. Margo and everyone up there needed not only help but also spiritual reinforcements.

"Please surround them with your angels and give them wisdom in all they do. Hide them in the shadow of your wings." Urgency as well as compassion rippled in Heidi's voice.

She seemed to read Joy's mind. The Holy Sprit's presence confirmed their agreement. "Yes, Lord, blind the eyes of those intent on evil. Let no weapon formed against them prosper." Though it looked like evil had gained a foothold in the area, Joy stood firm in her belief. God would ultimately win, no matter how desperate the situation looked. Ultimately, nothing could separate them from the love of God.

Not even death.

━━◆━━

Margo fumbled through the glove compartment for the third time, hoping to find the key. The seconds passed like hours. So much had gone wrong. She lost both stones, and now they were sitting here waiting around for the axe to fall. Had she failed to hear God's voice? Doubts nagged at her.

She heard a noise in the underbrush. "What's that?" She lunged toward Chris in fear and kept her eyes peeled. Her heart leaped into her throat.

As the bushes parted, Mike emerged. Margo breathed a sigh of relief. "Thank you, Lord!" The others, Lance, Ray, Dave and Mark, followed behind him. And they were carrying someone stretched between them, maybe Paul!

She hoped he wasn't hurt too bad. As they came closer, she confirmed his identity. Her hands flew to her face. Blood seeped though Paul's shirt and pooled near his chest. "Dear Lord, please let him live," she cried. She couldn't be responsible for yet another person's death. Not someone who didn't deserve to die. He had done so much for her. Saved her life that awful night in the cave.

Margo startled when Chris tapped her shoulder. Mike approached, and he was rolling one of the stones! She hobbled out of the truck on one foot to help him out.

"Get back in there," he scolded. "There's still a few guys chasing us. We gotta get outta here!"

Margo protested. "I can handle it." She wanted to help, but maybe it was better if she kept an eye out for the gunmen. Apparently, Mike knew the woods better than them. She watched as the three men maneuvered Paul onto the truck bed. He looked terrible. His face drained of blood, turning a chalky white. Craning her neck to see better, she wanted to jump out and help him. Put a compress on his head; get him some water—anything. But what could she do?

Maybe it was best if she prayed.

That's all she could do now. She'd been talking to God more than ever before, but sometimes she just wanted to get in there and get things done! But then she remembered what Joy told her. *Sometimes, prayer is the most important thing you could do.*

And didn't Lance say sometimes God puts us in the position where we're not in control, so all we can do is pray. *Okay, Lord, I get it.* She closed her eyes and implored Him. *Dear Father, Please surround us with your angels and protect us. Help us out of here, and get Paul to a hospital. Quick!* Her eyes popped open.

Mike lifted the stone into the truck. The familiar Egyptian symbols jumped out at her. So he had retrieved the one she'd dropped. Just when she thought all was lost. God knew what he was doing!

Mike climbed into the driver's seat next to her and slammed the truck into gear. He shot out of the woods and onto the road.

Margo couldn't keep it in any longer. "What happened back there, and how is Paul?"

"I'll tell you in a moment," he replied as he threw the truck into second gear and stepped on the gas.

The truck lurched forward, and threw Margo back against the hard seat. Her neck hurt, but she thanked God she was still alive!

As they drove Mike recounted everything that happened. "I have a feeling those boys are mystified by the whole thing," he said.

Margo hardly believed Mike's tale of the hit men, as he called them, being blinded and frozen in their tracks. He told her a similar incident occurred when a bear had chased his friend Bob. A bright light dazed the animal, and Bob escaped. Mike thought it was divine intervention, illumination from angels. Could that be possible?

Anyway, because of it, he retrieved the Egyptian stone. Had their petitions accomplished this? Was prayer really that powerful? In the past, she believed other people's appeals had such impact. But not hers.

Perhaps this was what God tried to show her.

As she mulled over the events, she worried about Paul. She didn't want to lack faith, but he looked awful. Maybe it was because she wasn't use to seeing people shot. She hesitated to ask. "How badly wounded is Paul?"

Mike scratched his beard. "It's hard to say, but it doesn't look good. Bill's henchmen shot him pretty bad. Depends if he got hit in his heart or not. But we better step on it if we want to stay alive."

⋙◆⋘

A trail of five police cars followed Bob's truck as he turned down the side road that led to the hideaway. Their flashing red lights reflected off the dark pines, casting an eerie light into the woods. He had rounded up several state troopers he thought were honest—a team of Special Forces from the jail and a few local cops. Bob instructed them to keep their sirens off until they were on the place. The Special Forces planned to attack from the woods.

Bouncing along the dirt road, Bob saw a red truck heading their way. He thought it might be his buddy's, but his eyesight wasn't what it used to be. As they got closer, Bob recognized the vehicle and Mike's cowboy hat. He wore his favorite one.

Just then, one of the cops in an unmarked car behind him got on a microphone and announced to the oncoming Chevy, "Pull over to the side of the road."

Bob spat. "Stupid fools." He picked up his CB radio. "Okay, boys, these guys are my buddies. Roger that?"

Meanwhile, Mike brought his pickup to a halt.

Bob lumbered out of his truck and ambled toward them, yelling, "Lay off, it's my buddy."

The cops shouted for him to get back into the vehicle, but Bob paid no attention. They let him go, but they jogged to the truck as Bob lagged behind.

Mike called out to him. "Boy am I glad to see you. We got Paul in the back, hurt pretty bad."

Bob stopped dead in his tracks. Mike had told him all about Paul. Probably deserved what he got, but if he was Mike's buddy, then he was not to be messed with.

The cops shouted and waved their gun at Mike. "Don't move. Stay where you are."

Bob pushed himself to move faster. "You dang fools," he shouted. "Put those guns away. You're gonna hurt somebody. Someone's already banged up back there."

Mike repeated to the approaching officers. "We have an injured man in the truck bed. He needs medical attention quick."

One of the policemen ran to the back of the truck.

The other turned to the people inside the cab. "Put up your hands up slowly. Don't reach in your pockets."

Bob shuffled closer. He saw a young girl in the front seat. The woman yapped loud enough for him to overhear. "What are you doing? I'm not some common criminal. Besides, you should be calling 911." The policeman gestured for them to get out, then quickly searched the vehicle.

Bob huffed as he reached the door. "Listen, you knucklehead, these are the people I told you about, not the criminals. Besides you need to get my buddy's pal to a hospital."

The state trooper ran past Bob to the police car. *Now that's more like it*, he said to himself. He figured the police were finally calling an ambulance. Bob turned to the tougher-looking cop, but he stuck his head in the truck cab. "Oh yeah, I think we found the missing stone."

Bob waved his hands in the air. "Now listen, you whippersnappers, I didn't report it missing. I said they were in danger of being hurt because they needed to protect the stone."

Margo also tried to explain, but the cop cut her short. "We don't have time for this now. We have our orders. You two come with me." He pushed Chris and Margo ahead with his club. "The cowboy can stay behind with the injured criminal. My partner will take care of them."

⸻◆⸻

While the dark forces of this destruction were getting drunk on their transient victory, a multitude of angels descended upon the vile creatures.

Zuriel shouted to them as he swooped down upon the thick cloud. "Keep your swords ready at all times." His wings covered a legion of demons.

Blades glinted light as they approached the blackness and thrust their swords in to the unsuspecting horde. Screams and howls erupted as Zuriel's legions struck hundreds of whimpering imps. Clouds of sulfuric smoke oozed from the mass.

Two large demons came swooping up behind the attackers, and the prayer warrior immediately recognized Prince Division and Witchcraft . He sliced the two-faced creature with the tip of his sword and tore into his hinged wings. Division hurled a host of obscenities and spewed forth a noxious odor, knocking over both the creatures of light and darkness. Witchcraft attacked from behind inflicting a blow, but Veritas came to the wounded angel's aid and pierced the slimy scales of the occult. Zuriel dealt Division a blow with the hilt of his sword, which sent him tumbling down a long dark tunnel.

A swarm of men in black uniforms emerged from the woods. As they came into full view, Lance spotted the words *SWAT Team* emblazoned on their backs. He recognized them as a special division of the police force.

As they swept through the trees surrounding the house, they looked like a pack of panthers stalking their prey. Their rifles gleamed like sharp fangs. "It's a good thing we're on their side," Lance whispered to Dave. Lance certainly wouldn't want to encounter one on a hike through the woods.

The men crept to the edge and spied as one group took the left flank and another the right. "Where had all this help come from?" Ray asked.

"I don't know, but God sure provides…just in the nick of time." Lance looked at the house. "I don't know how much longer those guys are going to hold up in there."

As they retreated a little farther back into the woods, Lance saw several men in outfits, like the Ku Klux Klan, emerge using a side door. Where had they come from? Apparently, they weren't aware of the police presence as they began to walk around the grounds hunting for something, but not for long. Lance hedged a little closer.

One of the teams spotted the strangely attired men with hoods and vestments and swooped down on them. Even though the men attempted to escape and run off, they were no contest for the highly trained SWAT team. Within a few minutes, they were handcuffed and dragged off, protesting all the while.

Lance heard one of them say, "You idiots, you got the wrong guys. We're unarmed, you fools. We demand a lawyer. You better read us..." Their voices trailed off and were interrupted by the sound of a bullhorn coming from the front of the house. "Come out, if there's more of you. We've got you covered!" But only silence ensued.

<hr />

"Where are we going?" Margo asked, annoyed as the policeman prodded her and Chris. They hadn't gotten this far to be stopped by some cops who got the story all mixed up, or had they?

Margo didn't like this one. Something didn't ring true about this cop's demeanor. Now she and Chris had to stay behind with these jokers.

The tougher-looking one kept moving them along. "To the police station for questioning."

Chris walked next to Margo, and she leaned over and whispered to him, "I don't trust these guys, especially this one." She gestured to the cop behind her.

"Neither do I. We better—"

The other officer sidled next to them and surprised Margo. "What are you two talking about?"

Margo blushed. "I just feel terrible leaving our companions, especially the one who's hurt." She turned back and stared into his cold eyes. It was the truth. She prayed the ambulance would arrive soon and hoped Lance and the rest of them would make it out alive.

"Can't we wait until the ambulance arrives?" she pleaded.

"No. I told you, my partner will stay with him. Just cooperate."

Margo studied the hard lines of his face. He must've dealt with a lot of criminals.

Chris turned to her. "When we get to the station, let's just tell them everything we know and ask them to release us so we can go help."

The policeman forced Chris into the backseat. "Hey, cool it. I'm getting in," he protested. Margo followed suit, and the cop kept his hands off her. When the officer sat in the driver seat, the locks clicked shut. Margo felt uncomfortable, trapped. The same eerie presence she felt in the cave threatened to overtake her.

"Which station are you taking us to?"

The cop didn't answer and turned the car around. Margo wondered what he was doing. They were heading back in the direction of the hideout. Maybe he changed his mind and would let them help. She tapped the window. "Where are we going?"

The officer turned around and slid the glass aside. He grinned but didn't say a word.

"You can't do this," Margo protested.

The cop slid the window back and stepped on the gas.

She and Chris lurched forward. Margo pounded on the glass. He ignored her.

"What can we do?" she asked Chris.

He tried to roll down the window but couldn't. He pushed against the door, but it didn't budge.

"You're holding us against our will. Let us out, now!"

The cop slid the pane aside. A crooked smiled curled his lips. "Where do you think you're going?"

"Back to the hideout, but why?"

He took a sharp left and headed down a dirt road. Maybe he took a shortcut, but it didn't seem right.

She looked over at Chris "What direction are we going?"

"West."

Fear washed over her in waves. Were they heading in the direction they left Bill?

She swallowed. "Are we heading for the cliffs?" Her eyes met Chris's and held them there for a long moment.

He hugged her and answered in a whisper, "Yes."

Joy beseeched the Lord as she had never done before. She sensed the presence of angels, but the ghastly faces of demons kept assailing her also, as well as the horrid stone. She sang a chorus to drown out their images. "Let God arise and his enemies be scattered." By now, both of them were on their feet. They closed the curtains and marched around the living room. Joy felt like Joshua marching around the walls of Jericho. Glad no one else was around to see them, she began to clap and dance.

"If God be for us, who can be against us, If God be for us, who can stand?" Heidi declared.

Joy couldn't agree more, though the vision of the bloodstained stone kept plaguing her. Was God trying to tell her something? A verse came to mind: *Finally be strong in the Lord, and in the strength of His might. Put on the full armor of God, that you may be able to stand firm against the schemes of the devil.* "That's it!"

"What?" Lance's wife stopped dead in her tracks.

"We need to put on the armor of God to stand against the enemy's plans. In all this excitement, I forgot to put on my spiritual protection."

"Your what?"

"Spiritual armor, the helmet of salvation, the shield of faith, and the sword of the Spirit."

"Yes, Lance told me about that."

"We need to do that before we go on." She bowed her head. "Lord, we put on Your helmet to protect our mind from thoughts that are not from You. We take up the shield of faith, trusting that Your will would be done and the sword of the Spirit, which is the word of God."

"Amen," Heidi declared then added, "Open Margo's and Chris's eyes to Your plans."

"Let's keep marching!" Joy believed praise was also needed. As they continued, she gained more confidence. Her faith grew even stronger. On the seventh time around, a huge stonewall appeared in her mind. Unlike a fortress, only one wall stood between her and the enemy. It seemed more like a mountain, and then it came into focus...the rock cliffs of Lookout Point.

Did God want that to come tumbling down? But why?

Mike watched as a policeman pushed the heel of his hands near Paul's heart. "Should you be doing that?" Mike asked.

"He's bleeding bad. Get me a shirt so I can wrap it around his chest."

Mike took his off. "Here, have mine."

The officer grabbed it. "Hold him up so I can get this underneath him." He slipped the shirt around Paul's chest as he mumbled something about Bill. Mike didn't hear the whole thing, but it seemed as if the cop knew this guy. Maybe he did. Paul probably had been in jail a number of times.

Paul had passed out, and it looked as if he was going into shock.

Mike hoped the pressure was enough to stop the bleeding from the near-fatal gunshot wound. The officer had radioed an ambulance, and they waited for its arrival.

Mike paced the ground, praying and pleading with the Lord. His ears strained, hoping to hear the whirring siren of the ambulance. Finally, he thought he heard the unmistakable whining advance toward the secluded road. He raised his hands and shouted, "Thank you, Lord." The officer looked sideways at him and shook his head.

Mike looked down at his new friend. His shirt had soaked through with blood.

The police officer pulled off the road and parked the vehicle. Margo swallowed hard. They were still in the mountains. Had her suspicions been correct? Thoughts swirled in her head. All hope seemed lost. So were the stones. It didn't seem like Mike would be able to hold on to it, and only Chris knew where the other lay. What was the real story behind these stones? So many unanswered questions, so little time left.

The cop turned around and barked at them. "Out of the car."

"Why?" Chris asked. "I don't see any police station."

He pulled out a gun and pointed it at them. "C'mon, get out, and put your hands up."

Chris protested, "Hey, put that away. We're not criminals." Chris opened the door and motioned for her to follow.

What else could they do? Run for it and get shot? Margo stepped out onto the cool air and looked around. She needed to stall for time. "What are we doing here?"

The man grinned. "Put two and two together."

The cliffs lay about a quarter of a mile away. Maybe Chris would come up with an idea. *Dear God, what now?*

Chris gestured to stop, and the phony cop jabbed the gun in his side. "Get walking." He took a few long strides, and the impostor followed, but Margo remained in place.

"Hey, no funny business!" When he spun around, Chris knocked the gun out of his hand. The cop dove for it, but Chris had a head start. He lunged and grabbed the weapon first then shot to his feet. Margo watched in horror as the impostor flew at Chris's legs, toppling him to the ground. Her husband fell with a thud, and the cop scooped up the pistol.

Margo ran to the safety of the car. A shot rang out, and she spun around. Chris lay on the ground.

The guy pointed the gun at her. "Get over here, or I'll shoot your husband."

Margo trembled. Chris's plan had failed. *Dear Lord, please don't abandon us now.*

Margo winced as the cop tightened the rope around her hands, but no one heard the muffled sound. Chris lay knocked out.

If only she'd never gotten involved in all of this mess. All she wanted to do was find her missing relative, or had she? She still didn't know if they were truly related. But why did she have to go traipsing after that blasted stone?

Margo shook her head and scolded herself. She knew exactly why. God wanted the truth to be known, the evil to be revealed. But how could she help? Especially now?

As the impostor opened the car door, he shoved her out. "Start walking." He jammed a gun in her back. She hated to think he was a crooked cop. She preferred to think he was a fraud.

Margo looked around. They weren't far from the cliff. Is this how her life was meant to end?

An accident victim.

Dear Lord, she cried. *Save me!* Margo marched to the scene of the crime-to-be. She walked slowly hoping to avoid the inevitable. Panic rose in her throat and nearly choked her. Gasping for air, she broke out in a cold sweat.

The officer pushed her closer to the edge. The cliff lay only a few yards away. He started to loosen the knots.

Yeah, though I walk through the valley of the shadow of death, I fear no evil. Thy rod and they staff comfort...

Margo fell to the ground as a body slammed into her. She tried to cushion her fall but hit her head on rock. *Yow!* It stung.

"Are you okay?"

Her head throbbed, yet she forced herself to open her eyes. A blurry image swam before her. Slowly it came into focus. Chris!

He knelt down beside her and stroked her hair. Blood covered his hand.

"I thought you were out cold," Margo said, surprised. She looked over and saw the phony cop sprawled next to her.

"I was at first, but then I heard someone call my name, and I jolted awake. I ran right to the cliff and rammed into the impostor."

As Chris spoke, another uniformed officer emerged from the woods. "Get up," Chris alerted her. They tried to scurry from him, but he raised his gun. He ran over to them. Margo ducked.

"What's going on here?" He looked down at the other cop. He was out cold. The officer turned him over. On seeing his face, he changed the position of his weapon and turned it on him. "We've been looking for this man. He's wanted for impersonating an officer."

Margo breathed a sigh of relief.

42

On Saturday morning, Margo picked up the Friday edition of the *Kingsland Freedman* from the coffee table and examined the picture of her and Chris on the front page. He had retrieved what was dubbed The Celtic stone, and the reporter snapped a picture of it beside him. She stood next to the Egyptian half. Margo wrinkled her nose at the awful snapshot and read the headlines again. "Local Couple Busts Big-Time Crooked Cops and Criminals." Margo laughed to herself. *What a cover-up. If only they knew the real truth.*

The story read, "High atop Lookout Mountain, Christopher and Margaret Pierson, aided by friends and the local police force along with other authorities, helped to apprehend a number of well-known criminals and police impostors in a heist of two valuable stones, supposedly worth millions. The origins of the pieces have not yet been disclosed, but the authorities reported that an Egyptologist from the Metro City Museum in New York and the Order of Hibernians from the Irish coalition would be examining them for authenticity.

"During a chase involving Christopher and Margaret Pierson, Bill Eville, a Manhattan businessman, plunged to his death. Several prominent businessmen were taken into custody under protest of foul play. They claimed Mr. Eville had framed them. A well-known associate of theirs, Paul Cambio, was shot and seriously wounded. The stones…"

Margo huffed. The story was partially accurate but left out a lot—like no mention of the businessmen being involved with the Royal Order of Freemasons or the satanic practices associated with the stones. They didn't even divulge the fact that names had recently been etched on it. Margo realized most editors wouldn't touch that topic, but couldn't they at least include some of her story? If the others weren't apprehended, people's lives were still in jeopardy. Or would the loss of the stone end the rituals?

She tossed the paper on the table. Who would believe a story like that anyway? She hardly did, except for the fact she saw it with her very own eyes.

Satisfied the facts weren't falsified, she thought back to a long time ago when the ruling class of New Covenant concealed the existence of the stone and perpetuated a lie. A lie covered up the true cause of Margaret Dubier's death. Margo felt certain she was murdered by the same society of people who had almost eliminated her.

It amazed Margo that God had brought this stone across her path. Her visions and dreams had been real, not just the delusions of an oversensitive artist. Somehow God had engineered the circumstances for her to stumble upon all this.

And now she knew why: to uncover the "diabolical evil stalking the town." Perhaps for a very long while. If only someone would write about this and expose this terrible wickedness.

But who?

Margo examined a picture of the stones on the front page, but they were unclear, and the etchings blurry. Perhaps it was best that way. By Friday afternoon, several historical societies had called and wanted to look them over. There was much dispute about the hieroglyphics' authenticity, and they anxiously awaited the arrival of the Egyptologist. The specialist would arrive on Monday to check it over.

The Celtic half of the stone, with the strange symbols and designs, caused a stir among local historians as some believed it to be a fake and others authentic, brought over by the Irish who settled in Kingsland. Though the local press covered the story, it didn't receive as much national press as the Egyptian half, which they considered much more valuable.

Margo thought otherwise. The Celtic half also had great power. Ever since she saw the stone in the cave, she worked on deciphering the letter. The darkened photocopy had helped a lot, but she thought she could figure out a few more missing letters farther down the page.

Margo ran to her bedroom to retrieve the original. In her rush, she knocked over her mother's antique jewelry box from the dresser. *Drat!* Bending down to pick it up, she realized the box had sprung open, and a secret compartment lay visible. A folded paper stuck out. She retrieved it and unfolded the aging document. Unbelievable. A family tree!

As Margo scanned the names, she gasped when she came to her grandmother's maiden name—Dubier! Strange how there were no more Dubiers after hers, but DuBois and Bevier seemed to replace the name. Interesting. Margo also noted that the handwriting was the same as the letter she discovered. So her great-grandmother had written the warning and probably safely tucked away the family tree. The truth nearly knocked the breath out of her. Margo was indeed related to Margaret Eltin Dubier!

After the realization had sunk in, Margo retrieved her great-grandmother's letter.

> There is a diabolical evil that stalks this town. They are closer than you think. Beware! Though few are aware, they are hateful, evil men who scheme against anyone who loves the Lord God. They worship their own gods of ancient civilizations and of power. I believe one of our ancestors, a true-blood Dubier, was once one of them and others before him. But you must not speak of it, or they will discover who has revealed their S—— Society. And you will suffer a frightful d—— along with your daughters. I know this because one day he renounced this abominable

> society but lived only a few months more! Though he left a
> diary, we discovered it was burned; only one page survived.
> It told of this society of S——, their lust for power and the
> meaning of their Divi—— Stone.

Now she knew the two words that gave her the most trouble. The *s* she decoded earlier meant Satan, but the last one had evaded her. At least she narrowed it down to two choices: Divining or Dividing. Either way, that's what the stone was meant to do, divide Christians. The evidence was clear. Obliterate anyone who stood in their way and divide the rest.

It was apparent that the Egyptian stone was the original one, but why had the two been welded together? What was the connection between the Celts or Irish and Egypt? And how did the French Huguenots, the Dubiers' ancestors, fit into the picture? The Irish settled a little farther north in Kingsland. At that time, the Huguenot settlement stretched halfway to the King's land. It was only another five miles to the small city that boasted a river port, which brought valuable items to the New World. The French and Irish bought and sold goods from each other on a limited basis, so they had contact here and in Europe.

In her readings, Margo discovered that some of the Huguenots had fled to Scotland and then to Virginia, but did any migrate northward? She also recalled reading an article linking Egyptian artifacts to France. Was it true? Perhaps the Huguenots brought the Egyptian stone over to America. She just couldn't figure out every detail on her own. More important, what about the strange open rectangles on the other stone, what did they mean? It would take time and research to know the whole truth, unless some other evidence could be found.

Later in the afternoon, she headed for the police station. She knew she had to get the stone to examine it more carefully. Was Margaret's name on the Celtic part also? Since the Egyptian piece was presumed older, the authorities might say it was another Margaret. But if embedded in the symbols of the Celtic half, she could then prove Ms. Dubier's murder with cold, hard evidence, and the fact that this society had existed for years.

⟫◈⟪

At the station, Margo was met with indifference and impatience. The officer in charge propped his arm against an old wooden desk and looked down at the stack of paperwork. "Lady, we don't have time or manpower to shuttle this stone back and forth at your convenience. We're just tryin' to do our jobs."

Margo composed herself. "Well, what I'm doing is very important," she explained. "My investigation might save the lives of people in this community. You wouldn't want to be responsible for their deaths, would you?"

The chief shuffled papers back and forth.

Margo hoped she had gotten to him with the responsible part.

He sighed. "Listen, the best I can do is let you take a few pictures, but that's it. You're not allowed to even touch it."

"But I was the one who found it!" Margo's patience felt as threadbare as her old jeans.

"Lady, no one takes evidence home. It's bad enough your fingerprints are gonna be all over it. Probably keep us from finding out the real killers." He glared at her.

"Umm, true." Margo didn't want to waste any more time. "Okay, I'll take some pictures."

He pushed the chair aside, and it banged into his desk with a thunk. He tromped down a narrow corridor, which led to a room cluttered with evidence sealed in plastic bags and labeled. The stone lay on a metal table with several filled vials next to it.

"Oh, I'm sorry. I didn't make myself clear. I don't need the Egyptian half. I've done a rubbing of it already. I need the Celtic side."

"Well, why didn't you say so in the beginning, lady? I think we may have handed it over to the Historical Society already. We took some samples and sent them over to the crime lab, but since that wasn't what the criminals were after—"

"What? Didn't anyone inform you that names were etched on it and some of those people had been killed?"

"I saw the stone myself. I didn't see any name on it."

Margaret pointed to the stone. "Do you see names on this?"

"No, just pictures, but I know they stand for words."

"Well, it's the same principle. The Celtic stone has symbols too, rectangles and dots, which could also stand for letters that can represent words and names. And it has other strange symbols I need to research."

"That doesn't matter. It's over a hundred years old, and I'm not solving any murders from back then. I have enough to deal with in taking care of the here and now."

Margo didn't have the time to explain the connection between the two right now. Neither did she think he would believe her if she told him about Margaret's murder. "Well, thank you anyway, Officer. I hope you can apprehend and convict the other criminals." She backed out of the office and flew out the door.

—————◆—————

Margo couldn't believe it. They were so close to having the stone, and it slipped through their fingers...again. She hoped the Historical Society had held on to it and that no one had accidentally or on purpose walked away with it. She looked at her watch, only three thirty. They should be open. Margo stepped on the gas just in case they kept banker's hours.

Her car skidded into the gravel parking lot. Nearly out of breath with anticipation, Margo ran up the stone walkway to the office. The sign said Closed. She knocked anyway. No answer. She rapped harder. Still no reply.

She twisted her fingers around her hair. What should she do? She couldn't wait around wondering if the stone lay in the wrong hands. Margo ran back to the car and pulled out the rubbings of the millstone she had brought with her. Since she wasn't far from the spot where this had all began, she decided to take a look around.

Not to be conspicuous in broad daylight, Margo strolled, rather than raced, to the historical home of the Dubiers. The day was sunny, but chilly, icy wind from the north howled through the valley. As she walked along the cobblestone street, a gust picked up her rubbing and nearly blew it out of her hand. When she reached the old stone house, she examined its exterior and tried to imagine Margaret living there.

Instead of going directly to the well and the stone wheel, she walked around the front of the house and back along the garden path. The stone walkway ended in an herbal garden filled with rosemary, sage, and thyme, which hadn't yet succumbed to the cold. Margo inhaled the fragrant smell. She sat down on a little wooden bench and looked around for a clue. Nothing jumped out at her. If only Margaret could talk to her. But the dead don't speak.

She walked over to the well. To her surprise, the millstone wasn't there. Why? She took out the rolled paper and spread it out beside the well. She studied the faded letters and tried to unlock the rest of the code. Over the last few weeks, she was able to decode some of the words. Early on she had deciphered "killed Margaret." She felt certain of that.

When she discovered rituals were performed with it, she decoded "pr" to be *priest*. What had bothered her was the C——t——. Before, she dared not think it meant Christian or Catholic. With the newest information on the origins, the C—t— now fell into place. The Celtic priests, like druids, practiced magic and cast spells. Some could be linked to satanists who killed people like Margaret. Yet where did the Masons with their inscriptions come in? Margo paused to think. It took longer for her to gather her thoughts as she was still recovering from the trauma.

What a minute! I can probably research online.

After much praying and pleading, Margo convinced the mayor of New Coven to allow her to borrow the Celtic stone. The events of the last few weeks, coupled with the letter from her great-grandmother, had given her the leverage she needed to convince him the town was at risk. Since the police had regained possession of it from the local historian and brushed it for fingerprints, the mayor's phone call clinched the deal. Margo knew the police chief was infuriated the prints were smudged, but they had enough of them on the Egyptian stone to convict who they needed, except for their so-called *Master*, who had conveniently slipped away.

Sitting in the police station, Margo fidgeted and looked at her watch. It was almost an hour and the chief wasn't back. He hadn't left word that it was to be released to her, and they wouldn't call him. Finally a tall, young officer came out from the side office and approached her.

"I'm sorry, ma'am, but you'll need to come back tomorrow."

Margo shot to her feet. "Oh no, you don't. I made arrangements to get it today." Margo's face flushed red. *Sorry, Lord.* Her temper could be such a problem. "That's not possible, I must have it today."

The policeman looked down at her. "Sorry, can't go against Chief's orders."

Margo burst out in a sweat. "Could you please call the mayor? I know he talked with him and—"

"What's all this commotion?" The chief burst through the door and brushed past them.

Margo trailed behind him. "Don't you remember me?"

He spun around. "How could I forget?"

"Well, didn't you tell your men I could pick up the stone?"

"No, I wanted to be here. Didn't want you convincing them"—he eyed her up and down—"that you could have the other one."

"That's absurd. I'd never do that!" Margo protested in the squeaky, high-pitched voice of hers when she got excited. She hated it.

The chief snickered. "You don't seem to be the type to give up on what you want."

Margo hesitated. "Guess not."

"Well then," his eyes softened. "Come back here and I'll see what we can do for you."

Margo stared at the stone in the trunk of her car. An electric shock, like a bolt of lightning, ripped through her. How many lives were lost because of it? How many marriages destroyed? She shivered and slammed the trunk. She needed to get home quick and do some research to decode the designs. She felt sure they were more than decorative and held meaning.

She looked down the street but didn't see Chris's car. She slipped her phone from her pocket and speed-dialed his number. He answered, "Coast is clear."

Margo laughed nervously. "Where are you?"

"Parked behind a telephone pole. You can't see me, but I can see you. It sure took a long time."

"Well, I've got it…finally."

Margo looked over her shoulder as she got ready to exit. No one seemed to be watching, but she felt paranoid, as if the whole town knew the secret. Chris trailed, just in case anyone was watching. She didn't fear the hit men; they were jailed. However, the satanic priests and their sacrificial altar was the source of her anxiety.

389

"How's your head?" Joy asked.

"Much better." Margo rubbed the bump on her noggin left over from the fall. "Jo, do you think you could call all the people you know who prayed for us during this whole ordeal? I want to come against everything connected to it."

Joy sounded happy to do so. "Sure. I've already started making some calls."

"You're so efficient. Listen. You won't believe this. But I just met someone from the college who just accepted the Lord, and guess what? She was involved in…let's say, 'dark activities.' I'll invite her also."

"And I'll call the other young man Paul told me about."

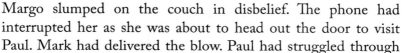

Margo slumped on the couch in disbelief. The phone had interrupted her as she was about to head out the door to visit Paul. Mark had delivered the blow. Paul had struggled through the night to survive, but he gave up in the early hours. He passed away at four fifteen in the morning!

Margo breathed a heavy sigh, and her lip quivered. Tears welled in her eyes then spilled over, making a path down her face. Shaking, she reached for a tissue in her bathrobe pocket and wiped her cheek. She had grown to love the unrefined and newly converted ex-con and bodyguard. Why did he have to die? The verse, "He who lives by the sword will die by the sword" came to mind. Could that be the reason? Whatever, she was thankful Paul had given his life to Jesus Christ.

Within moments, Margo sensed a comforting presence and a warm glow in the room. She still mourned his death, but now she rejoiced in the new life he would enjoy in heaven. Margo felt the opposite about Paul's former companion, Bill. His body hadn't been found yet, probably scattered all over the rock cliff, though a search party was sent out to find it. What a relief she would never see his face again.

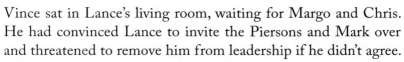

Vince sat in Lance's living room, waiting for Margo and Chris. He had convinced Lance to invite the Piersons and Mark over and threatened to remove him from leadership if he didn't agree. Vince intended on confronting all of them.

When they arrived, Vince was disturbed by the presence of a young man with a pierced ear, but no Mark. "Hmmm, may I talk with you?" He took Margo aside. "Who's this guy? I didn't invite him. I want to talk to you and Mark, as well as Lance."

Margo waited to reply, "Boswell is someone who knows firsthand what I'm talking about. Don't worry, I'll answer your questions, but I wanted him here to back me up." Vince grudgingly complied.

The interrogation lasted for over two hours. Vince didn't like what Margo had to say about almost everything, but he couldn't refute what her companion said. He objected several times to their story. "I think you're attributing too much power to Satan. Are you going to spend your life looking over your shoulder? You yourself admit the blood of Jesus is more powerful then their curses, so how can you say they are responsible for the recent indiscretions of our couples and the divisions in the church."

Boswell spoke up. "I'm new to all of this Christianity stuff, but how I see it is God lets people make choices, and some choose to get help from the other side. Others don't know there's power over there, so they ignore it until it smacks them in the face. Some Christians just don't know they can be influenced by Lucifer. He was once an angel of light and can disguise himself in many ways."

Vince recanted, "You're right about those who don't know Christ, but Satan has no power over Christians, so how can curses work?"

Margo slumped in her chair. "I wish I knew the answer to that. I'm not completely sure, but I have an idea. Satan attacks us where we are weakest, especially when we think we aren't. Look at Rich, he was full of pride. And Mark, even though he might be trying to change, he has a really bad temper and is not always reliable. As far as Jessica and Melanie, you know where they were at spiritually, riding on their husband's coattails."

Vince didn't like what he heard, but he had to admit she might be right. "But if we talk all the time about demons and Satan, respectable people, along with many Christians, will think we are wacky."

So the truth is out, Margo thought. *That's what the problem has been all along.*

Lance finally spoke up. He had been silent most of the time, although he previously made a few comments in their favor. "I believe Margo is on the right track."

Chris nodded in agreement. "If I may add something," he interjected. "You don't have to focus on Satan, but you need to be willing to confront him. Those who don't believe in his powers are going to be tricked by him."

Vince jumped back into the conversation. "Well, it's one thing to talk about the devil in an abstract way, but then when you start pinning the blame on him for breaking up marriages, I think you're running into trouble. I'm not going to mention it from the pulpit, and I will not allow you"—he pointed to Lance—"to preach about it either. You may be right, but I'm not jumping on this demon-frenzy bandwagon you guys are on. I'm maintaining my position that Jesus is Lord, not Lucifer."

With that, Margo bolted upright. "We never said Jesus wasn't Lord, but His word tells us Satan is the prince of the air."

Vince scowled. "We are Christians and not under his dominion. You and your friends, young lady, are preaching heresy, and I will not allow that in *my* church." He turned to the recent convert. "And you shouldn't even be allowed in any church. You're trying to deceive people to believe that your little potions and fake curses had any power. It's all just a bunch of sleight of hands and trickery." He repeated, "I will not allow that in *my* church."

Vince stood up like a bolt of lightning. "Until you realize the evil of your ways and the falseness of your scare tactics and so-called prayer meetings, I don't expect to see you in church. There are very few in the fellowship who sympathize with you, and it will be better this way." Turning to Margo, he added, "And personally, I hold you accountable for the death of Bill Guiles."

Margo was stunned by Vince's vehemence. She knew it was a touchy subject, but she thought the three of them had explained it to him; but apparently, he didn't really hear her. She ventured one last time. "I don't believe in focusing on the devil. My focus is on Jesus. But neither am I ignorant of Satan's ways. Contrary to what you believe, Bill wasn't a good person. He died in a struggle to cling to evil." On that note, Margo stood up and walked out of the room. The others followed.

Lance shook his head. "I don't know what's gotten into him lately. I didn't expect him to react so vehemently."

"I thinketh he protesteth too much, to quote Shakespeare," Margo said.

"You just might be right," Chris said as he started the car.

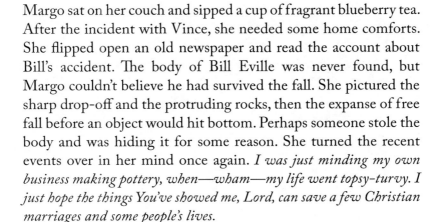

Margo sat on her couch and sipped a cup of fragrant blueberry tea. After the incident with Vince, she needed some home comforts. She flipped open an old newspaper and read the account about Bill's accident. The body of Bill Eville was never found, but Margo couldn't believe he had survived the fall. She pictured the sharp drop-off and the protruding rocks, then the expanse of free fall before an object would hit bottom. Perhaps someone stole the body and was hiding it for some reason. She turned the recent events over in her mind once again. *I was just minding my own business making pottery, when—wham—my life went topsy-turvy. I just hope the things You've showed me, Lord, can save a few Christian marriages and some people's lives.*

She put down the newspaper and thought about issues closer to home. Her heart ached with the news about both Mark and Rich's recent separations from their wives. Jessica had been her friend, but she wouldn't talk to her after Mark had found the goat's head. She wanted nothing to do with the church either. Unfortunately, their names were on the stone, and she knew from a firsthand account that their marriages were cursed. She hoped at tonight's meeting, the curse would be reversed.

Margo finished the tea and Googled "rectangular shapes with dots." An alphabet popped up, one the Masons use to send secret messages. *So that's the connection.* She knew little about them but immediately went to the stone and applied the cipher. It took some time to translate, but names from the past became evident: Dubiers, DeVitts, Bevier and Eltins, among others.

Wanting to know more, she clicked on information about the other ciphers, and a whole page of satanic symbols matched the ones on the stone. Bingo, the Masonic code and the satanic signs were, without a doubt, intertwined. Her mind wandered to Vince. She was saddened at his response, but not entirely surprised. He disagreed with several of her recent prophecies. "They were not uplifting or encouraging to the body," he had told her.

But how can I change the prophecies God gives me? she reasoned. *Am I supposed to edit them for palatability?* She was only the vehicle for their delivery, the messenger, and not the author. Now she saw them coming true before her eyes. Not only had division caused separation in Christian marriages but also in the body of Christ.

43

Saturday evening, the Piersons' house brimmed with people. The overflow from the living room spilled into the dining area and even the kitchen. Margo didn't realize the impact these last weeks had on the Christian community. Many were called upon to pray for her and her companions. Though she didn't know all of the couples, she was excited to see them.

Margo stood in the hallway and watched as Joy ushered people into the living room. The Celtic stone had been examined by the Hibernians and given back to the Historical Society, which lent it to her for one more day. It was placed on a circular table at the entrance of the room. People glanced at the circular stone as they passed by, but it was not the center of attention. Instead, a small table with an open Bible placed on it attracted people.

Margo had highlighted Ephesians 6:12: "For our struggle is not against flesh and blood, but against the rulers, against the powers, against the world forces of this darkness, against the spiritual forces of wickedness in the heavenly places." People stopped to read it and commented about the beautifully engraved sign above the Bible. "Devote yourselves to prayer, keeping alert in it with an attitude of thanksgiving" (Col. 4:2). Margo wanted people to focus on prayer and not on the enemy.

After everyone settled down, Joy stood up. "Our first guest today is Boswell Newman."

A tall, young man with unkempt jet-black hair and multiple piercings stood up.

"Some of you may not know this, but Boswell is a new Christian." She hesitated. "However, he'd previously been involved with NOW, the National Organization for Witches and Warlocks."

A few people fidgeted in their seats.

"As some of you may know, this group believes in *good witches*. Boswell is here today to tell you a little about their activities in the area and how it relates to us."

The young man didn't smile. "There are a lot more of us around here than you think, and they don't all look like me." A few guests laughed nervously.

He looked over the audience. "Some of them are prominent men and women in your communities—businessman, politicians, even teachers. I don't know their real names, and I don't know what all of them look like, but I know what they want. Power. Some of them think they are good people, but they practice magic in many forms. I just kinda flirted with the stuff, but some are into it big time, and not for good."

A number of people raised their hands.

Boswell looked over at Margo with a penetrating look and then continued, "I used to date a girl from one of the churches around here, Ashley Dart. She died in a car accident not too long ago. I found out later someone had put a spell on her."

Several people gasped.

"After that, I started thinking I might want to get out of this. I didn't get involved to start hurting people. It wasn't my intention."

He continued to inform them about different practices from *The Book of the Dead*, *The Book of Shadows*, and other rituals targeting Christians, like praying against the success of Christian marriages.

One woman wanted to know what rituals were associated with this. He explained, "Goat's blood or cat's intestines are often used. Prayers are offered up on an altar along with incense."

Then another guest stood up. She had long, straight blond hair. She walked over to the table and pointed to the stone.

"Objects like this have been used in the ancient arts for thousands of years. The rituals that surround them are known by only a few. The group my friend spoke of was considered amateur. The majority used white magic. Ours, the satanists, practiced black." Her eyes met Margo, and the young potter shivered.

The guest continued, "It is intended to harm or eliminate those in their way." Several people stirred. Margo sensed their fear. "Some of us worshipped Osiris, the Egyptian god of life and death. Others worshipped Ra the sun god, Horus, the falcon headed man, Ankh, and many others."

The group held their breath as she spoke. All eyes focused on the petite figure.

"I was one of them."

People exhaled loudly.

"I say this because though I was once ensnared by these powers"—she pointed to the cold stone—"I have now been washed clean."

At this, people clapped vigorously.

"It would take me hours to divulge the secrets behind such sorcery as this, but we are here to pray."

Another round of applause broke out.

"I've come to tell you what Margo and her friends experienced was very real. They're not exaggerating. Their lives were at stake. A real enemy, who still exists, pursued them. And they have joined forces with an elite group of Freemasons who are rich and powerful, the Illuminati. The people behind bars are just the ones who do their dirty work. They will go undercover for a while. Perhaps they will move their base of operations. I do not know.

But one thing I do know: prayer is what saved Margo and the others on their list."

People raised their hands in thanks to God.

"Let me close by saying I am here as living proof that God saves even the most vile and wicked, if they will repent. Because of Margo and the work of Jesus, I am a new creation."

Her testimony nearly brought the house down with hallelujahs.

After Margo quieted everyone, she shared the names of those she and Joy had deciphered from the recent etchings on the Egyptian stone. All Christians. Some of them were well known because of their willingness to stand up for their faith and strong beliefs. Others were considered weak and easy targets. A few in the meeting recognized the names and cried out loud.

Margo walked over and put her arms around a young woman who was sobbing. "I know how you feel. At first I was overwhelmed." She reached in her pocket and took out a tissue and offered it to her. "To think these people were targeted to destroy their marriages or their lives was frightening. But now, I understand who has the true power to overcome these curses by the blood of the lamb. Remember, Satan is a counterfeit. His power is only transitory, temporary. What we must remember is not to give the enemy a foothold, an edge in our lives."

Chris agreed. "Yes, we must pray that we will allow God to purify our lives. We should think and act in accordance to His Word. Our thoughts need to be monitored by the Holy Spirit. Of course we cannot do this of our own accord, and this is why we need to pray and stay alert."

With that, the group bowed their heads. After a few minutes, the doorbell rang, and Margo went to answer it. A young woman with long mousy-colored hair stood at the threshold. "Is there a prayer meeting here tonight?"

Margo asked for her name, and she answered timidly, "Susan, Susan Long."

The hostess stood frozen for a minute as she recognized the name etched in the stone but had never met the woman. After an awkward moment, Margo ushered Susan into the living room. The group was already praying, but Margo brought her over to Joy and quietly introduced her. She took the young woman's hand, and Margo went to get her a seat.

After only a few minutes of prayer, she broke down in tears.

"I don't understand what's been happening to me lately. I've always loved my husband, but I felt a little neglected, so I got involved with another man. The other day I planned on running away from him with this other guy, but then something changed."

Joy stroked her back.

"This wonderful woman"—she held Joy's hand—"who probably thought I was a good Christian, called and asked me to pray for Chris and Margo Pierson. She told me about the terrible things that happened to them and invited me to this meeting." She pointed to Margo. "I read the story in the newspaper and called them to find out more about it, but no one knew anything. So I just had to come here to find out." She sobbed. "But now I feel an amazing presence here like I used to know."

Joy hugged her. The young woman burst into tears and buried her face in her hands. Everyone prayed silently. She lifted her head, and Margo handed her several tissues. "I've been so confused lately. I don't know what else to say, but I really need your prayers."

Joy comforted her. "You've come to the right place. We will pray for you. All of us need to be willing to change." Everyone agreed.

Margo already saw the curse dissolving before her eyes, and the etched name of Susan Long, once covered with animal blood, appeared bathed in the blood of Jesus.

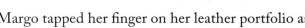

Margo tapped her finger on her leather portfolio as she waited in the police station for the arrival of the Egyptologist from New York. Ms. Haddad was from Cairo and an expert in her field. They were fortunate to procure her services since she was working on the new Egyptian Exhibit at the Metro City Museum. Probably the reason she was late. But other reasons made Margo's stomach do flips.

Finally a petite, dark-haired woman dressed in a beige suit opened the door. Margo recognized her from the pictures. "Hello, I'm Margo Pierson. The one who found the stone."

Ms. Haddad nodded politely and introduced herself. "So pleased to meet you." She turned toward the desk. The receptionist greeted her with her usual cold stare as the woman explained her identity. Unlike Margo's treatment, she was ushered into the chief's office with no hesitation. Margo trailed behind. This woman might know the connection between the two halves. And Margo wasn't going to miss a second of what she had to say or what her face registered when she saw them.

As usual, the chief sat behind a stack of papers, but as soon as Ms. Haddad entered, he stood to his feet. He extended his hand, but she kept hers clutched to her briefcase. The chief retracted his as he looked at his cluttered desk. "There's been a lot of commotion and a trail of paperwork involving this case." He glanced at Margo. "I assume you met the woman responsible for all of this." The chief smirked.

Ms. Haddad nodded.

"She can fill you in on the details after, but right now, we want you to examine the article in question."

The woman arched her eyebrows.

"The stone," Margo said as she pointed to a desk along the sidewall. It sat surrounded by plastic bags filled with vials, pieces of clothing, imprints, and other assorted evidence. The woman put down her briefcase and walked over. "I assume you've gathered what evidence you want off of it?"

Margo watched as Ms. Haddad looked at it, but she didn't look shocked. She ran her hand over the surface and along the sides, her fingers tracing back and forth.

"The stone is common, limestone, found in many pyramids near Memphis, but also here in your valley." Then she stopped. Her face darkened. "But these hieroglyphs"—she pointed—"are recent, not ancient, and the names, unusual, not Egyptian, but Western." She rubbed two fingers together. "Obviously traces of…blood. The probability of a crime."

"Yes, more than just a crime," Margo said, anxious to tell her more.

The chief held up his hand. "I'll explain this briefly. This young woman"—he pointed to Margo—"was abducted and almost murdered during a ritual involving a group of unidentified, umm, suspects."

Margo didn't like being silenced this way, but at the same time, she realized she might get involved in explaining too much.

The chief finished. "The proper authorities are investigating the crime, but we also need to know the stone's worth. Can you tell us if it's authentic?"

She opened up her briefcase and pulled out a shiny metal knife and three plastic bags into which she scrapped some of the lime into a vial. "It will need to be tested, but I don't think this is from Egypt, although it is made to look as so."

She took out a small magnifying glass and bent close to the surface. "I can tell you the newer carvings are made with modern tools. They leave a different mark." She looked up. "As for the earlier ones, they are cruder, but not the implements of the ancients." She put the vial in her case. "I must examine it further, preferably in my own headquarters."

The chief shook his head. "No, no, lady. This stone is a piece of evidence in a criminal investigation, and you can't take it with you. I've already got the other half housed with the local historian." He walked over and leaned on the table.

"Another half?"

"Yes, there was another stone welded beneath this, but it wasn't as old. I was hoping—" Margo managed to slip in this detail, but then the chief interrupted.

"Remember, we don't have time for that now."

The archeologist looked confused. "This is getting very complicated. I must examine this stone further." She fingered the sides. "The Egyptians did not weld stones together unless—"

"The other one wasn't from Egypt. But it doesn't matter. This one has the evidence, and it's staying here." The chief hovered over the stone.

She glared at him. "Yes," she hissed. "I am aware of this." She looked at the chief, but he didn't flinch.

"Then I must scrutinize it with care. Please turn the stone over." She softened her tone. "I must inspect its back." She smiled. "First, please help me turn it over."

The chief knit his eyes, threw up his hands, and walked over.

Margo joined them. She hadn't thought about the bottom, but then again, when it separated, she'd been running for her life. Then the police took custody of it.

The three carefully slid the stone and turned it over. It looked like a plain, cement-like surface. Nothing worthy of examination.

Ms. Haddad ran her fingers over it and along the sides. "This is just a covering to stick the two stones together. I must remove it with care and see what is beneath." She opened her black bag again and retrieved two small picks, a tiny hammer, and what looked like a scraper with a file.

She began to tap and gently hammer, removing small pieces then chunks of the cement. Underneath looked like a layer of wax or rubber. Its sheen looked somewhat like a latex substance Margo had used in sculpture class.

When Ms. Haddad had uncovered part of it, she stopped and rubbed the surface. Bits of the milky material began to peel off. Looking over her shoulder, Margo saw parts of falcons, eyes, and birds begin to appear.

The woman gasped and looked up at Margo. "Where did you acquire this tablet?"

Margo didn't know where to begin. How much of the story should she tell this dark-haired Egyptian? "It was found it in a local cave discovered by a man from church."

She seemed interested. "Please continue."

Margo recounted some of the details, but didn't include her horrifying experiences.

Ms. Haddad interrupted. "Up until now we were looking at just another imitation, and not a good one. Just names etched in stone—no historical significance. Maybe something linked to a crime." She began to peel another layer of the rubber. "Now we are looking at an Egyptian tablet, perhaps from antiquity."

The thought made Margo's spine tingle. Had this stone been used in rituals for thousands of years, or had its original intent been perverted? Had some pyramid grave robber discovered this?

Ms. Haddad ran her hand along its surface. "It is possibly worth millions. But I cannot know for sure." Her eyes narrowed, and she brought down her briefcase with a thud. "I must do some carbon testing." She smiled slyly like a cat. "Unless of course the police would like to do the carbon dating themselves."

The police officer hesitated. "I'll have to talk with forensics about that."

Ms. Haddad smirked. "Then please do. Until then, I'll take some pictures and some more samples for myself. This is most likely what your criminals wanted." She deftly scraped some of the other stone's surface into another vial and took more photographs. She handed the police chief a black embossed card from the Overlook Mountain House.

Margo's eyes grew wide as she registered recognition at the unusual card. The same color as Bill's.

The woman turned to Margo. "And no more tampering with the evidence." She smiled at the chief.

403

—————⟫◆⟪—————

Margo heard her cell phone chirp, and she recognized the number. "Hello, Chief. To what do I owe the pleasure of this call?"

"Just that Ms. Haddad called and wanted us to donate the stone to the Metro Museum in New York City. She said the results were in and the tablet is thousands of years old, but from one of the later, weaker dynasties. I wanted your advice. She said it's worth—now hold on to your hat—over fifty million dollars!"

Margo nearly fell over. "Fifty million! No wonder those master criminals didn't care about mowing down anyone who got in their way, including me." Margo thought for a moment about the chief's question. "But isn't it county property? And don't you have to keep it for evidence?"

"Yeah, of course, but after the trial and the dust settles. Who knows what? You might wind up with some rights to it since you unearthed it. Depends on the lawyers and all." The chief's voice changed tenor midstream. "Fifty million could sure help this county. Probably be worth sixty million after the trial with all the publicity. The museum already has so many Egyptian rocks dating back much further."

Margo had other things on her mind. "Sorry, I don't know what to say except we'll just have to wait and see. Think about it. A donation might look good and be the best idea." Margo didn't want to be anywhere near the stone. "Well, I have to go. I'll pray about it." She could just imagine the chief's face after that last comment. "Bye, Chief, I'm sure I'll see you soon."

Margo hung up the phone and turned to Chris. She related what the chief said and then leaned on his shoulder. She still felt the pain of Paul's loss. "It's a shame Paul died because of this whole ordeal."

Chris stroked her hair. "He didn't die because of the money, but to save you and others."

Margo felt rebuked, but her heart was still troubled. "That's true, but there are so many people affected by this *type of activity*.

Remember what those two guys said, this is not an isolated incident. Sure we can help those directly involved and pray for the others, but it's so much better to be aware of the enemy's tactics than to go along blindly until you fall into his trap."

"But you told me yourself you can already see the hand of God at work." Margo stopped and thought about the young woman who came to the meeting. "Yes, you're right, God is already doing a work in people's lives. I'm so thankful one marriage is saved already, but I can't help but think who will be the next one to fall prey."

The Wednesday night prayer meeting gathered at the home of Ray and Joy Hopelyn, and the Piersons arrived later than usual. As Margo entered the living area, she glanced at the Celtic stone. Margaret Dubier's name was etched on it along with other names she didn't recognize. It had unnerved her before, but now, its effect wasn't as overpowering. Margo had realized she needed to trust God more…and her husband. She looked up at him and smiled. *He had believed her through all this and kept her safe.* She squeezed his hand as they sat down.

Pastor Dave was speaking. He used a scripture taken from Luke 20 verses 17 and 18: "Jesus looked directly at them and asked, "Then what is the meaning of that which is written: "'The stone the builders rejected has become the capstone'"? Everyone who falls on that stone will be broken to pieces, but he on whom it falls will be crushed." Dave pointed to the Dividing Stone. "We know this one is an imitation of the true rock, and a defilement. Jesus is our capstone. No other. In a building, the cornerstone is laid first, and then every other stone is aligned to it. This is a picture of how our lives should line up to Jesus. He is our measure."

Margo was thinking about how Bill rejected God. His pride had gotten in the way, and he wanted to be like God, just like

Lucifer. Instead of falling on the Rock of Jesus, it fell on him and crushed him. Now Dave's word zapped her.

What about her?

She needed to line up her life with Christ. Not an easy thing to do. She had to be careful not to become prideful. Just because God revealed these things to her didn't mean she was better or more special than anyone else here. She also needed to trust her husband's judgment more.

Margo tuned back to what Dave had to say. "This is a strong portrait of God. If we are to survive spiritually, we need to fall on Him, to allow him to break us, which is not easy. But if we don't, then in the final judgment, we will be crushed."

The young potter knew there was much in her life she needed to allow God to change. She realized if she continued to treat Chris as beneath her spiritually, she would leave her marriage open for attack. Her marriage had been prayed against, and rituals were performed to oppose it. She would have to allow God to mold and shape her to counteract these deadly curses.

Being a potter, she thought about the biblical analogies in her own profession. Margo wanted to be clay in the Potter's hand, but she thought it was easier to be the potter than the vessel. She remembered the evening only a few weeks ago when she tried to throw pots with clay mixed together with pieces as hard as stone. *Oh no, Lord,* she cried out in her heart. *Please don't tell me this was a picture of me—soft sometimes yet hard as stone when I want to be.*

She felt an affirmation of her thoughts, but a comfort at the same time. Margo was becoming more consistent and soft in the Potter's hand, though she realized it required a complete commitment to Him, not a halfhearted attempt to live like a Christian.

As Margo examined her life, the rest of the group turned to 1 Peter 2:6–7: "Behold I lay in Zion a choice stone, a precious corner stone, And He who believes in Him will not be disappointed." Margo's spirit leapt within her. *Wow did I need to hear that!* Immediately, Margo pictured the stone she had detested, but now, she saw it as a grinding stone—the stone she'd seen by Margaret's house. Since her father was a miller, Margo pictured her long lost relative making bread as a young woman.

A flash of insight showed her how all the stones related. The grinding stone is meant to refine us, to make us useful to others, to provide bread; but the devil, being a liar and thief, tried to make it a means for destruction, division, and death. The secret society had replicated a millstone and inscribed their ciphers and then melded it to the Egyptian stone tablet acquired by someone with a great deal of money. Probably to increase its power and hide their identity.

Contemplating this, Margo stood up and asked Chris to join her. They walked behind the circle of chairs over to the Dividing Stone. She no longer called it Celtic, since they discovered most of the symbols were satanic, and the others were Masonic ciphers, decoded as names of various gods, an inscription to the Great Architect of the Universe, and people's names from the past. A few watched as she stepped by the table and ran her fingers over it. She stood there for a moment. *Well, Lucifer, the Bible says, "He who falls on the cornerstone of Christ will be broken to pieces, but whoever the stone falls on, it will shatter him like dust." It is you who will be pulverized.* "No matter what it looks like," she said aloud. "The Rock fell on you, Bill, but Paul chose to fall on the Rock."

All eyes were on her.

Dave turned to Margo. "So you were listening after all, even though you had a faraway look?"

Margo blushed. "Yes, of course." A vision of light consuming darkness played before her eyes as Margaret came into focus. She saw the millstone in the center of a table and Margaret bound. Then a blazing white light appeared and annihilated the darkness.

"Did you just see something?" Chris turned to her, his eyes round with wonder.

Margo jumped up, excited. "Yes, I saw Margaret lifted into heaven accompanied by angels. Then I saw the devil descending into a deep pit, and when he reached bottom, *the Rock* fell upon him and crushed him and all his demons once and for all."

Chris nodded in agreement. "Isn't God amazing?"

⟹◆⟸

A chorus of angels sang the Lord's praises for the revelation of the truth on earth. As it reached a crescendo, Margaret Eltin Dubier joined them and whispered a thank-you to Margo. A warm feeling spread throughout Margo's body, and she sensed something happening in the heavenly realm. She looked up and smiled as Margaret gazed down upon the assembly of believers.

Chris turned to his wife, and she squeezed his hand. "Yes, He is truly amazing."

Everyone contemplated what Margo declared and nodded in agreement, the heavenly host included.

DISCUSSION QUESTIONS

1. What character do you identify with in the story? Why?

2. Do you think Margo is overly sensitive to spiritual matters? Why or why not?

3. What scenes resonate most with your life?

4. What do you believe are three major causes of divorce?

5. What demonic powers do you think were operating in the New Way Fellowship of New Coven?

6. What do you believe about spiritual warfare? About the role of prayer?

7. Do you think Christians should take into account evil and/or demonic forces? Why or why not?

8. How can Christians lead a balanced life if they believe what the Bible says about Satan?

9. Do you think division in the church is a major issue? If so, what do you believe is the cause? Are some differences acceptable? What kind?

10. Do you believe Satan tries to interfere with peoples' lives? If so, how? What are your beliefs based on?

11. Do you think there are secret societies that wield a lot of power and control people and countries? How do you reconcile this with your Christian and/or other beliefs?

12. What do you think is the major theme of the *Dividing Stone?* Give reasons for your opinion.

If you have any questions about this book, you can e-mail the author at anitawriter7@ yahoo.com or visit her blog @ http://anita-thoughtsonchristianity.blogspot.com/